DEATH'S BRIGHT DAY

DEATH'S BRIGHT DAY

A REPUBLIC OF CINNABAR NAVY NOVEL

DAVID DRAKE

TITAN BOOKS

Death's Bright Day
Print edition ISBN: 9781785652172
E-book edition ISBN: 9781785652189

Published by Titan Books
A division of Titan Publishing Group Ltd
144 Southwark Street, London SE1 0UP

First edition: June 2016
2 4 6 8 10 9 7 5 3 1

A CIP catalogue record for this title is available from the British Library.

Printed and bound in Great Britain by CPI Group UK Ltd.

What did you think of this book? We love to hear from our readers. Please email us at: readerfeedback@titanemail.com, or write to us at the above address.

To receive advance information, news, competitions, and exclusive offers online, please sign up for the Titan newsletter on our website:

www.titanbooks.com

To Cecelia Holland, one of the two
good things I found in Cambodia in 1970.
(The other was Jane Austen.)

AUTHOR'S NOTE

As always in this series, Cinnabar weights and measures are given in English units while those of the Alliance are metric. I use them merely to hint at the variation I expect would occur in a future in which humans have spread across the stars.

Despite my saying this, I will probably get a note from someone telling me that the metric system is *much* better. For scientific purposes I agree, but logic isn't going to rule our distant descendents any more than it does us. (And for weather information, Fahrenheit beats Celsius all hollow.)

The historical incidents on which I based *Death's Bright Day* come largely from the Greek world at the close of the 3rd century BC. The empire of Alexander the Great had broken into three parts within a few years of his death in 323 BC. Now the large fragments were shrinking or crumbling. There were new players—Sparta, the Kingdom of Pergamum, and, overwhelmingly, Rome—and a world of opportunists at the edges and in the spaces between.

People at that time made short-term decisions based on short-term urges, among which pride, greed, and envy were prominent. And also fear; fear was a big one.

Perhaps this is the only way things ever happen in human societies. Current events seem to me to support that view. It's a milieu which creates many backgrounds for action-adventure. (I used only a few of these. My original plot had nearly twice the number of incidents, some of them quite dramatic, but I trimmed it for length.)

Speaking as a writer, this is a wonderful milieu. Viewing it as a member of humanity, though, I often wish that we were better as a species at taking a long view. The Greek world of 200 BC wasn't a safe place for anyone or a happy place for most, and things very rapidly became worse.

I would prefer that the reality my son and grandson will face were a better one, but my field is history. I don't find much hope there.

—Dave Drake
david-drake.com

They have forgotten all that vanished away
When life's dark night died into death's bright day
　　　　　—Alfred Noyes
　　　　　　The Progress of Love,
　　　　　　Canto III

CHAPTER 1

XENOS ON CINNABAR

Daniel Leary waited to board the rented tramcar which would carry him from the Pentacrest to Chatsworth Minor, the townhouse which had been his home in Xenos ever since he became friends with its owner, Lady Adele Mundy. He didn't spend much time in Cinnabar's capital city—or anywhere on his home planet, for that matter—but it was good for his state of mind to know that there was a comfortable, convenient burrow whenever he needed it.

Because of the crowd noise he bent slightly toward Miranda, his bride of approximately five minutes, and said into her ear, "I don't believe I've ever seen a car this fancy. What isn't wood inlays"—he recognized the tigerwood, but some of the exotics were beyond even his naturalist's eye—"is gilt."

He pursed his lips and corrected himself: "Or possibly solid gold, I suppose."

Miranda hugged herself even closer without turning toward Daniel. "I've never been so happy," she said. "I've never dreamed of being so happy."

She turned then and kissed him, which made the crowd cheer even louder; try to cheer louder, at any rate. "I'll try not to disappoint you, love," said Daniel. *Or disappoint myself or the Republic of Cinnabar Navy or Adele or the crew of whatever ship I command at the moment. Or anyone else I care about.*

Which included the Republic itself, he supposed, though Daniel didn't often think in political terms. The Learys had been involved in Cinnabar politics since before the thousand-year Hiatus in interstellar travel, if the family records were to be believed. Daniel had always been drawn toward the stars instead, and any urge he might have had toward a political career had ended when he was sixteen and had broken violently with Corder Leary—Speaker Leary; one of the Republic's most powerful politicians, and Daniel's father.

"The car doesn't have the Bantry crest," said Mon, his best man, splendid in his dress uniform. For years Mon—though still a half-pay lieutenant in the RCN—had been managing the Bergen and Associates shipyard for Daniel, who had inherited a half interest from his Uncle Stacey. "We could have knocked out the three fishes for you in the yard, easy enough."

Mon grinned. "In gold, if you like. A gift from me and the crew."

Not only had Daniel given Mon a ten percent stake in the shipyard but also a free hand in hiring his personnel. Most of them were ex-RCN, and many had lost limbs in the service. There wasn't another yard on Cinnabar which could match the staff of Bergen and Associates for skill or loyalty, and Mon had become very wealthy on his share.

Uncle Stacey's silent partner—and now Daniel's—was Corder Leary. The elder Leary earned the most from the yard, but for him that income was too small to notice.

"I directed that the car not carry any crest," Daniel said mildly. "We're going to Chatsworth Minor now, after all. When we have a second ceremony at Bantry, there'll be plenty of fish present. A few of them will be symbolic, I suppose, but I suspect that my tenants will be more interested in the wedding banquet." *And the wedding ale, of course.*

Adele, Lady Mundy, had boarded the lead car of the procession with her bodyguard Tovera and with Miriam Dorst, Miranda's mother. No one else had gotten on, and the usher stationed at the door had turned several would-be riders away. Something was going on, which made Daniel uncomfortable; but he would learn about it in good time.

He liked his new mother-in-law and got along well with her; as for Adele—Daniel had no closer friend. Whatever Adele was doing was for his benefit, or at worst not to his detriment...but he liked to know what was going on, and he didn't this time.

Daniel glanced toward the line of trams waiting behind his own. It was a very long procession.

As though Miranda were reading his mind, she said, "How many cars are there, Deirdre?"

Her maid of honor, Daniel's sister, shrugged. "I told the transit authorities to be sure there were enough to carry all those attending the ceremony to the reception," she said. "Only the first forty will be new, but I'm confident that there will be a sufficient number. Service in the suburbs may be delayed, but—"

She smiled, though there was very little humor in the expression.

"—after all, how often does a daughter of the late Captain Timothy Dorst get married?"

The four of them laughed, Miranda as brightly as ever. "Only once, I expect. And since I don't have a sister, I suppose our neighbors in the suburbs can accept the delays for one afternoon."

Daniel realized that his sister had been testing Miranda to see how she reacted to what was at best black humor. Captain Dorst had been a respected RCN officer who had died of a stroke not long after his last promotion. Perhaps if he had lived longer he would have plodded his way to admiral rank and modest wealth; as it was, his widow and children had a social position without enough money to sustain it.

The son, also Timothy, became a midshipman in the RCN and served under Captain Leary. Midshipman Dorst was a model of a fighting officer: brave, active, and as thick as a brick. He was also unlucky: his cutter had taken a direct hit from a twenty-centimeter plasma cannon which would have vaporized most of a corvette.

Timothy's bad luck had turned out to be very good luck for his mother and sister, because his former commanding officer had visited them to convey his personal regrets. Meeting Miranda Dorst had been good luck for Daniel Leary, also.

He hugged Miranda closer without looking at her.

"Looks like they got 'em loaded," Mon said, giving the crowd a practiced eye. He added with a grin, "Though nobody's going anywhere till you're ready to start, of course."

Deirdre—or more likely, one of the businesses which she controlled—had provided the ushers who were loading the trams, but Lieutenant Cory and three long-service warrant officers were overseeing the work. Some of the spacers who had attended the wedding of Captain Leary were too ragged to pass the scrutiny of a doorman borrowed from the Shippers and Merchants Treasury, but if they'd served with Six—Daniel's call-sign aboard the *Princess Cecile*—there'd be places in the wedding for them.

Perhaps thinking the same thing, Deirdre said, "Daniel, how do you know that some of those spacers claiming to have served with you aren't just bums looking for a free drink? Not that I care, of course."

"You can't fool a veteran, Deirdre," Daniel said. He felt suddenly saddened. "I don't remember the name of every tech who's served under me and I doubt my engineering warrant officers do either, but the phonies are all heroes. They don't say, "I was an engine wiper on the *Milton* and I haven't shipped again since that missile took everything off from three frames astern of the power room."

Thirty-three of his crew had died that day. Daniel didn't remember anything after the impact, because flying debris had knocked him silly. If the jump-seat had struck an inch lower, it would have broken his neck and there would have been thirty-four dead.

And I wouldn't have gotten married today, which I would regret. He squeezed Miranda's fingers and said aloud, "I think we can board now. If board is the correct word for a tram?"

Daniel handed his bride into the car. Mon offered Deirdre

his arm. She accepted it with a bemused look. Deirdre was used to toadies, but meeting a gentleman was probably a new experience for her. The RCN was old-school in many ways, which Daniel—grinning—thought was just as it ought to be.

Daniel also wore a first class uniform, his Dress Whites. He was far more splendid than Mon, however. Daniel's rig included flashy foreign honors which he would have been embarrassed to wear in a strictly RCN gathering. Deirdre touched the scarlet and gold sash over his left shoulder and said, "What in the world is this, brother?"

"That indicates I'm a Royal Companion of Novy Sverdlovsk," he said. "I have the right to wear a scimitar in the presence of the monarch."

"Do you have a scimitar?" Mon asked.

"I'm sure Hogg could find him one if Daniel ever visits Novy Sverdlovsk," Miranda said primly.

"Speaking of Hogg—" said Deirdre.

She paused as the tram rocked to a start a moment after the lead car. The monorail vehicles weren't coupled, but the central computer was moving the procession as a unit. Ordinarily it directed the trams to call boxes and then by the most efficient route to the riders' destination.

"—why is he riding on top of the car? And there's someone on the lead car also."

She gestured through the front windscreen. A Xenos tram with unscratched windows was at least as remarkable as one with wood inlays.

"Ah," said Daniel. He coughed into his hand. "That's Midshipman Hale, who served with me on two recent voyages.

She and Hogg"—Daniel's servant, mentor, and father figure since his earliest days on the Bantry Estate—"thought they'd have a better view from up there in case of trouble. A needless precaution, but if it pleases them to do it..."

He shrugged. He didn't mention that the long blanket-wrapped bundle Hogg had beside him was a stocked impeller, nor that the slightly built Hale's shorter bundle was a carbine. Within her range, Hale was as good a shot as the countryman who had been poaching game all his life.

Above them the tram's magnetic suspension rattled over junctions. The streets were still lined with cheering citizens.

"I wonder if they'll stretch all the way to the townhouse?" Deirdre said. "You're a famous man, brother."

"It's just the spectacle that draws them," Daniel said uncomfortably. "There'd be as many people if I were being carried in the other direction to have my head cut off and nailed to Speaker's Rock."

"Don't you believe it!" said Mon. "Listen—they're shouting, 'Cacique! Cacique!' They're cheering the man who beat the Alliance above Cacique and brought peace after decades of war."

"Daniel?" Miranda said, scanning the lines of shouting, happy faces along the route. "How will they all fit in Chatsworth? It's a big house for the center of Xenos, but...?"

Deirdre smiled. Daniel gestured toward her with an upturned palm and said, "I'll let my sister answer that. She was in charge of the arrangements."

"Mistress Sand, Lady Mundy's colleague, had as much to do with it as I did," Deirdre said in a nonchalant voice. Bernis Sand was the Republic's spymaster. She wasn't precisely Adele's other employer, because Adele didn't take money for the work she did on Sand's behalf. "In addition to Chatsworth Minor, all six houses on the close have opened their ground floors to the reception, and refreshments will be served in the street itself."

"How the bloody hell did you do that?" Mon blurted. "Kidnap their children?"

Daniel felt his lips purse. He'd had the same thought, but he hadn't asked because he'd been afraid that he wouldn't want to have heard the answer.

"No, no, no strong-arm," Deirdre said.

Her easy smile implied that the notion was absurd. It wasn't absurd.

"One of the owners was kin to Lady Mundy on her mother's side," Deirdre continued. "Distantly enough that he survived the Proscriptions, but happy to do her ladyship a favor. Another neighbor was enthusiastic to help the Hero of Cacique. You may get a dinner invitation, brother. You're not obliged to accept it, of course."

"I will," said Daniel. Miranda nodded crisply.

"Apart from those, there was a little extra time on a mortgage, help with a client's legal problems, and an invitation to a party at which neither you nor I would be caught dead, brother. It will be the achievement of a life's social ambition, however."

Deirdre coughed. "Finally," she said, "Mistress Sand arranged for the suppression of certain information. I don't know precisely what the information was, but we were suddenly offered free use of the house on the south corner for as long as we wanted."

The tram slowed for the stop at the head of the cul-de-sac

on which Chatsworth Minor was located. Three passengers were getting out of the leading car. The pavement within the close was packed with people, all shouting.

Miranda leaned closer. "Welcome home, darling," she said into Daniel's ear. "Welcome home, hero."

Adele took a front-facing corner seat in the lead tram. She wasn't surprised when Miriam Dorst followed her and Tovera: Miranda's mother had to ride somewhere, after all. Two middle-aged couples, dressed in up-to-the-minute fashion with ruffs at their wrists and necks, started to get on.

Miriam blocked them. Miranda played field hockey; her mother was fit and had the same stocky strength. "The bride's family has reserved this car," she said in a sharp tone. "Please find other places."

"We're friends of Captain Leary!" said the leading woman. She wore a striped top and a stiffly conical skirt, a combination that made Adele think of a shuttlecock.

"No, you are not," Adele said, looking up from the display of the personal data unit in her lap. "Mistress Dorst has requested politely that you find other places. Please do."

"Would you like me to shoot them, Mistress?" Tovera said. She gave the intruders a bright smile.

"I'll call an usher if necessary, Tovera," Adele said. The question was an example of Tovera's sense of humor: if she had really thought that shooting the civilians was a good idea, she wouldn't have bothered asking.

Tovera *would* shoot them if asked, of course. She was a

sociopath who rather liked killing people, to the extent that she had any emotional involvement at all with people.

The woman who had spoken froze. Her husband tugged her backward; the second couple had already backed away. As the speaker—Mistress Ethyl Smith with her husband the Honorable Edward Smith, according to image recognition software in the data unit—left the car, she snarled, "You're *sick*!"

Miriam closed the door. Tovera giggled and said, "If she only knew."

The tram started off. Miriam said, "I suppose you wonder why I'm here. I decided it was the best way to have a private conversation with you, Lady Mundy."

Adele looked up again, frowning; she'd been searching to learn the Smiths' relation to the bridal couple, not from any need but rather for her usual reason: she liked to learn things. Miriam hadn't seated herself. She looked stern and very possibly angry, which was puzzling.

"It's none of my business where you ride, Miriam," Adele said. They had been on a first name basis in the past; Adele far preferred to remain informal with Daniel's mother-in-law. "It hadn't occurred to me to wonder."

Adele's mouth twitched in the vague direction of a smile. She suddenly realized that if she had been watching imagery of this scene, she *would* find it interesting. She needed an interface between herself and information before it really touched her.

Miriam looked puzzled, as Adele had found people often did when she answered their questions. In order to ease the situation further, she said, "I was glad that you requested that the Smiths leave. I haven't found any connection between them and Daniel yet. I suppose you would know if they were friends of your family?"

"What?" said Miriam. The tram jounced between connectors hard enough to rattle the suspension against the overhead railing. She grabbed a support pole, then lowered herself onto the seat across from Adele.

"Oh, Ethyl Smith was an admiral's widow before she remarried," Miriam resumed. "Quite full of herself when she was Mistress Admiral Colfax. I suppose Daniel might have served under him at some point. If so, I sympathize. Timothy did, and it wasn't a happy posting."

"Daniel did *not* serve under Admiral Colfax," Adele said with satisfaction. She shrank the holographic display of the data unit and transferred both control wands to her right hand, then looked Miriam directly in the face. "What was it you wanted to discuss, Miriam?"

"Oh," the older woman said. She swallowed. "What I was going to say is that Daniel, that Captain Leary, has been very supportive of, well, his friendship for you. He's having the initial ceremony here in Xenos. He's even taking his bride to the Mundy townhouse, *your* house, ah, Adele. Instead of at the Leary estate, Bantry."

"Yes," said Adele. She didn't add "of course" because she found that just as silly as stating the obvious in the first place. Miriam Dorst wasn't stupid, so there would be a point coming sometime.

"Well, why then did you refuse my daughter's request that you be her maid of honor?" Miriam said. She grimaced and said, "Are you angry because Miranda married your friend?"

Adele started to bring the data unit's display up again. There was nothing she wanted to check on it, but it would be a normal thing for her to do. When faced with an absurd situation, she very much wanted to return to normalcy.

Retreating into the data unit would be a better choice than drawing the pistol in the pocket of her tunic, the other tool that experience sent her to when reality seemed to be coming apart. Nonetheless, the best choice was the usual one, to answer the question calmly—and to be ready to deal with whatever the reaction might be.

"No," Adele said aloud. "I'm pleased that Daniel is marrying someone whom I like and respect, unlike the bubbleheads whom he favored before he met Miranda. Though if he had married a bubblehead or a *dozen* bubbleheads, it wouldn't have been either my business or a matter of concern to me."

"Why, then?" Miriam said. She was gripping her own hands fiercely; her knuckles were white as her fingers writhed together. "Why did you refuse to be Miranda's maid of honor?"

"I didn't have any feelings about the matter," Adele said. "I thought it would be more politic for Miranda to involve Daniel's sister. I believe Deirdre thinks well of your daughter, but the honor would mean something to her."

Tovera was smiling from a third corner as she watched them. *I'm glad somebody's finding this funny,* Adele thought; but Tovera's expression wasn't necessarily connected with humor.

Miriam sagged. "I'm sorry," she muttered to her hands. "Miranda said that you weren't insulting her, but . . . I feel very foolish now."

You should, Adele thought. It was as though Miriam had

told her she believed Adele dined on murdered children.

"Miranda has had more opportunity to get to know me," she said aloud. "In another instance"—*which I sincerely hope will never occur*—"you might reasonably be guided by her judgment."

The older woman straightened in her seat. "Well..." she said. Then, more briskly, "Well. I'm very glad we had a chance to talk. I feel much better now. I was very much afraid that you felt that Miranda was your enemy and, well, you're Captain Leary's closest friend. That would have been terrible."

"Yes," Adele said, rising to her feet. She slipped her personal data unit away in the cargo pocket in the right thigh of this dress suit. She had a similar pocket in every pair of trousers she owned. "That would have been terrible."

It would also have been terrible if a giant invisible asteroid struck Xenos. To Adele the one seemed as likely as the other, but she had learned long ago that her world view differed from that of most people.

The car slowed as it neared their stop. Adele had wondered whether the crowd would overflow onto the tram line, but Deirdre had planned for that with a human barrier which—

"Those people are wearing liberty suits," Miriam said, peering through the forward window. "They're RCN?"

"Yes," said Adele. "Instead of hiring civilians to control the crowd, Deirdre"—or possibly Daniel himself—"seems to be using spacers. I hope they're not carrying batons." Or wrenches and mallets.

"The people who're most likely to get pushy are other spacers," Tovera said. "They're not going to complain about getting their heads thumped at a party. They're used to it."

As Miriam had said, the spacers were in liberty suits: RCN utilities tricked out with ribbons and patches commemorating every landfall the spacers had made and every ship they'd served aboard. Senior personnel wore rigs whose mottled gray base fabric was almost completely hidden.

Woetjans was in charge. She had been Daniel's bosun from before he captured his first command, the *Princess Cecile*. Well over six feet tall and strong even for her size, Woetjans was the perfect person for the job, but she could have been among the wedding witnesses in the temple had she wished. This was what she preferred. Pasternak, the chief engineer, and two bosun's mates had helped Cory advise the civilian ushers at the temple.

The tram's door opened automatically when it stopped. Adele gestured Miriam out and followed with Tovera. The joyous roar echoed from the building fronts, amazingly loud. The transit computer shunted their car out of the way to make room for the vehicles following.

"Miranda has married a great man," Miriam said. She was looking back, so that Adele as much read the words on her lips as heard them over the cheering. "I only hope he is also the husband who suits her."

Adele nodded. "Yes, I hope that too," she said. It didn't really matter to her, of course: Daniel was her friend regardless of his private life. He would be happier if his marriage went well, and Adele genuinely did like Miranda.

She stood facing the close, viewing the sea of faces past the wall of gorgeously beribboned spacers. She had seen similar scenes from the window of her bedroom when she was a child and her father was addressing an election rally of Popular Party supporters from his fourth-floor balcony. That had been the same sound, the same mass of people so enthusiastic that they seemed to blend into a single organism.

Those cheers had ended a matter of days after sixteen-year-old Adele left Cinnabar to continue her studies at the Academic Collections on Bryce, a member world of the Alliance of Free Stars. The speaker of the Senate, Corder Leary, had accused Lucas Mundy and his closest supporters of plotting against the Republic. He had moved quickly to crush the conspiracy by summary executions and the confiscation of property.

Now the close below Chatsworth Minor was rocking with similar enthusiasm for Speaker Leary's son, Daniel, and his new bride.

Adele turned to face the tram which immediately followed her own. She smiled as the bride and groom got out to redoubled cheers.

I don't believe in omens, she thought.

CHAPTER 2

XENOS ON CINNABAR

Adele would rather have been in her library with the door shut, but today she was a hostess. Lady Mundy therefore stood on the steps of Chatsworth Minor where she could be seen.

A rigger named Chabat lurched out of the scrum at the nearest refreshment tables. She had a mug of ale in one hand and the other arm around a civilian youth who would probably look better after a few more drinks.

"Hey, Mistress!" Chabat called. "Anything I can bring you? So you don't get your dress mussed, you know?"

"Thank you, Chabat," Adele said. She waved, since she wasn't sure the rigger could hear her even though she was—by her standards—shouting. "I'm all right."

Chabat turned away. The young man seemed bored but willing.

Even better than being in her own room would be to be transported to the Academic Collections and her carrel on the top floor of the Old Stacks. Nobody came there....

Deirdre approached, escorted by a much more impressive man—but also a professional. The blue of her dress complemented her reddish hair. Like Daniel, she fought a tendency to plumpness; which was odd, Adele realized, because Corder Leary was a lean, craggy man and considerably taller than his children as well.

"I hope my brother doesn't do this again for a long while," she said. "I've merged three trading houses with less effort."

She climbed the three steps to stand beside Adele. Tovera moved to the sidewalk to make more room.

A group of people—three couples, none of the six familiar to Adele—came out of the building and moved past, talking brightly without apparently listening to one another. Spirits were available on the ground floor for those who chose to ask, and these folk had clearly been sampling them.

"I was surprised when Daniel asked that only beer be served in the open and that he'd direct his spacers not to go into the houses," Deirdre said. "Don't spacers drink?"

"RCN ships use ninety percent ethanol as a working fluid in the power rooms," Adele said, allowing herself another slight smile. "It's ethanol because the crews are going to drink it anyway, so it may as well be a poison to which the human species has acquired a degree of resistance."

"But?" said Deirdre.

"Mixing drunken spacers with drunken civilians is a separate problem," Adele said. "As a matter of loyalty I would bet on the RCN, of course; but it wasn't the sort of entertainment Daniel wanted for his wedding. His only wedding, I hope and believe."

A young man approached but waited politely on the

sidewalk until Adele noticed him and met his eyes. He moved to the bottom of the steps, nodded to Tovera and then to Deirdre, and said, "Lady Mundy? A friend said she hopes to talk with you today if you have a moment."

"Ah?" Adele said, glancing at Deirdre.

Deirdre gestured her toward the messenger and said, "By all means. I'm sure I'll manage to occupy myself."

"You're to guide me?" Adele said as she joined the young man.

"If you don't mind," he said, turning toward the head of the close. Adele didn't know his name but she had seen him working as the doorman of Oriel House, the Sand residence. He had been a very good doorman, but she doubted that he considered that his primary occupation.

Behind them two men and a very mannish woman converged on Deirdre. Lady Mundy's presence had kept others at a distance, but as soon as Daniel's sister was free they moved in with their Very Important Questions. Presumably Deirdre really liked that sort of environment or she would live a different life, but Adele found the fact hard to fathom.

Aloud to her guide, she said, "Deirdre probably wouldn't be happy researching pre-Hiatus texts."

"Probably not," he said equably. "But judging from Mistress Leary's performance in other lines, I expect she would be good at it."

He gestured toward the steps of middle house of the three on the right of the close. The entrance was on the side rather than facing the street. A young civilian—another of the "servants" at Oriel House—and Midshipman (Passed Lieutenant) Cazelet stood on opposite sides of the doorway.

The civilian—if he was one—bowed to Adele, and Cazelet drew himself to attention with a grin. He was the grandson of Adele's mentor and protector when she arrived on Bryce as an orphan, though she didn't realize her status until the news from Cinnabar arrived by the next ship. Cazelet's parents had incurred the wrath—or possibly just the greed—of Guarantor Porra, which was as fatal a condition as plotting against a government led by Speaker Leary.

Adele had gained a protégé, and the RCN had gained a very useful junior officer.

"I'll leave you on your own, your ladyship," Adele's guide said. "She's waiting on the top floor." He bowed and was gone into the crowd.

Cazelet pulled open the door to the house for Adele. "Good to see you, ma'am," he said.

She nodded. If Cazelet had a fault as an officer, it was that his training had come from working his way up in the family shipping business. He treated Adele with the respect he owed a skilled colleague, not as a person of a particular rank in the RCN. Since Adele was of a similar mindset, they meshed well.

There were a number of people sitting in the entrance hall, including two RCN officers in their Whites who were drinking spirits and talking to the much younger women seated to either side of them. Bottles clinked down the hall to the right, and voices came from the drawing room directly ahead.

A plush rope closed the staircase beside the hall, but the servant waiting there unhooked it when Adele entered. She didn't recognize him, but he was cut from the same polite, well-born cloth as her guide and the man outside with Cazelet. When she and Tovera had started up the stairs, the servant dropped the loop back over the newel post behind them.

This house was three floors rather than the four of Chatsworth Minor, though there may have been a windowless garret under the high peak. Adele rather liked climbing stairs. They reminded her of her youth in the Old Stacks when she had no responsibilities except to learn, and—because warships had companionways rather than elevators—of the *Princess Cecile* where for the first time in her life she was part of a family.

Another servant, a trim young woman this time instead of an athletic young man, stood by the closed door to the left of the stairhead. She bowed to Adele and walked down the hall into an open room.

"I'll go chat with her," Tovera said, nodding after the servant. "Maybe we have friends in common."

"All right," said Adele. She tapped on the closed door.

Tovera was not a spy. She had been trained by the Fifth Bureau as a bodyguard and killer, support staff for the spy she had accompanied to Kostroma. When her previous principal died, she had attached herself to Adele.

This wasn't a change in allegiance: Tovera had been a tool of the Alliance when she worked for the Fifth Bureau, and she was a tool of Adele Mundy now. She had no more patriotism than the pistol in Adele's tunic pocket, and she was just as willing to kill whoever Adele pointed her at.

Tovera did have a degree of self-preservation, though; she had become Adele's retainer because she saw a familiar ruthlessness in Adele. Adele would supply the direction which would keep Tovera within social norms: an external conscience for a killer with no conscience of her own.

Adele's smile was cold. She had a perfectly good conscience, one which regularly awakened her in the small hours of darkness with a parade of faces she had last seen over her pistol sights as her trigger finger took up the final pressure. Tovera's character flaw allowed her to sleep soundly.

"Come in and sit down," called a familiar voice.

Adele entered what had probably been meant as a servant's room. The original furnishings had been replaced with a table, two straight chairs, and a side table with a decanter, siphon, and glasses. Mistress Sand was in the chair across the table from the door; a half full glass sat on the table in front of her.

"I ought to get up," Sand said with a lopsided smile, but she made no attempt to move. "Will you have one yourself?"

If I drink, she'll drink with me, Adele thought. *And she really doesn't need more.*

"I'll have a short one," she said aloud and sat down. *I'm not responsible for Mistress Sand's private life.* "I saw your husband earlier to nod to, but I wasn't surprised to see him—either of you—at Daniel's wedding."

Mistress Sand took a second glass and poured into it a more than the two fingers which Adele had meant by a short one. "If this hadn't come up," she said, "I would've arranged to see you anyway. Just to talk."

She set the decanter back on the serving table, then slid the glass toward Adele without picking it up. The decanter was down by about a third, but it might not have been full when it was brought here.

She looks older every time I see her, Adele thought as she sipped the drink; as expected, it was very good whiskey. *But then, I suppose I do too.*

Sand stared at her own glass. "I'm cutting back," she said—to the glass rather than to Adele. She raised her eyes and went on, "I decided I'd been putting away more than was good for me. It's . . ."

Sand smiled, looking more like the woman who had recruited Adele not so many years ago. She leaned back in her chair: stocky and solid in a dark suit for the occasion rather than the tweeds she had favored most of the other times Adele had met with her.

"You'd think that with the Republic at peace things would be easier," Sand said. Her hand touched the poured drink, then snatched back. "That's not . . . not what I feel. Before the Treaty of Amiens, you knew where you stood with the Alliance. Now I'm certainly not ready to consider Guarantor Porra our friend, but in some cases the policies of his government may be aligned with the interests of the Republic. . . ."

"Yes," said Adele, sipping more of her whiskey.

Mistress Sand knew that she and Daniel had worked with Alliance officials in the past; she probably realized that they would do so again if circumstances required it. Daniel was better about following orders than she was, but neither of them cared much about the judgment of a fool in authority.

"You've made it clear in the past . . ." Sand said, keeping her eyes on Adele by sheer determination when she obviously wanted to look away. "That you don't work for me or for the Republic. Nothing you do has to be taken as an expression of Cinnabar policy. You have a long history of acting on your own."

Adele's personal data unit wouldn't tell her any more about what was going on than her pistol would. Instead she squeezed the whiskey glass and wished she were somewhere else.

Aloud she said, "Mistress, if there's something you'd like me to do, tell me. As you say, I've never felt a great respect for Cinnabar policy in the abstract."

She pursed her lips as she considered her next words, then said, "To be honest, if the Republic has ever had a consistent policy, I've missed it in my reading of history."

"You're consistent," Sand said. She touched her glass again but she didn't raise it. "Someone who didn't know you would think that consistency would make you easier to deal with."

"Mistress, tell me what you want," Adele repeated. She wasn't sure she knew the person she was talking to any more. "I need information. When you give me that information, I will make my decision."

"I don't *want* you to do anything," Sand said fiercely. "I want you to know that if someone makes you a proposition which in your opinion would be to the benefit of the Republic, I hope you will follow your own judgment in the matter."

"I see," Adele said, sipping a little more of the whiskey.

She did see. Her friend, Bernis Sand, had told her what Mistress Sand, the head of intelligence for the Republic of Cinnabar, could not have said. A task would shortly be offered to Adele, and Bernis Sand hoped that Adele would accept that task.

"You realize..." Sand said, speaking to her drink again. "I won't be holding my present position forever."

She looked up and met Adele's eyes. "I would like to believe," Sand said, "that I would be succeeded by an experienced person whose judgment I trust."

Adele put down her empty glass and rose to her feet. "I hope matters go well for you, Mistress," she said. "Speaking for myself—"

She was turning to the door as she spoke.

"—I hope I'm not around when that question has to be decided."

Adele closed the door behind her. Out of the corner of her eye, she saw Mistress Sand raising her glass.

Daniel and three officers he knew from the Academy—Commander Vondrian and Lieutenants Pennyroyal and Ames—linked arms and bellowed, *"Then he kissed her on the lips, and the crew began to roar...."*

Though Daniel had lived at Chatsworth Minor for several years, whenever he was in Xenos, he didn't recall ever having been in the kitchen at the back of the ground floor in the past. Servants had guided him and his friends here where the cabinets had been converted to sideboards for the reception.

It would have been churlish not to join old friends when they wanted something harder than ale to drink. They'd started with Oriel County rye—Pennyroyal's choice; she came from Oriel County—and proceeded according to the whim of whoever's turn it was to pick.

"Oh! Oh! Up she goes! We're bound for Baltimore!"

Vondrian commanded a destroyer flotilla with Ames as his

flag lieutenant and Pennyroyal the first officer of his flagship. They were attached to the Cinnabar Squadron, the portion of thc RCN still in commission after the Treaty of Amiens. Vondrian had family money. Going on half pay wouldn't have seriously affected him, but he also had enough influence to secure an active commission. His friends Ames and Pennyroyal would have been up against it if they'd been landed on the beach for any length of time.

"So then he kissed her on the nose..."

Daniel hadn't partied like this in years. When he'd happened to share a landfall with his friends on Tattersall, they'd hoisted a few—more than a few—drinks together, but they were in the presence of their direct superiors and a number of admirals. Here on Xenos they were friends attending the wedding of one of them, and nothing that happened would be seen as adversely affecting the good name of the RCN.

"—and the crew began to roar!"

Hogg came into the room from the back, the door onto the alley. He was dressed like a Bantry tenant, which is how he'd been raised, with an enormous budget to buy finery for the Squire's wedding. His blue pantaloons and loose green shirt were bright and of thin, hard fabric, and his high leather boots and belt were dyed the same shade of red.

The same was true of the brimless leather cap which he took off and waved to catch Daniel's eye.

"Oh! Oh! Up she goes! We're bound for Baltimore!"

Daniel squeezed his friends' shoulders—he stood between Vondrian and Pennyroyal—and muttered, "Duty calls!" as he disengaged himself. He felt younger than he had since, since—

Since I was given my first command, he realized. A road had forked then, and Daniel Leary had been very fortunate in the direction his branch had taken him; but...But. There was always a "but" in life.

His friends closed together and resumed singing. The dozen or so others in the kitchen made way for Daniel, but nobody paid particular attention. He bent close so that Hogg could speak without raising his voice.

Hogg spoke loudly enough to be heard by anybody on this side of the room anyway: "There's a fellow out back wants to see you, Master. Name's Huxford, and if it was just him he could get his ass gone. He says he's from Lord Anston, though, and I know that's different."

"Ah," said Daniel, nodding. He wished he'd gone a little lighter on the spirits, but he was glad he had old friends. "Yes, that's different. Let's see Commander Huxford."

Admiral Anston had been in frail health since the heart attack which had forced his retirement as Chief of the Navy Board. Daniel had been pleased to see him on a wheelchair in the temple, but he hadn't expected the older man to attend the reception.

He tugged his uniform tunic down and settled his bright sash. Well, Anston had seen a half-drunk officer before. Like as not he'd been one a time or two.

"I saw Forbes here too," Hogg said. He blocked the door with the side of his foot and straightened the aiguillette of feathers and tiny diamonds on Daniel's right shoulder. "Nice to see that she hasn't forgotten who put her where she is."

Forbes had lost the Speakership of the Senate and had been sent—had been exiled—as envoy to Karst to greet the new

Headman who had just succeeded his uncle. The embassy had not gone well through no fault of Forbes—or of Daniel, who was captain of the ship which carried her to Karst.

"We were very fortunate to have the ambassador with us when things went belly up, Hogg," Daniel said mildly. "The good result was as much political as naval, you know."

"That's not how *I* remember what happened at Cacique," Hogg growled. He put his hand on the doorknob, then paused and met Daniel's eyes. "There's one thing I'll give her, Master," he said. "Forbes put the mistress in charge when you got knocked silly, made her an admiral. She knew to do that, at least."

Daniel followed Hogg into the alley. He'd heard what happened while he was unconscious above Cacique. Adele knew nothing about shiphandling or naval tactics or any of the other subjects which the instructors at the Academy taught, but she knew a more important thing: to go for the throat.

You can't really teach that, but the great commanders are born knowing it. Forbes had indeed showed her ability when she brevetted Signal Officer Mundy to admiral in the chaos of the damaged flagship.

The alley at the back of Chatsworth Minor ran between two major thoroughfares and served six culs-de-sac—three on either side—for garbage pickup and bulk deliveries. There were twenty or thirty people crowded into this one; mostly men, mostly servants, and most holding liquor bottles. Those who saw Daniel, or anyway recognized his uniform, grew quieter, but they weren't really doing anything wrong.

Daniel grinned. Or anything he hadn't been doing himself a few minutes before.

Commander Huxford was wearing his Grays, a second class uniform; proper garb for public functions—including command of a ship—but not formal wear for any officer who could afford a first class uniform. Even hopeless officers who had been on the beach for decades tried to scrape up enough florins for a set of Whites when they sat in the Audience Hall at Navy House, hoping against hope that their names would be called for a posting.

"Thank you, Hogg," Huxford said. "Captain Leary, his lordship requested that I bring you to him—for the privacy, of course, but also to avoid the—"

He nodded toward the house, presumably meaning the crowded cul-de-sac beyond.

"Yes, of course," Daniel agreed. He'd never met Huxford, though he'd seen him twice. Huxford had acted as messenger for people in the same line of work as Mistress Sand, though probably in a parallel organization out of Navy House.

Huxford had a history with Adele, which had ended in Adele's favor. Hogg probably knew more of the details than Daniel did; Tovera certainly knew them, and the two servants talked. All Daniel cared was that it had ended and that his friend was satisfied with the outcome.

They walked out of the group behind Chatsworth Minor and to Daniel's surprise turned into a feeder alley serving the close facing a parallel boulevard. A husky looking man with naval tattoos stood at a back door, which he pulled open when Huxford approached.

"I'll leave you now, Captain," Huxford said. His salute was curt but proper—they were both in uniform. "His lordship asked me to invite you, but his business is none of mine."

Daniel paused in the doorway. He would show due respect for any superior officer, but he *felt* respect for George Anston beyond anything to do with a uniform. Anston had kept the RCN operating during fifteen years of grinding war with the Alliance, finding crews where there were none and convincing the Senate to build ships with money that had to be squeezed out of taxpayers—much of it from the wealthy senators themselves.

"Hogg," he said, "why don't you wait here? I...that is, I don't need help to see the admiral."

"Right," said Hogg, eyeing the burly spacer. "We'll chat about opera, shall we, buddy?"

"Down the hall and second on the left, sir," the guard said, ignoring Hogg. He closed the outside door behind Daniel.

The man waiting in the hall was as tall as Woetjans and *big* where the bosun was rangy. He opened the door beside him and stood rigidly, staring over Daniel's head as though he were being inspected by his commander in chief.

The hinges squealed slightly. That was the only sound Daniel heard. The other doors onto the hall were closed; either the house was empty or the inhabitants were holding complete silence. Daniel was feeling a little uneasy as he looked in, but there was Lord Anston. He'd rolled his wheelchair beside rather than behind the central table.

"Close the door and sit down, Leary," Anston said. "When you're fixing yourself a brandy and soda—"

He gestured to the paraphernalia in the center of the table.

"—you can fix me one too. You drink brandy, I hope?"

"Sir, I'm RCN," Daniel said. "I drink anything. Some things

I won't drink—" he was thinking of peppermint schnapps, which had tasted even worse when it came back up than when it had topped off a night of drinking "—unless I've got a load on already."

Which I do now, come to think.

He squirted seltzer into two brandies and put Anston's beside him before sitting down. He was pretty sure that the older man wasn't supposed to have alcohol, but that was a matter between him and his doctors—none of whom were in the room at present.

Anston looked frail enough to have dissolved in the drink. Daniel would regret that, but it might be the kindest thing that could happen.

Anston sipped the brandy with relish. He set the glass down and said, "Well, Leary, I'll get to the point in good RCN fashion. The Republic is in a bad state, a *bloody* bad state, and the politicians are pouring us straight down the piss tube."

Daniel stiffened and sat upright; he'd been leaning toward Anston without being aware of the fact. "Ah, I, ah . . ." he said. "I don't pay much attention to politics, sir. I'm a serving officer and I'm, ah, forbidden to be involved in politics."

Telling Anston that was like offering to teach a bird how to fly. The words were a measure of how disturbed Daniel was.

"Well, it's time and past time for that to change," Anston said forcefully. "The Senate will shortly be replaced by a Supreme Council drawn from the RCN and the Land Forces of the Republic. I'll be President of the Council, but you can see that I'm a clapped-out old crock. That's where you come in, Leary."

Daniel stood up, sliding his chair back. It fell over. His skin prickled as it had when he regained consciousness after pinching a nerve.

"We need you to run operations," Anston said. "All the real power will be in your hands, and no one better to use it, *we* think."

"I'm very sorry, Admiral," Daniel said. His ears were buzzing. "I've suddenly been struck deaf. I haven't heard a word since I sat down. I'm off to find a doctor immediately."

He had to get off Cinnabar; he couldn't possibly remain neutral if he stayed. Indeed, he probably needed to get out of the Cinnabar sphere of influence.

Do I tell Adele? I have to. But do I tell Deirdre, which means telling my father; which means ...

"Leary, come back here," Anston said, somewhere in the far distance.

Daniel jerked the door open. The doorman stood in his way.

"Now, the gentleman says—" the big man said.

Daniel head-butted him, breaking his nose, backed a step, and kicked the guard in the crotch. That would have been more effective with heavy boots, but the low quarters he wore with his Whites had rigid soles, unlike the spacer's boots worn with utilities and meant to fit within a rigger's suit.

"Hogg!" Daniel shouted, hurling the doubled-over guard into the room. He wouldn't have had a chance against the bigger man in a fair fight, but the guard hadn't expected the mindless fury Daniel had unleashed on him. He couldn't hit Anston—he would die before he hit Anston, even if the old man had gone mad—but hitting anybody else was a relief.

They can't let us live now, Daniel realized. If he could get to Harbor Three, he might have a chance. There were spacers who would help Captain Leary regardless of what the high brass were saying, but the chance of getting there in torn Whites—he'd burst the seams of both his tunic and his trousers—wasn't good.

There was a loud thump from the alley and the door swung open. The outer guard was down. Hogg held his folding knuckleduster knife open in his right hand. Daniel didn't see blood on the blade, but that didn't necessarily mean the guard was still alive.

"Leary, come back!" Anston called. "I apologize for being a bloody fool!"

The door to the left between Daniel and Hogg opened. Hogg shuffled forward, his knife held low to stab through a kidney toward the heart.

Mistress Forbes stepped into the hallway.

"*Stop, Hogg!*" Daniel shouted, but Hogg had frozen when he saw the Minister of Defense. He put his back against the wall and darted glances in both directions.

Daniel looked over his shoulder. Admiral Anston was out of his chair and standing in the doorway, gripping the jamb to stay upright. "It's my bloody fault," Anston said, but he was wheezing now.

"No, it is not," said Minister Forbes. "I'm the one who insisted, because I didn't trust the admiral's certainty that no offer could shake your loyalty to the Republic."

Daniel felt weak with reaction and relief. He braced the flat of his hand on the wall.

"Well, Mistress," he said. "I'm not the Leary to be tempted by offering to make me a politician."

"I'm glad to hear that," Forbes said. "Now, can we join the admiral in the room with the brandy and discuss the real proposition I came to offer you?"

CHAPTER 3

XENOS ON CINNABAR

The big guard who had tried to block Daniel's way out of the interview room had managed to stand, though he was leaning forward and cupping his groin.

"Tester, get Riddle in the alley and help him to the car," Forbes said. She was small and sharp-featured; her voice sounded like breaking glass. "Stay there until I join you."

"Your man may need looking after," Daniel said hoarsely. He had to pull the words individually from the jumble in his mind; adrenaline had shaken everything together.

"Naw, he'll be okay," Hogg said. His voice hadn't settled either. He'd folded back the knife blade, but he hadn't returned the knuckle-duster to his pocket yet. "He don't deserve it, but he will be."

"Well, wait in the hall," Daniel said. His throat was dry. "Give Tester a hand and then come back."

"S'okay," Tester said, walking into the hallway and passing between Daniel and the minister on his way toward the

45

outside door. He stood a little straighter with each step. "I'll get Riddle."

He didn't look at Hogg on his way past.

"Let's have that drink." Anston said. He took Daniel's arm and walked back to the wheelchair.

"Sit," Forbes said, pointing to the chair Daniel had knocked over. She took one of those by the wall and dragged it to the table.

Under other circumstances Daniel would have gotten the chair for her himself, but he was still trembling from recent events and—the smile didn't quite reach his lips—still quite irritated with the minister. This had been unpleasant, and it could have gone much worse. Though Forbes would probably have hushed up even a killing.

"Well..." she said as she put down her glass of brandy. "Let's get down to business. Are you familiar with the Tarbell Stars?"

She sounded quite cheerful; either she didn't realize what could have happened or she didn't care. That seemed to be a necessary attitude for a politician. At any rate, Daniel had never heard his father express regret at what any of his successful schemes had cost other people.

"I've heard of them," Daniel said cautiously. "I'm not familiar, no. I believe that though the cluster is independent, it's well within what the Alliance considers its sphere of influence."

"Yes, that's right," Forbes said, bobbing her head like a bird pecking seeds. "I'm sure your friend Mundy can give you all the information you need. Well, there's a civil war going on there now."

"I see," said Daniel. There was nothing unusual about

small governmental units fracturing, generally as the result of a leadership conflict. "I...Ah, Minister? I trust the Republic isn't planning to get involved in a matter that has far more importance to the Alliance?"

Because that would certainly mean a return to full-scale war between the two superpowers. Neither had recovered from the decades of grinding war which had paused with the Treaty of Amiens. A complete victory by either the Republic or the Alliance was almost impossible. It was far more likely that renewed war would cause both to collapse, which would lead directly to chaos and barbarism across all of human space.

The previous time war had come to that point, it caused a hiatus in star travel which had lasted a thousand years.

"The *Republic* isn't involved, no," the minister said brightly. "But there are some intriguing aspects to the matter."

Unexpectedly, Lord Anston clacked his glass down on the table. When the others looked at him, he said, "Leary, I have no business in this discussion. I was asked as a character reference, that's all, and to be honest I'm sorry I went any farther than that."

He thrust out his hand; his grip felt frail in Daniel's.

"I'll talk to Hogg about fishing," Anston said. He looked at Forbes for the first time since setting the glass down, glared, and added, "Leary, whatever you decide, may Heaven be with you. And with Cinnabar!"

He rolled to the door and let himself out. Only when it had latched behind him did Minister Forbes say, "Leary, there's a considerable risk to you in the proposition I'm about to broach; that goes without saying. But I swear to you that if

I thought there were real danger to the Republic, I wouldn't have entertained the overtures."

"Go on," Daniel said. "Please," he added, remembering that he was talking to the Minister of Defense.

Forbes nodded. Daniel's reserve and Anston's obvious disapproval seemed to have dampened her enthusiasm slightly. She resumed, "You're correct in saying that the Tarbell Stars are within the Alliance sphere of influence, but you perhaps realize that Guarantor Porra regularly creates competing chains of command to divide potential opposition within his own polity?"

"Yes," Daniel said. The space officers of the ships and ground establishments of the Fleet were paralleled by political officers of equal or greater rank. In the civil sphere, governors were watched and could be overruled by the residents of the Fifth Bureau, which reported directly to Guarantor Porra.

"Extraterritorial jurisdiction of the Tarbell Stars," Forbes said, regaining her animation, "is under the Fifth Bureau... but it has been divided between two separate dioceses. One of these is the diocese directed by General Storn, whom I believe you have met?"

Daniel's face went very still. "I have, yes," he said. "But only to have exchanged a few words with."

A few words, and a salute.

"You would have to discuss the matter with someone else—"

With Adele.

"—if you want substantive information."

"I don't," said Forbes. She was wearing a satisfied

expression. "General Storn is backing, at least is interested in, the Tarbell government forces. The rebels call themselves the Upholders of Freedom. They're supported and may have been created by a General Krychek. Krychek directs the other Fifth Bureau diocese involved. He is a professional rival of Storn, and they appear to be personal enemies as well."

"All right," said Daniel, because the minister was waiting for him to say something. He didn't know where the conversation was going, and he was unwilling to say anything which might imply an opinion until he knew more and had discussed the matter with Adele.

From her expression, Forbes wasn't best pleased with his noncommittal response. She nonetheless went on, "General Storn is unwilling to oppose the Upholders directly, since it's at least possible that Krychek has the support of Guarantor Porra. There are numbers of mercenaries fighting on both sides of the conflict, however. General Storn has suggested through intermediaries that it would arouse no concern in Pleasaunce if the Tarbell government were to hire the *Princess Cecile* and her full complement."

"I see," said Daniel, since at last he did. Quite a number of questions remained, but only one had to be answered—if he were not going to walk out of the room right now, regardless of how the Minister of Defense might feel about it.

"Minister Forbes," he said, "forgive me if this seems impertinent, but why is a high official of the Republic of Cinnabar bringing me this offer?"

"The Republic has no interest in the Tarbell Stars," Forbes said. She didn't sound offended or even surprised. "It has been suggested to me in my public capacity that if I could help General Storn in this matter, that it might aid the Republic in matters which *are* of interest to us."

Daniel smiled wryly. If Minister Forbes were to secure concessions to the Republic from the Alliance, it would be a considerable benefit to her in the next leadership contest in the Senate. She had narrowly lost the speakership election a few years previously, which was why she had been sent as envoy to Karst.

There was nothing improper in that. A Minister of Defense who benefitted the Republic might reasonably expect her efforts to be noticed.

"It seems to me . . ." Daniel said aloud, mostly as a placeholder. "that a corvette like the *Sissie*, even ably crewed, is unlikely to be an overwhelming factor in a rebellion of any size. The Tarbell cluster involves nearly a hundred stars, does it not?"

"Seventy with any population or government worth mentioning," Forbes said, nodding agreement. "My suspicion is that Storn believes that you and Lady Mundy will be of more value to the Tarbell government than your armed yacht will. I haven't discussed the question, but that's how I would think if I were in his position."

The trouble with doing things that others said were impossible, Daniel thought, *is that people keep coming up with other impossible things. Eventually they're likely to be right.*

Aloud he said, "I'll think about the matter, Minister. I need to discuss it before I come to a decision."

Forbes smiled and rose to her feet. "Very well, Captain," she said. "I await your decision with a great deal of interest."

The minister left the door open behind her as she walked out. Daniel heard her exchange a quiet greeting with Admiral Anston. Hogg looked in from the hall without saying anything.

Daniel joined Hogg. He'd expected Forbes to press him, perhaps even plead with him. Instead she had demonstrated that she had read his character during the Karst mission and that she was treating him with respect and intelligence.

He grinned. Forbes was manipulating him in the fashion she'd decided would be most effective. Forbes was doing her job.

Hogg backed away, waiting for Daniel to give him direction. Daniel said to Anston, "Sir? Is there anything we can do for you?"

"Did Forbes leave the brandy in there?" Anston said, nodding toward the room Daniel had left.

"Yes, she did," Daniel said. "Would you like help drinking it?"

"No, just leave me with the decanter," Anston said. He barked a laugh. "I owe Forbes thanks for one thing. I've got a battalion of nurses that ordinarily worry me like I was a kitten in a dog pen. Forbes got *them* off my back for the afternoon."

Anston wheeled himself into the doorway, then rotated his chair and looked up at Daniel. "I was a bloody fool to have gone along with this game, Leary," he said.

Daniel shrugged. "Sir," he said, "when RCN officers stop taking orders from our elected masters, the Republic is in sad shape. Anyway, no harm done."

He saluted. The ripped back of his tunic flapped when his arm rose.

Anston returned the salute and disappeared into the

drawing room. He closed the door behind him.

Daniel took a deep breath and said, "Hogg, it isn't Admiral Anston who's the bloody fool; or about to become one, anyhow."

Hogg shrugged. "I guess you'll make it work out well enough, Master," he said. "Anyway, that's not my business to say."

Clearing his throat, Hogg added, "I guess you need to chat with the mistress now?"

"Shortly," Daniel said. He grinned widely. "But before I discuss matters with Adele, I need to talk to Miranda. I need to talk to my wife."

Adele stood in the street outside Chatsworth Minor, talking to—mostly listening to—three women whom to the best of her knowledge she had never seen before. She held a twenty-ounce mug of Bantry ale, wishing that she had gotten four ounces of spirits instead; her wrist was getting tired.

"Now she married Cousin Sandor," said the tallest of the three, a woman with blonde hair, a brightly youthful face, and eyes that might have been a century old. Her voice had the brittleness of old age as well. "That's my cousin, not yours, your ladyship."

All three women laughed in affected tones.

One of the reasons Adele held the mug in her right hand was that it prevented her from instinctively taking the data unit out of her pocket and losing herself in it. That would be discourteous. So would reaching into her left tunic pocket and shooting the women dead with the pistol there, but that notion looked increasingly attractive.

"Now, Priscilla—and how amusing that her name sounds so *much* like the name of your ship, Lady Mundy! Now Priscilla married—"

Daniel and Miranda were approaching, followed by a troupe of well-wishers, which reminded Adele of her father's clientele at the height of his political power. That wasn't an altogether positive memory—Adele's smile was too slight to be noticed by anyone looking at her—but she wasn't superstitious.

"Ladies, you must excuse me!" Adele said. "I must speak with Captain Leary!"

That is the cold truth, because if I stay here any longer I will behave ungraciously.

"Adele, might I speak with you for a moment?" Daniel said before Adele was able to get out her very similar words. "Ah, perhaps with a little privacy?"

Miranda squeezed his shoulder and turned to their entourage. "I'll try to deputize for both of us with our guests," she said. She looked as happy as Adele had ever seen her.

Miranda's face was framed by a halo of white gauze, and her dress was a cloud of similar material. The individual layers of fabric were so fine that Adele wondered if there was a membrane of some other material to prevent the ensemble from being transparent in bright sunlight.

"Yes, we'll go up to your suite," Adele said. "You arrived at a good time for me."

She wouldn't really have shot the women. She might have overturned the beer onto their feet, however. She would have regretted that afterwards: her mother's ghost would be horrified.

Hogg cleared a path through the people on the steps, all

of whom wanted to say something to Daniel. He was more diplomatic than Adele would have expected.

If she hadn't seen Hogg a moment before, she wouldn't have doubted that he really was as drunk as his slurred, "Clear ta way fer mashter!" sounded. He swung his mug back and forth, but the drops he sloshed out never quite stained the finery of importunate well-wishers.

Tovera was bringing up the rear. Adele could only hope that she too was on good behavior.

"There are so many people," Adele said as Daniel led her into the house. "And they seem happy."

"Yes, they do," Daniel agreed. "You and Deirdre have done a wonderful job, Adele. I won't forget it."

He had missed the point of the comment, which was Adele's wonder that *any*one could be happy when there were so many people around. It was evidence of how distracted she was that the fact surprised her.

A servant with a Leary flash on his collar—not one of the normal house staff—passed them through the plush cord at the staircase. Hogg stepped aside to wait at the base of the stairs, where Tovera joined him. Adele wondered what the two of them discussed. It was good that they got along; it would have been—briefly—disastrous if they had not.

Adele had her personal data unit out even before she was through the door of Daniel's suite on the first landing. Inside she sat on the nearest chair. Her control wands quivered, manipulating the holographic screen by their attitude and position. Daniel watched, patient if perhaps bemused in the glance she spared him.

"The woman who was speaking to me," she said, "the tall one. She's the widow of my father's brother's brother-in-law. Her name is Henriet Krause."

Instead of speaking, Daniel raised an eyebrow. With a shock of embarrassment, Adele realized that he didn't have—she hadn't provided—any background to explain why that was worth mentioning.

"I'm sorry, Daniel," she said. "Mistress Krause is probably my closest living relative, and all I could think of while talking to her was how much I wished I were somewhere else."

She pursed her lips and added, "Mistress Krause isn't *very* close, of course."

Because if she were, the Proscriptions which Speaker Leary had ordered would have led to her execution as well.

"I'm sure you can renew your acquaintance at a less busy time," Daniel said mildly. For the first time Adele noticed that his first class uniform had been torn along the seams and—the decorative wall mirror gave her a glimpse of his back—between his shoulders as well. "But since we *are* someplace else at the moment...?"

"I'm sorry," Adele repeated. "Please tell me what it was you wanted to discuss."

"There's a revolution in the Tarbell Stars," Daniel said. "Rivals in the Fifth Bureau are backing—secretly backing, I gather—the opposing parties. Your friend Storn is backing the Tarbell Government."

I wish everyone knew how to provide information as clearly and succinctly, Adele thought as her wands sent information streaming onto her display. Daniel waited patiently. As a courtesy she muttered, "Ah," but Daniel knew her too well to imagine that she was ignoring what he had just said.

"General Storn believes that if the government were to hire the *Sissie* and her crew as mercenaries," Daniel said, "you and I would be able to advise them usefully." After a pause, he added, "It seems rather nebulous to me."

"We would be reporting to President Menandros?" Adele said. She was sorting through material recently added to the suspense folder of her base unit here in Chatsworth Minor. The file came without a provenance, but the format was that of Mistress Sand's organization.

"I don't know any details," Daniel said. "I'm not sure there are any. If Storn is keeping his involvement secret, he may not be able to influence how we'll be used. It looks like a real mare's nest."

"Um," said Adele, again being polite. Operations beyond the borders of the great powers—the civilized states, Cinnabar and the Alliance—were always mare's nests. The fact that she and Daniel would be operating under the titular command of a local potentate wouldn't change that either way, because they would simply ignore any orders with which they disagreed.

She and Daniel had been known to ignore orders from their superiors in the Republic a time or two also. That wasn't going to change either.

Adele looked up at Daniel, holding the wands still for a moment. "Does Admiral Anston support this involvement?" she asked. She had seen the admiral's wife arrive at the reception with an escort of RCN officers, but Anston himself had not been present.

"The admiral thinks it's a foolish and dangerous operation," Daniel said. "Minister Forbes, on the other hand, thinks that the potential value to the Republic and the great potential value to her political ambitions more than outweigh any dangers to you and me."

He smiled broadly, suddenly relaxing. "What *I* think," Daniel said, "is that if Anston were my age, he'd knock me down to get at the chance. Well, he'd try."

"Are there any restrictions on how you're to act after you reach the Tarbell Stars?" Adele said as she returned to her screen.

"Not that anyone has mentioned," Daniel said. He shrugged. "Anyway, if I'm to be operating as a private citizen with no support from my government, I'm bloody well not going to be taking orders from politicians."

"I presume you would be given a full briefing if you were willing to undertake the task?" Adele said.

"I'll certainly *get* a briefing before I hare off to the Tarbell Stars," Daniel said. "Off-planet somewhere. If I'm not, *we're* not, satisfied with the terms, then the matter is closed and nobody needs know that it was even raised."

He cleared his throat again and said, "Adele, we've talked about what other people think. What do you think?"

She continued to go through the file which Mistress Sand had supplied. There were points which would require clarification, but for the most part it was remarkably complete—given the physical and political distance between Cinnabar and the Tarbell Stars.

"I was told to use my judgment," Adele said. "I see no disadvantage to me in attempting the task."

"Well, you might be killed," said Daniel, frowning.

Adele shrugged and continued to work. "I see no disadvantage to me," she repeated.

"In that case..." Daniel said. "I'd like to make an announcement from your balcony. With Miranda. She said that she'd support any decision that I made."

"Yes, she would," Adele said. She looked up, then put the data unit away in its pocket. "And of course you may use the balcony. The acoustics of the close are very good, as I remember from hearing my father addressing his supporters here."

She wondered what Lucas Mundy would think about Corder Leary's son speaking from the balcony from which Lucas had so often roused Popular Party supporters.

It didn't matter: Lucas Mundy was dead. His surviving daughter was pleased at the current use.

The main stairs of Chatsworth Minor were wide enough that Daniel and Miranda could walk up side-by-side. She pulled him closer and said, "Don't worry about the dress. It won't crush. Mother and I know fabric."

"You're lovely," Daniel said, a safe thing to say but not exactly true. Miranda was striking and extremely fit, but she wasn't a classic beauty. Her hair was usually brown, though bright sun brought out auburn highlights; her features weren't quite regular; and her torso would be described as sturdy rather than curvy.

Daniel Leary had known a good number of women. He'd never known one who was more alive than Miranda, and he'd never known one who made *him* feel more alive.

Adele was already waiting on the fourth floor, in what was now her library. It had been the master suite during her father's lifetime. While Daniel was fetching his bride, Adele and Tovera had moved piles of information in various forms off two chairs.

That hadn't been necessary: all Daniel cared was that there be a path to the wrought-iron balcony facing the close and the crowd there. Still, it showed that Adele was trying to be hospitable.

Daniel turned to Miranda and said, "Now, you're sure—"

That was as far as he got. Miranda touched his lips with her right index finger and said,"Yes, I'm sure. I told you I was sure. Now let's do what we planned."

Adele's face was as still as glass, but Tovera grinned. Daniel thought about it and grinned back.

He opened the balcony door and stepped out, holding Miranda's hand. The crowd noise built to a roar as people looked up at the couple above them.

Daniel raised both arms to their full length. After a calculated moment, he brought them down abruptly. The result wasn't complete silence, but it was close enough that he could expect to be heard when he called, "Shipmates!"

The response was shriller and even more enthusiastic, though the volume may have been reduced from its earlier peak. Daniel heard someone *Yee-hah!* quite clearly.

He gestured for silence again, grinning. There was an enormous number of people below. More were pouring out of the houses—or at least they were trying to get out—when they realized that Daniel was speaking. The small porches were already clogged by people talking in the doorways.

"And friends!" Daniel said. He was used to making himself heard on a starship under circumstances in which lives depended on people doing what he said. The tuned acoustics of the close helped, but he was doing his part now.

"In two weeks my bride and I are making a honeymoon cruise to Jardin," Daniel said. "We'll be travelling on the *Princess Cecile*, and for that we'll need a crew."

Miranda had mentioned several times during their relationship that her father had loved Jardin. Her delight when Daniel suggested that they honeymoon there proved that he'd been right to hear wistfulness in that recollection of her father.

Jardin was independent and a popular destination for people—for wealthy people—from all across human space. It was a perfect location in which to meet the envoys of General Storn for a detailed briefing.

"All former Sissies are welcome to sign on for the voyage," Daniel said. "I can't promise prize money this time—"

More cries of enthusiasm, but they died back before he had to quell them.

"—but I'll pay honest wages. I've been told that Jardin's a good landfall for a spacer with a little pocket money."

When the noise settled again, Daniel said, "I hope that sober Sissies will in the morning pass my offer on to their shipmates who've already got a load on. If there are any sober Sissies here!"

He turned to Miranda. They embraced as the crowd roared and continued to roar for a very long time.

CHAPTER 4

BERGEN AND ASSOCIATES YARD, OUTSIDE XENOS

Daniel eyed the *Princess Cecile* in her slip and felt the usual rush of ... well, love was the best word he could come up with. He smiled at Lieutenant Vesey and said, "The first time I saw her, she was passing overhead and shooting off fireworks in a parade on Kostroma. That was probably the only sort of action she'd have seen if she'd stayed in Kostroman hands."

"I came out of the Academy ..." Vesey said. She was also looking at the corvette. Her eye might have been more critical, but it was affectionate also. "Thinking that unit-body construction was so much stronger than modular that no one in her right mind would use modular construction for a warship."

She grinned at Daniel. "A voyage on the *Sissie* convinced me that I'd been wrong," she said.

Because the *Princess Cecile* was a private yacht in this commission, she was being fitted out and stocked by civilians. Vesey, Daniel's long-time first lieutenant, was waiting for dry stores to arrive from the suppliers she had chosen with only cursory oversight by the owner and captain.

Foodstuffs would have to wait for Chazanoff and his crew of missileers to finish striking down the main armament. The *Sissie* carried two missiles in her launch tubes and twenty reloads when her magazines were full. A corvette couldn't put out the volume of metal that a larger warship could, but a direct hit from a five-ton projectile at terminal velocity would wreck even a battleship.

The chance of a corvette's missile getting through a battleship's defensive armament was very slim: a bolt from an eight-inch plasma cannon vaporized enough of a projectile to shove the rest of it off in a harmless direction. Even so, a skilled missileer—or a lucky one—even in a corvette, was a threat. Daniel was both skilled and lucky.

"How's the crew coming along?" Vesey asked.

The question—from Vesey—meant more than the words themselves; but it was a polite way to ask, and there was no reason not to give her the full background. Daniel smiled until the lengthy *crash crash crash* of missiles rolling from a lowboy into the *Princess Cecile*'s magazine hatch had died away.

"I've got Rene in the office to take the names of any latecomers," Daniel said, "but we're already staffed at war complement and maybe a little beyond."

He said "Rene" instead of "Midshipman, Passed Lieutenant, Cazelet" because on the ground Vesey and Cazelet lived together. Cazelet had come to the Sissie as Adele's protégé, but he had from the first been an asset to the ship and to the RCN generally. With the present peacetime reduction in the RCN establishment he might have a very long wait before he got the lieutenant's commission which his abilities amply justified, but the prize money which had come the way of Daniel's crews meant that Cazelet was better off than many senior officers who didn't have family money.

"Rene said that you'd accepted some applicants who hadn't been on the *Princess Cecile* herself," Vesey said. "The *Milton* had the complement of a heavy cruiser."

Daniel's grin went hard. Not all of the *Milton*'s crew had survived the battle above Cacique, of course, but far more had than a corvette could carry.

"Of course, you can afford the paybill, sir," Vesey said, embarrassed to have pushed for what had not been volunteered. "I'm not prying."

"I'm at fault for not being more honest with my officers," Daniel said, a polite way to say that he expected her to talk with Cazelet. "I'm signing extra personnel now in case some want to leave when we make landfall on Jardin. I'll arrange passage back to Cinnabar for them, of course."

Vesey frowned, but she didn't ask why he thought they might lose more than the usual few spacers who might overstay liberty because they were in jail, in hospital, or dead.

"As soon as we're in orbit," Daniel said, "I'm going to explain that I expect the *Princess Cecile* to take a contract as a mercenary warship in the navy of the Tarbell Stars. I won't expect personnel who signed on for a honeymoon voyage to accept a posting to a civil war."

Vesey's frown didn't change. "You're concerned," she said in a deliberate voice, "that spacers who've served with you arc going to balk when you tell them that you may be taking them into battle?"

"Put that way it does sound pretty silly," Daniel admitted. "Still, I think they ought to have the choice."

A gondola marked MCKIMMON CEREALS had arrived at the entrance to the yard. The driver of the tractor pulling it had gotten out of his cab to continue his discussion with Midshipman Hale from the ground.

He might as well have stayed where he was. Shouting in Hale's face wasn't going to make her change her mind, and the train of lowboys hauling missiles was in the way regardless.

People like to think that their convenience is important. Daniel had found that as a general rule the universe didn't agree, and that other human beings tended to be a subset of 'the universe' in this regard.

"I think the crew expected that they were signing on for more than a honeymoon cruise," Vesey said, looking toward the cereals vehicle and then away: it would come when it came, and she would check the supplies in when they arrived. "With the exception of Pasternak I think they're all *hoping* for action again. And Pasternak was probably the first to sign on."

Vesey had mousy hair, an excellent mind, and an earnest personality. Her features were unremarkable, but they were sharpening as she aged. Surprisingly that added character and made her more attractive.

"Pretty close," Daniel agreed. "I'm lucky to have him. We're all lucky."

Chief Engineer Pasternak was a quiet man with the skill and seniority to run the power room of a battleship at a much higher base pay. He would have been subordinate to a commissioned officer on a large warship, however, whereas Daniel left him to his job.

The fact that he had earned a fortune in prize money as a senior warrant officer under Daniel Leary seemed to bemuse Pasternak From what he had said, though, it was very important to his wife that he was the richest and most important man in Wassail County. The risk that came with being chief engineer to a fighting captain was for Pasternak far outweighed by his freedom from the social demands of staying home.

"I saw Lady Leary come on board yesterday," Vesey said. "Is that really all her luggage?"

"*Mistress* Leary," Daniel corrected mildly. "I'm not the heir, thank heavens, and I'm sure my father feels the same way. And yes, Miranda insisted on packing like a midshipman. I told her she had all the volume she wanted—I'd land a missile if I needed to and pick one up for ready money on route to Peltry, that's the Tarbell capital."

"A strong-willed woman," Vesey said, looking toward the gate and speaking without emphasis. "I suppose she'd need to be."

"I suppose she would," Daniel agreed.

He wasn't sure how he felt about that—how he felt about Miranda or even about marriage. He'd always taken his duties seriously, but he'd lived his personal life at his own convenience. Over the years since Daniel met Miranda when he delivered the news of her brother's death, he'd found that he was happier with her presence in his life. Keeping her there imposed reciprocal obligations, not because Miranda demanded them but because he was a Leary of Bantry and *honor* demanded them.

Needing something means that I might lose it. Daniel cleared his throat because he didn't like the direction his thoughts had been going.

He said aloud, "I'm glad to have so many qualified officers, because I'm not sure what we'll find in the Tarbell Stars. You may find yourself in command, Vesey, as you're more than capable of being."

Vesey turned to face him. "Sir," she said. "I studied every battle in the Academy syllabus, and I've watched you a dozen times ripping the heart out of enemies that should have flicked you away, flicked *us* away. But I'll never be as good as you are. I'll never be as good as Tim was when he was a midshipman, because he had the instinct and I don't!"

Daniel met her eyes. His first thought was to say something reassuring, but that would be an insult to someone as smart as Vesey was.

"Vesey," he said. "If you have to command in battle, you'll do everything that study and experience can provide. That puts you ahead of nine out of ten captains in the RCN."

He swallowed. "Killer instinct is an important thing to have in a fight, sure," he said, "and Tim Dorst—"

Who had been Vesey's lover until an eight-inch plasma bolt stuck his cutter.

"—had that in spades. But luck is even more important than instinct for a successful commander, and Midshipman Dorst was terminally unlucky. I'd rather have you as captain of the *Sissie* in my absence than Dorst, because I trust you to bring her safely home if anybody can do that."

The final two missiles rumbled into the corvette's magazines.

The last lowboy began to crawl away, and Hale stepped out of the way of the delivery gondola.

Daniel squeezed Lieutenant Vesey's shoulder and let her get on with her job.

Adele was in her library, not so much cleaning up details before she left as making sure that every scrap of information which might bear on the Tarbell Stars was coming along with her. She could study files during the voyage, but a log book or a personal reminiscence which was still in Xenos would do her no good on Peltry.

She could never be sure she had everything possible. She could never be sure she had done her job: even if the *Princess Cecile* and her complement returned successful, that didn't mean that Adele Mundy hadn't missed some datum which would have made it easier or cheaper.

The library door was ajar so Adele probably could have heard the whispering outside in the hallway, but as usual she was lost in her task. A fingertip tapped on the panel; then Tovera pushed it open enough to look in.

"Mistress," Tovera said. "Miriam Dorst is here to see you, if that's possible."

Adele looked at the remaining pile of chips which she was copying to her base unit. They were the office copies of logs from a shipping consortium based on Twig in the Alliance. None of the ships she had viewed thus far had traded into the Tarbell Stars, and she saw no likelihood that any of the others would have done so either.

"Yes, all right," Adele said, rubbing her eyes. "Tovera, have them get us something to drink, will you?"

The door closed, then reopened for Miranda's mother. Adele nodded, wondering if she ought to get up. She decided not to. Miriam had arrived without invitation, so merely agreeing to see her was being sufficiently courteous.

Besides, I've been sitting in so cramped a posture that I might fall back if I tried to get up abruptly.

"I'm sorry to disturb you when you're so busy..." the older woman said, holding her hands lightly together. She was more heavy-set than her daughter, making Adele wonder if Miranda would fill out similarly as she aged.

"I said I would see you," Adele said, hoping she didn't sound as peevish as she felt. "I'll never be able to finish what I'm doing here"—she gestured—"so the interruption doesn't really matter."

No matter how long Adele worked, there would be information she hadn't copied into files where she could access it off Cinnabar. She was probably foolish in considering that a goal, but she didn't see any reasonable point short of that to draw a line on her efforts.

Unexpectedly, Miriam smiled. "Miranda told me that you didn't do small talk," she said. "Well, I was going to explain that I was here to apologize again for the way I accused you when we were going to the reception, but that would be silly on my part."

"Yes," said Adele. "I heard you the first time."

She realized that Miriam was still standing and said, "Sit down, please, I think there's a chair—"

There wasn't.

"—well, move the pile on the one beside you to the floor and sit down. Please."

When the other woman hesitated, Adele stood; she'd been working her legs beneath the table since she realized how stiff she was. Before she could act, however, Miriam had set the pile neatly out of the way and seated herself.

"What I really wanted to do," Miriam said, "was to ask you to help my daughter if she needs it. She will be—"

Her voice caught. She swallowed and resumed, "Miranda will be the only civilian on a shipload of RCN personnel. I realize that you're RCN yourself—"

Adele gave an almost-smile. "Not really," she said when Miriam paused. "I'm not a spacer, and I certainly haven't internalized the forms of military discipline. Or the need for it, to be honest. But continue."

"Yes, I think that's what I was trying to say," said Miriam. "Miranda won't really fit in, so I hope that you'll be able to appreciate that and, well, look out for her."

"From all I've found," Adele said, reflexively bringing up the file into which she had transferred all the data she had on their destination, "Jardin is a pleasant world with very little crime. The government is an oligarchy and autocratic. Potential troublemakers are denied entry or are shipped off immediately, and if they do manage to break the law they're put to forced labor."

She tried to execute a smile. She was probably no more successful than she usually was, but she hoped Miranda's mother would give her credit for the attempt.

"It appears to me," Adele said, "that Miranda will be safer

DAVID DRAKE

on Jardin than she would be in Xenos. I'll further add that she is an extremely capable young woman and in as little need of watching over as anyone I know of her age."

The girl's mother sighed and seemed to hug herself more tightly. Looking toward a stack of file boxes on the floor to Adele's right, she said, "Timothy, my husband, used to talk about Jardin as though it were paradise. He was only there once, when he was a midshipman on a replenishment ship. I thought we might visit—before Miranda was born, or even later as a family. We never did."

"It's an expensive landfall, I suppose," Adele said when she realized she ought to say something to show that she was listening.

"We could have managed something while he was alive," Miriam said, meeting Adele's eyes. "After he died, things became—well, you know how things became. But until then we could have gone. I always suspected that he was afraid of ruining his memories of Jardin by facing the reality. The reality—"

Her voice became forceful, almost harsh, and the muscles in her cheeks drew tighter.

"—was that Timothy wouldn't have been twenty-two with a career ahead of him if he had gone back to Jardin. But he always kept a hologram of the port on our wall. I've kept it in the living room after his death."

Adele had the data unit out anyway. She picked up the wands and brought an image live in the room between them, using the larger display of her base unit. They were looking out to sea from a moderate vantage. A city—probably Cuvier, the capital—of red roofs and white walls was scattered up

70

the slope toward them from the shore below. The broad natural roadstead had been improved with stone moles which narrowed the entrance considerably.

The harbor accommodated forty-odd starships as well as a number of good-sized surface vessels. One of the starships was noticeably plainer and larger than most of the others.

Daniel would be able to identify it by eye, Adele thought, whereas she had spent her time learning other skills than memorizing ship profiles. Her wands isolated the ship, then ran it through a sorting protocol. She remembered that Miriam had referred to 'a replenishment ship,' so that saved a fraction of a second—Adele smiled mentally—from the search.

"A Leaf Class vessel, probably the *Orangeleaf*," Adele said aloud. That was bragging, but she was proud of her skills.

"Yes," Miriam said. "Your ladyship? How did you do that? How did you bring the picture on my wall to here?"

For a moment the tension in the older woman's voice surprised Adele. She said, "The base image is resident on your apartment's control system. I simply—oh."

It hadn't occurred to Adele that there might be reason to conceal what she had done. She wouldn't have concealed it anyway, of course, but she might have explained in a more—

No, she wouldn't have tried to sound more apologetic either. She was who she was.

"Mistress Dorst," Adele said. "Your daughter is important to Captain Leary, and he—Daniel—is important to me. And to the RCN, I suppose. As a matter of course I set up links with Miranda's residence in case someone attempted to put pressure on Daniel by threatening his fiancée."

She coughed. "Now that Miranda has moved out, I can remove the links," she said. "I should say that Daniel had nothing—knew nothing—about my precautions. I didn't bother to waste words on something in which I trusted my own judgment."

"Yes, of course you trust your judgment," Miriam said as she relaxed. "As I do, Adele. It startled me, but it shouldn't have."

She gestured to the hologram. The projection was omnidirectional, clear to her as well as to Adele. She went on, "Yes, that's the *Orangeleaf*. It was Timothy's first cruise. We were married the day after he graduated from the Academy."

Miriam was smiling, but her eyes weren't focused on Adele or even on the image of Jardin. "He was so full of dreams," she said. "We both were. And we had two wonderful children. Promotion wasn't quick, even in wartime. Timothy wasn't a lucky officer like..."

"Like Daniel," Adele said to close the embarrassed silence. "He's been very fortunate."

That was true, of course, but it was also true that Daniel made a great deal of his own luck. Very few junior lieutenants would have turned a disaster like the Kostroma Revolt into a triumph and a springboard to greater triumphs.

Miriam nodded apologetically to Adele. "And that's very fortunate for Miranda," the older woman said. "For me as well, of course. But I recognize that my daughter is always going to be...well, Daniel Leary is a very dominant person."

"I've found that to be the case with most RCN officers," Adele said. "Haven't you? The successful ones in particular."

She shrugged. "If you mean that Daniel will continue to

make decisions for himself," she said, "yes, I think and hope that will be true. He'll often ask advice, but I've never known him to take orders except from someone who has the right under RCN regulations to give him those orders."

And even then we've been known to cut corners, Adele recalled. She didn't suppress her smile as she normally would have, since she thought it would have a good effect on the tone of the discussion.

"Yes, of course that's right," Miriam said, stiffly again; perhaps the smile hadn't been a good idea. "Life isn't fair, after all."

"I don't know how to define 'fair,'" Adele said, feeling sudden anger at the situation, at life. "I've killed many people, I don't know how many. And some of them were doubtless as innocent as my little sister Agatha."

For a moment she saw again the crowd blocking their way as they broke out of the cells beneath the Elector's Palace in Kostroma City. They were civilians who happened to be in the way of Adele Mundy and her new friends, so she shot as many of them as she could to panic the rest. There was no time to do clear the way in any other fashion.

"At the time I did it, at all those times..." Adele said, hearing the harshness in her voice. "I thought it was the best available option. Given the same situations, I would again shoot men, women and children. I'm sure there were children in the crowd in Kostroma, and even if I didn't shoot them some must have been trampled in the panic that I caused. So that we could escape. It wasn't a bit fair, it was necessary."

She was on her feet, though she didn't remember standing;

Miriam had risen also. Adele hoped she hadn't raised her voice, but the courtesy Esme Rolfe Mundy had instilled in her children should have prevented that.

Miriam stepped forward and hugged her. Adele tried to step back by reflex, but the desk caught her at the upper thighs.

"Lady Mundy, Adele," Miriam said. She was apparently crying, though Adele couldn't be sure. "Thank you. My little girl couldn't have a better protector in the life she's chosen. Thank you for being her friend."

Miriam moved away, snuffled, and wiped her nose and cheeks with a handkerchief. "I'd better go now. Thank you so much."

Miriam closed the door quietly behind her. A moment later Tovera looked in but didn't speak.

I didn't say I was Miranda's friend, Adele thought. *But I suppose I am, everyone aboard the* Sissie *is.*

She looked at Tovera and said, "I believe Miranda is fortunate. In her friends."

CHAPTER 5

BERGEN AND ASSOCIATES YARD, CINNABAR

Adele settled comfortably at the signals console of the *Princess Cecile*. Because the ship was well overstrength, every seat on the bridge was taken. Tovera would normally have been in the striker's seat on the back of the signals console; for this voyage she was on a jumpseat against the aft bulkhead and Midshipman Hale shared Adele's console.

The *Sissie*'s bridge was more of a home to Adele than the library of Chatsworth Minor was . . . though when she thought about it, she didn't think of anyplace as "home" in the sense that other people seemed to do. She lived in her own mind.

That had been as true while Adele was growing up as the child of the powerful Senator Lucas Mundy as it was now as a respected member of the crew of the *Princess Cecile*. In the years between she had lived hand to mouth as an orphan and a penniless scholar. During that time her ability to ignore external reality had been a valuable survival tool.

"*Testing thrusters One and Eight*," a voice from the power

room announced over the PA system and the general channel of the ship's intercom. Adele didn't think Pasternak himself was speaking, but the sound quality was too poor for her to be certain.

Two of the eight thrusters lit, shaking the ship and blasting iridescent plasma into the water of the slip. Their nozzles were flared open to minimize impulse; even with the leaves sphinctered down to minimum aperture, two thrusters weren't enough to lift the corvette from the surface.

Adele brought her display up and began sorting communications inputs. There wasn't any reason to do that here and very little benefit to the practice anywhere else, but it was Adele's habit to know as much as possible about her surroundings. Not because of possible dangers, but simply because she liked to know things.

A telltale showed her that Hale was echoing Adele's display. That wasn't a problem—if Adele had wanted privacy, she would have enforced it—but it reminded her for the first time that her console mate was a colleague who in theory she might be training.

Adele pinned a small real-time view of her face to Hale's display; the top register of her own display already had images of all the personnel seated at consoles. On a two-way link to Hale she said, "I intercept signals as a matter of course and put them through a mechanical sort. If we were on another planet, even if it weren't a potentially hostile one, I'd give a quick look at the findings in case I saw something that the algorithm didn't."

The power room continued to announce thruster testing,

working in pairs through the set. The big pumps in the stern throbbed, replenishing the reaction mass tanks from the harbor. The same tanks would be distilled to provide drinking water: impurities mattered very little when the fluid was being stripped to plasma and spewed through the thrusters.

The impurities mattered even less when the mass was being converted to antimatter before being recombined with normal matter in the High Drive motors. The High Drive was more efficient and provided much higher impulse, but it could only be used in the near vacuum of space: in an atmosphere, the inevitable leakage of antimatter which had escaped recombination flared violently and devoured everything nearby, including the hull.

"*Do you have any information about Jardin beyond the* Sailing Directions *which might be useful, ma'am?*" Hale said. Though their faces were only about forty inches apart on opposite sides of the immaterial barrier of a holographic display, only the intercom made it possible for them to communicate without shouting. "*I don't mean restricted information, just ... anything that would let me do my job better.*"

Since they were able to see one another, there was no need for the ponderous communications protocols which the RCN drummed into its signals personnel. Adele had no training: she was in civilian life a librarian whose skills fitted her for far more subtle uses of electronics than remembering to mutter "Over" and "Go ahead" and similar procedures.

"Yes," Adele said. She brought up an image of Cuvier and Cuvier Harbor on Jardin; Hale could manipulate the scale and orientation on her own display if she chose to. The harbor would have been an open roadstead, dangerous in a storm from the west, had it not been narrowed by moles from each headland. There was a passage through which surface vessels could enter.

"*We'll be landing here at the capital?*" Hale said.

"We'll land at Cuvier because it's the only starport on Jardin with proper facilities," Adele said, highlighting twenty-one points in and around the city; she had to increase the scale slightly to capture two outliers. "It's the capital by convenience, but Jardin really doesn't have a government, just a management reporting to the First Families who own the planet. Each family has a house near Cuvier though many of the principals live on distant estates. Here they are."

"*Closing main hatch*," Vesey announced. She was in charge of liftoff from the armored Battle Direction Center in the stern. Personnel at the duplicate controls there could control the ship if the bridge were out of action; or as now, when Daniel Leary at the command console was explaining procedures to his bride in the striker's seat.

The *Princess Cecile*'s main hatch clanged. A rapid-fire ringing followed as bolts dogged it tight. Other hatches were still open, including two on the bridge itself. Ozone from the thruster exhaust made Adele's eyes water, but she was too used to the experience to be consciously aware of it any more.

"*The* Sailing Directions *didn't say anything about political problems*," Hale said.

The *Sailing Directions* for each region of the human universe were compiled by Navy House for the guidance of spacefarers. The RCN personnel doing the work paid no attention to planetary sensitivities: if in the opinion of Navy House a ship landing on Jardin risked being caught up in a revolution, the *Sailing Directions* would have said so. That was true even for worlds within the Cinnabar empire, let alone neutrals like Jardin.

Hale added, "*I'd think a setup like that was a bomb waiting to go off.*"

"Perhaps if Jardin were more crowded it would be, Hale," Adele said. "The First Families have a tradition of service to the community. Ordinary citizens have a high standard of living, and Jardin doesn't allow immigrants. Agriculture and the service industries are largely staffed by foreigners, but they're on two-year contracts which are rigidly enforced. I gather the workers"—laborers and whores—"are also well treated and well paid, but so long as they're shipped off promptly, that isn't important."

"*It sounds like paradise, doesn't it?*" Hale said.

"Perhaps," said Adele dryly. "There are no libraries that I've found in the records."

Jardin was ideally placed to gather information. Ships came from all portions of the human universe, bringing the rich and powerful to relax. The logs of those ships contained unique information which could be compiled into an unequaled database.

No one on Jardin was interested in doing that. Adele felt her lips quiver. Despite what she'd said to Hale, it was possible to gain Jardin citizenship by the unanimous agreement of the First Families. Perhaps Lady Mundy could arrange that on her retirement from the RCN.

"*Ma'am?*" Hale said. "*Ah, you're smiling?*"

Was I? Apparently she had been. Aloud Adele said, "I expect to be dead when I leave the RCN, Hale. But it seems to amuse my subconscious to consider what I might do if I remained alive."

She paused thoughtfully and added, "Of course, that leaves the question of providing for Tovera."

Thinking of her own retirement was a grim joke. Imagining that Tovera would survive was more of a farce.

"*Ma'am?*" Hale said.

"Sorry," Adele said, realizing that she had drifted off in the middle of an exposition. "The daSaenz family"—she focused down on a highlight immediately to the north of the city and harbor—"isn't very politically active, but it's among the wealthiest of the First Families. They own the Starscape Caves in the limestone under their mansion."

She continued to increase the magnification on a courtyard building perched on a peak. It was almost a rectangle, but the angles had been adjusted slightly to allow for the contours of the ground. The end overlooking the city was a four-story tower, but the other walls were only two.

The slope immediately below the building was forested. Scattered city housing continued some distance up from the water, but the straight terminus implied a boundary line.

"Mistress Leary's father spoke with enthusiasm about the caves, so Daniel—" should she have said, "Captain Leary?" Too late now. "—contacted the present head of the family to be sure that he'd be able to take Miranda through. She's Carlotta daSaenz, and she was very gracious."

Hale's image was frowning. "Six"—the captain's call sign and the crew's usual nickname for Daniel—"sent a communications ship to Jardin?"

"There's enough traffic between here and Jardin that he didn't need a dedicated vessel." Which would have been enormously expensive, even for Daniel. "An admiral taking his family on holiday to Jardin carried the message there as a favor, and Lady Carlotta sent her reply by a returning yacht—a favor to her. It arrived two days ago."

All eight thrusters were alight together. Though their nozzles were flared, the corvette bucked and pitched. Plasma vaporized divots in the slip, and water surged in from the harbor proper to replace it. The *Sissie*'s hull and outriggers responded to the flow. Hydraulic rams closed the bridge hatches, but other hatches remained open. The sting of ions became sharper, and there were occasional sparkles in the air.

"*These caves weren't mentioned in the* Sailing Directions," Hale said, indicating both that she was listening and that she wanted to hear more. Active damping kept ambient noise from overwhelming their conversation, though loose objects were jouncing against every surface.

"There are animals in the caves which give off light," Adele explained. "Metazoans, which I suppose means insects—multicelled creatures, anyway, but they're spread in flat patches on the walls. They glow in the dark, which is why it's the Starscape Caves."

She shrugged, though she wasn't sure that the gesture was visible on the tight head shot she'd put on Hale's display. "It doesn't sound very interesting to me," she said, "but it impressed Captain Dorst. And I'm sure Daniel will be pleased to see the animals for himself. I forwarded all the information I found on them"—which wasn't very much—"but I don't understand any more than I've told you. If that."

"*Ship, prepare for liftoff!*" Vesey said.

"*Ma'am,*" Hale said. "*Thank you. And thank you for getting me this opportunity to serve with Captain Leary.*"

"*Liftoff!*"

Vesey sphinctered the thruster apertures to minimum diameter. The mass flow was already at full, so the concentrated jets began to lift the corvette in a bubble of steam and free ions.

Adele settled onto her couch. Plasma thrusters didn't crush people down, but the *Sissie* could exceed two gravities once it had overcome inertia. She was thinking about Hale's words.

Adele had met Hale, an out-of-work midshipman, and had suggested to Cory that he tell his former classmate that Captain Leary was hiring crew to take a freighter to Corcyra. Hale had applied and signed on as a common spacer. She had been an asset for that voyage, and she was aboard the *Princess Cecile* now as a midshipman.

That had certainly been what Hale wanted, but Adele wasn't sure it had been a favor to the young woman. Service on a warship was dangerous even in peacetime, and there was rarely peace where Daniel Leary took the *Princess Cecile*.

Everyone dies, Adele thought as the ship roared and trembled into the sky. *Which means that we're all racing on the way to our deaths*.

She smiled.

* * *

THE MATRIX: BETWEEN CINNABAR AND JARDIN

Daniel walked out on the hull of the *Princess Cecile* ahead of Miranda. He wore a rigging suit, armored against knife-edged fractures and hawsers worn into bristles of spearpoints; Miranda was in an air suit of tough fabric.

The Matrix, a panorama not of stars but of universes, flared above them. The *Sissie* was in a bubble universe of her own. The sails stretched on her four rings of antennas blocked Casimir energy and shoved her from one bubble to another. It was impossible to exceed the speed of light, but constants of velocity and distance varied among universes. By using those variations a starship could travel great distances in the sidereal universe, making a series of relatively short voyages in other universes.

Getting used to a stiffened hard suit required practice; until then the user was both uncomfortable and clumsy, which increased her danger. An air suit was safe for any regular use except running up and down the rigging to clear jams or to splice cables, and even for those tasks it was sufficient for anyone who was careful. A rigger in a crisis couldn't be careful, not and do his job.

Daniel worried about Miranda, but—he grinned within his helmet—he was going to do that anyway. He didn't hold Miranda directly, but he gripped the safety line which connected their suits. So long as one of Miranda's magnetic sandals was planted on the steel hull, she should be fine; but it was her first experience outside a starship, let alone a starship in the Matrix.

The *Sissie* would continue on her present course for the

next seventeen minutes, so the antennas and yards were motionless; there was no chance of a broken sheet whipping anyone off the hull. The riggers on duty—the starboard watch under Dasi—were at their scattered stations.

When hydromechanical equipment changed the area and aspect of the sails, the riggers watched to be sure that the result was what the semaphores indicated that the astrogational computer had intended. If a cable jammed or a gear didn't rotate by the right number teeth or if any of a myriad of other possible things went wrong, the riggers corrected the problem with whatever tool was required.

Daniel stopped ahead of the Dorsal A Ring antenna on the *Sissie*'s bow. He waited until Miranda halted beside him, then took out the thirty-six-inch brass communication rod which the tool shop of the Bantry Estate had manufactured to his specifications. He placed one end against Miranda's helmet, then moved his own helmet against the other end and said, "This is all existence."

He swept his free arm across the pulsing ambiance. The dense liquid filling the sealed rod vibrated to carry his words to Miranda without the awkwardness of touching helmets. An electrical impulse impinging on the sails, even a low-powered radio wave, could send a ship in the Matrix wildly off course. Riggers used hand signals—and experience—when a problem required coordination.

"These are every universe which has ever existed. This is the cosmos," Daniel said. He took a deep breath and added, "This is paradise."

He smiled, though Miranda couldn't see his expression

while he was facing forward. Perhaps she could hear the flush of contentment in his voice.

Miranda took her end of the rod to connect them firmly. "I can't take it in," she said. "I suppose that's as it should be, since it's well, everything. Each of those dots is a universe?"

The Matrix was a wash of pastels, the color of each bead varying according to its energy state relative to that of the universe in which the corvette was travelling at present. The astrogation computer of a starship could plot a practical course between any pair of points entered into it.

A really skilled astrogator, however, could shave hours or days off a course by studying the Matrix and choosing subtle gradations which better suited the ship's purposes than the one-size-fits-all course which the computer provided. Daniel had been trained by his uncle, Commander Stacy Bergen, who had opened more routes than any other single explorer since the Hiatus in star travel had ended a millennium before.

Daniel had heard himself described as his uncle's equal as an astrogator, which he knew was not true. He liked to think that Uncle Stacy wouldn't be embarrassed by his nephew's abilities, however.

"Daniel?" Miranda said. "You know you're famous. Do you think about that?"

Daniel felt his stomach tighten. *Does she know what I've been thinking?*

But of course she didn't, and anyway she hadn't asked whether he was proud of his skills. She'd asked how famous he wanted to be.

"I don't think about fame at all," he said. "Well, that's not really true—I'm human, I like to be praised, I like to be able to get seats when we go out no matter where we go. But I've never done anything because I thought, 'People will praise me for this.' Never. I've done things because I thought they were the right things to do."

Or maybe because they were in front of me and I thought I'd try them. Much the way I used to pick up women at parties....Daniel didn't say that, though it wouldn't have surprised Miranda to hear.

He turned his head so that he was looking out his right sidelight toward Miranda. Hardsuit helmets were fixed to the torso piece and did not rotate with the wearer's neck.

"Love," Daniel said, "it's like money. I like it and I like to spend it; but I spent money when I didn't have it, so nothing much has changed there. As for power, I never wanted any except the power to run my own life."

He grinned again, broadly. "I actually have less of that now than I did when I was a cadet," he said. "There's thousands of people that want a piece of me; at the Academy I only had to worry about my instructors and the cadre."

The void before them was gradually turning green though the shade was barely bright enough to be called a color. The *Princess Cecile* would shortly transition into another universe. Since there was only a slight energy gradient, even a complete newbie like Miranda would be safe on the hull. Daniel intended to get her inside nonetheless.

"What about friends?" Miranda asked.

Daniel had been about to suggest they return to the forward airlock, but the question stopped him. "I..." he said.

"Miranda, yes of course friends matter, more than anything else, I guess."

He wasn't sure that was true: a lot of things mattered to him, duty and Cinnabar and Miranda and the Leary name and a score of other things that were now fluttering around in his mind. But certainly friends.

"Having, well, *being* famous," he said, "hasn't brought me more friends, not real ones. It doesn't work that way, you know that. The only real peer I have now is Adele. She doesn't care what I've done for her or what I might do for her. None of the things that other people look at matter to her."

"But at the reception . . . ?" Miranda said.

The yellow-green ambiance was becoming more saturated, though it was still so faint as to be almost subliminal. Daniel shrugged mentally and said, "Vondrian and Ames and Pennyroyal, you mean? We knew each other at the Academy and knocked around together afterwards whenever we were all in Xenos—sitting in Navy House waiting for an assignment, often enough. We didn't really spend a lot of time together."

He felt a tingling as the corvette neared the boundary layer. "There in the kitchen," Daniel said, "when we tied one on . . . that's the closest I've come to carefree friendship since I was promoted. It's not exactly that we were carefree at the Academy. We worried about grades and promotion and money, all that sort of thing. But we were mates, and getting drunk with mates is . . . there's no strings on it. And it'll never be that way except maybe once in a while, like at the reception."

"Let's go inside," Miranda said, her voice very soft. She released her end of the commo rod and hugged him carefully.

Daniel led the way back to the hatch. The *Sissie* was already pulsing as they began the transition, but they would be inside before real discontinuity.

He closed the airlock behind them. Air pressure began to build, but before the light indicated it was safe to open the inner lock he leaned his helmet against Miranda's. He said, "I keep thinking of Lord Anston, darling. An old man, frail and alone. But he was the greatest fighting captain the RCN ever had, in his day."

"You won't go that way, Daniel," Miranda said. "You won't be a lonely old man."

Then she said, "One way or the other, my love, you won't be that."

CHAPTER 6

CUVIER HARBOR ON JARDIN

"*Opening main hatch*," Vesey warned over the PA system. Daniel, at the back of the boarding hold, squeezed Miranda's hand and released it. Landings on distant worlds were part of his normal routine, but this was the first time his wife had been off Cinnabar.

The bolts locking the main hatch into the *Sissie*'s hull withdrew with as much racket than they had made when ringing home. When dogged shut, the hatch was a stressed portion of the corvette's frame. Now the ship sighed, shaking herself as the hatch pivoted slowly downward to become the boarding ramp.

Steam and ozone sucked into the hold; Miranda flinched slightly. Exhaust from the plasma thrusters was quenched in the harbor when ships made normal water landings, but in still air a miasma of steam and ions hung about the vessel for as long as an hour. The atmosphere was safe within a few minutes of landing so ships rarely waited more, but the first experience of plasma-laced steam and harbor sludge was—literally—breathtaking.

Normally the liberty party would have cheered, but today the Sissies packed in the hold were showing their company manners—Daniel smiled—for Six and his lady. Miranda no more needed to be coddled than Adele did, but the crew was erring on the side of courtesy. That was always proper behavior.

Woetjans and four riggers carried the extendable boarding bridge down the ramp while it was still lowering. Jardin's triple moons were too small for their gravity to matter, but solar tides raised and lowered the harbor surface by as much as six feet.

The quays of most ports provided ladders to deal with tidal variations. The sort of passengers—and yacht owners—who visited Cuvier were provided with stone steps rising to the top of the quay so that they didn't get their hands and clothing slimy. Even the nonskid surfaces of the steps couldn't protect the soles of their shoes from filth, but there were probably mats at the top for cleaning them.

The *Sissie*'s boarding bridge was a roll of light-metal pontoons which the crew inflated. It connected the ramp with the floating stage attached to the quay by a track. Two members of Woetjans' team bounced across the bridge while it was still filling and clamped the free end. They trotted up the steps and waited on the quay.

Daniel grinned and murmured to Miranda, "They're showing off."

"They have a right to," she replied. "They're better than acrobats to be able to do that without falling into the water."

"They're riggers," he said. "If they make a mistake in the Matrix they have worse trouble than getting wet."

He didn't add, "Regulations aside, riggers don't wear safety lines. You'll drift for all eternity if you get separated from your ship." Miranda probably knew that already, from her brother or her brother's friends.

"*The liberty party is*—" Vesey's voice began.

"Hold up a bloody minute!" Woetjans called from the edge of the ramp. She was used to shouting over the noise of a dockyard; the Sissies in the hold could hear her easily. The spacers going on liberty had begun to surge forward in anticipation of release, but they settled back now.

"This isn't like the usual landfall!" the bosun said. "You're not working for the RCN now, you're working for Six himself. If you show your asses, you embarrass Six and you embarrass me."

She paused, letting her words sink in. "Nobody's saying you can't have fun," Woetjans said. "I'm going to get outside a couple jars of good liquor and find a man who's drunk enough that he don't mind looking at me. *But*—no problems, you got that? You may think Six is a soft-hearted git who won't go at you too hard, and maybe that's true; but I'm not. You embarrass me and we'll discuss it, understood? And it won't be going on the charge sheet, it'll be personal."

The bosun grinned. To call her plain would be undue praise at the best of times, but her expression now was terrifying.

"*Now* the liberty party is released!" she said.

Cheering, the spacers filed out of the hold and across the boarding bridge two abreast. Ribbons with ships' names and landfalls fluttered from the seams of their liberty suits.

"I've split the liberty parties into three at fifteen-minute intervals," Daniel explained. "I'm giving liberty to everybody but the anchor watch, and they'll go as soon as the first group returns to replace them. These are the senior people."

"Why split them if they're all going shortly?" Miranda asked.

"So that the five of us—" Daniel said, nodding past her toward Adele who stood a little apart with Hogg and Tovera "—had room to breathe before the first tranche disembarked."

The liberty party stopped at the marquee over the base of the quay. Four young women were processing the spacers through without undo delay. A pair of husky men stood behind the marquee, but they weren't armed even with truncheons.

Daniel frowned. He reached toward the bellows pocket of his tunic where he'd slipped a pair of RCN goggles. They had all the functions of a commo helmet's faceshield, so he could magnify the scene to get a better idea of what was going on.

"The authorities use facial recognition software on all visitors," Adele said, correctly interpreting Daniel's expression. "Anyone whom their database thinks is a threat to good order is denied entry. And if you're wondering, there's an emergency response squad on alert at all times. They're quite heavily armed."

"We could handle them," Tovera said straight-faced. "Even without the turret guns."

Miranda burst out laughing and hugged Daniel with the nearer arm. She obviously knew Adele's servant well enough that Tovera's dry humor didn't bother her.

Daniel wasn't sure humor was quite the word. Tovera created humor by studying what ordinary people thought was funny, much as she based her actions on what Adele did. The latter seemed to be an adequate substitute for the conscience which Tovera lacked.

"I think we can start off," Daniel said, having judged the rate at which the liberty party was moving through the marquee. "Then Vesey can send the second section down."

They were all in civilian clothes; Daniel wasn't even wearing the saucer hat that would mark him as a ship's officer. His dull yellow tunic and trousers were loose-fitting with many pockets. Miranda's outfit was similar but in a shade of pale green printed with a chain-link pattern.

They were as clearly *not* uniforms as Daniel could find without going to colors so bright that he would stand out, since he didn't want that either. Adele and Tovera were in suits of cream and tan respectively, and Hogg wore blue slops instead of the garish finery that was really to his taste.

At the boarding bridge Daniel looked at Miranda and said, "If you'd like to go ahead?"

"There's room for both of us," she replied, squeezing closer but breaking her stride so that their feet syncopated one another instead of landing in unison.

Daniel nodded mentally in approval. He had seen a bridge undulate when a squad of soldiers marched over it—halfway over, because it had flung them off. Miranda didn't have personal experience of spacefaring, but she had read and listened to those who did—and she was very smart.

A heavy ground-effect ship had been running its engines

up in the separated harbor for planetbound transport. Now it moved forward, its speed building from a crawl. The nose lifted as the craft came onto the first hull step, and by the time it had reached the outer mole it was on the second step and still accelerating. The trailing edges of its short, broad wings curved down to boost the craft the rest of the way into full ground effect.

"Do you know where it's going?" Miranda asked, her eyes following the big vessel. "It's a passenger ship, isn't it?"

Daniel glanced over his shoulder. "Adele?" he said.

"It's the dedicated coach to Paradise Beach," Adele said, "though the management calls it a 'conveyance.' It's carrying a party of ten from Tabriz, plus their luggage and seventeen personal servants. And a pair of deogales, which are..."

Her voice paused. She was having a little trouble manipulating her control wands accurately as she walked.

"Deogales are six-legged omnivores from Humara," Daniel said. "The *Swiftsure* ported there on my training cruise. They're as much at home in brackish water as they are on the shore. They're affectionate little things to their masters, but—"

He felt himself frowning without meaning to.

"I hope they're not a mated pair," he said. "Without grillards"—six-legged carnivores; the young ate sprats and insectoids, the yard-long adults preferred deogales if they couldn't get domestic cats—"to keep them in check, they could spread over the whole planet."

"Paradise Beach is an island," Adele said. "At what the Khan of Tabriz is paying the Bruckoff family for this vacation, they can sterilize and replant."

Daniel winced. He knew Adele was correct; most of the outlying leisure compounds on Jardin had already been sanitized for their guests' comfort. That was good business ... but he had grown up in the forests and marshes of Bantry under Hogg's tutelage. The discomfort—the itching, the thorn pricks, the bites and kicks and occasional real danger—had made him a part of nature, of life.

But this wasn't Daniel's world or even Cinnabar's world; and few Cinnabar citizens would have agreed with Daniel anyway.

They had reached the marquee and the smiling attendants. On the boulevard beyond was a rank of ground vehicles, but at least half the initial liberty party was crossing to the strip of bars and clubs facing the harbor.

A natty looking young man approached the marquee from the street side. The male attendants saw him first and jumped to attention. The fellow was dressed in Pleasaunce fashion—a suit with narrow, broken, vertical stripes in tones from yellow to russet.

"Just step to the footprints in front of the barrier, sir," the professionally perky woman at the nearest counter said to Daniel. She and her colleagues weren't as young as he had thought from a distance, but they were extremely attractive. There were four passages through the line of counters, each with a crossbar.

"Captain Leary, isn't it?" called the well-dressed young man. The female attendants stiffened just as their male colleagues had done a moment before. "And that would be Miranda Dorst Leary, would it not?"

"Sir ... ?" said the woman who had spoken to Daniel. She

turned her head and torso but kept her feet where they were planted. "Are these friends of yours, sir?"

"They are indeed, friends and guests of the daSaenz family," the young man said. "I think we can dispense the formalities, can't we, girls."

Without waiting for an answer—if he had even been asking a question; Daniel hadn't noticed one in his voice—the man lifted the bar and stepped through. The attendants remained at attention.

"I am Timothy daSaenz," the man said, clasping Daniel's forearm with his own in Pleasaunce, and more generally Alliance, fashion. "My mother Carlotta sent me to greet you and bring you to the house."

"Pleased to meet—" Daniel said. Before he could complete the phrase, daSaenz had turned to Miranda, clicked his heels—his calf-high boots were of pebbled leather—and bowed at the waist.

If I tried that, Daniel thought, *I'd fall on my face.*

Then he thought, *And I'd deserve to for acting like a prat.*

"I've brought the aircar," daSaenz said, turning and lifting his right hand to shoulder level. His index finger gestured forward. "Please come with me. Mother was insistent that you be shown the caves at once."

"Ah, Master daSaenz..." Daniel said. He led Miranda between the counters but then put a hand possessively on her waist when there was room enough to walk abreast again. "Thank you very much for the offer, but we're staying in the Ultramarine here in Cuvier. We'll be happy to join you after we've settled in, but—"

"Nonsense," daSaenz said. "I can't possibly allow you to go to a public hostelry. That would be an insult to my mother and to my family."

He stopped at a small aircar at the end of the row of ground vehicles. Its body shimmered between blue and silver. There were two comfortable seats in the back and a driver's cockpit in the front.

"Master daSaenz," Daniel said. He was used to bumptious young aristocrats. *I rather was one myself.*

A mental grin broke his mood. Instead of going on as he had been about to, Daniel said, "We'll be back as soon as we've freshened up and I've taken care of some of the ship's business here. We really appreciate—"

"Come," daSaenz said with a smile. "Mother has closed the caves for you and your bride. You look particularly lovely, Mistress Leary—"

He clicked his heels again, but at least he didn't bow.

"—and I assure you that the glowworms will not complain about your toilet."

"My business—" Daniel said.

"Captain Leary," Adele said. "Your officers can handle the business, I'm sure. You'll recall that I am one of your officers."

"Ah, Miranda . . . ?" Daniel said, looking at her.

"It's entirely up to you, Daniel," she said. "But I've never looked forward to a hotel room, and I've dreamed of the Starscape Caves all my life."

"There's only two seats," said Hogg. The words were neutral, but nobody who heard him would have thought he was happy about the situation.

DAVID DRAKE

DaSaenz frowned slightly. To Daniel—he didn't look at Hogg—he said, "I'll arrange ground vehicles for your servants, though of course they won't be necessary at the manor."

This is not *what I want to do*, Daniel thought. He hoped his irritation didn't show on his face.

"Mother isn't feeling quite well this morning," daSaenz said. "And of course she's seen the caves many times. She's sure she'll be ready to greet you after a brief rest, however, and she looks forward to doing so after I've guided you through the caves."

It is *what Miranda wants to do, and that's why we're on Jardin to begin with*. Of course Adele could by herself handle the initial meeting with their prospective employers...and from her comment, it sounded like she would prefer to do so.

"I think we'll be all right without you for the time being, Hogg," Daniel said, meeting his servant's eyes. "You can follow in a cab if you like, or you can spend the afternoon on your own. I'll be back by evening to check on matters, regardless of where Miranda and I decide to sleep for the next few days."

He looked at daSaenz. "You can arrange that, I trust?" Daniel said.

"Yes, of course," daSaenz agreed. "I'll put a car and driver at your disposal for as long as you stay on Jardin."

"I guess I'll check out one a' these bars," Hogg said. He wasn't happy, but he knew better than to argue. He slouched away.

Adele nodded crisply and, with Tovera, started back toward the *Princess Cecile*. Daniel wasn't sure whether or not she had already arranged a meeting with General Storn or his agents.

She was probably right in believing it was better that

the initial contact be in her hands. Spies made Daniel uncomfortable. He got along with Adele by consciously ignoring that other aspect of her life.

"Very well, Master daSaenz," Daniel said. "We'll be pleased to accompany you."

He took Miranda's hand and helped her step into the rear of the aircar—there were no doors. Miranda didn't need help, but if Daniel hadn't done so their host would have offered his arm.

And Daniel wasn't going to have that.

The store—*The Compass Rose, Rare Manuscripts*—was nestled between a high-end dress shop and a jewelry store with a uniformed concierge whose eyes had seen a great deal. He and Tovera traded glances as she followed Adele into the bookstore.

The shop was empty except for the fat man behind the counter. He looked up from a handwritten ledger and smiled. Glazed shelves resting on map drawers covered the sidewalls. There was a door into the back beside the counter.

"I'm told you have an original Thomas Middleton manuscript?" Adele said.

"Yes, ma'am," said the proprietor. He was mostly bald, but his fringe of hair and small moustache were black. "Go through to the viewing rooms, please."

He gestured to the door. "It's laid out in the room to the right."

Adele entered the back; the shopkeeper had returned to his ledger. Tovera stepped in front of her and opened the door. A bundle of stained paper, written on in spiky age-browned ink, was open on the table; above it was the faded ribbon with which it had been tied.

The stocky man who had been looking at the document nodded to Tovera, then to Adele when her servant retreated to the short hallway. Adele closed the door.

"Is that really a Thomas Middleton manuscript?" she said.

"Apparently," the man said. "Jardin isn't thought of as an intellectual center, but there's a great deal of money here. There are whimsical collectors of all sorts, passing through as well as among the First Families themselves."

He was probably in his late twenties, but he looked scarcely out of boyhood when he smiled, as he did now. "I'm Mikhail Grozhinski," he said.

Adele set her data unit on the table, being careful not to disturb the manuscript. She began checking the name against her files.

"Your records will indicate that I'm a major in the Fifth Bureau, Lady Mundy," Grozhinski said calmly. "They may or may not tell you that I am the son of General Storn, whom you know. In this instance I'm acting as his envoy."

"They didn't tell me the relationship," Adele said, entering new information in the file. When she delivered her report to Mistress Sand, the addition would be part of it. Without looking toward Grozhinski she said, "Are you here in your official capacity?"

"I am not," said Grozhinski. "Lady Mundy, your participation in this affair has been cleared at the highest levels of your government—not, of course, that you'd be safe if things went really wrong. I am acting as a traitor to my own government, though in turn I'll be a hero if we succeed. If you succeed.'

He plucked his loose-fitting tunic. It was a darker blue-gray than his gray-blue trousers. "I'm here on vacation with my friend Stephen," he said. "He's in a bistro, now, while I'm doing something boring. Stephan has nothing to do with my work"—a wry smile—"or any work, if it comes to that. But he amuses me."

"If things go really wrong, as you put it," Adele said, "I would expect to be dead. Political embarrassment is farther down my list of concerns."

The risk of death had never concerned her very much. Personal failure concerned her a great deal.

She looked up at Grozhinski. "Why is General Storn unofficially involved in the Upholder Rebellion?" she said.

"The Fifth Bureau's Diocese Three has extended jurisdiction over about half the Tarbell Stars, including Peltry, the capital," Grozhinski said. "Diocese One oversees the remainder of the cluster, including Ithaca, the center of the rebellion. Our brief—the Bureau's brief—is to put down anti-Alliance feeling in the Tarbell Stars but not to involve ourselves in the cluster's internal politics."

Adele listened as she compared the words with the information in her files. She didn't really have to look at the files; she had absorbed the important points before the *Princess Cecile* lifted from Cinnabar. She preferred the feeling of viewing a situation through an electronic filter, though, to getting the data firsthand.

"Krychek is aiding the Upholders, however," Grozhinski

said. "My father suspects he's actually behind the rebellion."

"This is why Porra divides regions for observation, isn't it?" Adele said. She entered the new information as she spoke. "Why hasn't General Storn simply reported the situation instead of involving himself—"

She looked at Grozhinski again, this time for effect.

"—in treason?"

"General Storn ... fears, I think, rather than actually suspects," Grozhinski said, speaking for the first time with obvious care. "Fears that Krychek has mentioned his intention to the Guarantor and has not been prevented from going ahead."

"If the Alliance were to absorb the Tarbell Stars," Adele said. "It would be a clear violation of the Treaty of Amiens."

"It would if the Cinnabar Senate were to view it as such," Grozhinski agreed. "It is not certain—"

If he had been circumspect in suggesting that Guarantor Porra might know what Diocese One had under way, he was doubly that now.

"—that the Guarantor fully appreciates how badly the prolonged state of war with Cinnabar has strained our economy. The risk of complete economic and political collapse *might* not weigh as heavily on him as it does on my father. Collapse of both Cinnabar and ourselves, of course."

"I see," Adele said as she entered more information.

For the first time Adele understood why Mistress Sand had encouraged her to get involved in this mare's nest. Like Storn, Mistress Sand was concerned about the political effect of renewed war. The Republic had come very close to breaking up in class conflict before the Treaty of Amiens; and if Cinnabar itself lost cohesion, the planets it now ruled would go off in a hundred different directions.

That said, Cinnabar agents meddling in a region which was clearly within the Alliance's sphere of influence constituted a cause of war also. Sand wanted Krychek's plotting to fail, but not if that meant the Republic's obvious involvement. She must be hoping that a corvette in private registry—and her crew— would not be enough to catch the attention of Pleasaunce.

Grozhinski set an eight-by-four-inch case on the table; it was less than two inches wide. "These are the log chips of a hundred and thirty ships trading in what is now Alliance space," he said. "My father said you collect such things, so you might like them. The oldest is that of the *Wideawake*, which is pre-Hiatus."

Adele set her wands down and opened the case. The chips were of varying sizes and appearance. The case must have been purpose-built, as each pocket precisely fitted the log in it.

"These aren't copies," Adele said.

"Father returned copies to the archives," Grozhinski said. "But yes, these are the originals."

He cleared his throat. "There is additional material—the background on matters we discussed here—at the end of the *Wideawake* log," he said.

Adele closed the case, then put her personal data unit away. "Thank you," she said, "and thank your father. I do indeed like them."

She swung toward the door, then stopped and met Grozhinski's eyes again. "If I may ask," Adele said. "What is it you expect us—Captain Leary and I and the *Princess Cecile*—to do?"

"I haven't the faintest notion," Grozhinski said. "And if my father does, he's kept it from me. What he said—"

Again the young man's voice became careful.

"—is that though he has no idea of what can be done, he has seen ample evidence of Lady Mundy's resourcefulness and that of her naval friend."

Adele sniffed as she went out. *A mare's nest*, she thought. *But a flattering appraisal nonetheless.*

CHAPTER 7

DASAENZ ESTATE ON JARDIN

DaSaenz flew the aircar well. That was a relief to Daniel, though it hadn't crossed his mind before they took off.

He'd ridden with some very bad drivers without worrying particularly about it. An aircar ride, even with Hogg driving, didn't make the top ten most dangerous experiences of Daniel's normal life. Miranda was sitting beside him this time, however.

"Would you like the top up?" daSaenz called over his shoulder.

Daniel looked at Miranda. "No, I like the breeze," she said.

After a moment she added, "This is a wonderful way to see the country. I've, well, I've never ridden in an aircar before."

Daniel squeezed her hand. He hadn't realized that, though it shouldn't have surprised him. Miranda and her mother had lived in Xenos where trams made personal transport unnecessary and flight was banned save for emergency vehicles. Daniel didn't own or drive an aircar, so he and Miranda had always taken the monorail when they visited Bantry.

They were swinging around the hill above Cuvier. DaSaenz stayed about three hundred feet up and kept his speed down to fifty miles an hour, though the car was obviously capable of going much faster—especially with the top up to smooth the airflow.

"That house on the peak is where you live?" Daniel said, leaning closer to the driver. They got only occasional glimpses of the building's buttresses through the tops of the native trees. The foliage grew from a base of filaments which rose in a slender cone over a hundred feet above the ground. The road at the bottom of the valley was the only other human construction now that they had left Cuvier behind.

"Yes, we just call it the manor," daSaenz said. "It's Starscape Manor in town, I'm told. There's an elevator down from the house, but we'll enter at the bottom and go up to mother when you've seen the caves."

Ahead was a twenty-foot-high rock face too sheer for vegetation to take root. In front of it was a gravelled parking area onto which daSaenz sent the car in a descending arc. A sturdy kiosk was built against the cliff. Nearby a metal door was built into the rockface.

"That's the entrance to the caves?" Miranda said. "It looks like the door of a bank vault."

"Supposedly my ancestor Captain daSaenz had the door made from the colony ship's sheathing," daSaenz said. He flared the aircar neatly, hovered an instant, and settled the last six inches to the ground in front of the entrance. "The caves are dangerous to people without an experienced guide."

He shut off the fans and turned in his seat. "I suppose there was a certain amount of pride of ownership too, of course," he said. "And initially I don't believe the colonists realized that the glowworms were confined to this cave system. At least, in seven hundred years, no other occurrence has been found."

Close up, what Daniel had thought of as a kiosk looked more like a pillbox. The walls were of closely fitted stone; the windows were small and now covered with armored glass which appeared to have replaced the original bars, as the slits in the masonry had been widened slightly. The door on one side was of the same heavy metal as that of the cave entrance.

DaSaenz was coming around to Miranda's side of the car before Daniel could get there. She hopped out on her own and smiled at their host. Miranda still practiced with school hockey teams to keep fit—which she certainly was.

The kiosk's door opened. A middle-aged man got out and bowed. His uniform was the same shade of red as the aircar, and it was piped with gold.

"Good evening, sir," he said. The guard didn't have a gun, but the baton hanging from his belt was a meter long. "How may I help you, sir?"

"Open the cave for me and my guests, then close it after we've gone in," daSaenz said. "We'll leave through the manor. Oh—and we'll need one of the lanterns."

The guard trotted obediently back into the kiosk. The cave door—it was four inches thick—began to open with the high-pitched whine of a hydraulic pump.

A moment later the guard returned with a flat six-inch lens of yellow crystal. It had a loop handle on top, but there was also a strap, which daSaenz hung around his neck. The power supply must be part of the backing plate.

"I'll lead," daSaenz said to Daniel. He completely ignored the guard, who was waiting for further orders. "Keep with me. That shouldn't be difficult since I'll have the light."

Daniel and Miranda could have walked abreast through the cave entrance, but he took the lead so that he was between her and their guide. The worst you could really say about daSaenz was that he was brusque, as aristocrats by birth often are.

Daniel smiled faintly. *As I have been in my time, particularly if I've been drinking. I still don't like daSaenz.*

The entrance started as a tunnel, clearly artificial. It was high enough that Daniel could walk upright, but daSaenz ducked slightly. He probably would have cleared the ceiling also, but his caution was an instinctive response.

"According to legend there was just a narrow fissure here," daSaenz said. "A boy, one of my distant ancestors, crawled in. When he came back with stories about the lights—the glowworms, of course—his father blasted the rock wide enough that he could get in himself. The present entrance was built within that first generation."

The outer door closed and blocked the final leakage of sunshine, daSaenz switched on the lantern he carried. Its deep yellow light flooded the tunnel ahead—they had almost reached the end—and spilled out into a much larger chamber beyond.

DaSaenz stepped aside so that the others could join him. "Why is the light this color?" Miranda asked.

"It doesn't harm your night vision," daSaenz said. "And it doesn't seem to affect the glowworms either—ultraviolet is fatal to them. But I'll turn this out in a moment after you've had a chance to view the cave itself."

The chamber was a hollow spire rather than a dome, reaching higher than the lantern could illuminate even when daSaenz pointed it straight up. The base was a near oval measuring seventy feet by a hundred at an eyeball estimate.

Lowering the lantern again, daSaenz tapped an object with the toe of his boot. "Notice this?" he said. "It was a plastic food container. And that—"

He tapped a wrinkled rectangle about eight inches square.

"—was a piece of paper, a wrapper I think. Though there may have been writing on the upper side, which of course can't be viewed now."

Daniel squatted and tapped the second item with his fingernail. It was a sheet of metal, just as he had thought from its gleam in the lantern light.

"Look at the bottom," daSaenz said.

Daniel raised the piece between his thumb and forefinger and turned it over. The underside *was* paper. The top had been plated with metal.

"There are other bits of human trash here," daSaenz said, gesturing toward the cave floor. "These are enough to show you what happens. Now I'll show you *how* it happens."

He switched out the light. Daniel grabbed daSaenz's arm by reflex; his other fist was cocked for a memory-guided punch to their guide's belly.

Before Daniel swung, his eyes noticed irregular pastel blotches all around. The larger blurs contained scatterings of bright points.

"It's what Daddy described," Miranda said quietly. "Like

being in the Matrix, surrounded by stars."

It's nothing like the Matrix! Daniel thought, but Miranda's hand touched his hip. He quickly released daSaenz and edged toward Miranda.

"Sorry," he said to their guide, embarrassed at his reaction. "I was startled."

The glowworms ranged in size from the pad of his thumb to a few that were the size of his palm. There had been no sign of them before daSaenz turned out the lantern. A number clustered close by on the floor, including a pale blue patch under Daniel's right boot. In fact—

He jerked his foot back. The blotch came with it.

"It's on my foot!" Daniel said, hoping he didn't sound as panicked as he felt. He bent to release the closures and kick the boot away. Could he hop back to the entrance without stepping on another with his bare skin?

"Glowworms are quite harmless on your clothing," daSaenz said. The scorn Daniel heard in his tone was probably not just imagination. "Here, I'll see if I can coax it onto the lantern. Hold still."

DaSaenz bent at Daniel's feet; Daniel felt the lantern case pressing against the toe of his boot. The glow had stopped where it was; in fact Daniel had never seen it move, just realized that there was a blob of light on his foot. By effort of will he kept from kicking out violently.

"Are they amoebas?" Miranda said, holding Daniel's hand firmly. She was changing the subject, bless her heart.

She's afraid I'm going to turn her childhood dream into something unpleasant, Daniel realized. Aloud he said,

"They're true multicelled animals, dear. They eat sulfur from the limestone and give off light."

"There!" said daSaenz, rising. The smear of light had transferred onto the back of the lantern; it seemed to have contracted into a brighter version of itself at half its previous inch diameter. "It seems to me that if you know that, Leary, you should also have learned that the glowworms are harmless."

"I accept that they're harmless," Daniel said, keeping his tone pleasant for Miranda's sake. "I was just surprised to find something crawling on me when I hadn't seen it until you turned the light out."

"They etch the rock with mild acid," daSaenz said. "I suppose a glowworm could burn your bare skin slightly, though I don't recall hearing of that happening."

DaSaenz waggled the lantern, visible for the glow, then let it hang back against his chest. "Daylight kills them, turns them to fine dust. I'll leave the lantern in the sun when we return."

The glowworms didn't illuminate the chamber, but Daniel saw daSaenz's silhouette turn toward Miranda as he said, "Your husband isn't quite correct, Mistress. There's no sulfur in limestone, but there are inclusions of iron pyrites, fool's gold, in this bed. The glowworms ingest the pyrites, separate the sulfur from the iron in the crystals, and excrete the iron on objects which contain no sulfur themselves. I've forestalled—"

He gestured again with the lantern.

"—this one from plating the toe of Leary's boots, since he was concerned about it."

Daniel said nothing. He knew very little chemistry.

"They give off light when they crack the sulfur out of the

fool's gold," daSaenz said. "One of my great-uncles had read geology. He told my father that he thought more of the cave is a result of the glowworms eating away the stone than just rainwater like most caves. From photographs the chamber has continued to grow in the past seven hundred years, despite the manor being built on top and blocking further drainage."

"Don't you worry that the house is going to fall in?" Daniel said. He immediately felt like a fool.

"No, I don't, Leary," daSaenz said. "But if you're concerned about your safety, you're welcome to return to the entrance and wait for us."

"Sorry," Daniel muttered. He was making a fool of himself in front of Miranda. *This young pup is making a fool of me!*

He gave himself up to the moment. The worms, so called, must be only a few cell layers thick. Daniel had seen no sign of the creatures in the lantern light, even though he must have been standing on the one which then crawled on his boot.

Because their glow was faint even in absolute darkness, Daniel couldn't judge how near they were. Some of them seemed infinitely far away, though he'd seen the cave walls in the lantern and knew that the farthest were within a hundred feet of where he stood.

"They're beautiful," Miranda said. "They're wonderful. Thank you, Daniel, for bringing me here. And thank you, Master daSaenz."

"This is the least that my family can do for such important people," daSaenz said. "A famous Cinnabar captain, and the daughter of Midshipman Dorst. Who was well-known here on Jardin even if not so famous on his own world."

"My father is known here?" Miranda said, her grip on Daniel's wrist tightening. "Known for what, please?"

"I'm sure my mother can give you all the details when you speak with her," daSaenz said. "Midshipman Dorst visited in my grandfather's time, of course, so I have only scraps of knowledge."

He coughed and said, "This was a little thing, as I said. This is the anteroom where the public is allowed. Now I'll show you a portion of the caves that very few even of my family have seen."

DaSaenz switched on the lantern. Daniel turned his head and found that he could still see ghosts of the glowworms on the back wall and floor of the chamber behind him, opposite the broad cone of light.

"Unless perhaps you're afraid, Leary?" daSaenz said.

"No," said Daniel. Though he kept his voice calm, he was clenching his right fist behind his back. "But Miranda may not—"

"I'd like to go on, Daniel," she said. "If that's all right with you?"

"Lead on, daSaenz," Daniel said, his voice raspy. "Anywhere you go, I'll keep up. We will."

DaSaenz walked toward the end of the chamber opposite the entrance tunnel, his lantern spreading a broad fan of yellow on the floor ahead. Even knowing they were there, Daniel saw no sign of the glowworms. What had looked like a shadowed fold in the rock became a narrow passage about five feet high when they approached it.

DaSaenz turned sideways and pulled the lantern out on its strap to move it from his chest. He slipped into the passage, sending flickers of lanternlight back to those in the chamber.

Daniel thought quickly. "I'll lead," he said, following their guide before Miranda could. He half-knelt to give his waist more room in the triangular passage. It was awkward and uncomfortable and *extremely* embarrassing, but he did it.

Five feet into the crack, Daniel came out into a tunnel with squared walls and a six-foot ceiling. A metal door was inset in the sidewall.

DaSaenz waited beside it until Miranda sidled into the tunnel with less difficulty than Daniel had. "This is the elevator to the manor," daSaenz said, tapping the panel. "We'll be going up in a moment. But if you're still willing and able, Leary? It's going to be quite narrow at the beginning."

"I'll manage," said Daniel. His voice was gruff. *Even if I've got to strip and rub my skin off on the rock.*

The rock had been carved out only in front of the elevator. The crack leading to the next chamber must have been left unimproved to deter visitors. It continued out the far end of the elevator landing. DaSaenz squirmed into it.

"Go ahead," Daniel said, gesturing Miranda on. If he got stuck, he would back out and decide what to do next. He didn't want to force her to back out also, and he didn't want anybody, even Miranda, to be staring at him as he made up his mind about what to do next.

He'd beat it, one way or another. He wouldn't have been so successful had he not kept clear in his mind the number of ways things could go wrong with a plan, though.

"Are there other openings in the anteroom, Master daSaenz?" Miranda said. Her voice was muffled by her own body.

Daniel got down on all fours and squeezed himself into the

passage. His upper shoulder blade—the right one—brushed repeatedly against the rock. The fabric was supposed to be tough, though he didn't care if this jaunt converted his outfit to wiping rags.

"Eighteen," said their guide. Daniel could barely hear him. "Most of them are just cracks, but you can crawl a distance into four of them."

Daniel was in complete darkness. He assumed daSaenz had kept the lantern on, but none of the light leaked back past the two bodies ahead of Daniel and the kinks in the passage. At least it didn't seem to be narrowing.

DaSaenz said something. Miranda paused and Daniel's left hand touched her foot.

"Daniel," she said. Her head must be turned, though Daniel couldn't see even the foot he was touching. "It's going to get tight in a moment, but it's just a short place. Will you be all right?"

"*Keep moving*," Daniel said. How in hell was he supposed to know if he'd be all right until he reached the pinch? He certainly wasn't better for talking about it in a tunnel tighter than a grave!

Miranda moved on. Daniel waited a moment, lying on his side and trying to control his breath. The air wasn't bad, though it had an odd mustiness. There couldn't be much circulation down here.

"Daniel, I'm through," Miranda called. "It opens up when you get through."

"I'm coming," said Daniel. He was already sorry for feeling so angry a moment before. He hadn't said the things he'd been thinking, but Miranda knew him well enough to have heard them in his tone.

She knows me well enough that it won't have surprised her either. Well, if she'd wanted a saint, she'd been looking in the wrong direction. He was still embarrassed.

The triangular passage narrowed side to side, and the peak lowered also. Daniel thrust at the rock with his toes, squirming forward almost as though he were swimming.

It was definitely getting tighter. He pulled his left arm back along his body and twisted slightly to make his body as slim as he could. He didn't think about it, just kept thrusting ahead. There was a way out, maybe not for him, but he'd keep going forward until he got there or died. Going forward...

Fingers touched his outstretched wrist. Daniel squirmed a little further and he could get his left arm free also. He opened his eyes—he didn't remember closing them—and the lantern made the wide chamber a yellow ambiance. DaSaenz and Miranda were waiting, she with a concerned expression. With another wriggling push Daniel was out.

He got to his feet. Miranda hugged him, probably from affection. It was a good thing regardless, because otherwise Daniel would have toppled backward.

"I'm all right," he wheezed, and in a moment he was.

"How did you find this place, Master daSaenz?" Miranda said, holding Daniel firmly. The ceiling was flat and much lower than that of the conical antechamber, but the floor had at least three large lobes. Its total area was considerable.

"I've been studying the caves all my life," their guide said. "I've had robotic mappers for the past fifteen years. I've explored every passage I've found and mapped them to the end, then built up a three-dimensional image."

DaSaenz made a broad gesture. "There are forty caves opening off this chamber," he said, "and I know them all. I've seen things that no one has seen for hundreds of years, and I *know* the caves as no one else ever has."

"That's very impressive," Daniel said. He was breathing normally again.

"It's my life!" said daSaenz. "These caves are the daSaenz heritage. No one but a daSaenz really has a right to be here! Ah, though you, you're my mother's guests. That's why I'm about to show you the greatest wonder of all."

"What would that be, Master daSaenz?" Miranda asked quietly. Her fingers were massaging the point of Daniel's right shoulder.

"I found a room which is *alive* with glowworms," daSaenz said. "When I was last there a year ago, more of the rock was covered by them than was clear. You noticed that the tunnel we came through to get here didn't have any glowworms in it?"

Miranda nodded; Daniel grunted. He probably wouldn't have noticed anything even if he'd kept his eyes open. He hadn't been panicked, but squeezing through the passage had been an extremely unpleasant experience.

"Because that stratum had no pyrites in it," daSaenz said, nodding enthusiastically. "And there are very few in the present chamber, see?"

He turned off the lantern. Daniel felt Miranda's body shift as she turned to scan the whole chamber. He saw a pink blur on the floor in the middle distance. There seemed to be prickles and sparkles of light all around them, though they were too faint for him to be sure that he wasn't seeing ghost images within his retinas.

"But if you have the courage to come with me," daSaenz said, "I'll show you a hollow which must have been a huge pyrite crystal before the glowworms began to devour it. *Huge*."

"We'll follow," Daniel said. "Go on, then."

Miranda squeezed his hand again and stepped slightly away. DaSaenz turned on the lantern and led the way into a left branching...though when they were well within it, Daniel saw that what he'd thought was a solid wall to the right seemed rather to be a massive pillar standing in a single large bay rather than a divider between two. He couldn't be sure in the side-scatter from the lantern.

Their guide led them into a series of passages, some wider than others, but none really narrow. The ceiling remained high enough to clear their heads, though from caution Daniel put his left hand on his forehead. A scraped knuckle could be ignored, but a whack on the scalp was apt to be bloody and distracting.

There were multiple branchings, but daSaenz never hesitated. He really did know the caves.

"We're coming to the wonder," daSaenz called back over his shoulder. He got down on all fours and led into a branching to the left which was only about three feet high. Miranda hesitated; Daniel sent her in ahead of him, but he followed on her heels.

"Here," said daSaenz. He stopped and shifted in the passage. It gleamed when brushed by lantern-light: the rock was metal-plated.

DaSaenz shifted again and slipped waist deep into the rock: there was a hole in the floor of the passage. The remainder of his body and finally his head disappeared also. The lantern from below lit not only the opening but also the rope ladder hanging down into it.

"Come, if you will," daSaenz called. "I'll turn out the lantern when you're here."

"Wait," said Daniel. He turned onto his left side to edge by Miranda as she shrank herself against the opposite wall.

The ladder hung from a wooden bar. Daniel felt the ends and found they were held securely by U-bolts hammered into the rock. The fasteners and the rock were both glass-smooth with iron deposited by the glowworms, but the bar hadn't been touched: wood must contain some sulfur, though not enough to tempt the creatures when pyrites were available.

There were glowworms—a violet one and a red one, both more vivid and filled with bright sparks than those Daniel had seen farther back in the caves. He ignored them as he tested with his bare hands both the bolts and their grip on the crossbar. He had to be sure that the structure was solid before he trusted Miranda's life and his own to it.

Daniel couldn't feel the creatures, though the vivid glow beneath his thumbs proved he was touching them. He shifted his grip onto the bar and let himself down into the opening. He kicked his feet until one boot found a rung; he settled his weight onto it, then walked himself down the rest of the way on the ladder. The rungs were wooden battens; the rope stringers seemed to be woven from some slick synthetic fiber.

DaSaenz kept the lantern aimed at Daniel's shoulders on

the way down. The floor of the lower chamber was about ten feet below that of the passage from which they had dropped.

Daniel gripped the ladder to hold it steady. "I'm clear!" he called up to Miranda. She descended with the supple quickness he had noticed in all her movements.

DaSaenz swept his light around the chamber. It was an irregular polygon almost thirty feet across at its widest point. There were patches of bare rock in the floor, but the walls had a metallic luster deeper than the shimmer of deposited iron nearer the anteroom of the cave.

"I suggest you keep very quiet after I turn the light off," daSaenz said. "I'm going to move against the wall behind me, but you'll get the best view if you move to the other end of the chamber."

Daniel nodded and walked away from their guide. Miranda was half a step ahead of him.

"Are you ready?" said daSaenz.

"Yes." "Yes." Daniel's voice was curt, Miranda's musical.

The lantern went off.

The darkness was alive. The glowworms were not only brighter than those Daniel had seen before, they were larger—some of these were two hands across—and the concentration of bright points in the glow was greater. All the colors of the rainbow mingled, and the violet ones hinted that their light extended deeper into the spectrum than human eyes could follow.

"Oh, Daniel," Miranda said. "Oh, Daniel. Oh, this is so wonderful."

As daSaenz had said, glowworms covered more than half the surface of the chamber. They did not quite touch one another except in a humped mass along the edge near where Daniel and Miranda stood. There the glowworms had concentrated like an oil slick on the surface of a harbor.

Daniel bent to the mass without speaking. He touched it, finding metal which was too thick to bend under the pressure of his hand.

He felt lower to get to the edge from which he could lift a piece and feel the bottom. He expected to find bits of rock which had spalled off the wall when supporting pyrites had been eaten away.

Daniel lifted a glove.

He stood holding it. "DaSaenz, turn your light on!" he said. "I've found something!"

DaSaenz didn't reply. A moment later Daniel heard the click of battens knocking together. He ran back to where they had left their guide but as he feared, he was too late.

"Daniel?" said Miranda.

"The bastard's pulled the ladder up behind him!" Daniel said.

CUVIER HARBOR, JARDIN

Adele was lost in her work, pretty much as always. Some of the material in the files which Major Grozhinski had provided duplicated or at least supplemented Mistress Sand's files, but Cinnabar could only guess at what the Fifth Bureau was doing in the Tarbell Stars—let alone what they intended.

The plural in speaking of the Fifth Bureau was necessary

here. Storn had laid out in detail the cluster assets both of his diocese and that of his rival Krychek. Storn's activities had been limited to observation and to increasing his ability to observe—particularly on the worlds overseen by Krychek's diocese.

The First Diocese had been encouraging separatist movements on the more important worlds of his sector. That hadn't been quite as useful as Krychek might have hoped when rebellion against the Tarbell Government had broken out on Ithaca.

There was a great deal of hostility to President for Life Menandros throughout the sector, but the planetary leaders didn't care for one another much either. The rebels formed a Council of the Upholders of the Freedom of the Tarbell Stars, but it was a talking shop which spent its time in ill-natured squabbles. The council could not have successfully maintained a rebellion even against a foolish coxcomb like Menandros if Krychek had not provided personnel for administrative positions among the Upholders.

Does Krychek think they won't be noticed if they're not officially in command? Adele wondered. Another possibility was the one which concerned General Storn: that Krychek had Guarantor Porra's support, so that he didn't have to be concerned about Pleasaunce learning of his plot.

Under other circumstances Adele would have been sharing her task with Cory and Cazelet, not so much to reduce her workload as to bring them up to speed about the situation. This was the first night of the landfall, however, and both her deputies—their position unofficial but beyond any question—were sampling the entertainments of Cuvier City.

Both men would be working beside Adele if she had asked, and their companions, Hale and Vesey respectively, would have been uncomplaining if disappointed. They all felt they owed Adele more than she thought they did, and they trusted her judgment implicitly.

Her lips quirked. Adele was demonstrating her good judgment by not calling them away from their fun. She didn't believe she had ever been young in the sense that people seemed to mean it, but she had observed humanity closely enough that she understood the concept.

The watch officer was Chief Engineer Pasternak. He was competent for any question involving the power room or the propulsion system. Astrogation was a closed book to him, and Adele would probably be as useful as Pasternak if the *Princess Cecile* had to leave the planet.

There would be plenty of time for Cory and Cazelet to study the Tarbell Stars on the twenty-day voyage from Jardin. And if there wasn't, then Adele herself would be enough as she had always been enough in the past.

I have flaws. I don't have the flaw of false modesty.

She was looking at the military and particularly naval strength of the Upholders, since that was probably the most significant factor. It would certainly be the first concern of her colleagues.

For the most part the Upholder fleet was the collection of scraps and antiques which Adele had learned to expect in hinterlands like the Tarbell Stars, but there were exceptions. The three destroyers were of recent Alliance construction, and the officers and crew of one of them were ex-Fleet. That didn't prove Krychek's connivance as there was a considerable number of Fleet and RCN spacers freed by the Treaty of Amiens. Some of them preferred naval duties to those of the merchant service.

There was also a modern heavy cruiser. That—

Adele's holographic screen blurred. She came awake to her present surroundings, blinking in surprised anger. Tovera, standing beside the signals console, had just slid her hand through the display.

"Yes?" Adele said. She was still angry at having been dragged out of her studies, but she knew Tovera wouldn't have interrupted her without a good reason.

"Hogg wants to talk to you," Tovera said with her usual lack of expression. She stepped aside, though Hogg didn't move closer.

Is Hogg afraid of me? Adele thought. *Or is he simply deferring to Tovera's ownership interest?*

"Ma'am," Hogg said. His arms were at his sides, and he was standing as straight as Adele had ever seen him. "The master's not back and he hasn't called in neither. I know, you're not his mother and I don't worry about him normal like, but I been talking in some of the bars."

"Go on," Adele said. She had no idea of what time it was. She called up a real-time image on top of her screen and viewed Cuvier Harbor at dusk, much later than she had expected it to be.

"You see, the thing is, the cave wasn't open to strangers till seven years back when the current lady took over when her husband died," Hogg said. "It was daSaenz family and maybe friends after a big dinner or the like. Not something a junior officer from a supply ship gets invited to. Dorst was lying about being there, and that means I don't know what's going on. And the master's not back."

Adele began searching. She used the control wands through her personal data unit to access her console and through that the thirty-odd databases in Cuvier City which she had coupled during the time the *Princess Cecile* had been here.

Hogg said something. From the corner of Adele's eye she saw Tovera move him back so that he wouldn't again try to interrupt. When Adele was searching, she ignored the people around her. If they thought that she should give them a running account of the process, they were going to be disappointed.

Adele grimaced. She wasn't sure there was a definitive answer, but she had what was probably good enough for current requirements.

"I can't at present prove that the caves were not open to the public thirty years ago when Midshipman Dorst landed here in the *Orangeleaf...*" Adele said to Hogg and Tovera. Pasternak was in his office in the power room; only she and the servants were on the bridge. "But there are ample references to them being opened one day a week when Carlotta daSaenz became head of the family seven years ago. At her father's death, by the way; her husband wasn't a daSaenz, she was."

As she spoke, she shifted the material from Major Grozhinski into a separate cache, then threw the mechanical switch under her saddle to cut it off completely. It *could not* be accessed online; even Adele herself would have to snap the switch before she could get to the data.

"What's that mean?" Hogg said. He seemed bewildered as well as being angry.

"It could be nothing," Adele said, getting to her feet. She paused; she had been sitting in the same position for long enough that her circulation took a moment to respond to movement. "Dorst may have gotten a special dispensation, just as Daniel did. But we'll visit the caves and ask. Hogg, can you line up transportation?"

"I've got a truck up on the street," he said. "Six wheels, a lot like we used for hauling at Bantry. Do you want something fancy?"

"That will be fine," Adele said. Hogg wasn't a good driver, but a familiar vehicle was a safe enough choice under the circumstances. She strode off the bridge, heading for the down companionway. "Oh, and Hogg? Bring a long gun. I'm not expecting trouble, but it's as well to be prepared."

"There's an impeller in the back already," Hogg said. "And I've got a pistol."

Tovera laughed. The sound echoed in the armored companionway like the chittering of bats.

"If it's pistol range," Tovera said, "leave it in your pocket. That's for me and the mistress."

CHAPTER 8

DASAENZ ESTATE, JARDIN

"There may be another way out," said Miranda. Her voice was perfectly calm, but the fact that she'd spoken at all showed that she must think they were doomed.

"Oh, I think we're all right," Daniel said. He walked back to her, keeping his voice low. "You can stand on my shoulders, can't you? Though I think we should wait a few minutes in case he's waiting at the top."

"Oh," said Miranda. She hugged him fiercely. "I'm sorry I panicked. Yes, of course I can stand on your shoulders. Actually, with a boost I could probably jump through the opening; enough to get a hold, I mean."

"I'd rather you just climbed up on me," Daniel said. "I'll worry less."

It would be very easy for someone trying to jump through a hole in a stone ceiling to smash her elbow in this uncertain light. Several glowworms were on the rim of the opening, but even so it would be a tricky target.

After what he'd decided was a safe delay, Daniel walked with Miranda to the edge beneath the opening. He heard nothing from the level above.

The glowworms were softly attractive when he thought about them, but for the most part they were of no more interest than the curtains in a woman's bedroom. He was smiling as he cupped his hands and said, "I've made a step."

Miranda, facing him, put her left foot in the stirrup and raised her right onto his shoulder in the same motion. Daniel had expected her to steady herself by dabbing her hands against the wall behind him, but she hadn't needed to do that.

Miranda brought her left foot up. For a moment Daniel was supporting her weight on both shoulders; then it was gone. The loose cuffs of her trousers brushed his ears as she lifted herself through the opening by her arms.

"The ladder's still here," she called. "I'm letting it down."

Daniel stepped back with his hand up to catch the ladder when it dropped. Miranda let it down smoothly instead of just tossing it over to potentially whack him on the head. She was a girl in a thousand.

Daniel smiled. *And I ought to know. Well, not a thousand.*

Daniel pulled the ladder tight to be sure that it was still firmly attached, then mounted quickly. He didn't like the way he swayed, but he wasn't on the ladder long enough for that to matter.

When Daniel squirmed through the opening, he breathed a sigh of relief. "I kept thinking that daSaenz was really waiting up here and was going to clout me one as I put my head up," he said. "Now all we have to worry about is a hike, and not so very long a hike either."

"But Daniel?" Miranda said. "How will we find our way out?"

"The first thing Hogg taught me when we started going into the woods was how not to get lost. I was about three at the time."

"But it's dark?"

"Right," Daniel said as he squirmed out of his tunic. "But it's not pissing down rain, and we don't have to worry about a million vine-wrapped trees which all look the same even in daylight. Which it usually wasn't when we were checking the trap lines. Hogg being a poacher when he wasn't giving me fatherly advice."

He held out the tunic to her. "Here, take one sleeve and I'll have the other," he said. "That's easier than holding hands."

"I..." Miranda said. Then, obviously changing what she had intended to say, she said, "I'm very glad you can do that. I thought we were lost."

"DaSaenz apparently didn't expect it either," Daniel said. "I suppose it's not a skill which many Academy graduates share."

He touched the rock wall with his outstretched hand. "I'll wiggle through the hole here and take the tunic again on the other side," he said. "There's not much chance of you wandering off inside, is there?"

The passage through the rock was shorter and easier than Daniel remembered it being when he came the other way. Maybe he'd sweated off a few pounds. More likely it was just familiarity and the fact that going in this direction he had a clearly defined mission: to get out, and to settle accounts with Timothy daSaenz.

Daniel reached the end and waited in a hunching posture for Miranda to rejoin him. His fingers were spread at the edge of the opening to make contact.

Miranda's fist came out, thrusting the tunic ahead. Daniel took the trailing sleeve and sidled down the passage, straightening as the height of the rock permitted him to.

"I'm not concerned about finding our way to the entrance," Daniel said. "I haven't figured out yet how we'll open the door there, though. I didn't see a way of opening it from the inside, but there must be one. DaSaenz didn't intend to die here himself."

He was talking so that Miranda wouldn't be left with only her thoughts for company. He was used to moving in darkness—and a rainy night in the forest really was as dark as the interior of the caves—but she wasn't. She trusted him, but chattering to her in positive fashion cost nothing.

"There was a call button at the elevator," Miranda said. "DaSaenz told the guard that we'd be going up by that to the manor house."

"We can try that," Daniel said. "If that doesn't work, we'll go to the main entrance—careful here."

His right little finger reached a branching; he was feeling his way along by very light contact with the wall, holding his hand high enough that a sudden dip in the ceiling wouldn't take him by surprise.

They turned right and shortly turned left again. This put them in the great multilobed chamber Daniel remembered from when daSaenz brought them into the cave.

"As I said, we'll go to the entrance and see what we find

there," he said. He was keeping to a normal walk—strolling, not trying to cover distance. The floor was smooth and clear of obstructions, and a purposeful pace would do as much to calm Miranda as his voice would.

Daniel wasn't altogether comfortable either, to tell the truth. He'd seen his share of danger, but this was a new one.

"Worst case—here's where we turn. It's going to get narrow again, but we know where we're going. Worst case, as I say, is that we'll wait for a rescue party from the ship. In fact, they may be waiting for us when we get to the anteroom."

Daniel was being brightly cheerful, but it was true that he expected Hogg and the Sissies to come for them. That might not have helped if he and Miranda had been deep in the bowels of a labyrinth, though Daniel was pretty sure that if daSaenz's mapping had been entrusted to a computer, Adele would eventually find it.

"We may get a little hungry, is all," he added.

"I wonder if the glowworms are edible?" Miranda said. "At least gathering them will keep us busy."

The sulfur will make our urine stink, Daniel thought. He didn't say that aloud. *Like eating asparagus.*

"Of course, we don't have any water, so the sulfur won't be much of a problem," said Miranda in the same matter-of-fact voice as before.

"Are you reading my mind?" Daniel said.

"Umm," said Miranda. "We know each other pretty well, darling."

Daniel reached the narrow crack which led to the elevator chamber and from there to the anteroom. He felt a rush of pleasure: they'd reached their goal, or almost. Though he'd never consciously doubted that he could lead them back, his present relief proved that his subconscious hadn't been quite as certain.

"We've made it, love," Daniel said. "I'm letting go of the tunic again."

He got down on his belly and squirmed into the passage. The grit on the floor scraped him, and he was pretty sure that he'd rubbed through the skin on his right shoulder blade.

Cheap at the price. We're getting out.

Daniel reached the square-cut section that acted as a foyer for the elevator and stood. He knew that was where he was, but for the first time he felt the darkness.

"I'm clear," he called to Miranda, and he heard her rustle through the opening. He wondered how much blood from his shoulders was lubricating the rock by now.

Daniel found the elevator door and explored the smooth metal with the flat of his hands. He wondered in which direction it slid to open.

"It helps to remember it's beige," Miranda said from beside him. "It helps me."

Then she said, "Here's the call plate. There isn't a button, that is, a mechanical one. I saw a black dot when we went by, but it must be painted."

"Push the center," Daniel said, leaning his ear against the door panel. "I'll listen to see if I hear anything."

"I'm pushing," Miranda whispered.

The metal door gave no sign of anything. It was slightly cooler than the rock wall. Daniel couldn't hear either mechanical noises or the possible sighing of air in the shaft beyond.

He straightened. "Well, I guess we'd better try the main entrance," he said. "Nothing seems to be happening here. I'll take the sleeve again."

"I thought I heard something from that direction," Miranda said. "A humming?"

"It could have been the hydraulic door," Daniel said in sudden hope. "DaSaenz might not be very far ahead of us, you know."

If daSaenz hadn't closed the door behind him, this was going to end more quickly than Daniel had dared to hope. Regardless, it meant that there was some way of getting out by the way they had come in. DaSaenz's aircar was parked at this level, after all.

"Daniel, why do you suppose he did it?" Miranda said quietly.

"He could be crazy," Daniel said. "It might be that simple. But...Miranda, it might have something to do with your father."

"Yes, I thought that," Miranda said. "But Daniel, he really did love Jardin. I can't believe that he, well...that he had anything on his conscience."

"Well, daSaenz may tell us something himself in a little bit," Daniel said as he sidled through the final narrow passage. "I certainly plan to have a discussion with him. Until then we don't have enough information."

Captain Dorst may well not have had anything on his conscience, but Daniel had known enough RCN officers—and had *been* an RCN officer—to know that things that bothered civilians might well slide off an officer's conscience. The

Academy taught many things to cadets, but the absolutely necessary attribute for an RCN officer was one that wasn't taught: you had to be willing to kill. Once you've overcome that basic human inhibition, there's really nothing that you might not be willing to consider.

Except perhaps for cheating at cards. A cheater would not go undetected for three years and would not remain in the RCN for an hour after detection.

"The glowworms look brighter to me now," Miranda said. "I guess after being in the dark so long."

Daniel turned his head as they crossed the antechamber. His first view of the cave, only a few hours earlier, felt like something remembered from his childhood. The blurred patches in the uncertain distance of the walls and on the floor did seem sharper than they had initially. The glowworms here seemed scattered after the wall-to-wall splendor of the pit in the interior of the mountain.

"You know," Daniel said, "I haven't seen any of the glowworms move. Though they must, there was the one on my foot after—"

Movement.

Daniel dropped the tunic and was lifting his left hand when a blow stunned his forearm and cracked him on the head. He hit the stone floor. His right side was numb but his left forearm felt as though it had been dipped in molten lead.

Light flooded the antechamber. The lantern wobbled on daSaenz's chest as he raised the guard's long baton over his head in both hands for a finishing blow. There was someone behind him. Daniel kicked with his left leg, the only limb which was working at the moment.

DaSaenz gave a startled bleat and lurched forward. He no longer held the baton. He turned, lantern light sweeping across the chamber.

Miranda stepped into her blow. The baton flickered like black lightning, catching daSaenz on the top of the skull with a sound like that of a dropped melon.

DaSaenz sagged liquidly, falling on top of the lantern and plunging the chamber into darkness again.

Adele was on the passenger side of the cab, clinging to the frame of the open window with both hands; her left arm was across her body. With her feet braced against the firewall, her buttocks only touched the seat when the vehicle jolted over a particularly violent bump.

The seat had slapped her repeatedly.

"We don't know that there's a problem, Hogg," Adele said, raising her voice more than she cared to do in order to be heard over the road noise. "Until I have a chance to look at the situation, neither you nor Tovera are to do anything."

Hogg grunted. That might not have been a response to her words: the truck had bounced badly again. His hands were mottled with his grip on the steering yoke.

Tovera stood in the open truck bed, somehow staying attached to the vehicle. There were lugs for tiedowns along the sides. Perhaps Tovera had tied herself in with a length of cable from her attaché case.

Adele didn't turn to look. Hanging on was as much as she

could handle. Tovera had known what the ride was going to be like with Hogg driving. She had still insisted on being in the back where she had a better view of their environment and a quicker shot at any hostile portion of that environment.

They came around the corner between a rock wall and a dropoff. "We're here!" Hogg said.

In the glare of their single working headlight appeared a squat building and beside it the three-place aircar in which Daniel and Miranda had ridden off six hours before. No one was visible in the vehicle or nearby.

They skidded to a halt on the gravel apron, throwing a cloud of dust ahead of them. Pebbles bounced against the gleaming aircar, but Hogg might not have done that deliberately.

Adele got out. Tovera swung to the ground beside her, the attaché case in her left hand and her miniaturized submachine gun openly in her right.

"Hogg, watch the back!" Tovera called.

"Right," said Hogg, drawing the stocked impeller from behind the seats. "Get on with it."

He and Tovera had a working relationship, much like that between Daniel and Adele. Each led when it was appropriate; each listened to the other's advice. A task which required long-range firepower was Hogg's responsibility, however much he might want to shake his master's whereabouts out of somebody close at hand.

The attendant watched Adele through the armored glass as she approached the kiosk. "We're looking for Captain Leary and his lady," she said to the speaker plate under the window. "Where are they, please?"

Her tone was less polite than the words; but then, nobody who knew Adele expected warmth from her.

"Look, you'll have to talk to the manor," the attendant said, his voice tinny through the speaker. "I don't have authority to talk to you."

"I can open the cave up!" Tovera whispered urgently.

"No," said Adele. She looked at the entrance, closed by what appeared to be a vault door.

I doubt Tovera could get through that, she thought. *The hinges are internal.*

But there was no need of that anyway. To the speaker plate she said, "You. Open the cave at once. Otherwise I'll come in and do it."

The attendant vanished beneath the level of the window without responding.

"Tovera, get me into this bunker," Adele said. "Don't damage the electronics if you can help. I'll want them to open the door."

"I can shoot through the wall!" said Hogg, which was probably true. A single osmium slug from his impeller might not do the job, but two or three pecking at the same point certainly would. It would be a waste of time.

"No," said Adele without turning to look at him. "Watch your sector."

Tovera had been readying the charges since Adele told her not to try to open the cave. If she wasn't to blow open the cave, they had to get into the guardhouse. Tovera had reasonably assumed that the attendant wouldn't be any more willing to let them into his control room than he had been to open the cave for them.

DAVID DRAKE

Now she scampered back to Adele, facing the long side of the building; the door was on the short side to their left. "Ready!" Tovera said; she had a small control mechanism in her hand.

"All right," said Adele, covering her ears. "Hogg?"

"Blow it!" Hogg said.

The *crack!* was a single sound even though Adele knew that there were charges on both door hinges. A shard of metal struck the aircar's body and ricocheted off, humming. Adele and Tovera walked to the side of the building.

"My turn!" said Hogg as he pushed past them, his impeller slung. Neither woman was in a mood to waste her breath arguing with him.

Hogg wrenched the door free—it hung askew by its bolt—and went in, the knife open in his left hand. Hogg knew not to kill the attendant, though other than the mess that wouldn't have bothered Adele very much.

Hogg reappeared, dragging the attendant by the throat. Adele stepped into the building. The bitter haze of explosive made the fugg even more unpleasant. The attendant must have voided his bowels in fear.

She sat at the chair and explored the control system through her data unit; her holographic display was better than the building's cheap flat-plate screen. The installation was really a terminal of the manor system rather than an independent computer. It had a recording function which Adele would examine later, but for now—

She threw an electronic switch. "This should open—" she called to the doorway.

The cave's massive door began to whirr open. Miranda staggered out with Daniel. She was supporting him in a fireman's carry, his right arm hanging across her shoulders so that she could grip his wrist. Blood had trickled down his cheek.

Hogg stopped kicking the attendant and with Tovera ran to the freed couple; Adele entered the system of daSaenz Manor. To each her specialty. Hogg had a great deal of experience with the cuts and breaks that you got in agricultural work and field sports; he would do anything first aid could accomplish. Adele, however—

"Mistress, we gotta get him to the ship!" Hogg shouted.

"I'm just dizzy," Daniel said, his voice almost too weak to hear. "I'll be fine in a bit."

"There's a Medicomp in the house," Adele said, using the guardhouse microphone although the speaker plate wasn't aligned well for the purpose. "We'll use that. Can we take him in the aircar?"

"There's an elevator in the cave," Miranda said. "It goes right into the house, but it wasn't working when we tried before."

Daniel was sitting down. Miranda held him by the shoulders. His face was ashen except where blood from his scalp had leaked over it. He was mumbling something, probably that he was all right.

Adele found the control and turned it back on. "It's working now," she said. "But don't use it until we've made sure that the other end is clear. Tovera, you can drive the aircar?"

"Yes," said Tovera. She had clipped the submachine gun into a holster built into her tunic. She started for the vehicle.

"There's room for three, Hogg," Adele said. "Are you

coming or staying with your master?"

"Coming," said Hogg. He reached into his pocket and came out with a squat, short-barreled pistol which he offered to Miranda. "Here you go, Mistress. In case."

Tovera had the aircar's fans spinning. Hogg got in one side of the back as Adele entered the other.

She put her data unit away and brought out her pistol. *I might need either one at the Manor*, she thought. *But if I need the data unit, I'll have more time to get it out.*

Tovera didn't drive well, but she made an adequate liftoff and started up the slope with the fans screaming in overload. Which was exactly what Adele would have been doing if she could have driven.

CHAPTER 9

DASAENZ ESTATE, JARDIN

Where the hell am I? Daniel thought. He was seeing the interior of Starscape Caverns, but the glowworms were racing about like startled cockroaches. *What Hell am I in?*

Daniel opened his eyes. His head hurt, his left arm was an icy lump attached to his shoulder, and his vision was as blurry as if he were under water. He lay on a blue couch, his toes sticking over the open end and his head lifted on the low arm at the other.

His feet were bare and he was naked beneath an amazingly soft sheet.

"He's coming around," said Adele, seated near his head on a chair whose upholstery matched that of the couch.

Daniel turned toward her. There was a white flash inside his skull. It was a moment before he could see anything again.

"Not very far around," he croaked, closing his eyes and opening them again carefully after a moment. "The last time I felt this way, I'd been drinking power-room alcohol that we'd cut with spoiled grape juice."

Hogg and Miranda were across the room, placing someone in a side-loading Medicomp. Daniel couldn't see who it was. As blurry as his vision was, he couldn't have sworn to Miranda and Hogg.

"An hour ago you were telling anybody who would listen that you were all right," Adele said. "None of us *did* listen, of course."

"That's good," said Daniel, "because I was lying."

He relaxed again with his eyes closed. His voice was getting stronger with use, and the dizziness seemed to be going away. "What's the damage, then?"

"Your left ulna, that's in the forearm, was cracked," Adele said. "Your skull *wasn't* broken thanks to your having gotten your arm up so promptly, but you have contra-coup injuries to your brain. The Medicomp reversed the swelling before it did permanent damage, but the drugs will be affecting you for at least the next twelve hours. And you've got a splint on your left arm, of course."

Hogg and Miranda walked to where Daniel lay. Tovera and a woman Daniel didn't know moved in front of the Medicomp. They must have been standing farther into the room than Daniel could see without sitting up or craning his neck over the arm of the couch. The way he felt now, Daniel wasn't *that* interested in much of anything.

"That's daSaenz?" Daniel said quietly, hooking his thumb in the direction of the Medicomp.

"That's Timothy daSaenz," Adele said. She nodded to the unfamiliar woman who was now joining them. "And this is our hostess, Mistress Carlotta daSaenz."

Carlotta daSaenz must have had lush good looks when she was in her twenties, but she was nearly fifty now and was fighting a losing battle with her weight. Daniel winced, thinking of his own waistline. She clasped her hands together before her and said, "Captain Leary, on behalf of my family and myself. What my son attempted to do was..."

She shook her head slowly as though she was looking for a word in the pattern of the carpet.

"Insane," she said. "Unbelievable. Unforgiveable."

Carlotta raised her eyes and went on, "I am the head of the family so this was my responsibility, but I knew nothing of what Timothy intended. I swear to you as a mother!"

"What *did* your son intend?" Daniel asked. He felt and sounded calm, though raspy. The drugs probably had something to do with that, though in fact he was usually clinical about events in the past. He was alive and Miranda was uninjured; that was good enough.

"I met Timothy Dorst when I was a young woman," Carlotta said. "I was giving a party for my friends and I thought that an RCN supply ship might have something exotic that would give me a coup."

She had raised her head, but she was looking in the direction of a painting on the wall above Daniel's couch. From his angle it seemed to be of flowers, but he doubted his hostess had any real interest in it.

"I spoke with a young midshipman who agreed to provide forty servings of pepperfish," Carlotta said. "*If* I would invite him to the party also. And I did."

"Pepperfish is very tasty," Daniel said. That was true, at

least fresh-caught off the coast of Bantry. A replenishment ship probably carried it frozen in bulk, so forty missing servings weren't going to set off any alarms.

He had spoken to urge Carlotta along. She'd stopped to stare at her hands as she wrung them together.

"He was so handsome..." Carlotta whispered. "And so different from anyone I knew. Even my friends who'd been off Jardin had only seen people like themselves and places like here. Timothy was..."

Tears dribbled down her cheeks. Hogg startled Daniel by whipping a doily one-handed from under the flower arrangement on the table nearby and putting it into Carlotta's hands. The vase rattled but didn't fall over.

Carlotta blew her nose and nodded gratefully toward Hogg. She didn't resume speaking.

"Midshipman Dorst was the father of your son?" Daniel asked gently.

"No, no," said Carlotta. "Timothy was Jacques' son, my husband after I married. But Timothy, Midshipman Dorst, was the only man I ever loved or could love. I kept thinking he would come back some day. I *dreamed* that he would. But of course he had his career. And had his wife."

She turned to Miranda and dipped her head in formal acknowledgement. "And that was proper," Carlotta said, "because he was a man. I would not have loved Timothy if he were not a man."

Miranda nodded back, still-faced. She said, "Did you hate my father?"

"I love him, dear," Carlotta said. She seemed to have

144

forgotten that the two of them weren't alone in the room. "I loved him then and I love him now. My Timothy did not come back, but he sent his daughter who has his eyes and his smile. You make my heart well again, dear Miranda."

"Why did your son try to kill Captain Leary?" Adele said. She didn't normally interject when a subject was speaking freely, but perhaps she wanted to guide the discussion.

"That was why," Carlotta said with a sad smile. "I took my family name back after the divorce. I told Timothy that I would always love him as my son, but that I had never loved his father. The daughter of the man I still love was coming to visit me, and if I felt after meeting her as I did now, I would make her co-heir with him."

"So your son stood to lose a lot of money," Daniel said. He was still woozy and he wasn't sure that he'd fully taken in all he was being told, but the motive seemed clear.

"The daSaenz wealth is beyond computation!" Carlotta said. "Timothy doesn't have expensive tastes any more than I do. All he really cares about are the caves ... but he cared more about the caves than I understood."

She closed her eyes for a moment, then resumed, "He kept saying, screaming really, 'You can't give the caves up to an outsider, even part ownership!' And I said that I was head of the family, and that I would follow my heart."

"But didn't you ..." Daniel said, but he was losing the thought in the fog of his mind. "You sent him to greet us, I mean?"

"I did not," Carlotta said forcefully. "I knew Mistress Miranda was coming, but I didn't know when. 'In about another week,' I was told by our agents at the port; that was how long it would take a yacht from Cinnabar to arrive even if you lifted at the time you planned to."

"We radioed down when the *Princess Cecile* reached Jardin orbit," Adele said. Though polite, her voice was that of a displeased Lady Mundy.

"Timothy had directed that all messages regarding Captain Leary's arrival be given to him alone," Carlotta said stiffly. "He had given those orders to both the port agent and to my steward. He said it was a family matter and that I had told him to deal with it."

She paused and swallowed before saying, "The servants will be punished in whatever fashion you direct, Captain Leary."

"Oh, no!" said Miranda.

Daniel thought about what his father would do if faced with a similar situation. Corder Leary wasn't cruel, but he had been known to punish a mistake brutally to make others more careful in similar circumstances.

"Brutally" didn't mean the same thing on civilized Cinnabar that it might here on Jardin, of course.

"I don't think any punishment is called for here," Daniel said. "It appears that your servants made the same mistake you did, after all. As I did, for that matter: trusting the son of the house."

"I am so sorry," Carlotta said. "So *very* sorry."

"I gather that Timothy daSaenz attempted to lose Captain Leary and his wife in the depths of the cave," Adele said. "Where they wouldn't be found even when we learned what he had done. He didn't realize that Captain Leary had a pair of RCN goggles which not only allowed him to see in the dark—"

She raised the goggles in her right hand. She must have found them in the cargo pocket of his trousers.

Where I'd forgotten them.

"—but also have an inertial compass which allowed him to retrace his steps precisely."

"Oh!" said Miranda. "I didn't realize..."

Her voice trailed off. She looked down at Daniel in dawning surprise.

"No, that's wrong," Daniel croaked. "I'd forgotten they were there. I just went back to childhood when Hogg was teaching me always to know where I was in the woods and how I'd gotten there."

Adele's face went blank, but Miranda's expression was softening again.

"I went right back to basics," Daniel said. "I learned about goggles in the Academy, but the shock of being dumped in that hole—I just grabbed the first way out."

"And we did get out," said Miranda. "We came straight back to the entrance. I was never in doubt."

She bent and kissed Daniel on the forehead. He stiffened, but her lips were as soft as a warm breeze.

"Oh, did I hurt you?" Miranda said in concern.

"No, no," said Daniel. "Not you. I flinched for what it might be, is all."

"I'm so sorry." Carlotta repeated into the handkerchief.

"How is, ah, Timothy doing?" Daniel said. He was curious, but he was also trying to change the subject.

"He'll live," Tovera said as she walked to them from the Medicomp. She had put her submachine gun back into its nest in the attaché case. "He may even be able to feed himself one of these days. He's not going to walk, though, and I'll give long odds that he won't be able to speak complete sentences."

Carlotta made no sound except a gasp. She looked as though lightning had struck her.

"We can't be sure of that so soon!" said Miranda. "It's far too early to give a prognosis."

Tovera shrugged and smiled. Fortunately Carlotta wasn't looking at the smile. "Maybe so," Adele's servant said. "I've read a lot of Medicomp displays over the years, though. You've got quite a wrist on you, Mistress."

Carlotta sobbed. She ran to the Medicomp and hugged the cabinet. Miranda joined her, putting her arms around the shoulders of the older woman.

Daniel grimaced. *Why did Tovera have to say that?* But that wasn't a question you could usefully ask a sociopath.

And—Daniel grinned, mildly embarrassed at doing so—the truth was, he was just as glad that Timothy was in a bad state. Though he was sorry that Miranda apparently felt it was on her conscience.

Tovera grinned back at Daniel. That sobered him immediately.

Adele said, "I've checked the house security system. Carlotta wasn't informed that the *Princess Cecile* had landed. Today Timothy told her that he was going to a club in Cuvier and that he might not return to the manor until tomorrow. He has stayed in town overnight in the past."

Daniel almost shook his head but thought better of it. He'd been feeling better ever since he woke up, but that was a low standard. It would be some time before he could do normal things without remembering what had just happened.

"Do you think it was really about the caves?" Daniel said. "That seems a strange thing to care so much about."

He pitched his voice low as Adele had hers, though Carlotta and Miranda seemed engrossed in conversation. Neither was now crying.

Adele shrugged. "I don't have enough information to be sure," she said. "Nothing we know suggests that Carlotta is wrong, however. And it was the caves that Miranda's father spoke of."

"Sure, but he really meant—" Daniel said.

He stopped himself. He didn't know what Captain Dorst had really been thinking of. Certainly he might have been mourning the beautiful heiress or even his own lost youth when he spoke of Starscape Caves. But it was at least possible that the caves and their glowworms had hit him as hard as they later did Timothy daSaenz.

"The glowworms are interesting," Daniel said at last. "They're unique in my experience, but then a lot of life forms are unique. That's part of the marvel of being a spacer. But glowworms weren't anything special to me."

Miranda and Carlotta rejoined them. Each had an arm around the other's waist.

"Daniel," Miranda said. "Our plan was that I should return to Cinnabar when you left for your other business. That's correct?"

"Yes," said Daniel, wondering where this was going. If Miranda insisted on staying aboard the *Princess Cecile* after this experience, well, he couldn't blame her. "There's plenty of traffic so we ought to be able to find suitable passage for you. But if you don't—"

"I want to stay here," Miranda said firmly. "Carlotta and I have talked it over. There's nothing I need to do on Cinnabar and, well, I'd like to see more of Jardin. And the caves."

Daniel opened his mouth, then shut it. After a moment he said, "I think that's a good idea. And of course you can easily return to Cinnabar if you recall there's something you need to do after all."

Hogg looked at Carlotta and said, "You think that's safe, young Master?"

"I think you're forgetting who saved whom in the cave, Hogg," said Miranda sharply. "But yes, it's quite safe."

Carlotta had drawn herself straighter at Hogg's question. She smiled sadly and said, "It is right that the question be asked, Master Hogg. But yes, it is safe. Miranda is now the only child I have."

Adele coughed. "I think I should go back to the ship and inform the officers of the situation in person," she said. "Will you and Miranda be returning with me?"

"No, I'll stay the night—" he looked up at Carlotta "—if?"

"Of course," she said.

"Tomorrow we'll see how I feel," Daniel said. "I'll be back for a time, anyway. What do we have for transportation?"

"There are aircars up to ten-place and ground vehicles," Carlotta said. "Also drivers. Anything you wish is yours."

"Can we have the one I drove up from the cave in?" Tovera said unexpectedly. "I engaged the automatic stabilizer and it was very good."

"Timothy's car?" said Carlotta. "Yes, of course. Especially that."

"I'll stay," said Hogg. He wasn't asking a question. The stocked impeller was still slung over his right shoulder.

"Yes," said Carlotta. "You may sleep in your master's chamber, if you wish."

"That won't be necessary," said Miranda. "This is still our honeymoon, or it will be when Daniel recovers a little more."

"Come along, Tovera," Adele said. "I don't think we're needed here."

Daniel thought he saw the ghost of a smile on Adele's lips.

CUVIER HARBOR, JARDIN

The signals officer of a corvette didn't rate a private cabin, but Daniel had turned the captain's cruising cabin over to Adele. It was only a bunk and a terminal just off the bridge so that the captain had a place to sleep for a few minutes when a situation was moving too fast for him to go to his great cabin on D Level directly below. On a corvette the great cabin was pretty cramped also, of course.

Adele appreciated the kindness. She could work anywhere, but that very focus made her a difficult cabinmate for anyone else.

Tovera tapped on the hatch. It had to be Tovera because she was in the corridor outside.

"Yes," Adele called without looking away from her display.

She was determining the best way to access the fire and emergency services of Newtown, the capital of Peltry. They seemed to be wholly private and decentralized, which would make it difficult to take them all out of action if required. Adele didn't know why she might want to do that, but she never felt that time spent on preparations was wasted.

Tovera opened the hatch. Miranda entered.

"Oh," said Adele. She blanked her screen by reflex, but there was nothing on it that Miranda shouldn't see. For that matter, there was nothing on it that anyone was likely to be able to identify, let alone understand, at a glance.

"When Lieutenant Vesey told me that you were here, I thought I'd come find you," Miranda said diffidently. "I wasn't serving any purpose on the quay."

"That was what I thought also," Adele said. Miranda was easy to be around, which was an unusual thought for Adele. That didn't really matter: Adele had since childhood cultivated the ability to tune people out. It was a pleasant change, however.

Adele glanced at the real-time panorama which ran at the top of her display. Daniel had assembled his crew on the quay and had informed them from the boarding ramp that the *Sissie* would not be returning directly to Cinnabar. Instead he would be taking his ship on a dangerous undertaking which had only a small chance of profit. Those spacers who wanted out would have their passage paid back to Cinnabar with full wages and a bonus.

Daniel then shook the hand of each and every spacer who signed on. The line of those waiting to reenlist hadn't yet finished moving past the formalities to Daniel.

"Did anybody decide to go home?" Adele asked. Her first

impulse had been to check the feed from the terminal on which Vesey was enrolling spacers and compare the number to the original crew list, but that would be discourteous.

I mustn't disappoint my mother's spirit, Adele thought wryly. She didn't believe in an afterlife: all that remained of Esme Rolfe Mundy was in Adele's memory. But Adele had a very good memory.

"Several hung back at first," Miranda said, "but they seemed to be joining as the line moved."

She leaned over Adele's shoulder to peer at the flat-plate screen. "That's Brausher on the end, isn't it?" Miranda said, pointing. "She said she was going back because her daughter's pregnant. But she's in the line now."

Miranda straightened and moved back slightly. "It's going to be like this always in our marriage, isn't it?" she said. "Daniel shipping out and me staying behind."

"I suppose so," Adele said. She almost added, "I hope so," but she didn't need to say that. It probably wouldn't have surprised Miranda, though.

"This week here on Jardin has been wonderful," Miranda said with her face to the outer bulkhead. "Jardin really is a paradise, just as my father said."

Adele thought back on her week, spent mostly aboard the *Princess Cecile*. She had sifted Grozhinski's data and interfiled it with the material she had brought from Cinnabar. At each stage she had considered what the new situation meant for Daniel's existing plan, and what further information she should try to gather when they reached Peltry.

"Yes," Adele said. She smiled faintly. "It's been a good week."

"Adele, I have a personal question," Miranda said. "You don't have to answer me."

"Yes," said Adele. Of *course* she didn't have to answer a question. Under most circumstances refusing to would be more revealing than an answer, however.

The last figures on the harborfront had reached Vesey. Only Brausher remained to sign the crew list.

"Adele, do you ever worry that I'm going to take Daniel away from you?" Miranda said. "From you, from the *Princess Cecile*; from the RCN?"

"No," said Adele. Her frown was almost as slight as her smile of moments before. "I don't think about the future, to be honest, just the task in front of me. But even if I did think about the future, I wouldn't—Miranda, I don't worry about Cinnabar falling into the sun either."

Miranda laughed. "Yes, that is silly, isn't it?" she said. "Daniel will never leave the RCN, so of course you wouldn't worry about that. But I won't try, Adele. I wouldn't want to do that even if I could."

Daniel was addressing the newly enrolled crew again from the boarding ramp. Adele could listen if she chose to, but she knew the sort of inspiring talk Daniel gave his crews at times like these.

"I would miss Daniel," Adele said. "If he died, if he left for any reason. But I think I would miss the community even more."

Her lips smiled. Miranda flinched; she must have seen the sadness beneath Adele's expression.

"Daniel isn't the family of the *Princess Cecile*," Adele said. "But the community wouldn't exist without him to hold it together. And I would miss that very much. I'd never had a real family until I met Daniel on Kostroma."

The crew began boarding in a jaunty column, talking and apparently singing as they trotted up the ramp.

"But you grew up at your home until, until the conspiracy, didn't you?" Miranda said.

Until my parents and sister were executed on the orders of Speaker Leary, Adele added in her mind. Aloud she said, "My father cared very much about political power; my mother cared about the family name and prestige. I didn't care about either of those things, and they didn't care about me."

"I'm so sorry," Miranda whispered.

The words shocked Adele. She said, "Don't be. I have everything a person could want. Well, a person like me."

To change the subject and because she had just remembered it, Adele opened the cabinet beneath her seat and brought out the metal-plated glove. "Can you tell me what this is, please?" she said. "I found it in the trousers Daniel was wearing in the cave, stuffed into his pocket on top of the goggles."

Miranda took the object. The iron plating on the upper side was a quarter of an inch thick, so it was quite heavy.

"I don't..." Miranda started. Then, "Oh, yes—in the grotto. We'd found what must have been the body of one of the early explorers. Just then Timothy pulled up the ladder and I forgot all about it. Daniel must have stuck this glove in his pocket."

"I see," said Adele. "Do you remember anything about the body?"

Miranda made a moue. "Not really. There was no light except the glowworms, remember, and we didn't have long.

I think it was just the clothing left that the glowworms had deposited iron on."

Adele turned the object over. The bare underside was made of some tightly-woven synthetic.

"The reason I wondered," Adele said, "is that there are only three fingers. It doesn't seem to have been a human glove."

"I don't understand," Miranda said.

"It's a big universe," Adele said as she returned the glove to the drawer. "And a very old one."

Tovera tapped on the hatch and opened it enough to look in. "Six would like to see his wife before we lift," she announced. "Which is going to be soon."

Adele got up. "I'll walk with you to the bridge," she said as she gestured Miranda to the hatch.

Next stop, Peltry in the Tarbell Stars.

CHAPTER 10

ABOVE PELTRY

Adele found freefall very uncomfortable when she was aware of it, but she easily slipped into an existence outside her physical body when confronted with a fresh mass of data to be processed. There was a smile—or at least contentment—at the back of her mind as she began linking Peltry's communications networks to the *Princess Cecile*.

"*Cinnabar registry ship* Princess Cecile *to Newtown Harbor Control*," Vesey called. Newtown was Peltry's capital and main starport. Vesey didn't have a particular flair for communications as Cory did, but she would be polite, correct, and if necessary extremely patient with the local personnel.

It was usually necessary to be patient with ground control once one got outside the core planets of the Cinnabar and Alliance blocs. Adele had the skill and equipment to take over most port control computers. She could give the *Princess Cecile* authorization to land and could block other ships from landing or lifting off.

That would often have been easier than dealing with a numbskull on the ground—or waiting for someone to finally wake up in the control booth. It would also tell everyone with a modicum of awareness how great the *Sissie*'s capabilities were and how dangerous the ship was to anyone with something to hide.

The most Adele had ever done was to set off the tornado warning sirens in the port of Sisleen on Brookshire, a sleepy Friend of Cinnabar. The sirens continued to wind until someone in Port Control responded to the alert signal on the console— which was the *Sissie*'s request for landing authorization. Adele felt that this would be explained as unconnected computer glitch...but since then, unless there was a specific reason for her to perform as a normal signals officer, she thought it best to leave the task to others.

Besides taking over Peltry's networks, Adele was collecting the contents of official databases—those of the Newtown and Peltry administrations, as well as what passed for the government of the Tarbell Stars. The last was a mare's nest— or rather, half a dozen mare's nests which communicated badly or not at all with one another—but Adele was used to that.

The Department of War was a well-organized exception. There was even an attempt at security. Adele's software had been designed to penetrate Alliance systems. The Fifth Bureau data from Grozhinski had specific keys to the Department of War files, but Cory hadn't required them. A computer capable of guiding a starship through the Matrix could, with the right software, defeat almost any form of encryption.

Cory was sucking in data from the Tarbell Navy. There

were at least a dozen ships in the naval harbor separated by moles from the general harbor. The largest vessel was a heavy cruiser, but it appeared to be out of service.

Adele gave the naval material only a passing glance. Cory was fully competent with the process, and his Academy background gave him advantages. She would go over his gleanings at leisure, but she didn't expect to find anything Cory had missed.

"Princess Cecile, *this is Newtown Control*," a female voice announced. "*I'll be able to clear you to land in about five minutes. There's a freighter scheduled to lift ahead of you, over.*"

Cazelet was searching Port Control and the logs of the sixty-odd ships in the general harbor. He had worked all his youth in his family shipping business until his parents fell foul of Guarantor Porra. Cazelet had fled to his grandmother, who had in turn sent him on to Adele Mundy on Cinnabar.

Just as Mistress Boileau had fostered Adele on Bryce, so Adele took responsibility for Cazelet by placing him in the crew of the *Princess Cecile*. It had been a good bargain for the RCN, and a very good one for Adele herself. Cazelet's different training meshed well with what Cory had received from the RCN, and the two young men even got along well.

I've created a uniquely skilled staff for myself, Adele thought. *Without in the least intending to. And they both feel that I've saved them, which is true enough but wasn't part of a plan either*.

You could accomplish quite a lot—and do quite a lot of good—without goals. Focusing on a task and doing it well was as much as could be expected of anyone. Adele assumed that must be more difficult than it seemed to be to her.

Adele noticed three small civilian craft—the largest was under two thousand tons—clustered around a hulk. They were in the orbit of Peltry's outermost moon, about a million miles above the planet's surface.

From their electronic signatures the ships were barely functional. Adele turned the *Sissie*'s excellent optical sensors to the largest of the three. The imagery showed it just as decrepit as the electronics implied: one of the ship's four antennas was a stump, and a yard was missing on two of those remaining. A rocket basket had been welded to the hull beside the stub antenna where it would have the broadest field of fire.

She highlighted the image and checked Daniel's display on the command console, intending to pin an icon there for him to call up when she alerted him. Daniel was already observing the strange ships, but he had focused on the hulk.

A shaded triangle on his display alerted him that she was echoing his screen. He grinned and said, "*Adele, I'm looking at pirates.*"

Adele had set the system so that her name cued a two-way link. She said, "I thought that's what they were. But what's the hulk?"

When we first met, Daniel wouldn't have noticed that I was echoing his display, she thought with mild pride. *And I wouldn't have recognized pirates.*

"*They're using a junked freighter as a water buffalo,*" he said. "*They probably towed it through the Matrix from wherever their base is so that they can keep a way on while they're waiting for a target.*"

"Are we going to do something?" Adele said. It wasn't idle curiosity—she would have a part in any action. *Though I don't suppose I would have to apologize for being curious.*

"*I'd like to,*" Daniel said. "*But—*"

"Princess Cecile, *this is Newtown Control*," said the voice. "*You are cleared to land in the outer harbor. A tug will bring you to your berth. Over.*"

"*But there isn't time,*" Daniel continued, "*and it's not really our business. Not yet, at least. Still—can you get me a tight beam to the biggest pirate?*"

"Yes," said Adele, "but I'd be amazed if they had functioning laser or microwave receivers. I certainly don't see any sign of antennas on them."

"*Then shortwave will do,*" Daniel said.

Adele adjusted the hailing antenna toward the largest vessel and said, "Go ahead."

"*Unidentified ships,*" said Daniel, "*this is RCS* Princess Cecile. *Stand by to be boarded. If you offer resistance, you will be immediately destroyed, over.*"

Daniel hadn't alerted the *Sissie*'s crew to what he was doing, but the ship trembled as both gun turrets slewed to bear on the pirates. Sun had been monitoring radio traffic. In a moment he would lower the turrets and lock them for landing, but now the plasma cannon were ready to fire.

Lights winked in a corner of Adele's display. She knew if she checked she would learn that Chief Missileer Chazanoff was arming his weapons too. None of the pirates looked worth a missile, but Chazanoff wasn't going to miss any chance that was offered.

The pirates had been cruising at low thrust, just enough to maintain a semblance of gravity. There was no reply by radio, but two and then the third vessel came up to what was probably full power. As Adele watched, one vessel entered the Matrix. The other pirates followed a moment later.

"*I don't blame the locals for not chasing them off,*" Daniel said, back on the two-way link. "*But they ought to be able to smash the water buffalo. Still, it's not our business.*"

Adele was sure that Daniel *did* blame the Peltry forces. She understood that it was considered polite to be charitable to incompetents, but she had never been able to fathom why.

"Princess Cecile, *this is Newtown Control,*" the radio voice said unexpectedly. "*Is Captain Leary aboard, over?*"

Without hesitation, Vesey sent an alert to Adele's console, passing the call to her. Adele, feeling her voice harden further with each word, said, "Ground, this is *Princess Cecile*. Captain Leary is aboard. What is your reason for asking, over?"

"Princess Cecile," said Newtown Control, "*the Tarbell Stars have directed that Captain Leary and his staff report as soon as they arrive to Christopher Robin, the Minister of War. The ministry will send an aircar to pick them up, over.*"

"Message received," Adele said without discussing the matter with Daniel. "*Princess Cecile* out."

Instead of turning her head toward Daniel, Adele expanded his face on her display. Over the two-way link she said, "Well, it gives you plenty of time to change."

Daniel stretched at his console. "*It would,*" he said, "*but I think I'll wear these utilities, like the civilian captain I am. I'll wear a saucer hat, though.*"

He frowned slightly and added, "*You know, I think it might be just as well if you weren't with me. Though if you want to come, of course...?*"

"I can check with the local representative of our principal during the time," Adele said calmly. She knew that Daniel liked to keep a distance from her intelligence activities, but there was more going on here. "Is there any particular reason that you'd like me to be absent?"

Daniel laughed; the question seemed to have restored his normal good humor. "*Not really,*" he said. "*Well, the same reason you didn't give a real answer to the demand. We knew we'll be working with the Minister of War, but...*"

He frowned again and said, "*There are a lot of people who can give me orders. They all wear RCN uniforms. More to the point, none of them are jumped-up quartermasters like Christopher Robin, sitting behind desks in the back of beyond.*"

Adele smiled. Lady Mundy understood Captain Leary's reaction very clearly. Another person would have laughed out loud.

NEWTOWN ON PELTRY

"Captain Leary?" said the man waiting on the pier in a white uniform without rank insignia. "I'm Captain Walters. I'm to escort you and your staff to the Minister of War."

Daniel eyed the aircar behind Walters. It would seat twelve in the benches running along the sides of the passenger compartment; there was a cab in front for the driver.

"Is that Army?" Hogg said, frowning. "It sure looks like it."

"It doesn't have armor," Daniel said. "Police, maybe. A paddy wagon, I shouldn't wonder."

Walters was young and had a fluffy blond beard which contrasted with the flush of his skin. "His Excellency wasn't sure how many personnel you would be bringing. I thought it best to borrow a vehicle from the Quick Response Force of the National Police. It is *not* a prison van."

"I've ridden paddy wagons before," Daniel said mildly. "We can leave whenever you're ready, Master Walters."

Walters looked past Hogg and Daniel and frowned. "I'm to bring your staff with you, Captain Leary," he said.

"That's me," said Hogg, sauntering past Walters toward the aircar. The female driver watched him silently. She had shut down her fans.

"I distinctly remember His Excellency telling me there would be a woman!" Walters said.

"Then he's going to be disappointed," Daniel said, walking around the aide's other side. He had told Hogg about the summons from Minister Robin, but he probably wouldn't have needed to. Hogg automatically got a chip on his shoulder when he had to deal with what he considered uppity foreigners—who were basically anybody who wasn't a Cinnabar citizen.

"Say, but if you find one," Hogg said, "see if she's got a friend. I don't know anybody yet on this pisspot world."

"Drive to the ministry!" Walters called to the driver as he got in behind them. He banged the door shut. The back had a cage of heavy wire. It could be covered with a tarpaulin, but at present the mesh was open to the sky.

The driver balanced her six motors and lifted. The two beneath the stern squealed loudly at idle. *Probably why she'd shut down while she waited*, Daniel thought, but the sound muted once the oil was at full pressure.

"I was expecting to call on the president as soon as I'd changed," Daniel said truthfully to Walters. He raised his voice only slightly.

Walters had seated himself on the back end of Daniel's bench. He slid closer so that he didn't have to lower his dignity by shouting and said, "You're welcome to see President Menandros, but if you want to discuss the war you'll be very disappointed. If you're a wine connoisseur, the president is your man."

Daniel nodded with a smile. For the first time the aide sounded like a real human being instead of the puffed-up retainer of a puffed-up bureaucrat. He said, "Then perhaps I'll get on better with Master Robin than I feared I would from his summons."

Walters flushed again. "He *is* the Minister of War of the Tarbell Stars, Captain Leary," he said.

"Right," said Hogg. "And me and the young master is Cinnabar citizens. So now we've decided who's the class act on…what's the name of it again? Peltry."

The driver flew them around a large courtyard building, three stories tall like the square structures to either side of it. The front entranceway was covered by a cornice supported on full-height pillars, but the back was an alley not much wider than the aircar. The driver settled to the alley pavement skillfully, keeping a degree of forward motion to steady the vehicle despite the currents eddying between the buildings. She shut off the motors.

"His Excellency thought it would be better for you to arrive without fanfare," Walters said. "There are spies in Newtown, you see."

Yes, Daniel thought. *We're working for some of them.*

Storn's officers weren't the only spies on Peltry, of course. But it was equally obvious that entering by the back door wasn't going to keep Daniel's presence a secret from the Upholders and their Fifth Bureau backers.

I wonder if Robin is hoping to hide us from his president?

The aircar had landed just ahead of an unobtrusive door in the back wall of the War Ministry. Walters removed an electronic key from his breast pocket and inserted it in the lock. The heavy door opened outward; it wouldn't have cleared the side of the car if they'd been directly in front of it.

Walters gestured Daniel and Hogg into a dim-lit anteroom. "There's no guard," the aide said, "because there's only this one key. His Excellency keeps it himself. Being entrusted with it was a great honor for me."

Hogg sniffed, but Daniel was glad that he didn't say what he was obviously thinking: *if you think an electronic lock will keep out anyone but the key-holder, you haven't met Adele.* Which was true, of course.

The anteroom was tight for three people. Daniel wondered what would have happened if he had brought a staff of ten.

Walters pressed a button in the wall. A green light winked above the inner door, which he then pushed open. "Your Excellency, the visitors are here. They're both male."

There hadn't been a lock. The light was simply to indicate that the person within was free.

Christopher Robin had risen from his wooden desk. He faced Daniel and Hogg with a noble expression. The large office beyond was empty of furniture except for three chairs and the smaller desk set near the door to which Walters went.

Robin was large without being really fat. He would have been an imposing man even without the white leather uniform glittering with medals and braid. Adele's briefing mentioned that Robin was the Marshal Commanding All Military Forces of the Tarbell Stars. Apparently it was in that guise he had decided to meet the Cinnabar advisors rather than as the civilian Minister of War.

In official Tarbell records Robin was a former Admiral of the Kostroman Navy. Kostroman naval ranks didn't rise to admiral, and the captains had to be members of the ruling families; Robin's father had been a dockyard welder and his mother a schoolteacher.

Robin *had* been in the Kostroman navy, as a quartermaster. He had left his position and Kostroma ahead of an investigation. That said, Tarbell's Ministry of War was well organized and well run—uniquely among the government bureaus.

"Seat yourselves, please," Robin said, gesturing to the chairs facing the front of the desk. Daniel walked around to take one.

"I'll stand," said Hogg. He leaned against the door they had entered by.

Robin laughed and sat down on his own chair though that left Hogg glowering at his back. He said, "Captain Leary, I've heard a great deal about you and Lady Mundy."

"Friends of the Tarbell Stars thought the *Princess Cecile* could be useful to your government in fighting the Upholders,"

Daniel said. He ignored the reference to Adele.

"Indeed, indeed," Robin said. He took off his saucer hat—leather as well, it appeared—and set it on the desk. "The Upholders have three modern destroyers, one of which has a crew of Fleet veterans. Not so very impressive, you might say, but we have only three destroyers which are really serviceable, plus the destroyer which recently came to us when Nabis decided to join the Tarbell Stars."

That hadn't been in the briefing materials, Daniel thought. Aloud he said, "When did Nabis join? I'd understood they were taking a strongly independent line?"

"The former ruler, Peter Langland, certainly was independent," Robin said with a chuckle. "He asked for help from us and from Karst to resist pressure from the Upholders. Karst sent a regiment—which promptly assassinated Langland and started looting the capital. The locals rose up and slaughtered about half of them. The provisional Nabis government was happy to join Tarbell when our troops arrived."

That was too recent to have been in the briefing materials. No doubt Adele would be getting an update from her sources right now.

"Anyway," Robin said, "I'd like you and your officers to transfer to the Nabis destroyer, the *Katchaturian*, and whip her into shape. I'll provide Tarbell officers for your corvette. I think that's the most efficient way to use the available resources."

A number of ways to respond riffled through Daniel's mind like the pages of a flipbook. "I don't think we'll do that," he said mildly. "I think we'll be able to work out something satisfactory when I've got a little more information, though."

Daniel coughed into his fist, enough of a pause to allow Robin to absorb the idea but not to respond, then said, "You mentioned the Upholder destroyers but you didn't say that the rebels are also believed to be negotiating for a heavy cruiser. Can your own cruiser be readied in time to meet it?"

Both of Adele's sources were certain that General Krychek was arranging the transfer of an Alliance cruiser to the Upholders. On paper the rebels were buying a hulk for scrap value. The reality was that the paperwork had been switched with that of a sister ship which was old but fully functional.

Robin certainly knew that. Either he was testing how much Daniel knew, or he was simply trying to hide the real situation from his new advisor.

"The *Maria Theresa* can't be returned to use," Robin said without hesitating. "What I *can* do is configure a pair of modern transports as missile ships. The Upholders can't fight a battle of maneuver. If we can overwhelm the cruiser they may be getting, the n any surviving ships will lose heart and flee. The war's over then."

That's a good plan, Daniel thought. His opinion of the Minister was going up.

"We're getting the missiles from Cinnabar stocks," Robin went on. "I suspect you may know more about that than I do."

You're wrong, Daniel thought.

"Anyway, they're Alliance missiles captured in the recent war and being shipped to us as scrap. I've just been informed that they've arrived on Danziger, which is the usual transfer point for the cluster."

"My crew and I can help in refitting the transports as warships," Daniel said.

Robin grimaced and spread his hands in a dismissive gesture. "We have dockyards here," he said. "Perhaps when it comes to fitting the fire control a specialist might be helpful. The *Katchaturian* is too important a ship for me to just hope that Langland did a good job of maintaining it and training its crew!"

Daniel pursed his lips. Robin was being forceful, but he didn't repeat his initial error of trying to give orders to someone who wasn't under his command.

"I think we can find a useful compromise," Daniel said. "Give me command of the *Katchaturian*. I'll treat her and the *Sissie* as a small squadron and work them up together. That is, if I have a free hand with the *Katchaturian*'s crew?"

Robin snorted. "You have it," he said. "Hang a few of them if you think that'll wake the others up. The officers are Nabis gentry, so that might be a good idea. The crew is whoever signed on, of course. Some Nabis, most not."

"All right," said Daniel, rising. "You'll arrange that I have any authorizations I need?"

"Walters, see that Major Berners gives Leary whatever he wants," Robin said. "And guides him around personally."

"Yes, your Excellency!" Walters said. "I'll take him straight to Berners."

"Say, Leary?" Robin said. "I know the destroyer's under strength. How would you like to take over the Nabis ground troops too? I shifted the Nabis Capital Regiment to Peltry and put a Tarbell regiment on Nabis, just for safety. The Nabis troops really are from Nabis, you see—Langland was trying to make the planet great, the way it was before the Hiatus."

"Yes," Daniel said. There were many questions, *many* ways that could go wrong. His assumption was to assume he could deal with whatever luck or the gods threw him. There were always too many potential side-effects to prepare for all of them.

"Then I think we're done here, Leary," Robin said. "Walters, take him to Berners."

They left by the front door of the office. Daniel wondered how he was going to get back to the *Princess Cecile*, but he would deal with that when the time came.

CHAPTER 11

NEWTOWN ON PELTRY

Adele stared at the text from Guy Mignouri, the Fifth Bureau Resident in Newtown, for some seconds longer than the words themselves required: IT IS NOT SUITABLE TO MEET NOW. I WILL INFORM YOU FURTHER IN A FEW DAYS.

Adele cued the link to Tovera, who sat opposite her on the striker's seat of the signals console. "Tovera, we're going visiting. It's possible this will involve forced entry."

"*Should I bring something bulkier than the usual?*" Tovera said.

"No, it's likely to be very short range if it comes to that," said Adele. Neither she nor Tovera was skilled with long arms, and Tovera's miniature submachine gun had always proven as satisfactory as one throwing heavier slugs could have been. "But now that I've thought about it, I should have backup. Break. Captain Vesey, this is Mundy."

Adele did not refer to herself as "Signals" or "Signals Officer Mundy" as she might have done at other times when she was being formal. Her present request had nothing to do with her RCN duties.

"*Go ahead, Mundy,*" Vesey said. Though Vesey was in command of the *Princess Cecile* during Daniel's absence, she chose to remain at her normal duty station in the Battle Direction Center in the stern.

"I'm going to visit associates," Adele said. "They didn't respond as I expected when I informed them of my presence. It's possible that there's something wrong. I would like a squad to back me up at a short distance. Six should be enough. I hope to wave them off after the door is opened to me normally."

"*Do you want Woetjans to lead?*" Vesey said. "*And what sort of tools? Over.*"

"I'll have Hale to lead if you don't mind," Adele said, adding the junior midshipman and sending her the early part of the call. "She's here at the navigation console at the moment. Woetjans is checking the A Ring antennas, and I don't see that I need her for this."

That was true, but it was also true that Woetjans tended to act quickly and with great force, as a bosun was required to do. Hale was cool in a crisis, but she was much less likely to get physical.

"And I don't want to march through the city like an assault force," Adele said. "I don't want any weapons visible. I truly don't expect serious violence."

"*We've got collapsible handcarts in a locker,*" Vesey said. "*One of them will hold guns politely, over.*"

Hale was already alerting spacers for the duty, pinging them individually instead of using the general push. She was the kind of officer which the RCN needed.

"That will be very satisfactory," Adele said, rising to her feet. "I'll inform you of the results on my return. Over; that is, out."

"Sun is opening the arms locker," Hale said. Sun was the gunner's mate—the *Sissie* didn't rate a gunner—and doubled as armorer. "And I told Evans to bring a long-handled maul. That will fit in the cart also. We'll meet the squad in the entry hold."

Evans was a short, broad power-room technician who was good-natured and extremely strong. Almost as strong as he was stupid, Adele would guess.

"There shouldn't be any shooting," Adele said as she strode quickly to the down companionway. "If there is, Tovera and I will start it."

Unless they've shot both of us in the head, Adele thought. She couldn't help being precise, but at least she had learned not to say everything she was thinking. At that, she could imagine Tovera shooting back after being killed the way a headless chicken ran about.

Barnes was still closing his boots as he stumbled into the boarding hold a moment after Adele. Dasi, his partner and fellow bosun's mate, was helping Sun shift two submachine guns, two stocked impellers, and a carbine—Hale's weapon of choice—into the cart which Evans and Bledsoe had assembled. The maul was already there.

It was a remarkable performance. Aloud Adele said, "It makes me proud to be a Sissie." Or at least it would have if she hadn't already been proud.

"Can you tell us what to expect, Mistress?" Hale said.

Other spacers were looking toward the group from hatchways and the quay; that was inevitable and not a problem.

"What I'm *afraid* of," Adele said, "though I don't expect it, is that agents of the Fifth Bureau have taken over the office of my associates."

She didn't bother explaining that her associate was also a Fifth Bureau agent. The details didn't matter to the Sissies; all they needed was to be told the situation they might be facing.

"It's only three blocks," Adele added. "And I hope just to knock on the door and be admitted. If you stay fifty feet behind me, you'll be close enough to call if I need you."

Adele was wearing a civilian suit in light green, cut much the same as a set of utilities. Tovera's suit was on the tan side of cream; her attaché case was brown and looked like leather even from quite nearby. The material was actually an expensive composite and would stop anything short of a slug from a stocked impeller.

The ground floors of the buildings facing the harbor were ship chandleries and bars, while the upper stories were spacer's lodgings, brothels, and pawn shops. The next block inland was inexpensive shops below civilian apartments. By the third block back from the water, the buildings were duplexes and private residences, many of them with a ground vehicle parked on gated driveways.

The residence looked like a single-family home—and probably was that as well as containing communications equipment. The walls were of dark blue brick, fired from a local clay, and the curtained windows seemed normal unless you recognized the frames as being much wider than the outer glass alone would have required.

Tovera pushed the button on the call plate and said, "Mistress Simmons and her secretary to see Master Mignouri." When she got no response, she rapped sharply on the panel—and still got no response.

Adele was holding her data unit. She keyed the "execute" button to signal the door's electronic latch. There was an internal *clunk* and the panel swung open. It was five centimeters thick and made of armor plate.

Both Adele and Tovera had their weapons out, but beyond was only a second door, this one opening inward. It had a latch but no visible lock. The handle rotated easily, but the panel rattled against a bolt on the other side when Tovera shoved against it.

Adele turned and called, "Evans!" The squad of spacers was only ten feet back instead of fifty, but there hadn't been much traffic on the street—and anyway, it didn't matter.

Hale had removed the tarpaulin covering the handcart, but Evans didn't bother to reach in for his maul. He rushed to the door, lowered his shoulder, and slammed into it. The panel broke lengthwise in the middle.

The halves dangled—one side by the hinges and the other by the bolt near the top edge of the panel. Evans' mindless straight-ahead smash had been the best way to deal with the problem, which Adele found disturbing.

A cabinet had been slid against the inside of the door, but Evans rolled it back—it was on casters—in the same rush that had taken him through the door panel. Beyond was a reception room with chairs against the walls and a small table holding a vase of flowers probably picked in the front garden. A woman leaned on the table, weeping into her hands.

"Don't shoot!" Adele shouted as Barnes and Dasi rushed past her brandishing weapons. Evans was picking himself up from the floor when the cabinet—a musical instrument, Adele now saw—rolled back.

Tovera took the weeping woman by the hair and shouted, "Who else is in the house?" while looking up the staircase. The woman continued to sob.

"Bledsoe, with me!" Hale said and started up the stairs, holding her carbine forward in both hands. The tech following her had one of the submachine guns.

"Don't shoot my husband!" said the woman who had been crying, the first intelligible words she had spoken.

"Hold up, Hale!" Adele said. "Tovera, let her go."

Tovera released the woman's hair and stepped against the wall. She kept her weapon raised, but she had stopped pointing the muzzle at the stairs when Hale started up.

"Who are you, Mistress?" Adele said. "And who is your husband?"

"I'm Yvette Mignouri," the woman said. She closed her eyes and wiped her nose with the back of her hand. She was younger than Adele had guessed—probably mid-twenties—and would be attractive after she washed her face and calmed down. "My husband is Guy Mignouri. Please, why have you attacked us? There's nothing here to steal!"

"Call your husband down," Adele said. "Tell him not to carry a weapon."

"He can't come!" Yvette cried. "He can't move! He's had

a stroke! Please leave us alone!"

Ah!

"I'll check!" said Tovera as she slipped past the spacers on the stairs. The other spacers were backing to the nearest wall and pointing their guns upward—with the exception of Evans, who didn't have a weapon. He was scratching his crotch with a puzzled look.

"I was directed to call on Guy Mignouri, the Fifth Bureau Resident in Newtown," Adele said. "When I didn't get a satisfactory reply to my queries, I came to view the situation for myself. Why didn't you report that your husband was incapacitated?"

"He's here, all right," Tovera called from the stairhead. "Hooked up to what I'd call a first-aid machine. It seems to be keeping him alive, but he's not going to get better any time soon. If he ever does."

"Guy *will* get well!" Yvette said with a quaver that suggested she might be about to resume crying. "He'll be removed if they learn, and this is his first field posting. He'll never get another if he's removed now!"

He can't do his job so he has *to be removed*, Adele thought. She didn't say that out loud. She had learned long before Mistress Sand recruited her that other people didn't see the obvious as clearly as she did.

"Where's the station?" Adele said aloud.

"In the basement, but the files are all locked," Yvette said. "I have the key to the communications console, though."

"Thank you," Adele said. The electronic files wouldn't have been a problem even if Grozhinski hadn't given her the keys, but there was no reason to tell the wife that. "Hale, I'll take a look at the equipment. Then I'll probably have you stay here while I return to the *Sissie* and discuss the matter with Daniel. Oh, and I'll have an ambulance sent here to pick up Mignouri. Mistress Mignouri, you'd better pack a case. Whether you go with your husband or not, you can't stay here any longer."

"Right, Mistress," Hale said. She braced to attention unconsciously.

"You can't walk in here and do that!" said Yvette.

"Mistress," said Lady Mundy, speaking with the icy certainty that her mother would have displayed in similar circumstances. "I am here at the behest of your husband's superior's highest superior. You have nothing to say to me but 'Yes, sir!' And if you're wise, you might add, 'And thank you for not shooting me for treason, sir.'"

Yvette's mouth fell open.

Tovera had opened the door under the stairs. Adele strode to it.

Behind her Evans said plaintively, "Bledsoe, are we supposed to shoot this lady?"

"Good evening, gentlemen," Daniel said, speaking clearly and without the need of amplification to be heard by his audience of the forty-odd officers and noncoms. "I am Captain Leary. The Minister of War has put me in command of the Nabis Contingent of the Forces of the Tarbell Stars."

Daniel had changed into clean utilities with RCN rank tabs and his saucer hat for this introduction. It was the garb he would have worn on the bridge of the *Princess Cecile* when she was in RCN service, though on larger ships, officers were expected to be in second class uniforms.

All the officers before him were men, which was the usual case in the military on planets at such a distance from the centers of civilization. Gender discrimination wasn't unheard of even on lesser worlds in the Cinnabar and Alliance spheres. It was one more excuse for residents of Cinnabar and the core worlds of the Alliance to consider their subjects from the fringes to be higher animals rather than real human beings.

"Minister Robin put me in charge because he wants the Nabis Contingent raised to the level of the RCN," Daniel said, keeping his tone informal. His audience had been nervous at the start, but there was nothing in his delivery to worry them further. "That's going to be a change, as some of you have already learned."

He smiled gently as he looked across his ranked audience. A dozen of those facing him were not in full uniform, and one was wearing pajamas. Further, some were the worse for drink. They hadn't all been on duty at the time Daniel called the meeting; but most had, or should have been.

"Now, a spacer is a spacer," Daniel said. "There's good ones and bad ones, but the RCN isn't great because our crews come from Cinnabar—which mostly they don't. What makes a military force great is the quality of its officers, commissioned and warrant both. That means you."

He smiled again. This time his expression wasn't so friendly.

"You're going to come up to RCN standards," Daniel said. "Then you and I together are going to turn the Nabis Contingent into the finest fighting force in the Tarbell Stars."

Only two of the commissioned officers and half a dozen of the noncoms—warrant officers and sergeants depending on the service—had been at their duty stations or in their official residences. The spacers' ground billets and the regiment's barracks were filthy.

The reason the personnel were here facing Daniel was that Cory had located them using a console on the *Princess Cecile*. Adele had apparently connected the databases and communications networks in Newtown—and probably throughout Peltry—to the *Sissie*. Knowing that wouldn't have helped Daniel himself very much, but to Adele's protégés it was as good as a street map to the missing officers. Teams of military police backed by two or three Sissies each had brought the officers to the parade square between the Nabis barracks and the *Katchaturian*'s berth.

Angry bluster probably wouldn't have gotten Nabis citizens very far with military police, none of whom were from that until-recently independent planet. It got nowhere at all with the Sissies, nor did any claimed rank that wasn't in the RCN.

"You're going to train..." said Daniel, raising his voice slightly to override the sudden buzz of voices. "By performing as common spacers under officers of the RCN. On Cinnabar, RCN spacer is a respected position. That's because every citizen knows that the RCN is a collection of the best."

Vesey and Major Berners, the Minister's representative, stood to Daniel's left. Woetjans was on his right, but a pace back out of the bosun's own sense of decorum.

Hogg stood at the side of the square along with common spacers from the *Sissie* and the *Katchaturian*; both ships were moored in the same slip. Hogg had wanted to be closer to Daniel, but the whole point of this address was to create a dichotomy between the military and civilians.

The best way to weld the two crews into a single fighting force was to give them third parties on whom they both could look down: mere civilians. Daniel wasn't a philosopher. He didn't try to reform human nature, he just used whatever aspects he could when they helped him toward a goal.

"Now, you're going to train as hard as you need to to come up to RCN standards," Daniel said. "It's not going to be a picnic. You'll take orders from whoever your officers—*my* officers—put in charge of you, and you'll learn to jump when you do it. That means—"

"How *dare* you?" said a man as he pushed his way forward from the third row. "How dare you, you Cinnabar ponce!"

"You're Lieutenant Feilson, I believe," Daniel said pleasantly. He adjusted his stance slightly.

"I bloody well am!" Feilson said. He was properly dressed—but in a civilian suit of good quality rather than the uniform he should have worn as the duty officer of the *Katchaturian*. "I'm an officer of the Fleet and a gentleman of Pleasaunce. If you think some yob from Cinnabar is going to give me orders, you're bloody wrong!"

"Get back in line, Master Feilson," Daniel said, his voice still friendly. "You're on duty and I'm your commanding—"

Feilson was a little taller than Daniel and in good condition; he swung for Daniel's jaw. Daniel blocked the fist with his open left hand. Instead of counterpunching as he normally would have done, Daniel shoved the Pleasaunce officer backward.

"An officer of the RCN doesn't brawl with his crew," Daniel said, trying to sound a little bored. He wanted to shake the sting out of his left hand, but he controlled the urge; Feilson had been stronger than Daniel expected. "Master Feilson, you have—"

Feilson cocked his arm to swing again. Woetjans caught him by the neck and jerked him aside. Feilson got out one squawk before the bosun slapped him with her right hand. She could drive nails with her callused palms.

Feilson's eyes glazed; Woetjans tossed him to Barnes and Dasi. They dragged the unconscious man away.

"As I was about to say," Daniel continued to the remainder of his audience, "Master Feilson has chosen to resign rather than become a real officer. At this moment you all have the option of resigning. I don't know or care what your obligations to the Tarbell Stars may be. If you're not willing to become an officer who I can respect, I want no part of you."

"Does she beat the crap outta us if we quit now?" said a scarred, wiry man of fifty in the front row. He wore utilities but the rank tabs were on the underside of his collar.

Daniel didn't recognize the fellow by name from the briefing materials, but he didn't need to. "No, she doesn't," Daniel said, "but I hope you don't quit anyway. Senior warrant officers with the balls to speak up aren't thick on the ground around here. What's your specialty, spacer?"

The little man braced to attention. "Gunner Gabriel Wright, sir!" he said. "Late of the Fleet, late of a lot of other places that needed somebody who knew how to make a plasma cannon sing!"

"At ease, Wright," Daniel said. "Do you know how to take orders too?"

"Yes, *sir*," Wright said. "Even if I think the guy giving 'em is about two brain cells short of being a moron. As I did Lieutenant Feilson, *sir*."

"I'll hope I measure up to your standards when the time comes, Wright," Daniel said.

His expression sobered as he looked at his audience again.

"Gentlemen," Daniel said, "I've told you that you'll learn to be officers under me, and that's important. But this is your chance to learn something even better. I'm giving you a chance to be part of an elite combat unit. Until you've felt that, you can't imagine what it's like. You trust your fellows and they trust you, because you know every one of you will do his job."

Daniel felt his throat getting husky as it always did when he thought about this. He continued, "You'll have trained with the Sissies and you'll be as good as the Sissies, and there's no better in the human universe than my Sissies."

Daniel swallowed. "Gentlemen, I'm going to dismiss you for an hour," he said. "After that, you'll assemble again and we'll enroll you in the new Nabis Contingent, all of you who've got the balls."

He grinned and said, "Which I hope a lot of you do, because we've got a real fight ahead with the Upholders. Dismissed!"

CHAPTER 12

NEWTOWN ON PELTRY

"Mundy of Chatsworth to see the president," Adele said to the uniformed doorman. "He's been informed of my visit."

She had come to the presidential palace in civilian clothing as Lady Mundy. The outfits Adele had brought from Cinnabar reflected her own taste, very dull by Peltry standards, but fortunately Yvette Mignouri was both young and from the more flamboyant Pleasaunce. The garments the resident's wife had left behind included some which suggested a basic tawdriness as well.

Adele had sent two of the most likely suits to the ship to be converted into Peltry-style court dresses: most spacers were expert tailors. In this case Woetjans had insisted on doing the sewing herself for the honor of it.

Adele could imagine her mother's reaction: "Go and change at once! You look like a common prostitute!"

Adele smiled faintly. She didn't, of course. Even wearing an outfit of saturated red and blue, she was no more sexually enticing than a similarly painted tramcar.

"Ah, a moment, please," the doorman said, looking worried. He pressed a button. The fellow wore a pistol as part of his uniform, but it may never have been out of its holster.

Tovera was in gray today. She was as unobtrusive as one of the *Sissie*'s bunks.

A big man, blond where he still had a fringe of hair, bustled up from the interior: Dumouret, the butler, as Adele knew from Mignouri's files. "Lady Mundy!" he said. "Come through, please. President Menandros will be so pleased to see you!"

"I'm glad to hear that," said Adele, walking past the relieved-looking doorman. Visits from foreign dignitaries were obviously not part of his routine.

Adele's statement was true. Besides, her parents had been prominent politicians. She had grown up hearing much greater lies than the one Dumouret had just told.

Dumouret took them—took Adele; he seemed oblivious of Tovera beyond the fact that Lady Mundy had brought her maid—through a door to the left and then down a long corridor. The windows on the left opened onto a courtyard whose bushes had been trimmed into balls and pyramids. Fresh growth blurred the topiary with bright green tendrils.

The room at the end of the hallway had a front wall of ornate grillwork instead of being solid. There were upholstered chairs and couches along both sidewalls, but at the opposite end of the room three young women were playing cards with a man wearing loose garments of pink and orange in vertical stripes.

The gate had a latch mechanism, but Dumouret swung it open without hesitation; either it had not been locked, or the butler had an electronic key in his ornate signet ring. "Your Highness," he said. "Lady Mundy of Cinnabar is here to pay her respects."

President Menandros looked up with a frown. Ignoring his master's obvious displeasure, Dumouret ushered Adele through the gate. "You'll recall, your Highness," the butler said, "that Lady Mundy is passing through the Tarbell Stars and wished to make your acquaintance."

Menandros grimaced, but he got to his feet. Like the furniture—and despite the generous cut of his clothing—the president was overstuffed.

His face suddenly brightened. "Lady Mundy, I wonder if you'd like to try some of my wine," Menandros said, gesturing to a sideboard with bottles and glasses. "Dumouret, pour her ladyship some of the Saturnia!"

"At once, your Highness," the butler said.

Tovera was standing beside a chair near the grill. The wall panels were of gray wood with very fine grain. Adele wondered if Tovera had chosen her outfit with the present background in mind.

Tovera was direct—brutally direct—but she was also intelligent. She noticed minute details which might affect her own duties.

Dumouret handed the glass to Adele. There wasn't a chair for her at the table, so the butler stepped away to get one of those against the wall.

The three women—girls, rather—stared at Adele with vaguely petulant expressions. That didn't necessarily mean they had anything against the newcomer: in Adele's experience, women of a certain sort always looked petulant. Each wore a filmy pastel shift—blue, pink and yellow.

The wine was as pale as sunlight. Adele sipped it, feeling a tingle on her tongue and at the back of her nostrils. Menandros was watching her intently.

Adele lowered the glass and said, "I believe that my mother would have approved. I myself don't have the palate to really judge."

"Oh, do sit down," said Menandros, suddenly solicitous. He gestured to the chair Dumouret had brought up. "Your mother is a connoisseur, then?"

Adele sat down. The chair's wooden frame matched the room's panelling.

"She was a connoisseur," she said. "Mother has been dead for many years now."

Executed as a traitor and her head displayed in the center of Xenos, to be precise, but Adele didn't go to that level of detail. She had learned that it shocked people; particularly those who thought she was making a joke in bad taste.

Adele sipped more wine. The information she had received about President-for-Life Menandros was completely accurate—as she had expected. She wasn't here to observe the president.

Menandros settled happily back onto his chair. "We've been playing cards," he said, tapping the deck. "The girl who wins gets to spend the night with me."

He caressed the ear of the girl in yellow with the backs of his fingers. "Yevgenia is ahead," he said.

"How lucky for her," Adele said. She frowned slightly and

said, "What if you win, President Menandros? You're playing also, aren't you?"

"Ah!" Menandros said. "If I win, *I* get to choose. But Yevgenia is far ahead now. Do you play rummy, Lady, ah . . . ?"

"Lady Mundy, your Highness," said Dumouret. "Lady Mundy is here to discuss your views on the rebellion."

"I thought you said she was just paying her respects?" Menandros said sharply, glowering at his butler. This was the first evidence Adele had seen that the president wasn't quite as fuzzy as he acted.

"I *am* a private citizen paying my respects," Adele said. "But as a member of one of the leading families of Cinnabar, my impressions will be solicited when I return home. I would be remiss to neglect this opportunity to discuss matters of such import with the president of the Tarbell Stars."

"Well, I don't see that there's very much *to* say," Menandros said. "There isn't really a rebellion. My subjects are happy, why shouldn't they be happy? The Upholders are just stooges for the Alliance of Free Stars. It's that simple!"

"I'll certainly pass on your opinion, Mr. President," Adele said. "But how is the war—"

"It's not an opinion, it's the simple truth!" Menandros said. "Look, you're important on Cinnabar, you say? You've got to help us, then. The Alliance is attacking us and you're their enemy!"

"President Menandros," Adele said, "I am a private citizen. I know that we and the Alliance have been at peace since the signing of the Treaty of Amiens, however. I'm afraid you've been misinformed."

The girls didn't speak, but they picked up and put down their cards in a bored fashion. They kept glancing sidelong at Menandros, in case he should suddenly take an interest in them again.

"Are you a fool?" Menandros said, slapping the table with the flat of his hand. His cards jumped and several of them fell to the floor. "This treaty says that the Alliance won't increase its territory by conquest! And that's what they're trying to do, conquer my Tarbell Stars!'

Definitely not as fuzzy as he seems, Adele thought. Although Menandros hadn't been the subject of her visit to the palace, she had learned something that neither Mistress Sand nor the Fifth Bureau seemed to be aware of.

"I am not a lawyer or a diplomat—" she began.

"This isn't law!" said Menandros. "This is honor! If Cinnabar doesn't defend its honor, it is cowardly and all the world will know that Cinnabar is a coward!"

Adele stood up. She was here playing a part, but there was a point beyond which she could not go and remain believable. The president might not recognize that, but Dumouret probably did—and those to whom Dumouret reported certainly would.

"Master Menandros," Adele said. She poured the rest of her wine on the floor and set the glass on the table. "You forget yourself. *Nothing* that happens in a place as benighted as the Tarbell Stars could affect the Republic's honor."

Adele walked out without looking behind her. She thought that Menandros might lift himself from the chair to follow, but he only mumbled protests. The three women chattered in low, piping voices like birds after sunset.

Tovera pulled the gate open, her face turned backward to watch the president and his servants. *What would I have done if the door had been locked?* Adele thought as she set a dignified pace down the hallway.

She smiled. *Tovera could cut the ring off Dumouret's finger, I'm sure. And if that wasn't the key, it would at least encourage him to tell us where the key is.*

"Do you think they'll try to stop us?" Tovera asked in a low voice after they turned the corner.

"Dumouret has more sense than that," Adele said. "I suspect Menandros does also, though you can't be sure whether rulers in a backwater like this really understand how insignificant they are to the Republic. Still, Dumouret won't let the president tell the guards to detain me."

Tovera giggled. "A pity," she said.

The doorman had changed while they were with Menandros. This one merely nodded with a vacant expression as they walked out. His mouth was slightly open.

"Dumouret is an Upholder agent," Adele said. "I wanted to get a feel for him in his own element."

"A job for me?" Tovera said. She opened the back of the Mignouris' ground car for her mistress, then went around to the driver's side.

"No," said Adele. "Mignouri or his predecessors have planted a very thorough information-gathering suite on Dumouret. He's harmless in himself, and I'm sure the Upholders—or General Krychek—would easily replace him if they had to. This way we know what the Upholders know."

Tovera drove off, overcorrecting as they turned into the

street but managing to avoid the gatepost.

Adele was thinking of the new Headman of Karst, a boy and a fool. He had insulted Cinnabar's representatives, Senator Forbes and Captain Daniel Leary, and he had insulted the Republic itself. He hadn't realized how insignificant he was, but because of the war with the Alliance the Republic hadn't been able to do anything about it.

The war is over now, Adele thought as Tovera got out to open the gate of the residency.

As Daniel raised his hand to knock, Tovera opened the door. "The external security is pretty good," she said with a grin— her version of a grin, that was. "The Fifth Bureau brings in its own construction crews whenever it can. The plumbing may not work, but you'll be able to watch visitors a block away in any direction."

"I hope it's all right for us to drop by here," Daniel said. That aspect of visiting his friend at her new house hadn't occurred to him before. "At a safe house, I mean."

"Come in, please," said Adele, who had come up behind her servant. "It's not a safe house, it's the Fifth Bureau Residency on Peltry and we're not Fifth Bureau."

"Well," said Tovera as she closed the massive outer door behind Daniel and Hogg, "*I* haven't been for years, at least."

Adele led them through the entrance hall into a drawing room with upholstered chairs and a table on which sat a vase of dead flowers. She glanced at the vase and said, "Perhaps I should've directed the wife to stay here. I'm not a skilled housekeeper."

"There's some fresh ones out front," Hogg said, taking the vase by the neck in his left hand. "Come on, Tovera. Let's see what we can find in the garden."

They weren't in the way, Daniel thought as the servants went out. But he was just as glad to be alone with Adele. He was feeling wrung-out and—almost—overwhelmed, and he didn't like to hint at weakness in front of his old servant.

"I've been put in charge of training the crew of an ex-Sverdlovsk destroyer," he said as he let himself down onto a chair covered in deep red plush. "I can do it, of course, but it's scarcely going to change the course of the rebellion unless the Upholders are a great deal less formidable than they've been made out to be."

"I've downloaded full particulars on Nabis to the command console," Adele said. "I don't think there's anything you need, but I wanted you to have the background. Would you like a drink?"

I didn't say anything about Nabis. But she's Adele.

Daniel closed his eyes. It was relaxing to chat with Adele. "I wouldn't turn down a whiskey," he said. "But a small one or I'll fall asleep and Hogg will have to push me to the *Sissie* in a wheelbarrow. If you have a wheelbarrow here."

"The house inventory doesn't mention one," Adele said. "I believe there's a shed in back which you could check. Or Hogg could."

Glass clinked on the table beside Daniel. He opened his eyes and saw the bottle and tumbler which Adele had set there.

"I don't think the Mignouris had very elevated tastes," she said, "but I don't suppose it will poison you."

As Daniel poured—more than the small one he had asked

for, he realized—Adele continued, "Minister Robin is afraid of you. He's an adventurer himself, and he can't imagine that you don't plan to displace him in running the government here."

"Bloody *hell*," Daniel said. "What would I want with the Tarbell Stars?"

Adele shrugged and took a sip from her own tumbler. "Minister Forbes was concerned that you'd want to do that." she said. "Why shouldn't a Kostroman quartermaster imagine that it's the height of your ambition also?"

"I'd sooner go into banking," Daniel said, setting down his tumbler. He'd finished the whiskey in it, more fool him.

"I'm going to go ahead with the training," Daniel said deliberately, staring at the empty glass. "Split both crews between the two ships and pack in as many of the Nabis Regiment as I can. I've brought landsmen up to speed before now. I'm going to take them off to an uninhabited world where we won't have distractions and get me a feel for the people."

He looked at Adele and said, "Do you have a better idea?"

"No," she said. She sat in the chair across the table from him. "I'll look for a way around Robin's concerns."

Adele coughed. "I wonder, Daniel..." she said. "If you'd mind if I stayed in Newtown while you're training?"

"What?" Daniel said, sitting upright again. "No, of course not. I was already doubtful about asking you to give the Nabies some pistol training, because I thought you'd frighten them."

"If you don't mind, then," Adele said. "I'd like to look over the local files, which will take some time. There's extensive video coverage of the palace and all the ministries. And though of course I don't have any responsibility to General Storn in his official capacity, it would be courteous to have someone competent watching over the residency until Mignouri's official replacement arrives. The wife wasn't even keeping up with the correspondence in the areas within her capacity."

Daniel eyed the bottle, then turned his tumbler upside down on the table. He rose. "I'll sleep aboard the *Sissie* tonight," he decided aloud. "Tomorrow we start training for real and I probably won't be getting much sleep from there on out. Have fun with your files."

"I will," said Adele, the simple truth as Daniel well knew. She walked with him to the door.

Tovera opened it from the other side. Hogg stood with her, holding a vase refilled with flowers of a sort that Daniel's mother had grown. He didn't remember what they were called.

Daniel grinned. "And you know what?" he said. "I'll have a good time with the training. Langland gathered up some decent material on Nabis before he made the mistake of trusting Karst."

CHAPTER 13

ABOVE PELTRY

"Braking in five seconds," Daniel announced over the ship channel, piping his voice through every commo helmet and every PA speaker on the *Katchaturian*. He watched the countdown clock and said, "Braking—now."

He pressed the Execute button, which on this Sverdlovsk-built destroyer was a real button instead of being virtual like that of the *Sissie*. The twelve plasma thrusters roared in unison.

The ship shuddered—of course—but with a little more violence than Daniel thought was proper. He eyed the readouts, then used the vernier scale to adjust the attitude of both bow nozzles on the port outrigger. The vibration smoothed noticeably.

He grinned. Noticeably to him, at least.

"Power," Daniel said, keying a two-way link to Chief Engineer Pasternak. The 2 g braking thrust would be uncomfortable to walk in, but it didn't seriously affect anyone's ability to speak. "Chief, I think you solved the problems when you blew out Tank Three. "Good call, over."

When Daniel moved to the *Katchaturian*, he had brought the *Sissie*'s chief engineer with him. The corvette's propulsion systems were in blueprint condition, but he hadn't been confident that the same would be true for the destroyer.

In fact, neither the thruster nozzles nor the High Drive motors of the *Katchaturian* had excessive hours on them. On the voyage out to 5L13TTF—the uninhabited world Daniel had chosen for training—there had been niggling stumbles in both systems, however.

Pasternak had finally decided that the problem wasn't in the power units themselves but rather was debris in one of the destroyer's reaction mass tanks. The power-room crew had blown out the tank and the lines it fed while Daniel and his officers conducted training either on the ground or on the *Princess Cecile*.

"*Six, I don't think that tank had been drained in years,*" Pasternak replied. "*That bloody Riddle*"—the *Katchaturian*'s chief engineer when Daniel took over the Nabis Contingent; Pasternak had cashiered him on his first inspection of the destroyer's power room—"*was a lazy scut besides being a drunk, which was why I fired him. The ship made only short hops, and Riddle didn't rotate the draw so that they all got used. Over.*"

"Six out," Daniel said, smiling faintly.

The stutter in the thrusters as he brought the *Katchaturian* down on a rocky shoreline on 5L13TTF for the first time had been unnerving. The problem could have been in the ship's electronics—or worse, the wiring harness. The notion that trash in the reaction mass lines was randomly starving the thrusters of fuel hadn't occurred to him, because it was so easy to prevent.

Atmospheric buffeting began when the destroyer braked into Peltry's stratosphere. It grew worse as she dropped lower.

A starship couldn't be streamlined. Even with the antennas and yards telescoped and lashed firmly to the hull, a ship was a mass of irregular protrusions. At the speeds a starship entered the atmosphere, you could only hang on and hope that nothing—well, as little as possible—carried away.

The *Sissie* and *Katchaturian* had proceeded to their destination in a series of hops through the Matrix rather than the single insertion which was all that so short a distance really required. Daniel was not only giving the new personnel as much experience as possible, he wanted his Sissies to get a feel for people who would revert to being officers if they worked out.

Most of the Nabis officers had done pretty well, or anyway, well enough. An infantry captain—formally, the ground troops had been the Capital Regiment on Nabis—was probably a decent officer in his original slot, but he had proven unwilling to take orders from warrant officers or from women. Minister Robin might well have a use for him; Daniel Leary did not.

The *Katchaturian* handled well on reentry; better than the *Princess Cecile* if the truth were told, though Daniel didn't think he would ever say that aloud. They were actually slanting in short of his intended path to Newtown Harbor, so he angled the thrusters to emphasize lift over braking. The buffeting increased, but not seriously.

5L13TTF had a breathable atmosphere and a temperate climate at the equator. It had never been settled because there was no soil and plenty of more suitable worlds in this region, but it was a perfect place for firearms training.

"Marksmanship training" would have been overstating the process, because at the end of it most of the spacers—Sissies as well as the Nabis recruits—still couldn't be expected to hit a man-sized target much farther than they could have thrown the weapon.

They were less likely to be afraid of an impeller, however, and they were probably less likely to shoot things by accident. A technician had blown off his own big toe, but spacers regularly lost digits and even limbs. Daniel thought the fellow would be all right in the *Katchaturian*'s power room once he'd healed.

He halted the destroyer in a hover, then slid her sideways into position a hundred feet above her slip in the naval harbor. Flaring the thruster nozzles manually, Daniel set her down. Just above the surface their descent slowed. The ship wallowed for a moment, cushioned by steam licked upward by plasma exhaust. When the outriggers touched the water, Daniel chopped the throttles.

It had been a good landing, though a slight drift to port suggested that either thruster alignment or the sphincter balance wasn't as good as it could be. He and Pasternak with all the original Nabis officers would go over the propulsion systems in the next day or two.

It was also true that the *Katchaturian*'s greater length-to-breadth ratio than a corvette emphasized Daniel's sloppiness. Schnitker—the Nabis and later Tarbell captain, now Daniel's striker—would have said that the landing had been perfect.

Daniel grinned. *When I start judging my performance*

by the standards of an officer from Novy Sverdlovsk, now working in the back of beyond, it will be time to retire. Though in fairness, Schnitker was a decent astrogator and a better shiphandler than most recent Academy graduates.

The *Katchaturian* pinged and crackled as she cooled. The pumps in her stern throbbed, sucking harbor water to replenish the ship's reaction mass through fat hoses. For human use the water would be distilled, but inlet filtering was sufficient for the thrusters and High Drives. Any working fluid was adequate for the propulsion systems, but using water had benefits for the crews.

Daniel checked his readouts and found no red lights. Barnes, the bosun, and his crew wouldn't be able to check the rigging until the ship had cooled considerably, but at least they hadn't lost a whole antenna. The hull's integrity was as good as you could expect of a ship which had seen more than twenty years service, and only one of the High Drive motors was showing excessive wear. In all, a very satisfactory—

Cazelet was the *Katchaturian*'s acting signals officer. The slot was ordinarily that of a junior warrant officer, but Daniel had become used to having a signals officer who did more than pass messages.

Neither Cory nor Cazelet were the equal of Adele, but she had trained them to do many of the things she did—and more important, to *think* the way she did. When Cazelet sent an alert message to the command console, Daniel opened it immediately and scanned the contents.

"Cazelet," he said, opening a link. "What has the government reaction been, over?"

"*Sir, there hasn't been one,*" Cazelet said. "*Not to mention, I mean. Port Control alerted the* Alfonso, *the destroyer on standby, but the captain queried the Ministry of War and the ministry hasn't responded. That was five hours ago, over.*"

"Do we know who the pirates were?" Daniel said. He called up the recordings of *Katchaturian*'s Plot Position Indicator when they extracted above Peltry an hour ago. The hulk which held reaction mass for the pirates remained where it had been, a million miles above the surface, but the three smaller vessels had vanished.

There were several alerts on the command display—Barnes was ready to open the main hatch, Vesey was bringing the *Princess Cecile* down, and Pasternak had a detailed report on the propulsion systems. They could all wait until Daniel had sorted out Cazelet's report.

"*Sir, Harbor Control reported that it was the pirates from Benjamin that we saw before,*" Cazelet said. "*They're probably right, but I won't be able to confirm that until I've checked their records. Ah, sir? Do you suppose Officer Mundy might know, over?*"

"I'll never bet against what Officer Mundy knows," Daniel said with a broad grin. "But I think we can go with common sense for now. Break. Lieutenant Cory, do we have two weeks' stores aboard, over?"

"*Six, we've got thirty days of everything but dairy and fresh fruit,*" Cory replied. "*Is there anything in particular you're worried about, over?*"

"Negative," said Daniel. "Break. Ship, this is Six. I expected to give you all a day's liberty. That's not going to happen after all."

He was using the general channel, so everyone aboard the

Katchaturian heard him. Though the Nabis personnel would be upset, Daniel suspected that the announcement made the Sissies within the crew hopeful, because they had a notion of what would come next.

"Instead, all the Nabis personnel are released for six hours," Daniel said. "Former Sissies get three hours, port watch first. Starboard acts as anchor watch, then switch. When the crew has reported back aboard, we're going to see some action. Probably not a lot of action, but we'll be earning our pay."

The general push was locked in send-only mode so nobody could interrupt Daniel over the intercom, but cheers echoed from the destroyer's compartments. He continued to smile.

"Now, some of you may wonder what happens if some of you don't show up after liberty," Daniel said. "That's easy: you're off the ship. I don't come looking for you. I don't need spacers who don't have the balls for a fight, because if you serve with me there's going to *be* fighting. Ask the nearest Sissie if you don't believe me. Six out."

Daniel took a deep breath, then said, "Ship, I'm opening the main hatch. Barnes, get the gangplank out."

He pressed Execute. The dogs withdrew from their sockets and the hatch began to pivot down.

There were now a dozen desperate messages on Daniel's display, but there was another call he needed to make before he talked to any of his officers. "Cazelet," he said. "I want to talk to Officer Mundy. Can you—"

"*Six,*" Cazelet interrupted, "*you're connected. Signals out.*"

"Adele?" Daniel said. Cazelet was showing off.

"*Yes,*" Adele said. "*I'm looking at the report of the attack which Rene sent me. Can you track the pirates?"*

Cazelet has a right to show off.

"No," said Daniel, "not through the Matrix with that much of a head start. But we're pretty sure they're heading for Benjamin with their loot. I think with your help we'll be able to locate them on the planet."

Or even without. Adele's identifications through electronic signatures were valuable, but Daniel's own Mark 1 Eyeball ought to be good enough to spot the captured freighter among the ships the locals used in their asteroid belt—and for piracy.

"Are you up to join a live-fire exercise against pirates?" he said.

The destroyer rocked as the *Sissie* landed in the next slip, her thrusters thrashing the surface like eight miniature volcanoes. Daniel would make sure that Cazelet had sent the full report to Vesey, but he didn't interrupt his discussion with Adele to make the order explicit.

"*Yes,*" said Adele. "*Tovera and I will be with you in half an hour. Sooner, I suppose, if you need us.*"

"I've given the crew six hours liberty," Daniel said. "And I want to check the rig, though I don't expect any real deficiencies. You've got plenty of time."

"*Daniel, my specialist equipment is aboard the* Princess Cecile," Adele said. "*I can work from the* Katchaturian, *but it will be more efficient if I'm aboard the* Sissie.*"

"That's fine," Daniel said. "The ships will be operating together. Ah—will this be a problem for your other duties?"

"I'll lock the doors of the residency when we leave," Adele said. "The flowers may suffer, but other than that the operation here will be as productive as it was when Mistress Mignouri was in charge. Doing a favor for the Fifth Bureau doesn't take precedence over my duties to the RCN. And to you."

"I look forward to seeing you shortly," Daniel said. He broke the connection, smiling even more broadly.

ONE LIGHT-MINUTE ABOVE BENJAMIN

"Benjamin is a mining world," Adele said, speaking to both the *Princess Cecile* and by laser link to the *Katchaturian*, which hung in space next to the corvette. She wasn't sure how good the destroyer's commo suite was, but Cazelet and Cory were both aboard her. They would make something work so that the whole crew got the briefing.

"I suppose I should say that Benjamin is a metal processing world," Adele said. "The residents haul metallic asteroids to the planet's surface and process them with fusion plants. The work is easier for low-skill personnel to do in normal gravity and atmosphere, and they aren't concerned about waste products because Benjamin is largely a desert with oases in which most residents live."

"*The residents live like rats in brush hovels*," said Daniel, the only person whom Adele had permitted to comment; all other helmets and consoles were locked out. "*That's another reason they don't worry about wastes, over.*"

"Yes, that's correct," Adele said. She knew that she worried more about precise details than most listeners did; certainly she worried more than an audience of common spacers on a warship. In her heart though, Adele knew she was right and they were wrong, which made it very difficult for her to restrain the tendency.

She displayed a real-time image of the surface of Benjamin. Normally the necessary level of enhancement at this distance would have washed out details, despite the *Sissie*'s excellent optics. That wasn't a problem with Benjamin, because there were no details.

The surface of the planet was of a generally tawny color flecked with gray wedges downwind of smelter flues. No standing water was visible, though Adele knew that greater magnification would have picked up ponds at low points. The watercourses were underground, and only a light dusting of ice glittered at the poles.

"You'll notice the bright smears at various locations," Adele said, focusing down on one which was catching sunlight at an angle to display its metallic sheen. "The sharp end of each is a smelter. Ordinarily the settlement will be upwind of the smelter, though I have found exceptions."

Daniel's comments about rats living in hovels was unjust to rats. All rats would have moved out of the path of sulfurous fumes.

"That isn't a concern with the two villages we're interested in," Adele said, shifting the display to place the adjacent sites— they were fifteen miles apart—in the same frame. Huts were merely irregularities at this magnification, but the ships were brightly visible: one large and two small ones at the village on the left and a medium-sized ship on the right.

"The nickel-iron which the smelters produce must be

transported to other systems for use," Adele continued. "It pays for basic foodstuffs, generally processed algae. Higher value trace minerals are exchanged for luxuries from the small trading vessels which make periodic visits to Benjamin. All in all, it's a pretty miserable existence, so it's not really surprising that some miners have turned to piracy in neighboring systems."

Under other circumstances, Adele might have hesitated before she used a laser communicator to link the two ships, since it was important that they avoid notice from the planet below. Passive observation of ships a light-minute out would have been difficult from the surface even of a developed world, but when they were using active emitters detection became an order of magnitude easier.

That said, on Benjamin an order of magnitude didn't raise the risk to the level of real danger. The only laser receptor on the planet was the one on the freighter whose capture had brought the Nabis Contingent here.

"This ship..." Adele said, highlighting the largest vessel, "is the *Mezentian Gate*, a three-thousand-ton freighter out of Rosecrans, carrying a rolling mill to Peltry where she was captured in orbit. She is owned by her captain and in the past has carried a total of fifteen crew."

She moved the highlight to the pair of small ships near the captive. "Neither of these ships has a name," she said, "but one has the legend 'sixteen' painted on both sides of its bow. They are two of the ships which were loitering above Peltry. Captain Vesey"—as she was while in command of the *Princess Cecile*—"informs me that they are six-hundred-ton general purpose craft configured to tow cargoes in the Matrix.

Normally that means asteroids, but they towed a freighter full
of water to the Peltry system. And this—"

Adclc shifted the imagery to the other village and the
vessel there. "This is the *Roebuck*, an eighteen-hundred-ton
freighter," she said. "The third pirate vessel. The *Roebuck*
mounts a basket of eight bombardment rockets and is the only
armed pirate."

"*The* Mezentian Gate *was waiting for landing clearance
and was taken unawares,*" Daniel said, answering a question
that Adele hadn't thought to ask. "*A rocket hit near the bow,
starting seams. Captain Chidsey had the choice of landing a
damaged ship without ground control, or surrendering to the
pirates. The pirates put a crew aboard and brought the prize
to Benjamin, over.*"

"I have no evidence of where the crew of the captive is
being kept," Adele said. "I would be able to pick up radio
signals at this distance, but I don't find any evidence of such
signals. Though both villages have smelters, neither seems to
be using its fusion bottle to power electric lights. The residents
are subsisting at a very low cultural level."

She cleared her throat. "I believe that's all I have to say," Adele
said. "Captain Leary, I'm turning the briefing over to you."

"*Spacers of the Nabis Contingent,*" Daniel said. Adele
noticed again his way of sounding both friendly and in charge.
"*I'm going to keep this short, because we'll sort out the attack
details on the ground. We'll be setting down initially a hundred
miles west of our targets. If we're noticed there by locals, it
won't matter, since planetary communication on Benjamin is
at the smoke-signal level.*"

He paused, his image on Adele's display looking to right and left. Daniel had miniatures of the assembled crews on his screen, almost four hundred faces. That was too many people to see as individuals, but the same would have been true if they were on a parade ground in front of him.

"*When we go in, it'll be hard and fast,*" Daniel said. "*In the best traditions of the Nabis Contingent. For now, dismissed!*"

On the Sissie's command channel, Vesey said, "*Ship, prepare for insertion. We'll extract in Benjamin orbit. Out.*"

BENJAMIN

The captain's great cabin on the *Katchaturian* embarrassed Daniel because it was, well, *great*. It wasn't just that the destroyer was almost twice the size of a corvette like the *Princess Cecile*. The *Katchaturian* had been built on Novy Sverdlovsk, where the distinctions between commissioned officers and everybody else were extreme. A Cinnabar-built destroyer would have applied half this cabin's volume to crew accommodations.

Daniel looked around the table at his officers and smiled. Reforming the social structure of Novy Sverdlovsk was no part of his duties to either Cinnabar or the Tarbell Stars, and the cabin was extremely useful for Daniel to address all his officers in privacy and comfort.

"Fellow Sissies," Daniel said, and his grin softened: everyone in the cabin now was former RCN. "We'll be attacking the two villages simultaneously. The ships will lift from here, take curving courses and keep low, then land a mile from their targets. The *Katchaturian* will take the village we're calling Alpha where the captured ship is, the *Sissie*'s party will take Beta. The locals themselves don't have names for the villages, as best Officer Mundy can tell."

"Which means the locals don't have names for them," Cory said. Daniel joined in the chorus of chuckles around the table.

Adele was the only RCN officer not present in the flesh. She had said she could join in if needed through the cabin's display and that she didn't want to leave her console on the *Sissie*'s bridge. Daniel had deferred to her opinion, though it would have led to a short discussion if anybody else had said that to him. Nabis officers provided the anchor watches and were assembling the combined crews on the ground between the two ships.

"Six?" said Woetjans, her forehead wrinkled with the effort of getting her mind around a concept. "Why so far out? I mean, I don't mind a hike, but you and Vesey could drop right in the middle of the places, right? Or a hundred feet out so we don't burn 'em up, anyway."

"We don't want to burn the huts up, that's true," Daniel said, "because we don't know where the prisoners are being kept. We're all spacers, and the worst these poor bastards from Rosecrans did was sign on with a captain who was more concerned with making port than he was of being ambushed by pirates."

Nods and grunts of agreement greeted the partial explanation, but Cory and Hale remained still-faced. They clearly realized there was more to come.

"The mile is a compromise," Daniel continued. "It's far enough out, especially if we stay low, that it probably won't alarm the locals, but it's close enough for the assault parties to hoof it without being too winded by the time they get into position. Remember, we're landing on sand over rock, not water. Our exhaust will heat the ground molten. It'll be a good half hour before we can disembark."

Everybody nodded this time. Cory and Hale wore broad grins besides.

"The assault parties will include all our Nabis personnel and all the Sissies except an anchor watch," Daniel said. "I'll be leading Alpha Party, Cory will lead Beta. We'll—"

"Sir, why you?" said Cory. "I mean, we all know you're not afraid, but I think I speak for everybody—"

"You bloody well do!" from Dasi; nods and murmurs of agreement around the table.

"—when I say that if some drunken wog gets lucky and blows your brains out, this whole cluster wouldn't be a fair exchange."

"Thank you, Master Cory," Daniel said, "but you're missing the point. Our current task is to train the Nabis Contingent, particularly the officers. That means demonstrating what leadership means. I'm confident that there are already sufficient officers in the Tarbell Stars who can demonstrate sitting on their butts and sending other people out to die."

"Sorry, sir," Cory muttered, jerking bolt-upright and meeting Daniel's eyes. "*Very* sorry, sir."

As well you should be, Daniel thought, but he forced his lips into a smile and as usual his mind followed after a moment. He wanted his people to be cocky and sure that they were the best in the world, but bragging couldn't get in the way of doing the job. When you parsed out what Cory had said, he was bragging.

"Six," said Vesey. "I should lead Beta Party."

Bloody hell, she's right.

Vesey was seated to Daniel's immediate right; he stared at her without expression. She didn't flinch, which showed—Daniel's smile was internal—that she had guts. That hadn't been in doubt.

"Yes, you're right," Daniel said. "Cory—"

Across the table from Vesey.

"—you'll still transfer to the *Sissie*, but you'll remain in command of her. I want somebody experienced there, because Officer Mundy is our communications and intelligence base."

"Sir, may I request to accompany Beta Party?" Cazelet said. "I know I've had problems pulling the trigger in the past, but I'll be carrying a length of pipe this time instead of a gun."

Somebody chuckled. Woetjans glowered and said, "Bloody useful piece of kit, a pipe."

In the bosun's hands, that was certainly true. For the slightly built Cazelet—probably less so, but that wasn't the point. Cazelet didn't have the military indoctrination which trains its subjects out of the normal human hesitation to kill another human. He'd failed to shoot an enemy during a deadly struggle on Corcyra and he might fail again, but he could lead an attack just as well with a club as with an impeller.

Likewise Vesey. Daniel had been thinking of Vesey as the person whom he could best trust to take care of Adele and the *Princess Cecile*. He'd ignored the fact that she was an

RCN officer—and a human being, who had the right to resent Captain Leary's unintentional insult on her ability to lead.

Daniel smiled, relaxing his audience. "Yes, all right, Cazelet," he said. "That means I'm going to put the *Katchaturian* under—"

His pause may not have been noticeable to his officers, but it was very real in Daniel's mind. Cazelet's request had surprised him, though it shouldn't have: Rene wouldn't have been much of a man if he hadn't asked to accompany into danger the woman whom he was seeing when they were both off duty. He and Vesey had been together for nearly two years now.

"—Captain Schnitker, who commanded her in Nabis service. He's got a good deal of dry landing experience and has shown himself generally competent. What I *don't* know about him yet is how he behaves when bullets are flying. For that reason—"

Daniel grinned at Hale, seated beside Cory.

"—Acting Lieutenant Hale will be on the *Katchaturian*'s bridge during action at the navigator's console. Hale, if you believe at any point that the mission or the personnel on the ground are being endangered by Captain Schnitker's behavior, you are to shoot him and take over. Can you handle that?"

"Sir!" said Hale. "Yes, *sir*!"

"Draw a sidearm, then," Daniel said. Normally personnel turned in their weapons when they returned from detached duty. Not only were guns unnecessary, the steel bulkheads made ricochets from an accidental discharge a particular nightmare.

"If that's all our business here..." Daniel said. He waited a few beats to make sure that it *was* all the business. "Then we'll go outside and inform the crews of the plan."

He rose, bringing his officers up with him. Daniel gestured them out of the cabin so that they could join the ordinary spacers before Captain Leary addressed them from the main hatch of the *Katchaturian*.

"How much trouble do you think the wogs are going to give us?" Hogg asked over his shoulder as he led his master down the companionway. He carried his own stocked impeller and had slung a submachine gun for Daniel.

"I doubt there's half a dozen guns in either village," Daniel said, speaking over the echoes of boots on steel treads in a steel tube. "At Beta there might be a problem if somebody's awake enough to use the rockets on the *Roebuck*."

"Hey, Hogg?" Tovera called from behind Daniel. "You want to switch duty? A slug from that cannon of yours would take out the rockets. Maybe set 'em off, even."

"Naw, I'll stick with the master," Hogg said. "If the wogs get their fingers out in time, which I don't figure'll happen, then it'll show this Nabis lot that life has risks, right?"

True enough on all counts, Daniel thought. But he really hoped that it wouldn't happen. He'd be able to hear eight-inch bombardment rockets detonating even from fifteen miles away.

Reed and Nagata, both techs, were on watch in the boarding hold, standard operating procedure when the hatch was open. They muttered greetings as Daniel and the servants stepped to the top edge of the hatch. Gusts from outside whipped their clothes.

"Fellow spacers of the Nabis Contingent!" Daniel said. The loudspeakers on the *Katchaturian*'s spine were being fed from a parabolic microphone on the *Princess Cecile*, lying parallel to the destroyer and a hundred feet away.

The crews, assembled into squads, stared up at him. The spacers' expressions varied from anticipation through discomfort to outright concern. The Sissies who would be acting as squad leaders had done the sorting while Daniel addressed the officers who would command larger groupings. The attack parties weren't armies, but at least they were organized.

Daniel was uncomfortable too, if it came to that. Benjamin's air was thin and dry and cold. He knew he wouldn't notice it once they moved out to attack, but he didn't want to shiver and have the Nabis personnel think that he was trembling in fear.

"We're going to attack two peasant villages, capture the ships there, and free any prisoners we find," Daniel said. "Our job is *not* to kill peasants, though anyone who resists will be dealt with in the quickest way possible. People who surrender are not to be harmed."

He wondered if the spacers below could see his stern expression as he said that. Probably not, most of them; the wind flicked dust from the ground and made them squint. Benjamin was really a miserable place.

"Now that it's really coming to the point, some of you may be thinking that maybe you'd be happier in a job where nobody's going to be shooting at you," Daniel said. "You've got that option: anybody who decides he doesn't have the balls for this work can chicken out now. You'll stay on shipboard till we can carry you back to Peltry and land you on the beach. The Nabis Contingent has no room for cowards!"

Daniel gave his words a few moments to sink in. He didn't expect many Nabies to take up the offer, since crewing a starship was a dangerous job itself—more dangerous than rushing a couple villages full of startled peasants. Besides, even rcal cowards hated to admit they were cowards, especially in front of their comrades and a corvette-crew of foreigners, many of whom were women.

When nobody stepped forward, Daniel nodded and said, "I'm done here, then, but before we board the ships for deployment, my servant Hogg has a few words to say to you."

Daniel stepped back, taking the submachine gun which Hogg handed him. Hogg and Tovera moved to the edge of the ramp. Tovera carried a full-sized submachine gun from the *Sissie*'s arms locker.

"I've been looking after the young master for nigh-on thirty years," Hogg said. His gravelly voice boomed out from the speakers above him. "I'm still doing that. Now, the master knows that if we go in fast and everybody keeps moving, this is going to be a piece of cake. The only way it gets dangerous is if we funk it after we start; and by 'we' I mean 'you.' I'll be following the batch with the master, and Tovera here—"

Tovera raised her submachine gun overhead by the balance.

"—will be in back of those of you landing on the *Sissie*. What we'll do is kill anybody who runs away or tries to go to ground. If you think we won't do it or can't do it, you talk to your shipmates who served with us before. Believe me, we're a lot more dangerous than the barefoot wogs you're going up against."

Hogg and Tovera backed away; Daniel took center again and said, "Fellow spacers, if everybody does his job we'll be back on Peltry in three days, with liberty for all and a bonus—"

Paid out of Daniel's own pocket if the Ministry of War balked.

"—to spend. Dismissed to your ships!"

Sissies led the cheer, but Daniel saw that a gratifying number of Nabies were joining in. Tovera walked down the ramp to get to her action station on the *Princess Cecile*. Daniel moved to the side to let the *Katchaturian*'s crew reboard.

"I think they'll do fine," Hogg said, eyeing the squads of spacers.

"We'll know in a couple hours," Daniel said, wishing that he were as confident as Hogg sounded.

CHAPTER 14

BENJAMIN

Though in command, Cory was at the navigator's console, opposite Adele on the *Princess Cecile*'s bridge. The equipment was the same, and Cory had said he didn't need Six's seat to act as captain. When Vesey commanded the corvette, she remained in the Battle Direction Center where she would have been when Daniel was aboard.

That probably implied something about Daniel as a leader, though Adele didn't have any idea what. She observed human beings closely and could often predict their behavior, but as a general rule she didn't really understand *why* humans did things. Desire for money or power or sex were behind most human activities . . . and none of those things interested Adele in the least.

"Cory?" she said on a two-way link. Another person would have turned and spoken directly. "Do you know of a great deed that was done for the sake of knowledge?"

"*Ma'am?*" said Cory. He was echoing her display on the

lower half of his own, but he hadn't expected her to address him directly. "*Well, explorers like Commander Bergen, I guess. I'd say it was pretty great to open as many routes as he did, over.*"

Adele considered that for a moment. Daniel's uncle hadn't gotten rich from his work. He had retired as a commander while Academy classmates had become admirals because they had focused on paths to promotion while Stacy Bergen was finding routes through the Matrix. He had never married.

He *must* have been driven by a desire for knowledge.

"Yes, I see that," Adele said. "Thank you, Cory."

She had never paused in her task of observing the assault parties. The three hundred and some red dots were overlaid on a terrain map created from imagery which the ships' sensors had gathered during their landing approaches.

Benjamin didn't have enough water for oceans and continents. The elevation of this region didn't vary as much as a hundred feet in a mile, but six feet was sufficient to hide a standing human and a hundred would conceal the ships from the villages their crews were attacking.

That was fine, but it caused Adele a coordination problem since Benjamin had no satellite network. She was making do by having both ships raise a dorsal antenna high enough that the masthead sensors bore on the target village and also had a line of sight to the other ship.

A keen-eyed local could notice the distant glint on the horizon, but you couldn't eliminate *all* risks.

"*Beta Six to control*," Vesey said. She wasn't in sight of the ship; her signal was being relayed through several commo helmets until it reached one which had a direct link to the *Sissie*'s sensors. "*Beta is in position. Please confirm, over.*"

Adele checked her display. It was being echoed to Vesey's helmet, but the larger scale of the console might show something that could be missed on a face-shield display. *Besides, Vesey probably wants contact with someone who's on her side.*

"Beta Six, I confirm that your party is in position," Adele said. The hundred-plus red dots had advanced to within fifty yards of the village on the left of their line and of the *Roebuck* on the right.

The pirate ship's rocket basket was locked in a forward position. With optical sensors within a mile of the target, Adele could see that only two rockets remained in the launcher.

Village Beta was dead quiet. Only dust moved in the wind.

"*Acknowledged, Beta out,*" Vesey said.

"Alpha Six," Adele said. "Beta party is in position. Over."

"*Roger, Control,*" Daniel said. "*I think we're here also. Please confirm, over.*"

Adele checked her display again. She had split the screen vertically with Alpha on the left and Beta on the right; she had compressed the ten miles in the middle between the villages.

"Alpha Six," she said. "Your party is in position. Over."

She had created a do-not-cross line, yellow on the consoles and a yellow pulse on the face-shields of all spacers who reached it. That was the point beyond which the helmet was visible from the village according to the terrain map. In many cases it was closer for a spacer on her belly than it would be if she stood bolt upright.

"*Control,*" Daniel said. "*When you're ready, you may give the command to attack to both parties. Six out.*"

There's no reason to delay. "Nabis Contingent," Adele said. "Attack!"

"*Attack!*" said Adele's crisp voice in Daniel's commo helmet and the other helmets in Alpha Party.

Daniel got up from behind a sand-scoured boulder, waved his submachine gun over his head—he didn't shout; they were still unobserved as best he could tell—and began trudging across the hundred yards of wasteland toward the *Mezentian Gate*. Scrubby plants the size of a double fist studded the gravel plain at intervals of a yard or two.

Commo was a problem. The *Katchaturian's* Table of Equipment had never been to RCN scale, and what there was had been run down considerably. Pasternak's techs and a considerable amount of scrounging on Peltry had provided about half the original Nabies with something that would work.

The former Nabis officers had RCN helmets from the *Sissie's* stock. They were being judged on this mission, and Daniel was making sure his decisions were based on the personnel rather than on their equipment.

The *Mezentian Gate* was an ordinary tramp freighter for this region. She had a single ring of antennas and was missing the uppermost yard on at least the starboard set. A circle of bright scars around a broad dimple showed where the rocket had hit before she was captured, but so far as Daniel could tell the blast hadn't penetrated her hull.

He looked over his shoulder. His Sissies were keeping quite

a good skirmish line; probably better than they would have done if they hadn't been setting an example for the Nabies.

The village straggled off to the right. It was a line of shacks made from packing containers with the smelter was on the other end. It would give the locals an excellent strongpoint if they were organized enough to use it.

Daniel waved his submachine gun again and slanted toward the ramp of the *Mezentian Gate*. The ship was cold and silent, completely shut down.

Twenty spacers had been told off to capture the freighter with him, but it appeared that more were joining. That wasn't ideal, but Woetjans should've been able to round up all the villagers with half a dozen picked Sissies. Daniel had detailed a hundred and fifty for the huts and the two small pirate ships as training, not the job itself.

Just as Daniel reached the boarding ramp, a woman began to scream. He looked over his shoulder. A local wearing a shift had come out of a hut and seen the attacking spacers. She dropped her bucket and bolted back the way she had come.

The woman was a problem for Woetjans and her people. Daniel went up the *Gate*'s ramp at a run; they had crossed the hundred yards from cover at a steady walk so as not to reach their targets winded. He hadn't expected to get as far as this before being discovered.

There was a burst of gunfire from the village. Daniel hoped it was his people doing the shooting, but that was out of his control. It was always out of the commander's control when the shooting started, and he wished more politicians understood that.

He entered the up companionway and started for the bridge.

Wright, the *Katchaturian*'s gunner, was immediately behind him. Daniel was much more surprised to see in his glance backward that Hugo, a midshipman from Nabis aristocracy, was third in line with a determined look on his face.

Hogg had been staying far enough back to keep a lookout for stragglers. He hadn't caught up in time to bull past the pair of Nabies before they reached the helical staircase. He was probably furious, but Daniel suspected Wright would provide sufficient backup—especially since the Nabie carried a submachine gun. Hogg's stocked impeller was useless except as a blunt spear in the tight confines of a starship.

Daniel was breathing hard when he reached Level E, the freighter's highest deck. Because the *Mezentian Gate* had a tiny crew compared to that of a warship, the galley and all accommodations were on this level with the bridge.

He stepped into the rotunda which served both companionways and the freighter's dorsal airlock. A barefoot local in dungarees started out of the accommodation block behind the bridge; he bleated and jumped back when he saw Daniel.

Daniel lunged after the man and butt-stroked him in the ribs from behind. The local had been reaching for an impeller leaning against the wall; the blow pitched him forward into the rack of bunks welded to the outer bulkhead. The crash and jangle was welcome, at least to Daniel.

Men were wired to the bunks, though Daniel didn't have time to count to be sure all were present. "We need wire-cutters!" Daniel shouted as he started to turn.

WHACK-whang! Someone kicked Daniel hard in the left buttock.

He staggered and almost fell down. He hopped to the hatch—his left leg was going numb—and grabbed the coaming.

Wright faced into the bridge and fired a short burst. Somebody unseen cried out. Wright disappeared onto the bridge with Hugo following.

"Master!" Hogg said, grabbing Daniel by the shoulder and pivoted him back into the accommodations block. Somebody emptied a submachine gun on the bridge; a slug ricocheted into the rotunda and disappeared aft with a nasty keening.

"I'm all right!" Daniel said. "A ricochet hit me in the ass, but I don't think it even broke the skin!"

"It did," said Hogg grimly, "but I can see the metal. A good thing your butt's so fat, though. I wonder if this tub has a Medicomp?"

Daniel was getting feeling back in his leg, but his left hip was beginning to feel as though he were sitting on a hotplate. He wanted to sit in a bucket of ice water.

He said, "The *Katchaturian*'ll be incoming soon; she'll have lifted as soon as we attacked. Right now I need to see what's happening on the bridge."

The bridge had a single console and a flat-plate display attached to the aft bulkhead by a cable which was bolted to the floor. Wright held two submachine guns, his own by the pistol grip and that of Hugo by the sling; the barrel was fading to red heat.

A dead local holding a rusty impeller was sprawled beside the console. A second dead man, apparently unarmed, lay on the other side of the console; he had been shot at least a dozen times in the chest. The rest of the submachine gun's magazine had spanged directly into the forward bulkhead. Fortunately recoil had lifted the muzzle as well as pulling the weapon to the right, so the slugs had passed over the console instead of into it.

Hugo was down on all fours, still facing the pool of his vomit. He was weeping.

"Don't blame the kid," Wright said hoarsely. "He'll be all right. Fire discipline's a lot harder to teach than marksmanship."

"Agreed," Daniel said. He switched the console on. It took long enough to start to boot that for a moment he was afraid that it'd been damaged after all.

"I hear the *Katie* coming in, isn't that so?" Wright said. The throb of the destroyer's thrusters reflecting from the ground near below was making the freighter tremble. "You'll want to get your butt looked at, so why don't you head on out and I'll watch the kid here."

"Let me borrow that multitool," Daniel said, nodding to the pouch on the gunner's equipment belt. "I need to cut some wire. It'll take a while for the ground to cool so I can board."

Wright set down the empty submachine gun. He hooked the tool out of its pouch and tossed it to Daniel.

Daniel and Hogg reentered the accommodation block. They'd had to make their way through a handful of the members of the assault force who had followed them but were milling uncertainly.

"If that fellow wants a warrant from the RCN some day . . ." Daniel muttered. "I'll bloody well pull some strings to make it happen."

CHAPTER 15

BENJAMIN

Cory had lighted the thrusters as soon as Adele ordered the attack, but it was almost a minute before he was willing to tighten the sphincters. Adele felt the *Princess Cecile* lift as smoothly as if she had been on water. They rose vertically until they were comfortably above the lip of the swale which had sheltered the ship while Vesey's party advanced.

The message came from a laser emitter, but it was so weak and distorted that only a system as sensitive as the *Sissie*'s could have received and enhanced it: "*Beta Six to Beta. Cazelet down, need Medicomp soonest, out.*"

Adele forwarded it as a throbbing purple text crawl at the bottom of Cory's display. She didn't think there was anything Cory could do about it, and maneuvering a starship at low altitude was more than most captains could have managed even without distractions. It was all Adele could do, though, so she did it.

"*Command to Barnes,*" Cory said on the command channel.

"We're going to open up as soon as we get down. I want your crew in hard suits so you can lay the boarding bridge while the ground's still hot. We'll have a stretcher coming aboard and they won't have suits, over."

"Roger, out," said Barnes, the acting bosun while Woetjans was aboard the *Katchaturian*.

"Ship, this is Command," Cory said, keying the general push so that everyone aboard could hear him. *"We're going in hard, so brace yourselves. Command out."*

The *Princess Cecile* was at a hundred feet. They had porpoised slightly when they lifted off, but Cory had held the ship steady as soon as it had built forward motion. They sped up slightly as they slanted downward; Cory had adjusted the angle of his thrusters.

Adele switched her display to a real-time panorama, reducing her communications duties to a sidebar. Benjamin in closeup was the same gray-dun blur it had appeared from a light-minute out. Small bushes wriggled in the *Sissie*'s bow wave, sometimes releasing a fluff of white seeds before the plasma exhaust incinerated them.

The village Beta came in sight ahead. One of the huts was burning.

"Ship, hang on!" Cory repeated. The ship bucked as he opened the throttles. The *Sissie* was beginning to slow when the outriggers touched, first toward the stern.

There was a rending crash and one of the worst jolts Adele had ever felt aboard a starship. Automatic restraints clamped her about the waist, so that she wasn't flung off the console. *The only worse one was when a missile hit the*

Milton ... and that wasn't much worse.

Sand and dust sprayed up, filling Adele's display. The Dorsal A antenna, raised as a communications mast, carried away. The butt end rang on the *Sissie*'s bow on the way past, certainly hard enough to dent the steel hull.

"*Opening main hatch!*" Cory warned. The dogs withdrew; their hammer-on-anvil chorus seemed muted after the landing itself.

The ship shuddered. There was a muted shock and the hatch began to hum downward.

Though only a few feet away from one another, Cory and Adele sat back to back. He looked at her face in his display and said, "*I was afraid for a moment that the hull was so warped the hatch wouldn't open. I don't know what we'd have done then.*"

"We'd have found a way," Adele said. "Anyway, the hull didn't warp. You did a good job, a remarkable job."

"*Six'll have my commission for this,*" Cory said. "*I doubt either outrigger is watertight now, and the gods only know what damage the antenna did when it ripped loose.*"

"Daniel doesn't care about problems that can be solved by money," Adele said, deliberately emphasizing her personal connection with Captain Leary. "Neither should you."

The boarding ramp thumped into the ground. Three Sissies wearing gauntlets and the lower halves of rigging suits and one with just the suit bottom carried the boarding extension down the ramp at a dead run. The haze of dust and unquenched ions from the exhaust blurred them to ghost figures.

In a normal landing, the harbor water dissipated heat and

quenched plasma by conduction and boiling; this rocky soil would be too hot to touch for hours. Four figures with jackets wrapped over their faces were trotting out of the village. They carried a cloth-wrapped figure on a stretcher made from a tarpaulin and a pair of stocked impellers.

Adele rose from her console. She squeezed the acting captain's shoulder and said, "Cory, I'm going down to the hold. Handle communications, if you will."

"Yes, ma'am!" Cory said. Over the years he had developed more skill with communications suites than anyone Adele had met apart from herself. He already sounded brighter than he had while he was thinking about the damage he had done by skidding the *Sissie* in to save a comrade's life.

Adele started down the companionway. It was strange to hear her own feet on the steel treads without the sound of Tovera's footsteps in counterpoint. It took her back to her days in the Academic Collections, though the staircases in the stacks weren't in armored cylinders so the echoes weren't as noticeable.

Adele's smile was mostly in her mind; and mostly sad. She recalled a time when she had no problems except those of poverty, which really hadn't distressed her very much.

She opened the hatchway into the main hold and staggered. The shock of the hot atmosphere full of ozone and other ions. It was like being slapped in the face with barbed wire.

Barnes' landing crew had returned to the hold as soon as they had extended the bridge. A guard was still at the hatch, using her hands to shield her eyes as a submachine gun swung loose from her shoulder.

The stretcher bearers stumbled aboard. Barnes opened the internal hatch to the chamber which held one of the corvette's Medicomps. The main hatch was already rising; when it closed, it would at least stop the influx of air poisoned by the ship's exhaust.

People were shouting instructions. A half-suited crewman grabbed Dasi by the arm and guided him and his crew toward the Medicomp. The stretcher bearers were blind or the next thing to it; they would probably need medical attention also. Adele followed them into the inner chamber and closed the hatch behind her.

Crewmen who'd remained aboard tossed aside the jacket which had protected Cazelet's face during the trip through Hell; they loaded him into the waiting Medicomp. Adele was glad to see that Madringer was one of them; he was an expert in the unit. Like any other machine, there were better and worse ways to use a Medicomp, even though it was designed for the lowest common denominator.

Cazelet's right leg from mid-thigh was separate on the stretcher. Madringer arranged it carefully within the Medicomp, then closed the machine and let it get on with its business.

Adele realized that Dasi was standing beside her. The big bosun's mate's hands were swollen, and his red eyes looked ghastly.

"Dasi, you'd better get some help yourself," Adele said.

"Yeah, I'll do that," Dasi said. His words were slurred; fumes and ozone had obviously damaged his mouth and tongue even worse than they had the tough outer skin of his hands. "But I want to make sure the kid's okay first."

"Yes," said Adele. "I..."

She paused because she wasn't sure how to continue. "Feel responsible for him," was what she had started to say, which sounded extremely foolish when the words formed in her mind. Rene was a thoroughly competent adult who knew the risks of RCN service as well as she herself did.

"I was greatly indebted to his grandmother on Bryce, after I was orphaned," Adele said. "She sent him to me when his parents were arrested for treason."

"Madringer!" Dasi croaked. "How's he doing?"

"I'll tell you when I bloody know something, won't I?" Madringer said, bending over the display screen and adjusting the roller control beside it.

"Hell, he's gonna be all right," Dasi muttered. It was more a prayer than a prediction. He looked at Adele and said, "Half a dozen of us was just going up the ramp of the *Roebuck*, clearing her, you know? And some wog comes out of a hut and shoots at us, from behind, you see? And then he throws his gun down—the loading tube was jammed, Sun said afterward, but he got the one slug out and it took off Cazelet's leg neat as a snapped cable."

Under the circumstances, the villager might as easily have missed the ship itself, Adele thought. *And if he'd had time to realize how badly the attackers outnumbered them, he probably wouldn't have shot at all.*

But probabilities didn't change reality; and eventually everyone dies. Which Adele often found a blessing to remember.

Madringer had blond, curly hair, but he was developing a paunch and he seemed wrung out. He turned from the

Medicomp and said, "Okay. He's stable and he's going to make it. The leg, well, it's knitting and chances are most of the nerve cells are going to come back. Thing is, he lost two inches of bone. The 'comp'll rebuild it, but that's too bloody much for perfect, you know?"

"Right, right," Dasi said, bobbing his head. "Yeah, that's okay. Good job, Madringer."

"Yes, thank you, Madringer," Adele said, busy with her data unit. Rather than making a voice link, she sent a text to Vesey's face-shield: CAZELET RECOVERING.

That was everything Adele knew with certainty, and she didn't intend to speculate with Vesey about longer-term prospects. Vesey could discuss matters with Madringer if she wished to.

"Wouldn't of took much and we'd have whacked all the wogs when we saw how bad the kid was," Dasi said, now looking into the past instead of at Adele. "The leg lying there beside him. Vesey wouldn't let us, you know? And Tovera backed her, not that anybody wasn't going to take Vesey's orders."

"Yes," said Adele, wondering how she felt. She didn't seem to feel anything.

"He's going to be under at least six hours," Madringer called. "Everything's trending up, though."

"Thing is..." Dasi said, looking sidelong at Adele. "Tovera shot the fellow who did it. Just, you know, shot him. And then she slung her gun again. She said the mistress would understand. Is that okay?"

"Yes," said Adele. "My skills don't include bringing the dead back to life."

And even if they did, I'm not sure that I would want to do so this time.

"I'm going up to the bridge," Adele said aloud. "You'd better get your burns looked at, Dasi. You can use the unit on Level E."

She opened the inner hatch, wondering how well the environmental system had done in clearing the boarding hold. It was at worst a minor discomfort.

Especially compared with walking for the rest of one's life with a stiff, painful leg.

Daniel stood on the ramp of the *Katchaturian* and viewed the prisoners. There were about two hundred and fifty of them, placed under guard in the open not far from Beta. Men were in one body, women and children in the other.

On the horizon was a smudge of black smoke from the burning huts of Alpha. For the most part the wind whipped it off at an angle, but occasionally Daniel caught a bitter taste.

He didn't mind that. It was useful to remind the villagers exactly what their situation was.

"Sir!" called a man in urban clothing. He stepped toward Daniel from the group of men. "I need to talk to the person in—"

The nearest guard was Evans. There was a heavy wrench in Evans' belt, but instead of bothering with a weapon he hit the prisoner in the belly with his bare fist. The prisoner flew backward onto the ground. He lay so flaccid that he didn't even turn his head as he vomited.

The male villagers edged away from the man who had been

knocked down; their eyes were open and frightened.

"You people have raided in the Tarbell Stars," Daniel said. His voice boomed from the speakers on the *Katchaturian*'s spine. "You're pirates, and hanging is the proper way to deal with pirates, right?"

Everybody in the crowd who was old enough to understand the words began to speak; the infants bawled in response to the general outcry. A score of men and more women fell kneeling or threw themselves prostrate, but not even the ones who were blind with fear tried to rush forward. Evans had been a good teacher.

Vesey stood to Daniel's right; on his left was Chidsey, the captain and owner of the *Mezentian Gate*. The merchant captain was heavy and fortyish, with healing sores on his wrists where his bonds had cut. All the freed spacers had been spending time with the warships' medicomps, since the freighter herself didn't have one.

"I'm *not* going to hang you this time," Daniel said, "but that's for my own reasons. You deserve to be hanged. If the Tarbell Stars have to do this again, other people will be in command and I suspect they'll take a different line."

There was a burst of ringing from the *Princess Cecile*, where Cory was overseeing the reattachment of the Dorsal A antenna. They were bolting a new mast step to the hull with an impact driver.

The outriggers had come through better than Daniel would have expected, though Cory and Woetjans would need to check the undersides in space. He personally—as owner of the armed yacht—had gone down into the interior of both outriggers while teams resealed gapped seams with structural plastic.

Cazelet was making a satisfactory recovery. If he'd had to wait another half hour to get into the Medicomp, the recovery would have been less satisfactory.

Some of the villagers had begun shouting Daniel's praises when he announced he wasn't going to hang them. Others continued to wail, perhaps because they hadn't been listening. Those who had lived in Alpha had lost everything; the smarter residents of Beta probably realized that their hovels were going to be next.

"*Six, we've got the ships rigged, over,*" Pasternak reported. He was here at Beta, but he'd sent a team of techs to prepare the pirate ships at Alpha.

Daniel started to cut the parabolic mike but instead grinned. "Blow the *Roebuck* at Alpha when you're ready, Chief," he said—to Pasternak and to the crowd below. "Hold off on these two until we're ready to lift. Six out."

He expected a delay of perhaps several minutes before Pasternak executed the order. Instead a bright flash appeared at once on the horizon, swelling through the sooty blackness. The ground shock made the *Sissie* tremble noticeably before the dull *thoomp!* arrived through the air.

Power-room techs had run the fusion bottle of the pirate ship to full pressure. At Pasternak's signal they had vented the bottle into the *Roebuck*'s interior. The result was a fiery rupture, flinging molten bits of the hull in all directions.

The villagers hadn't stopped wailing since they began, but the sound changed tone. Chance or extremely powerful lungs brought to Daniel the cry, "We need the ships for mining!"

"If you'd stuck to mining, you'd still have the ships!" Daniel said. "If you'd stuck to mining, you'd still have your houses! If you'd stuck to mining, you wouldn't be hiking seventeen miles to your nearest neighbors with nothing but water and the clothes on your backs!"

He cut the microphone with a raised finger. He said to his two companions, "You'd think they'd run out of breath. Heaven knows my throat's dry enough and I'm not trying to shout over the wind."

"They're shouting against fate, not the wind," Vesey said. Her face looked as hard as Daniel had ever seen it. She'd been splashed with Cazelet's blood when the bullet hit him. Dasi had slapped the tourniquet on the boy's stump, but it had been Vesey who had the presence of mind to signal the corvette by bouncing a laser signal off the *Roebuck*'s hull.

Plasma exhaust created so much radio frequency interference, especially at low altitude, that not even microwaves would have been certain of getting through. Laser communications were less affected, but they were normally very tight beam and the *Princess Cecile* had been moving. Spreading the signal from a reflective surface was a brilliant way to make contact—so long as you had Adele on the receiving end.

Daniel cued the microphone again and said, "You'll be given a meal"—from the villagers' own stocks; the rest was being destroyed—"and an inertial compass with a bearing to the nearest village. If you don't get along with your neighbors, you should've thought about it before you became pirates. I figure they'll be willing to take in slaves, but I won't pretend I really care what happens to you after we lift off."

This time a woman carrying an infant did step forward, calling something unintelligible. A Sissie raised his impeller to butt-stroke her, but Wright—still a common spacer, but that would change as soon as the *Katchaturian* reached Peltry—caught the gun by the receiver and held it long enough for the woman to come to her senses and scramble back.

"We ought to hang them all!" snarled Chidsey. "They killed my son! Shot him down!"

"I'm sorry," said Daniel truthfully, "but my family has presided over one massacre in my lifetime"—the Proscriptions following the Three Circles Conspiracy—"and I don't choose to add a second."

Chidsey muttered curses as he watched the villagers marched off for the meal Daniel had promised them. The merchant captain had no more power at present than those villagers did, if the truth were told, but so long as he showed that he knew his place Daniel had no reason to jerk him to heel.

Chidsey's son had been the mate of the *Mezentian Gate*. He had either mouthed off or tried to take a weapon from the pirate boarding party and had been shot. It might have been possible to learn who the shooter had been, but it would have taken time. The Nabis Contingent wasn't going to spend any longer on Benjamin than it took to restep the *Sissie*'s antenna, and Daniel would have been willing to let that wait for Peltry if the job hadn't been going so well.

Daniel had never asked his father if he had any regrets over the Proscriptions. By the time Daniel was old enough to appreciate what it meant to send thousands of people to their deaths without trial, he was no longer on speaking terms with his father.

He probably had the answer already. So far as Daniel knew, Corder Leary wasn't on record as having expressed regret about anything.

The villagers were marching off glumly to the swale where they would be fed. Spacers watched them, some of them obviously eager to use their weapons. The spacers didn't have any particular malice, but this raid was the most excitement many of them had ever imagined. Daniel hoped that nobody would get trigger-happy, but this was war. Bad things happen in wars.

Two men remained between the warships under the guard of Evans and Dasi, the latter with bandaged hands. The trigger guard of Dasi's submachine gun was latched down as it would have been for use while wearing a rigging suit.

"Let's go down and take care of the rest of our business," Daniel said to his companions. He started down the ramp, noticing as he did so that Woetjans had left the corvette's spine and was coming over to join them.

The bosun called, "The *Sissie*'ll be ready to lift by nightfall, Six. Sooner if we jury-rig it without a base section, but we can get the kink outa the base if we have a little time with it."

"I want to get off Benjamin," Daniel said after a moment's consideration, "but we'll be here for that long anyway, refilling with reaction mass. The well here doesn't have as much flow as I'd like, but unless it dries up completely I want to top off both ships."

The two prisoners were watching Daniel expectantly as he talked with his bosun, though the former Nabis spacer's face showed a degree of nervousness as well. The city-dressed civilian had regained his composure, though handsful of gravel hadn't cleaned all the vomit from his tunic. He offered Daniel a bright smile and said, "Captain Leary, I—"

"In a moment," Daniel said, his eyes on the spacer.

"But—" said the civilian. Evans grabbed the fellow by the shoulder to anchor him with his left fist and cocked his right.

"Stop!" Daniel said, grabbing the big tech's right wrist. "I need to talk to him, Evans. Just not now."

"Sure, Six," Evans said equably. He smiled and let go of the civilian, who had lost the ruddiness of his cheeks again.

"You're Easton," Daniel said to the spacer, "and you're an engine wiper. Right?"

"Yeah, port watch on the *Katie*," Easton said, bobbing his head in agreement. "Look, I'm sorry about it all but I was drunk, you know?"

"What I know at this moment," Daniel said, "is that you're a rapist. Right?"

"If you say so," Easton muttered, staring at the ground.

"Not a lot a doubt about it," Woetjans said. "I came over because she was screaming like a stuck pig and dragged him off. She can't a' been but twelve."

"Look, I'd had a couple tots of working fluid," Easton said, snarling now but his eyes still on the ground. "I'm not a bloody soldier, and I didn't like the notion of going out and getting shot! Anyway, I relaxed some when things quieted down, all right?"

"No, not all right," Daniel said calmly. "I think the best thing to do with you is leave you on the ground here where you won't be tempted by engine-room alcohol."

"Hey, you can't do that!" Easton said, looking up in horror. "What am I going to do here on this pisspot world?"

"I'll take him," Captain Chidsey said. "I can use another tech. My boy handled most of the power room, and we're shorthanded besides."

"No," said Daniel without looking at the merchant captain. "If you want to come back for him later, that's your business; but not now."

"Look, I'm *sorry*," Easton bleated, dropping to his knees. From his tone, that was true, as sure as sunrise. "You can't leave me here!"

"If you don't chase after those villagers right away..." Daniel said. "Evans is going to hit you. And if he does that, you won't be able to get up before the line is well out of sight. I'm not leaving another compass with you."

Easton blubbered for a moment, but when Evans raised his fist slowly—it wasn't a threat; he was choosing the right target—the Nabie turned and stumbled off in the direction of the villagers. Daniel watched him for a moment.

"What do you suppose they'll do with him?" Vesey said quietly.

Daniel shrugged. "They might marry him to the girl," he said. "Or they might eat him because food's short. I don't really care, except that he's off my ship."

He turned to the remaining prisoner, who had lost his previous bonhomie. "Now, what's your name, fellow?" he said.

"I'm an Alliance citizen," the civilian said, "Charlie Platt, and I'm just here by accident. I'm sure—"

"He's the shipbroker," said Chidsey. "He was bargaining

for my *Gate*. He talked to the village chiefs on the bridge for privacy, that's how I know for sure. He was cheating them too."

"Pretty much what I thought, Captain," Daniel said, smiling faintly.

"Look, there's money in this for you!" Platt said. "Lots of money, more money than you can dream. All you have—"

"Shut up, Platt," Daniel said.

"—is take a message to my—"

"Hit him, Evans," Daniel said.

Evans smashed Platt instantly in the jaw; apparently he regretted not swinging in time to drop Easton. Platt flew backward. From the amount of blood, his tongue must have been between his teeth when the punch closed his mouth.

"There are things I won't do for money," Daniel said, his voice suddenly hoarse. "Quite a lot of things, actually."

He took a deep breath, then turned to Chidsey and said, "Captain, you said you were shorthanded. Would you care to take aboard a landsman?"

"How do you know I won't put him out the lock as soon as we make orbit?" Chidsey said, his tone challenging.

"I don't know, Captain," Daniel said, "and I don't care. Though I'll point out that Master Platt probably could make you very wealthy."

"Being rich wouldn't bring my boy back, would it?" Chidsey said.

Daniel smiled, for the first time warming to the merchant captain. "No, sir," he said, "I don't believe it would."

He hooked a thumb in the direction of the moaning Platt. "I'll send your crew down to you," Daniel said. "You can get him to the *Gate*, I presume. I've checked, and you've got plenty of reaction mass for the run back to Peltry."

"Then I guess we'll take ourselves off," Chidsey said. "I'd guess we'd lift to orbit in an hour at the outside."

"Then I'll leave you to it," Daniel said. He nodded to his companions and walked toward the ramp of the *Katchaturian*. He was whistling "The Fair Maid of Xenos Town."

CHAPTER 16

NEWTOWN ON PELTRY

"*Six, the boarding bridge is fast to the dock,*" Barnes announced from the main hold. He was bosun of the *Princess Cecile* for now because Woetjans was still aboard the *Katchaturian*.

"Release the liberty party, Barnes," Daniel announced, using the general push rather than replying on the command channel. Faint cheers came up the companionway. The bosun would still give the formal order, but it pleased Daniel to be an open part of the process.

He got up from the command console and stretched. He, Adele, and Cazelet at the astrogation console were the only officers on the bridge. Sun and Chazanoff had gone on liberty. Strikers in the Battle Direction Center with Vesey were covering the gunnery and missile slots, but that was to obey regulations rather than for any practical purpose.

Turning again to face the console's mike, Daniel said, "Ship, I am turning command over to Lieutenant Vesey. Six out."

He had switched back to the *Princess Cecile* on Benjamin

because he wanted to personally examine the outriggers in space. Cory was in titular command of the *Katchaturian*, but Daniel and Cory had agreed to let Captain Schnitker bring her back unless there was an unexpected problem.

The shakedown cruise had been a thorough success for both the destroyer and her personnel. Now that they were back on Peltry, Daniel would confirm most of the Nabis officers in their original ranks. He was still of two minds whether or not to leave some of his Sissies as warrant officers on the *Katchaturian*. In large measure that depended on the mission of the Nabis Squadron...when somebody told Daniel what that was.

"I'm off to the *Katchaturian* to accompany Captain Schnitker in his post-mission walkthrough," Daniel said, smiling at Cazelet. "Midshipman Cazelet, would you like to accompany me?"

Cazelet wasn't back to one hundred percent physically, but he never would be. The stiffness in his right leg might improve further; but equally, it might worsen. Some of the feeling in the leg was gone forever, and the flashes of phantom pain would always be with him also.

Daniel's personal response to a problem was to face it head-on: if a muscle hurt, use it more. He wasn't sure that was good physiology, but it was good for him mentally. Offering Cazelet a chance to push himself was the only thing Daniel could think of that he himself would be thankful for in the same situation.

"Ah, thank you, Six," Cazelet said, turning at the console, "but—"

Daniel was prepared to hear, "—I'll wait aboard until Lieutenant Vesey goes off duty."

What Cazelet actually said was, "—I'm to accompany Officer Mundy on business in Newtown."

"That's right," Adele said. She'd gotten to her feet. She had already changed into civilian clothes, Daniel saw; they were similar enough to the utilities Adele wore on duty that he hadn't noticed the fact until now. "Rene has kindly offered to give me some help while he's off duty."

"Oh!" said Daniel. *She's giving the boy a change of scene. She's his guardian, after all.* The guardianship was unofficial, but neither the Mundys nor the Learys needed an official decree to know their duty. "Well, you're in good hands, then, Cazelet. Ah—Officer Mundy, is there an update on Robin?"

"Master Walters says that the Minister of War will be able to fit you in at four P.M. today," Adele said. "That's three standard hours from now."

Daniel grimaced. "Did he say that the minister 'graciously agreed to see me'?" he asked.

"I took that as the implication," Adele said. "Minister Robin appears to be afraid of your competence, and of course the success of your operation on Benjamin isn't going to reassure him."

"*I* don't want his bloody job!" Daniel snapped.

"No, you don't," Adele said. "But you really can't blame a former quartermaster from Kostroma for thinking you'd be tempted."

Daniel grimaced. They were talking in front of Cazelet, which didn't disturb either of them. Daniel suspected that Adele's other employers might be distressed, but the less he thought about *them*, the happier he was.

"I'll be sure to arrive on time for my appointment," he said aloud. "If we leave the Tarbell Stars abruptly, it won't be because the Minister of War has rescinded my appointment for good cause."

He and Hogg started for the companionway. He was interested in Schnitker's assessment of the *Katchaturian*'s thruster nozzles, particularly the four on the aftermost truck.

"And who knows?" Daniel said over his shoulder to Hogg. "Maybe the minister will have had a change of heart in the time we've been gone."

Hogg snorted in contempt. That was probably the correct response.

The large gray ground car waiting at the end of the dock for Adele and her companions wasn't the vehicle the Mignouris owned. The man who'd brought it waited at the driver's door. He was the same one who had driven Adele and Tovera from the residency to the *Princess Cecile* for the mission to Benjamin.

"It's all right," Tovera said. "Hogg told me his friend couldn't return the blue one just yet but this one was nicer."

"It's a limousine!" said Cazelet. He was walking stiffly and the smile on his face looked forced, though Adele realized that she wasn't an expert on smiles. In any case, Cazelet was maintaining a normal pace and demeanor, which was all that anyone had the right to expect. Adele's own mental state probably wouldn't pass a psych evaluation, but so long as she did her job, that was her business alone.

"If you're satisfied that it's safe, Tovera," Adele said. "Worst case, I'm sure Hogg will avenge us."

Tovera giggled. "I trust Hogg's judgment," she said.

The driver tipped his billed cap and said, "She's got a full charge. I'll send word to Hogg when he can have the little 'un back. Or if you like, you can keep this 'un. The previous owner doesn't need it any more."

His short laugh sounded like a deeper version of Tovera's.

"Thank you," Adele said. "You'll be informed."

She didn't know what the Mignouris would want—or the widow would want, very possibly. This car was worth at least twice what theirs would sell for, but there might be other reasons not to accept the trade.

Cazelet handed Adele into the passenger compartment. She took one of the three front-facing seats; he sat kitty-corner facing her with his right leg stretched out straight. Tovera drove away sedately, though she overcorrected even more noticeably than she had with the Mignouris' smaller vehicle.

The wood inlays of the car's interior were real. "I'm guessing that this would cost four or five times as much as the car it replaces," she said aloud. "I suspect the Mignouris will find some way to accept what they're being offered, even if they believe it's a proceed of crime."

Tovera pulled into the parking space of the residency. She didn't hit either of the posts, but she did tap the wall of the house with her front bumper because she was concentrating on the sides behind her.

"This is a private house?" Cazelet said as they got out.

"This is the Fifth Bureau Residency in Newtown," Adele

said as she led the way to the front door. "It's administered through the Bureau's Third Diocese, whose director is General Storn. I suspect you've become familiar with that name, though I've never discussed him with you."

Tovera closed the door behind them. She immediately disappeared toward the garden with the vase of—now very dead—cut flowers.

"I..." Cazelet said. "Cory and I in our researches, ah, came across the name, yes. But we were just getting general background on the work we might be called on to do in the course of our duties."

Storn had been instrumental in the satisfactory outcome of Adele's business on Tattersall. Adele had been certain that she had trained Cory and Cazelet well enough that they would have followed up some of the loose ends of that operation and found where they led.

"The *Princess Cecile* and her personnel are aiding the government of the Tarbell Stars at Storn's behest," Adele said. "The Peltry resident was to help me in this task—he reports to Storn."

She shrugged. It bothered her to simplify the situation so coarsely, but her statement was accurate and sufficient for the purpose. "Unfortunately," she said, "the resident has had a stroke, so until he can be replaced I've taken it on myself to keep the residency running."

Cazelet began to laugh. He overbalanced and would have fallen had he not grabbed the pole of a floor lamp to brace himself.

"Adele," he said through gulps of air. "I knew that there was more going on than a contract to provide military assistance to a cluster in the back of beyond, but I didn't expect . . ."

He began laughing again.

Adele allowed herself a slight smile. This wasn't the reaction she had expected, but it was apparently a very good result.

"Yes," she said. "It *is* an incongruous situation, one which you're now an active part of. You may have believed that I brought you off the ship to entertain you. In fact, I want someone to provide this necessary support to our mission."

"You think that I'm a cripple but that I can do this?" Cazelet said with sudden harshness.

"The mistress *knows* that you're a cripple," said Tovera. She had just placed fresh flowers on the table. "And if she didn't think you could handle the job, she wouldn't have told you to do it."

His mood swings are probably because of the injury and the medications he's on, Adele thought. *At least he didn't behave this way in the past.*

"Yes," she said aloud. "Tovera's analysis is correct. The choice was between you and Cory, and your injury reduces your present capacity for normal shipboard duties."

Cazelet's expression went from anger to a hard blankness for a moment. Then he grinned and said, "Yes, and besides I'll never be the astrogator that Tom Cory is. Show me my station."

"Downstairs, I'm afraid," Adele said, leading the way. "No doubt the exercise will be good for your leg."

If Rene thought I was going to tell him that he isn't physically impaired, he's been damaged more seriously than I believed, Adele thought. She hoped it was a temporary aberration. She didn't exactly depend on Cazelet, but he was an asset to her and to her RCN family.

Her smile was mostly in her mind. *Besides, I like him as a person*.

Adele set Cazelet to reading in, starting with the files which Major Grozhinski had provided. Cazelet was starting from scratch, so it would be days or weeks before he had the full background. He was quick, however; and, having grown up and worked in the Alliance he had an instinctive grasp of structures which would be only words to Cory.

The hardened communications room was really intended for solo use, but the console had a junior position on the back like the striker's seat of warship consoles. Adele put Rene there and used the primary display to catch up on traffic which had arrived during her absence on Benjamin.

The Fifth Bureau normally communicated with its residencies using commercial vessels travelling to the desired location. Encrypted messages were implanted in ships' astrogation consoles, generally without the crews or owners being informed. When a ship reached its destination, the message was transmitted to the residency there.

Communications were therefore uncertain as to time and even arrival: a tramp freighter might change its planned course for any reason or none. From Adele's experience, informing merchant captains that they were carrying government messages would not appreciably increase the likelihood that they would be delivered in a timely manner. Important information was sent in multiple copies.

Adele had sent her warning that the Peltry resident had to

be replaced to three separate worlds where the Fifth Bureau presence was major enough to rate a courier missile. Even so there was no telling when the message would get to where it was supposed to go.

Hundreds of messages were in the console's suspense file. Many of them involved Mignouri's personal business, importing high-end office equipment from Pleasaunce and bypassing Alliance export tariffs.

Adele grimaced. That was grounds for dismissal, which in the Fifth Bureau meant execution. She could not fathom what made Mignouri think that the profit justified the risk, but human beings made a great number of choices which struck Adele as the next thing to insanity.

Having scanned the message traffic, Adele checked on the surveillance of Dumouret. Realizing that this was something nonstandard which Cazelet should keep on top of, she said, "Rene, echo my display and note the path. Dumouret is President Menandros' butler and an agent of the Upholders. There are cameras in his office and living quarters in the palace, but the audio leaves something to be desired."

Dumouret's office was empty at present. Adele ran the recording back so that Cazelet could see the butler's appearance. He appeared as he was walking out with two unfamiliar men, apparently taking them somewhere.

"His outfit must be a uniform," Adele said. "He wore the same red-piped blue suit when I met him."

"Let me see those men again," Tovera said from over Adele's shoulder. Her voice was sharp.

Adele locked on them and ran a facial recognition program.

This was linked to the harbor database—a Fifth Bureau system, not something she had put in place since she arrived.

"They're listed as citizens of Danziger," she said. "They arrived from there today on the freighter *Dubrovnic*."

Danziger was outside the Tarbell Stars but due to good connections in the Matrix had become a major transshipment point. Freighters broke bulk here for distribution throughout the cluster.

"Run them through the Bureau database," Tovera said. "I don't recognize them, but I recognize the type."

Adele did a separate search, wondering as she did whether she should have integrated the Fifth Bureau files into the general database. *No, because they include Mistress Sand's information as well as what Grozhinski provided. I won't put Cinnabar data on the residency system because I may die before I can wipe it.*

"The one calling himself Sadler is from Maintenance Section C on Pleasaunce," Adele said. "I don't find the one calling himself Scroggs."

"They're killers," Tovera said. "I was Section C."

"Tovera, let's see if we can get to President Menandros before they do," Adele said, swinging off the console's seat and heading for the stairs. Tovera was right behind.

"Cazelet, alert both ships for liftoff!" Adele called over her shoulder. "All liberty is cancelled!"

She had no authority to give orders. Fortunately, Daniel cared as little about that in a crisis as Adele herself did.

At the back of her mind Adele wondered if Menandros' death would really be such a bad thing for the Tarbell Stars.

It would disrupt the government, however, and anyway the Upholders seemed to *think* that it would be bad for the government. If Adele had had time to consider the effects and side-effects she might come to a different conclusion, but for now she would go with blocking the plans of her enemies.

Adele got into the passenger compartment because the limousine had only a seat for the driver in front. As she started to swing the door closed, Cazelet called from the doorway, "Adele! On the external security system, they're heading for the Ministry of War!"

Daniel is meeting Christopher Robin about . . . now.

"To the back entrance!" Adele said as Tovera switched on the motors. The limousine took off the left gatepost as Tovera backed into the street.

The waiting room of the Minister of War was scarcely bigger than Robin's office. Daniel had passed through it when he left the minister after their first meeting, but he couldn't have described it from that experience.

Thirty-odd straight chairs stood in rows with a center aisle that wasn't quite straight. Most of the chairs were occupied, but only a few of those waiting to see Robin wore uniforms. Most of the others had the look of salesmen of one sort or another. Wars were always good opportunities to dispose of unwanted merchandise.

The floor was littered and the walls hadn't been washed in too long. It wasn't an impressive sight to someone who had spent long hours in the Navy House waiting room in Xenos.

Daniel walked up to the front where a middle-aged male clerk sat at a console beside the door to the inner office. A soldier had pulled a chair nearby from the front row. He sat on it, his carbine leaning against the wall.

"I'm Captain Leary," Daniel said pleasantly. "The Minister of War requested to see me at four P.M. today. I seem to be two minutes early."

The clerk looked up. "Take a seat," he said. "I'll tell you if the minister wants to see you."

Still smiling, Daniel said, "May I ask who Minister Robin is with at present?"

"He's busy and that's all you need to know," the clerk said. "I told you to take a seat!"

"So you did," Daniel agreed. The door didn't have an external latch, but there was a large button on the right side of the console. Repeated use had worn the button's cream enamel finish through to the black base.

Daniel leaned over and pushed the button. The door opened outward.

"Hey!" said the clerk, loudly enough to alert the dozing guard. Daniel and Hogg sauntered through without anything more serious happening before the door closed behind them.

"Good afternoon, Minister," Daniel said as Robin looked up from the flat-screen display facing him at an angle on his desk. "I'm here as you directed."

Walters rose from his console, then sat back again. Robin made a sour face, but he gestured and said, "Yes, take a seat, Leary."

Walters eyed Hogg doubtfully, probably wondering what Hogg intended to do. Daniel wondered also as he took one of the chairs in front of the large desk, but Hogg remained at the back of the room.

"I've been very pleased with the progress the Nabis Contingent has been making, Minister," Daniel said, "and I hope you are too."

"Yes indeed, Leary," Robin said. He tapped his display repeatedly with a light pen. "Major Berners gave me a quick account of your recent training mission. It shows real initiative and an ability to work with material which must be well beneath the level you're accustomed to on Cinnabar."

"Actually, sir," Daniel said, leaning forward slightly, "the Nabies were solid personnel, very solid. All we cadre did was to show them what they were capable of doing. Ah, and working with the officers some to bring 'em up to speed."

"Well, you shouldn't be modest," Robin said, turning from his display to flash Daniel a bright, false smile. "President Menandros has decided to greatly increase your responsibilities. He's made you Governor of Nabis, reporting directly to him."

Are you out of your bloody mind?

For a moment Daniel thought the words had come out of his mouth. They hadn't, but Robin probably read them in his face.

"Your Excellency..." Daniel said. He closed his eyes for a moment to visualize his next words. Opening them he continued, "Sir, look. My father was the most powerful politician on Cinnabar; he's still pretty bloody important. My sister Deirdre gives every sign of following him into the Senate, and I've never known her to play a game that she didn't win at."

Daniel had straightened when Robin pronounced his exile to

a backwater. Now he leaned forward again and said earnestly, "Sir, if I wanted to get into politics, I'd go home and join the family firm! But I didn't, I wanted to be a naval officer and I'm a bloody good one. Put me in charge of *ships*. Or better, put me in charge of your navy, and I'll show you what I can do!"

"Captain Leary, I'm sure you're a very important man in Cinnabar space," Robin said, his voice rising. "But here in the Tarbell Stars, we're under the rule of President Menandros, and it's his decision—"

"President Bloody Nonsense!" Daniel said, rising to his feet. "Look, everybody knows you call the shots. Menandros probably knows, if he's got two brain cells to spare for any serious thinking! That's fine, but—"

"That's enough!" Robin said as he stood. He crossed his arms before him. Walters had gotten up also and was edging closer to Daniel from the side. *If he tries to jump me, I'll break his face.*

Hogg, glimpsed in the polished metal surface of the side of the desk, remained by the door; nothing in the present situation required him to intervene. Though Hogg acted the simple hayseed, he had a very sophisticated grasp of urban society. He wasn't going to precipitate a brawl which *could not* have a good result.

The door from the waiting room opened. The clerk outside was babbling something in a high-pitched voice. Walters turned to the disturbance, and Daniel glanced over his shoulder.

A heavy-set balding man in a blue servant's uniform had entered. A tall man and a short one, both in business suits, were behind him.

"Dumouret, what in bloody hell are you doing here?" Robin shouted.

"Minister," Dumouret said, "I'm very sorry to disturb you, but the President—"

The short civilian shot Hogg in the chest. Hogg flew into the wall behind him, thrown when his legs spasmed.

The shooter's tunic pocket was smoldering, ignited by the vaporized aluminum driving band of the slug fired from inside it. The taller civilian was taking a submachine gun out of his briefcase.

Daniel grabbed Dumouret by wrist and thigh. He pitched the butler into the tall man, who in turn bumped the shooter off balance. Walters had frozen for a moment with his mouth open, but now he lunged at the shooter.

The pistol was now clear of short man's burning pocket, and he shot Walters twice through the breastbone. He pivoted toward Daniel, who tripped over Dumouret's flailing legs.

The shooter sprawled forward, though he continued to turn. There was a fleck of blood on his right temple and a long bloody crease at the top of his head where the second pellet had gone a little high.

The taller man had risen to a kneeling position. At the crackle of Tovera's submachine gun, he collapsed again over his own weapon.

The door to the rear entrance hit the wall and began to swing closed again behind Adele and her servant. Robin peeked up from behind the desk where he had dropped to shelter.

The air stank of ozone and feces and fear. Also of blood: Walters lay on his back. He had stopped bleeding, but the tunic of his white uniform was a crimson which would darken as it dried. His eyes were open and his lips drawn back in a grimace of horror.

Daniel tried to get to his feet, then fell onto all fours and crawled toward where Hogg lay. He felt icy inside. He wondered if he'd been physically injured.

"Do we need the butler?" Tovera said. Daniel heard all sounds through a thumping that seemed to be synchronized with his heartbeat.

"Not really," said Adele, "but he's no—"

The burst from Tovera's little submachine gun cut off the next words. It sounded like an electrical fault. Dumouret had been curled in a ball. He twitched, and all his muscles relaxed.

The man with the pistol had fallen over Hogg's body. Daniel felt his strength return. He stood up, hauling the dead shooter with him, and hurled him out of the way.

Hogg's lips were moving slightly. There were bubbles of spit on them. He wasn't bleeding, neither from mouth or chest, but something had blasted a hole in the left side of his tunic on a level with his heart.

Daniel reached into the outer right side-pocket of Hogg's tunic and brought out the knife that Hogg kept there. He snicked the blade open, then plucked the collar of Hogg's shirt away from the skin and ripped the garment down to the belt, baring his chest.

The skin was unbroken but there was a welt the size of Daniel's spread hand at the point the hole had been blown in the tunic. It was fiery red and already swelling.

Hogg's eyes focused on Daniel. "I hope somebody got the

bastard who shot me," he said in a rusty whisper.

"Is there a Medicomp in this building?" Daniel bellowed into the noise and confusion. Hogg winced with every breath, but he *was* breathing. "Adele, alert the *Sissie*! I want a stretcher team here soonest!"

Leaning close to Hogg again, Daniel said, "Adele handled that problem. I think Tovera took care of his partner, but anyway it's taken care of."

Daniel slit the left side of Hogg's tunic and drew the pistol from the built-in holster concealed there. The slug had struck the receiver like a sledgehammer, almost severing the barrel from the butt and magazine.

"The bastard suckered me, played me for a right sap," Hogg said, tensing against the pain but getting the words out without gasping. "If the mistress fixed him, he won't be doing it again, though."

He laughed, punctuated by spasms of pain.

"There's a Medicomp in the next room to the left," Adele said, squatting to put her head on a level with Daniel's.

"There's a stretcher there too," said Robin. "I thought, well, I'd as soon there was a facility close to my office."

"I can bloody walk," Hogg said, but he wasn't trying to get up.

"You'll do what your master bloody says, Hogg!" Daniel said. There might be internal bleeding; there were *certainly* cracked ribs.

Daniel straightened. "Let's get the stretcher," he said to Minister Robin. "Then you can take the back end while we haul him to the unit."

Daniel felt enormous relief as he led Robin through the

waiting room, shoving people out of the way when they babbled instead of clearing his path. It felt good to work out some of the adrenaline surging through his system.

For the moment, Adele was alone in the minister's office. She sat at Robin's desk and slipped the pistol back in her pocket; she had laid it on the desk to allow the barrel to cool.

The carnage was familiar to her by now. The four bodies lay where they had fallen. Well, all but that of the man she had shot: that corpse lay where Daniel had tossed it away from Hogg.

Daniel and Minister Robin returned; Daniel looked haggard, and the minister appeared to be in shock. He'd seemed calm enough immediately after the shooting, but perhaps it hadn't sunk in.

Adele smiled faintly. She was trembling a little also, but that was a result of hormones rather than anything psychological.

The only thing unusual about this *room full of bodies is that I only killed one of them*, Adele thought.

The door banged shut behind Robin, muting the babble of voices from the outer office. Adele looked up from the display of her data unit; she hadn't been consciously aware of the sound, but the near-silence got her attention.

"Who are those soldiers?" Robin asked. He started toward the chair behind his desk, then realized that Adele was already sitting in it.

"They're spacers from the *Princess Cecile*," Daniel said, "under my bosun and Midshipman Hale. Lieutenant Vesey sent them here when Lady Mundy alerted her."

He cleared his throat and added, "Ah—my people didn't know precisely what was happening. Hale informed me that in their haste they did a certain amount of damage in entering the ministry."

"Knocked down doors?" Robin said, frowning. "That scarcely matters."

"I gather it was more a matter of people who wanted to discuss matters," Daniel said. "Hale didn't believe there were any fatalities,"

"Fatalities!" Robin said. "Well, I suppose that doesn't matter either."

He looked at the sprawled bodies, then looked toward the back door instead. "What was this? Do you know, Lady Mundy?"

"Dumouret was a spy for the Upholders," Adele said. She saw no reason to lie, but neither did she intend to inform the minister of all the background. "They apparently sent assassins to kill you."

The actual gunmen were Fifth Bureau, but the impetus might well have come from the rebel leadership itself. They were acting as the puppets of Storn's rival, but they might view themselves as more independent than Adele did.

"But how did you..." Robin said. "How did you even get in by my private door? This is all—it's a nightmare, *nothing* makes sense."

Cazelet had unlocked the door by cutting power to it while Adele and Tovera were on the way. The system's default was to spring open, which was scarcely ideal for security even with a battery backup. Cazelet had shut the backup down also.

"Captain Leary?" Adele said. "The Nabis Contingent has

been called to action stations at my request. Now that the danger appears to be over, would you care to release the personnel to liberty again?"

"Umm," Daniel said. "No, not till I see how the recall went. I wouldn't have done this deliberately, but it's quite a useful test of the training, don't you think?"

"Yes," said Adele. She continued to scan the updates she was getting from Cazelet and both warships in the Nabis Contingent.

"Minister," she resumed, "friends of the Tarbell Stars in Cinnabar sent Captain Leary and his staff to aid the Tarbell government in putting down the rebellion. We're doing that to the best of our abilities, though the training mission you've relegated us to very nearly caused us to miss this assassination attempt. On that subject—"

Adele considered, then looked up. "Captain Leary, I would appreciate it if you took charge of the situation in the outer office."

"Of course, your ladyship," Daniel said. His expression had just gone guarded. "Ah, your ladyship? Your servant is overseeing the Medicomp, but Hogg isn't in any danger. Should I direct Tovera to return to you?"

Adele felt her lips hint at a smile. "That won't be necessary, Captain," she said. "I can handle anything necessary myself."

She looked at Robin. She wasn't sure what expression she was wearing, but it seemed to disconcert the Minister of War. She was aware of the door opening and then closing by the sudden increase and cessation of babble from the outer office.

Robin said, "What do you want, Mistress? That is, Lady Mundy."

He was looking down at her because he was standing, but that didn't increase his confidence. She wondered how much he knew about her. He knew enough to bother him when they were alone together in a room full of dead bodies, apparently.

"I want to do my job, the job Captain Leary brought us all here to do," she said. "To defeat the Upholder Rebellion. You're making that needlessly difficult, because you're afraid that Captain Leary wants to supplant you."

"That's not true!" Robin said. "I have President Menandros' full confidence!"

"Stop yammering," Adele said. She didn't raise her voice; if Robin continued to bluster, she supposed she could fire a shot into the ceiling.

Or I could just shoot him dead.

The smile that accompanied that thought shocked Robin to silence as effectively as a shot would have done. "Thank you," Adele said.

"You'll note that despite your interference," Adele continued, "we've managed to save your life. We did that because you're quite skilled. Captain Leary tells me that your idea to convert freighters to missile ships was a very clever use of available resources and might be enough in itself to defeat the rebels under present conditions."

Robin seemed to relax slightly.

"Unfortunately," Adele continued, "elements of the Alliance bureaucracy are supporting the Upholders. That means the present situation is certain to change for the worse. You personally don't have the experience and contacts to deal with enemies outside the cluster."

"That's not—" Robin said, then shut up.

"Captain Leary and his personnel are capable of dealing with your new enemies on their own terms," Adele said. "If you are unwilling to let Captain Leary do his job, I will have you killed and find someone to replace you. I may have to replace you myself."

She felt her lips quirk. "Indeed, I may just kill you myself."

Robin's eyes drifted toward the bodies, then returned to meet Adele's. He smiled back. "I wouldn't care to have that happen," he said. "What do you want me to do to avoid it?"

He may be buying time, hoping to kill me or us, Adele thought. *But I don't think so, and I don't think he could plan it without my becoming aware of it.*

"You can appoint Daniel as commander of the Navy of the Tarbell Stars," Adele said. "After that, give him the resources and support he would have if you had no concern at all about him wanting to remain in the cluster after the Upholders have been defeated."

She shrugged and added, "That's the truth and I hope you believe it. You don't have to believe it, though, so long as you believe that I'll kill you if you don't do as I direct."

"I do believe you, Lady Mundy," Robin said. "If you care to call Captain Leary in, I'll make the appointment immediately. And then—"

Adele had gotten up, but she paused on her way to the door.

"—would you mind if I had these bodies removed and disposed of? I assure you, I don't need so vivid a *memento mori*."

"Yes, I don't need them any more," Adele said. She opened the door to the outer office.

The whole business had been quite unplanned, of course, but it had been even more useful than Daniel's test of how well the Nabies reacted to an emergency recall.

"Captain Leary?" she called past the backs of Dasi and Barnes who were blocking the doorway from the other direction. "Will you come in, please?"

As the bosun's mates made way for Daniel, Adele walked over to the first shooter's pistol and picked it up. It was a powerful weapon, not a light pocket pistol like Adele's own.

She would give it to Hogg as at least a temporary replacement for his own. He would appreciate the gift.

CHAPTER 17

NEWTOWN ON PELTRY

Tovera, wearing a chauffeur's uniform, opened the door of the limousine's passenger compartment for Grozhinski. He started to get in and only then noticed that Adele was inside waiting for him. The windows were opaque from the outside.

"Lady Mundy!" he said as the door closed behind him. "Have you been able to alert Minister Robin's guards?"

The freighter *Fisher 14* had reached Peltry orbit three hours before. Its astrogation computer had immediately sent an alert to the residency, warning that there would shortly be an attempt on Christopher Robin's life. The immediately following message said that the resident should arrange for Major Grozhinski to be picked up upon landing and meet Lady Mundy as soon as possible.

"We took care of that yesterday," Adele said. "The gunmen from Section C arrived before you did and went to work immediately. They were unsuccessful."

"I'm..." Grozhinski said. "Well, I'm very glad to hear that.

I was afraid I would be too late. As I gather I was."

Tovera pulled into the space at the residency. The top of the gatepost still lay in the yard. Adele wondered if she should call for brick masons in the Nabis Contingent and have them repair it. She had learned early in her association with the RCN that starship personnel included a wide variety of skills which had nothing to do with their normal duties.

Adele waited until they were within the shielded residency to say, "I gather that communication in the other direction, from me to your organization, has been delayed also. Master Mignouri has had a stroke. I've been acting as your resident myself. Yesterday I delegated those duties to Midshipman Cazelet. He's downstairs now."

Grozhinski stared blankly for a moment, then laughed. He seated himself at the table at the edge of the room and opened his briefcase.

"We've been having a run of bad luck, haven't we?" he said. Adele took the chair across from his. "And one piece of good luck, Lady Mundy: that you're on hand. Which seems to have been enough. Well, this next item isn't luck. This was a very clever move by General Krychek, and it took us by surprise."

The file appeared in Adele's data unit. She forwarded it to Cazelet upstairs before she even opened it. This was Fifth Bureau material—in a way, at least—and if Grozhinski had concerns about it being in the residency database, it was his job to remove it.

"Umm," Adele said as she scanned the material. "Danziger is outside both the Tarbell Stars and the Alliance. How were Krychek's agents able to embargo the missiles?"

The missiles on which the Tarbell Stars were depending had been captured by Cinnabar—captured by Daniel himself—after the battle above Cacique. Because they were of Alliance design and manufacture, the RCN had declared them surplus to requirements with the cessation of hostilities. Minister Forbes had arranged for their sale to the Tarbell government at the price of scrap metal.

"Danziger is independent, yes," Grozhinski said, "but when two Fleet investigators arrived with evidence that the missiles had been stolen from Fleet stocks, the local authorities probably didn't see any choice but to embargo them until the matter could be adjudicated. Which might reasonably be at some time after the Upholders have succeeded in conquering the Tarbell Stars."

He shrugged. "I don't say that no money changed hands from Krychek's agents to the locals," he said. "But it might not have been necessary."

"I see," said Adele. An independent world couldn't risk being seen as a receiver of war stocks stolen from a neighboring superpower. Cinnabar wouldn't regard an Alliance punitive expedition to correct the situation as a breach of the Treaty of Amiens.

The stock of top-grade missiles which Cinnabar was sending to the Tarbell Stars had permitted Robin to bypass the generation of neglect which had rotted the Tarbell Navy into a rickety joke. Freighters configured as missile ships weren't really warships, but they would be sufficient to defeat the Upholders—and that would buy time for the Minister of War to create a real, professional navy to maintain the central government's sovereignty against internal and external threats.

Without the missiles, the government had no time. Adele smiled faintly. It would be very tempting to add that the government had no chance, either.

"Very well," Adele said, getting to her feet. "The next step is to bring the matter to Captain Leary. He's at the dockyard, overseeing the conversion of the freighters *Montclare* and *Montcalm* into missile ships."

"What will Captain Leary be able to do?" Grozhinski said as he closed his briefcase and rose with her.

"If I could answer that question..." Adele said tartly. "I wouldn't need to talk with Daniel."

Daniel stood beside Pasternak and Captain Ealing on the platform of an out-of-service crane, looking down on the refitting of the *Montclare*. Arc welders snarled as they attached brackets to the hull. Hogg stood far enough back that the actinic radiation was blocked by the floor of the platform; otherwise it would have burned holes in his retinas. The three spacers wore goggles.

Six teams were working on the *Montclare*. There were four more in the next dock on the *Montcalm*, another fast freighter, to add to the racket.

"The ship's existing computer will handle missile computations easily," Daniel said. "My people"—Cory and Chief Missileer Chazanoff—"are installing the necessary software, and the yard is adding missile stations."

These were flat-plate displays rather than full holographic consoles, but they were sufficient for the present purpose.

The multiple alternate tracks that a warship's console could handle were unnecessary: the two government missile ships would only be targeting the rebel heavy cruiser, deluging her with missiles which would either overwhelm the vessel—the *Upholder*—or drive her from the battle.

"That's all fine…" said Captain Ealing. "But what if they shoot back? Are you adding cannon so that we can stop incoming missiles? Right now there's only the one gun station for pirates on each of these freighters."

Ealing was the civilian captain of the *Montclare* whom Minister Robin had hired when he bought the ship for the Navy of the Tarbell Stars. Daniel had kept an open mind about whether he would confirm the appointment now that he had been put in command of the navy. However—

Anyone who thought that plasma cannon could *stop* missiles was probably too ignorant for any naval appointment. Skillfully used, plasma bolts could nudge a missile in a direction which would not intersect with the track which the target vessel intended to follow.

A warhead weighed over a ton, however. Even if it were vaporized by direct hits, the ton of vapor would continue on the plotted trajectory and do equal—if varied—damage to the target should they intersect. The trick was to vaporize divots from the warhead's mass to thrust it out of the ship's course.

"We don't have time to fit plasma cannon," Daniel said, "or to train gunners to naval standards. The missile ships will be defended by the dedicated warships accompanying them."

He realized he was frowning. "Captain," Daniel said. "This is a war and there are risks. It is my job to minimize those

275

risks to the degree possible, and it is your job to carry out my orders promptly and to the best of your abilities."

A sharp *Clang!* punctuated the arc welders' pervasive nastiness, followed by another and at length a third and fourth. Woetjans was on the *Montclare*'s hull with a bronze maul, hammering a freshly welded bracket from both directions.

The shipyard here at Newtown didn't have enough portable magnaflux equipment to check each weld, so the bosun was using a field expedient: if the weld didn't crack when she slammed it with her maul, the chances were that it would survive liftoff while holding a missile. To reduce stress, the missiles wouldn't be filled with reaction mass until the ships were out of the gravity well and were accelerating at a fixed direction and rate.

"*Captain Leary*," said the bone-conduction speaker of Daniel's goggles. It wasn't as good as a commo helmet, but it was better than shouting. "*Lady Mundy has arrived at the base of the crane and wishes to speak with you.*"

"Roger, Signals," Daniel said. "I'll join you immediately in—" he thought for a moment. "In the crane house. It's as private as you could ask and it's insulated against sound. Six out."

He turned back to his companions and said, "Gentlemen, I've been called to an urgent matter but I was about done here anyway. I'll be in touch with you later."

The lift at the back of the platform had been crowded bringing the four of them up together. Daniel didn't offer to share it with Pasternak and Ealing going down.

"What's urgent?" Hogg asked, putting his right hand in his pocket.

"I didn't bother to ask," Daniel said, "but I assume there's something to bring Adele here rather than calling. Besides, I think I learned all I was going to up there."

I learned that I need to replace Ealing. Who his replacement should be was the tricky question.

At the door of the operator's cab waited Adele with a man whom Daniel had not met. The fellow wore civilian clothes, but that was the only thing civilian about him.

Tovera came out of the building which she must have been scanning. She grinned at Hogg. The two servants remained outside while Daniel followed Adele and her companion into the cab and closed the door after them. Outside, the lift was returning to the platform to pick up Pasternak and Ealing.

The only seat in the crane house was that in front of the control panel, but there was room for six to stand without crowding. Adele said, "Daniel, this is Major Grozhinski, our contact with our employer. If you'll sit at the display we'll feed you the data."

"It won't be resident on the dockyard system," Grozhinski said reassuringly.

Does he think that I worry about that? Daniel thought, smiling. He didn't have to worry about electronic security because he had Adele. *Which is good, because I probably wouldn't worry anyway, and one of these days that could come back and bite me.*

Daniel scanned the summary paragraph. *How the bloody hell did that happen?*

He grinned. That reaction was one stage better than trying to put his fist through the screen.

He turned and stood up again. The display wasn't the way he preferred to be briefed.

"Adele," Daniel said. "Master Grozhinski? Will it be possible to get the missiles released to us in time to fit them to the ships here?" He gestured vaguely toward the *Montclare* and *Montcalm* without actually turning his head.

"No," said Grozhinski. "They *are* Alliance missiles, after all. The Cinnabar government sent them to make its involvement deniable, but the Fleet investigators who demanded that the weapons be embargoed until they're returned may not realize that their documents are forgeries. Equally, of course, they may be Krychek's agents."

"All right," Daniel said, nodding to indicate that he'd received the information. "Do either of you know of a source for missiles in quantity, even if not the three hundred Minister Forbes provided?"

Outside, work on the freighters—which might not become missile ships after all—continued unabated. The cab's soundproofing was good—even the double-glazed windows must damp a considerable amount of noise—but it wasn't perfect.

"I do not," Grozhinski said.

"Nor do I," said Adele.

Daniel smiled. It was nice to work with professionals who provided information without hedging it to uselessness. *It's a pity that the information isn't different, though.*

"All right," Daniel said. "Adele, can you make these freighters appear to be heavy cruisers?"

"Electronically, yes," Adele said. She frowned. "Visually, only to a very limited degree. It's a matter of how good the personnel crewing the Upholder ships are. The optics themselves are of adequate quality—the three destroyers are ex-Alliance and the *Upholder* herself was the *Triomphante*, built on Karst but from Fleet service."

"One of the destroyers has a ex-Fleet crew and officers," Grozhinski said, picking up seamlessly where Adele had stopped. Daniel hadn't noticed a signal pass between them. "The crews of the other destroyers and the remainder of the Upholder forces generally are either locally raised or from Karst. I suppose they're equivalent to the Tarbell navy. All major offices in the ground establishment are Krychek's people."

Grozhinski glanced down at his data unit. It was live in his hand, but he hadn't been referring to it and probably wasn't now.

"The *Upholder*," he said, "is a special case. The commissioned officers are mostly ex-Fleet, though only the communications officer is Fifth Bureau reporting to Krychek. The bulk of the crew has been recruited from Cinnabar's empire, however. Most served in the Cinnabar navy during the recent war. Lady Mundy probably has better records than my organization does, but I assume they are skilled. The *Upholder*'s officers certainly are."

They're traitors! Daniel thought. But they weren't. They were spacers who preferred naval service to merchantmen and who, while the great powers were at peace, had found a corner of the galaxy that welcomed their skills.

They weren't fighting Cinnabar, and they weren't fighting *for* the Alliance. They were spacers taking jobs with piss-pot rebels fighting a piss-pot government, and they probably figured that with a heavy cruiser they were going to come out the winners.

"The rebels are offering considerable premiums to spacers

with RCN experience," Adele said. "I suppose Krychek has agents in most major ports in Cinnabar space."

"No doubt the pay is coming from the secret account of the First Diocese," Grozhinski said, nodding agreement. "But without a very careful audit, there's nothing to suggest Alliance involvement."

"Right," said Daniel. "Deniability, like the missiles. But how do the recruits get to Ithaca? That's the rebels' capital, isn't it?"

"It is," Grozhinski agreed. "Krychek's residency on Danziger acts as the transshipment point. The residency gathers recruits in quantity and ships them to Ithaca, where they're distributed among the Upholder vessels."

Daniel smiled slowly. "We were caught by Mistress Sand's care to be deniable," he said. "It strikes me that we might return the favor."

Adele's smile was probably invisible to anyone who didn't know her as well as Daniel did. Grozhinski looked from one to the other. He didn't speak.

"Adele," Daniel said, "what do you think about subverting the crew of a rebel heavy cruiser?"

"I have nothing better to do with my life," she said. The joke made her smile more noticeable. "We'll need a neutral ship."

"May I offer the *Fisher 14*?" Grozhinski said. "The owner isn't exactly neutral in this business, but his involvement would be as hard to trace as the First Diocese secret account."

They were all three smiling. *We must look like a pack of dogs about to start dinner*, Daniel thought; and he smiled more broadly.

CHAPTER 18

ELAZIG ON DANZIGER

Adele rocked both side to side and forward and back as Barnes drove them toward the Fifth Bureau Residency in Elazig. The big wheels were independently sprung. On this irregular pavement, the motion was less like that of a land vehicle than of a skiff on very choppy water—the latter an experience which Adele had no wish to repeat.

"This bloody thing has no bloody power!" Barnes snarled, his big fists gripping the steering wheel as if he were trying to strangle it. Indeed, they were proceeding at only about twenty miles an hour, but that was quite fast enough for Adele.

"We'll get there in plenty of time," she said aloud. "And our business won't take long."

The van was local, provided by Major Grozhinski, as was the similar vehicle carrying the backup team under Hale. She and her squad were already in position at the rear of the building; Adele hadn't set out from the *Fisher 14* until Hale had reported in.

Daniel, Hogg and Cazelet were in back, all of them somber, though for different reasons. Hogg said—muttering, though in a voice meant to be heard, "I sure wouldn't mind going in with you. You know, my ribs still hurt where that bastard broke my gun."

Tovera turned her head and grinned back at him. "What's the matter, Hogg?" she said. "You don't trust me and the mistress?"

Hogg snorted. "I trust you fine," he said. "I just want to come along."

"This is it," said Adele. "Drop us here and park."

The buildings on this street were mostly three or four stories high: retail on the ground floor with offices or apartments on the upper ones. The residency was an exception, the single floor above the local branch of Bank of Danziger. There were vehicles parked along the curb, all of them similar to Grozhinski's van, but there was a space near the intersection ahead.

Barnes stopped in the street. Tovera got out, looking in all directions in two quick seconds—a coldly pleasant expression on her face, not friendly but courteous. Only after she was sure the situation was clear did she step aside so that Adele could get out also.

The guard inside the bank barely glanced at them as they went up the stairs beside the entrance where he sat. Adele led; Tovera followed with her attaché case held in front of her on the narrow staircase. Behind them the van's diesel engine rattled as Barnes moved into the parking space.

The door at the top of the stairs didn't have an outside latch, but it was propped open at present. A man with naval tattoos had gotten up from his desk at the sound of the outer door and their footsteps. He looked down at Adele with growing puzzlement.

"Mistress?" he said. "This is the Stanfleet Organization."

"Yes," said Adele. She had her Fifth Bureau credentials in her right hand: she held them up, though the doorman couldn't see more than the fact of an open wallet in the light of the staircase. "I'm here to see Colonel Colmard."

The doorman backed out of her way. His expression ranged through half a dozen emotions; fear was prominent among them.

"There's no colonels..." he said, but he let the lie trail off, since he could see that it was pointless.

The room at the top of the stairs was a bullpen with six desks, three of them occupied and the fourth near the staircase where the doorman must have been sitting. A corridor led into the back; beside it was a blank door.

"Summon Colonel Colmard and Captain Passley," Adele said, holding her credentials before the young woman whose desk was nearest the back door. "And *don't* try to tell me that you'll see if they're in: they're in to the Inspection Service."

The men at the other two desks were ordinary office workers. One was young enough and fit enough that he could have been a problem, but he wouldn't be; the other looked older than his fifty-odd years and was too fat to get his bulk from behind the desk without more warning than he was going to have.

The doorman backed another step away, keeping his desk in front of him. The visitors were officers. Physical threats wouldn't have cowed that man, but Adele's persona did.

The back door opened inward. A man of forty with short hair stepped out, trying to straighten the jacket he had just put on. He wore civilian clothes, but he didn't *seem* civilian.

The younger man following him was blond, very handsome, and faultlessly tailored: a scion of nobility, a clever youth with all the advantages. He stayed a pace behind Colmard, moving to the side.

Colmard's eyes strayed to the credentials Adele held out in her right hand. He said, "If you'll come into my office, Mistress—"

Adele brought her left hand out of her tunic pocket and shot twice, aiming at the Colonel's right eye.

Colmard's nervous system threw him backward in a spasm. He was dead before he hit the wall beside his door. His body sprawled forward, onto his ruined face.

Passley was falling also, his blood spurting through the trio of holes in his upper chest. Tovera didn't shoot for the heart but rather for the major blood vessels above it, allowing the heart to work at its highest efficiency as it pumped the blood out of his body.

Movement—

Another man shambled out of the hallway to the back, still fastening his fly. He looked at Passley, hesitated, and doubled up, spewing vomit. It smelled of alcohol.

The doorman hadn't moved from where he stood, not even when Tovera turned her submachine gun toward him. His hands clenched and unclenched.

The receptionist sneezed violently, probably a reaction to the ozone from Adele's pistol being fired so close to her nose. Then she began to sob.

Adele lowered the muzzle of her pistol, though it was too hot to drop it back into her pocket. She looked at the civilians. The fat man met her eyes, but none of the others did or could. The doorman seemed to be in shock.

"You all know who you work for," Adele said harshly. "You know how he feels about traitors. This pair seems to have forgotten. Do any of you care to join them?"

Nobody spoke. The woman continued crying. The man on the floor was trying to vomit more from an empty stomach.

"If not," Adele said, "just continue coming to work and doing your jobs. Nothing has changed for you, you'll just have a different overseer. Is that understood?"

Tovera had entered Colmard's office. She came out again, then put her submachine gun away in the attaché case. The outside door opened and several people began climbing the stairs—Daniel and Cazelet, and either Barnes or Hogg, depending on who was staying with the van.

"I opened the back way," Tovera said. "The cleanup crew is on the way."

Tovera glanced at the clerks, never letting her smile rest long on any of them. At the doorman she paused and said, "You can sit down, buddy. I'd like you to sit down."

The doorman sat without looking behind him to be sure where the chair was. He must have been a rigger. They developed their situational awareness in an environment when a missed step or handhold meant a—brief—lifetime drifting in a bubble universe which was not meant for humans.

"Nothing has changed about your mission," Adele said to the clerks. The harshness in her voice was only partly a result of the ions parching her throat. She dropped her pistol back into her tunic. "You have been providing support for the rebels in the Tarbell Stars. That will continue. When is the next shipment to go out?"

She already knew the answer, but she wanted to calm the civilians by focusing them on their ordinary work. Colmard and Passley were the only Fifth Bureau officers in the residency. The others were merely clerks doing office jobs; the woman and the man on the floor had been hired here on Danziger.

"The *Flower* landed yesterday," the fat man said. "She's to carry missiles from the embargoed stocks to Ithaca."

Adele nodded. "There will be twenty-two personnel also," she said. "They'll be processed in normal fashion."

Hale's section arrived up the back stairs; Woetjans was in front swinging a length of pipe, but Hale with a carbine and four Sissies carrying sacks and cleaning equipment were right behind. Hogg led Daniel and Cazelet in from the street.

"In there," Adele said to Cazelet, nodding toward the office with the consoles. He stepped over Passley's legs before Hale's crew could stuff the body into one of their bags.

"That's Master Cazelet," Adele said to the staring clerks. "You report to him now. And so long as you do your jobs loyally and efficiently, you'll never see me again."

She started down the stairs toward Barnes and the van. Footsteps followed, Daniel and Tovera, but neither of them spoke.

I need to load a fresh magazine, Adele thought.

She walked by reflex. All she saw before her was the disbelieving face of Colonel Colmard, an instant before his right eye exploded.

* * *

Daniel stood with the other twenty-one Sissies before the boarding ramp of the *Flower of Cortona*, a three-thousand-ton freighter out of Piedmont—an Alliance world. It was in better shape than the *Mezentian Gate* had been—it appeared to have a full set of masts and yards—but there was nothing to set it apart from the better thirty out of a hundred tramp freighters.

Captain Dreyer was angry, but from her attitude during Daniel's brief observation of her, that was her normal condition. "There's supposed to be somebody from the hiring office along with you!" she said. "You're supposed to have been checked in by them and I just say that I've taken you aboard the *Flower*."

"This is what they told us to do, Captain," said Hale, acting as the transit officer for the intake. Her file showed her as Midshipman Garrett, who had been a classmate of Hale's at the Academy. "They said if we couldn't find our way to the harbor, the navy didn't need us, and if you couldn't check us in, the navy didn't need you either."

The rest of the intake was listed as warrant officers—Woetjans was a bosun's mate—technicians, spacers, and a smattering of specialists. Adele was a Communicator 2, Tovera was a clerk, and Hogg—who absolutely insisted on being part of the group—was a cook. He was actually a pretty good cook, better than many Daniel had run into in the RCN.

"Ma'am?" said Daniel—or according to his chip, Able Spacer Green. "I think they've had some turnover in the recruiting office. The new boss is trying to get a handle on things, but he did say he was going to send our jackets to the ship's system so you can access it."

This intake couldn't be processed normally because about a third of the faces had been involved with taking over the residency. The clerks might not suspect that the intake was working against the Upholders, but they would certainly know that something odd was going on.

So long as the files which Cazelet sent to the *Flower* corresponded with those the intake carried, no alarm buttons would go off. Two of the party, Evans and Yarnold, a rigger, didn't have files. That was normal too. They were holding paper identification sheets which Adele had run off before they lifted from Peltry.

"Bloody *hell*," Dreyer snarled, making a change in procedure into a problem. Daniel wondered how good her astrogation was. "All right, line up and board one at a time. Wessels, sign 'em in!"

A wizened man stood at a workstation near the main hatch. When he moved, Daniel saw that he was missing three fingers of his left hand. Hale walked up the ramp; the rest of the intake followed in a leisurely procession.

Adele looked back at Daniel and said, "I used to tell myself that it was necessary. I've stopped doing that."

What was necessary? Daniel thought, but the words didn't reach his tongue. He said instead, "I think things are going pretty well at the moment."

"Yes," said Adele. He knew the twitch in her lips was a smile. "And Colmard and his aide weren't much of a loss, except to General Krychek's plans."

That's what she's talking about. Because Adele didn't react to things that happened—to things that she *did*—it was easy to assume that they didn't touch her. It was easy even for a good friend to assume that, especially when he was trying to forget the things himself.

Aloud Daniel said, "It *was* necessary. We had no way to imprison them on Danziger. All the infrastructure here has been penetrated by Krychek's agents."

Adele shrugged. "Perhaps," she said. "But it doesn't matter. It's done."

The line was shuffling forward. Adele was in front of him and Hogg followed behind. Daniel reached the base of the ramp.

Captain Dreyer came out of the ship and walked down to Tovera and Adele. "Which of you is the communicator, Bethel?" Dreyer asked. She was younger than she'd looked from a short distance; the gray in her frizzy red hair was premature.

"I'm Bethel," Adele said. "I was a Communicator 2 in the Fleet."

"Well, on the voyage to Ithaca, you can take a look at our commo, right?" Dreyer said. "It cuts out sometimes and it's a pain in the ass."

"I won't be able to do much if it's a hardware problem," Adele said.

"The hardware all checks out but it's something in the programming," Dreyer insisted. "Can you fix it?"

"I'll take a look," Adele said. "If it's programming, I may be able to help."

The line moved forward, bringing Daniel to where Dreyer stood. He met her gaze with a smile.

"And you are?" Dreyer said, more harshly than she had spoken to Adele.

"Able Spacer Green," said Daniel. "I'm a rigger."

Dreyer grabbed his left wrist and slid his sleeve up above the elbow. "You've got the calluses," she said, fingering his elbow where a hard suit rubs against the bone. "You don't look right, though."

"Try me," Daniel said, treating the words as more of a joke than a challenge.

Dreyer dropped his hand. "I guess we'll do just that," she said. "The first thing we do when we get you lot enrolled is load as many missiles into the *Flower* as we can pack. I turn you over to the recruit depot when we get to Ithaca, but till then you're my crew. You'll earn your meals, never fear!"

"I've never been afraid of hard work," said Daniel. He smiled again.

His practice of conning his ship from the rigging had gotten him the right calluses. *It's been a long time since I helped strike down heavy cargo, though. Well, it ought to sweat some of the fat off my waistline, at least.*

CHAPTER 19

CORALVILLE ON ITHACA

Adele had examined imagery of Coralville from before it became capital of the Upholder Rebellion. It was a little place with only a thousand houses but extensive warehouses and grain elevators along the harborfront of Coral Harbor.

All that still remained, but the original town was dwarfed by the prefab barracks extending to the south and along the west side of the harbor. In addition to the rickety quays which had loaded the ships which carried Ithaca's produce across the Tarbell Stars, there were to the west extensive steel structures at which naval vessels were docked.

The new imagery was of poor quality, supplied by the *Flower of Cortona* as she landed an hour earlier. Adele would shortly be in the files of the heavy cruiser *Upholder*, whose naval-grade optics would do much better, but that probably wouldn't provide any additions that her work really needed.

"How long is this going to take you?" Captain Dreyer asked. She was sitting on a bunk as Adele worked at the command console. Tovera stood beside the hatch, watching both the bridge and the work in the main hold. The spacers there were unclamping the missiles which were to be offloaded by a travelling crane.

"As best I can tell, Captain," Adele said, "your communications system hasn't worked at full efficiency for at least two and a half standard years. I hope to have it repaired in less time than that."

"You don't have years!" Dreyer said angrily. "You should be at the recruit depot right now!"

"My truelove is being ironic, Captain," Tovera said. "And she is far too much of a lady to tell you that it will go faster if you don't disturb her as she works."

"Look, Michels, you've got no business here at all!" Dreyer said, rising to her feet.

"Tut," said Tovera. "Do you think I'm likely to leave my truelove alone with a harpy like you? *I* don't."

Adele didn't know anything about Tovera's sexual interests or even if she had any. Though Adele was generally curious about everything she encountered, she'd made the conscious decision to avoid that subject. She didn't imagine she would learn anything that shocked her, but she might well learn things that would make it difficult to work with her servant— and Tovera had become a valuable asset. As valuable as the pistol in Adele's pocket, and much harder to replace.

Adele allowed her lips to quirk into a smile. She was fairly certain that Tovera did *not* have a passion for her mistress. That would be awkward.

"What are you going to do if you're not assigned to the

same ship?" Dreyer said with a sneer.

"I suppose I'll waste away until I die," Tovera said. There was no emotional loading to her words, but there never was. "I will be praying to the gods of my family that such a tragedy does not occur."

It wouldn't occur, because Adele had just finished arranging for the entire intake to be sent to the *Upholder*. *I wonder if Tovera's family worships me?* she thought.

It was hard to imagine Tovera having a family. Knowing her well—and by now Adele did—one found it easier to imagine Tovera hatching with scores of siblings and slithering off into the grass.

"I'll be done very shortly, I think," Adele said aloud. "As soon as the updates are configured."

"What was the problem, then?" Dreyer said. She was still standing, though her anger seemed to have been replaced by irritated frustration.

"Incompetence," Adele said. "Updates were applied randomly, sometimes in the dedicated communications sector but more generally in other sectors of the ship's computer. There's plenty of capacity, of course, but portions of the program couldn't be accessed while the unit was working on course predictions. It probably didn't help your astrogation either."

She wondered whether Dreyer herself had maintained the equipment or if it had been done by outside technicians when the *Flower* was in harbor. It didn't affect how Adele answered the question; she just wondered.

Adele had falsely implied to Dreyer that she couldn't fix the commo problem during the voyage itself. In fact, she needed to be in harbor in order to access the rebel databases. After arranging that the personnel department would sort all the *Flower*'s intake onto the *Upholder*, Adele began to siphon the contents of the databases so that she could examine them at leisure.

She was storing the data on the *Flower*'s system for the moment. She would transfer it to one of the *Upholder*'s consoles once she was aboard and had examined the situation.

It would probably have been safe to drain the information directly onto the cruiser, but if Adele wasn't present at the time there was always the chance that somebody on the cruiser's bridge would notice the anomaly. The communications officer, Commander Braun, was actually Fifth Bureau instead of Fleet. Although that might mean that his familiarity with the equipment was lower than that of a real signals officer, he might also be more careful and paranoid.

"Is it going to do this again?" Dreyer asked. Her voice had lost its previous hectoring edge.

Adele looked at the captain for the first time since she had begun working at the console. Dreyer seemed to have softened. Very few female captains operated on the fringes. Even though the *Flower of Cortona* was registered in the Alliance, Dreyer's personality must have been shaped by the hostile environment.

"Not if you use basic care to keep all commo software in the designated sector," Adele said. "This is no more difficult than drinking filtered water rather than straight reaction mass."

Adele got up. "I think it's ready now," she said.

"Bethel, look," Dreyer said, looking at the starboard bulkhead. "How would you like a second mate's slot? The *Flower* isn't a luxury yacht, but you're better off than you will be with the Upholders. They're a bunch of wankers, let me tell you."

"Thank you," Adele said, putting her personal data unit into its trouser pocket. Her slight kit was bundled with that of Tovera beside the hatch. "I prefer a structured environment to that of a tramp freighter."

"I can find a slot for your friend, too," Dreyer called to their backs as they walked down the boarding ramp. Adele didn't reply.

When they reached the quay, Tovera chirruped a laugh. "I'm sure your duties on the *Upholder* will be very simple," she said.

Adele clicked her tongue. "I don't want to learn astrogation," she said.

Though it couldn't be very difficult to program an astrogation computer adequately, judging by the intelligence of many of the space captains she had met here on the fringes.

"I probably wouldn't have to kill anybody as mate on a freighter," Adele said.

The rest of the intake was involved in emptying the hold. Access plates on the spine had been laid aside so that the crane could hoist out missiles and transfer them to lowboys. Adele didn't see any reason to volunteer her slight body to brute force labor which was already being handled with skill.

"You don't *have* to kill anybody now," Tovera said. "Look at Cazelet."

Daniel rose into sight aboard a missile. He stepped onto the hull, then waved cheerfully when he saw Adele.

"No, I suppose not," Adele agreed. "And it wouldn't bring

back the ones I've already killed." *The hundreds, many hundreds, I've already killed*. "Which is a good thing, in a few cases."

She didn't often smile when she recalled the faces she had last glimpsed over her gunsights, but she smiled now. *Platt the child-molester, writhing in his own blood and filth as he boasted of his importance....* "Yes, sometimes a good thing."

Tovera sat on a bollard. It had been kinked when it stopped something large from rolling off the quay. "I've always heard that you should stick to work that you're good at," she said. She grinned at Adele and added, "And you're very good, Mistress. Very good indeed."

Daniel expected to be mustered aboard the *Upholder* by the First Officer—or even by a midshipman; twenty-two spacers weren't a very important increment to a cruiser with a crew of five hundred. Nonetheless Captain Joycelyn himself was here in the riggers' mess, though the enrollment would be conducted by the bosun, Wagstaff. A clerk sat at a lowered table beside them.

"Spacers, I'm Captain Joycelyn of the *Upholder,* your commander," said Joycelyn, a good-looking man with short blond hair. His Fleet second class uniform—field gray with dark piping—had Upholder red-and-blue shoulder flashes of an arm raising a torch. It was tight around the waist.

But so is mine, Daniel thought ruefully.

"I want to congratulate you for choosing the winning side in this affair," Joycelyn said. "It isn't really a civil war, it's a real government appearing in the Tarbell Stars where there's been nothing but a joke and a nest of bloodsuckers on Peltry for the past generation."

He gestured to the hologram over the serving line at the head of the room: the *Upholder* with all sails set, against the glowing background of the Matrix. It was an imposing piece of art, though the ship was too sharp and clean for reality and the colors of the Matrix were too saturated.

"*We* have a navy," Joycelyn said. "You're part of it, a big part of it—a heavy cruiser with a crew of real veterans. The so-called Tarbells have only a few destroyers, and *those* are mostly too rusted to lift. Their crews are the sort of sweepings you'd expect on junkers, *and* they haven't been paid for months. You've all gotten your signing bonus, and you'll get your pay regular by the month, not just at the end of the voyage. Ask your shipmates!"

Joycelyn looked around, but the Sissies didn't react. Daniel wondered what real recruits would have done; perhaps he should have coached his people on how to react, but he didn't know what to suggest.

Maybe silence was the best choice after all. People who had come this far to sign on to a civil war were likely to have seen quite a lot of life.

"Wagstaff will assign you to watches," the captain said. "File up to the table and give your name so that the clerk can sign you in."

The front rank began to shuffle forward. Hale called, "Sir? I'm an Academy graduate, Garrett. I was told you'd have a lieutenancy for me?"

"All right, Garrett," Joycelyn said. "Wait here with me, and when your colleagues are done I'll take you to the bridge and run you through your paces."

"How were the Upholders able to buy a heavy cruiser?" Daniel said quietly to Adele, standing beside him in the rear rank. "There's obviously money behind them, but I don't see the Fleet handing over a ship like this even though the Peace of Amiens has held now for a couple years."

"The *Galissonniere* was hit by a missile at Keeler's Planet," Adele said, her eyes on Captain Joycelyn. "She limped back to Pleasaunce, but she was scrapped as uneconomic to repair. The missile hit the starboard outrigger and splashed the hull as well."

Daniel frowned. Whipping from a missile strike, followed by being bathed with molten steel, certainly would make a ship unrepairable economically, but—

"This ship can't have been hit by a missile!" he said. He hadn't seen any evidence of serious damage when they boarded the cruiser. A hit like that should have stretched or crumpled every bulkhead on the ship.

"No, this is the *Galissoniere*'s sister ship, the *Triomphante*," Adele said. "The Alliance bought them both from Karst. General Krychek got the papers switched. An audit of the ships in ordinary will indicate what happened—though possibly not how it was done even then. There won't be an audit for a decade, judging from RCN practice. Unless war breaks out again."

"I wonder if overthrowing the Tarbell government is a violation of the Treaty of Amiens," Daniel said. "It isn't really the Alliance doing it, after all; just one official."

Adele shrugged. "It's grounds for the resumption of war if

the Republic wants it to be," she said. "If it's made public, of course, but I don't see how the plan can keep from becoming public if it succeeds."

"Do you think we will respond?" Daniel said.

Adele shrugged again. "By 'we' you mean the Republic, I suppose," she said. "You know as well as I do that there isn't *a* Republic, there are factions just as there are factions in the Alliance. Two of them are involved here, obviously, and I dare say Guarantor Porra would have an opinion of his own if he learned what his subordinates were doing. I don't know what would happen. What *will* happen, I suppose."

"Well, not if we stop it," Daniel said, relaxing slightly. "Which is why we're here."

"I've been the bosun's mate of a battleship!" Woetjans said from the front of the line, her voice rising with anger. "I'm not a bloody landsman!"

"You're a landsman on this ship!" Wagstaff shouted back. "Because I class you as a bloody landsman! Women can't do a spacer's job, and they *bloody* well can't do a warrant officer's job!"

Daniel thought of intervening, but he probably couldn't. He *certainly* couldn't intervene effectively without destroying the mission that had brought them to Ithaca. If Woetjans kept her temper and remembered they were really here for—

Woetjans bent enough to grab Wagstaff by both legs below the knees. Wagstaff shouted and punched down at the middle of her back.

Daniel thought Woetjans was going to throw the *Upholder*'s bosun, but instead she pivoted him as though he were a bat she was striking the floor with. Wagstaff got his arms up to save his head.

Woetjans kicked him in the face. Wagstaff moved his hands to block her. She drove his head down into the deck. The steel rang and Daniel was sure he heard bone crunch.

Woetjans tossed Wagstaff toward the hatch, limp as a half-filled grain sack. She straightened to attention, facing the bulkhead in front of her, and said, "Sir!" as if reporting to a new commanding officer. Her face was red and she'd torn off the right sleeve of her tunic, but she was doing a good job of controlling her breathing.

"What's your name, spacer?" Joycelyn said, looking Woetjans up and down.

When Woetjans didn't answer—possibly because she didn't remember her name for this mission—the clerk said, "She's van Arp, sir."

"Well, van Arp," the captain said. He was apparently taking her silence as a reaction to the fight; which indeed it might have been. "The *Upholder* has a vacancy at bosun. Do you think you're capable of filling it?"

"Sir!" said Woetjans. "Yes, sir!"

"Enroll van Arp as bosun, spacer," Joycelyn said to the clerk. He looked at Woetjans again, then around the intake generally. He continued, "Wagstaff was from Karst, he came with the ship. I find Karst generally to be behind civilized norms. Wagstaff was an extreme example of that."

"I'll have him landed on the dock, shall I, sir?" Woetjans said. She remained at attention.

"Yes, Bosun, I think that's a good idea," Joycelyn said.

"Garrett, with me. The rest of you, carry on."

He and Hale walked out of the compartment, stepping carefully over Wagstaff's outflung arm.

Daniel felt himself relax. "Just as well we didn't rehearse this," he muttered to Adele. "Because that *certainly* wouldn't have been my plan."

Adele had mistakenly expected the bridge of the *Upholder* to be very similar to that of the *Milton*, since they were both heavy cruiser hulls of similar vintage. Instead, the *Upholder* had two rows of consoles back to back down the center, with the striker's station of each relegated to the bulkhead. There was a corridor between the primary and secondary stations on each side.

"Sit at the communications console, Bethel," Commander Braun directed. He lowered himself onto the seat across the aisle from her. "I'll observe from the backup station."

The *Upholder* hadn't been built for the Fleet. The Alliance had purchased the cruiser and its sister-ship from Karst at the height of hostilities, when young Headman Hieronymous had succeeded his grandfather. Hieronymous immediately broke the long relationship between Karst and the Republic of Cinnabar.

His advisors were brothers who had returned from an exile in which they had become officers in the Fleet; they had brokered the sale. The two powerful cruisers were a useful addition to Fleet strength, and their sale had cemented the brothers' relationship with the Alliance. They had shortly murdered Hieronymous and, with Alliance support, had taken over Karst. The Treaty of Amiens left Karst outside both superpower blocs, however.

"I've read your file, Bethel," Braun said as Adele settled herself and brought the console live. "It says that you don't have any big-ship experience. Is that true?"

Almost a dozen people were on bridge at present, though only a few of them seemed to be on duty; several were in civilian clothes. Adele wouldn't be able to identify them until she had some time alone with the cruiser's internal systems.

"Yes, that's true," Adele said. She had proven herself able to lie when necessary, just as she was willing to kill when necessary. This wasn't a lie, though: the file of Communicator 2 Bethel, which Adele herself had written, showed her Fleet service as being in ground facilities or on a destroyer.

"Well, do the best you can with this test sequence," Braun said. "I'd like to be able to leave most of the ordinary commo to you while I'm occupied with other duties."

Krychek had picked several key officers for the rebel military, but Braun was high up in the ranks of the First Diocese itself; he reported directly to Krychek. Braun was aboard the cruiser as the political officer under the guise of a communicator.

In fact his background in communications wasn't any better than that of a normal Fleet—or RCN—officer. Braun could handle signals officer duties on a cruiser well enough not to arouse suspicion in his fellows, but he was obviously very willing to pass those duties on.

Adele's smile was tiny and very cold. *Braun was probably sent as a signals officer because his astrogation isn't much better than my own.*

"Respond to these incoming signals as though you were the communications officer, Bethel," Braun said, then turned to the flat-plate display at his own station and activated a program.

Adele took out her personal data unit, which she had already linked to the *Upholder*'s system. The test signals started with normal incoming for a ship in harbor—notice of deliveries, status requests, personal messages for named individuals— then progressed to communications regarding liftoff and from the ground to the cruiser in orbit.

Adele routed them without difficulty. The signals were always slugged properly, which made the job much easier than it would be in reality with an unfamiliar crew. Real incoming messages were likely to address "Daisy" or "Phil," and were made unintelligible as well as unfamiliar by the speakers' mushy accents.

"Commander...?" Adele said, using a link to Braun's station rather than turning and raising her voice. On the *Princess Cecile* she would have keyed the link verbally, but here she used manual controls until she had time to explore the system. "I'm dealing with real incoming messages as well as your test sequence. If you don't want me to do that, please tell me now."

"*What?*" Braun said. He turned, raising his voice, but his station properly routed the words as a reply on the two-way link. "*What real messages?*"

"Tomorrow's training schedule from Central Personnel," Adele said. "I sent that to the first officer. And a request for a fatigue party of twenty to aid with rerigging the destroyer *Truth*, which I sent to the bosun. Sir."

"*Ordinary messages are routed to the duty officer during this test*," Braun said, frowning.

"You set it to do that…" Adele said, wondering if she should pretend more respect than she felt. "But then you shut down the console. When I brought the console back up, it reverted to default programming and sent incoming messages to the signals console."

There didn't seem to be any reason to crawl to her new superior: Braun needed her even more than she had assumed from the beginning. *Besides, I'm not very good at pretending respect.*

"*I see*," said Braun. "*To be honest, this model of console is unfamiliar to me. Well, that's very good, Bethel. You can consider yourself acting signals officer of the* Upholder, *though that won't be formal since you don't have commissioned rank yet. You* will *have when you return to Fleet service, I promise you.*"

"Thank you, sir," Adele said. "Selkirk"—Tovera for this mission—"was my regular clerk on the *Z71*, so we're experienced in trading watches. You won't have to worry about signals with the two of us in place."

"*You had a clerk on the* Z71?" Braun said, frowning again. "*Is that SOP for destroyers?*"

"In most cases one of the technicians doubles as the signals officer's striker," Adele said, hoping that Fleet standard operating procedure was the same as the RCN's. "Selkirk and I made the connection more regular, and it works well."

Tovera, seated at the empty astrogation console beside signals, nodded demurely to Braun.

Braun stood up; Adele turned to face him but stayed at the

console. "All right," he said. "That seems a good system for the *Upholder* as well. You may carry on until I get regular watches set up. Your real duties will begin in a week when we make our first shakedown cruise."

"Thank you, sir," Adele said.

Braun frowned again and added, "I warn you, this will be work for you; I won't have leisure to give you much guidance. But in the end I think you'll find yourself quite satisfied."

"I expect I will, sir," Adele said. "And I've never minded hard work."

Braun nodded and walked off the bridge. Adele busied herself with learning the details of the system she now controlled.

On a two-way link, Tovera said, "*He certainly won't be able to give you much guidance. Personally, I'm really looking forward to the payoff.*"

"Yes," said Adele as she transferred her stored files from the *Flower of Cortona* to a walled-off portion of the signals console. "I think we all are."

TEN LIGHT-MINUTES FROM ITHACA

Daniel, perched on the second flange of the Starboard B antenna, reeved the final sheave of the new block. He extended the cable's free end, working hand over hand; it was stiff enough to be treated as rod for short distances. Beauchamp, farther down the rigging, walked the end to Schatt and held it while his partner clamped a bight in the end.

Daniel climbed down to the deck while the others coupled

the fall to the motor. He joined them as Beauchamp arm-signaled to Longridge, the bosun's mate waiting at the control point. Longridge obediently touched the power switch. Hydraulic motors hummed, tightening the fall along with three others. The topsail yard rose majestically into position.

Beauchamp clapped Daniel on the shoulder and gave him a thumb's-up. Schatt waved to Longridge, who responded with a dismissal signal; the three of them had worked well past the change of watch to finish changing out the block. Beauchamp was carrying the old block; it would have to be disassembled to determine where the damage was and whether it could be repaired.

They didn't wear safety lines. Most riggers didn't bother with them, and additional lines made working on the rigging itself almost impossible. They got tangled with the cable you were reeving or replacing.

Schatt and Beauchamp were riggers in their forties. They had met in the RCN while serving on the battleship *Revenge*. When she was put in ordinary after the Treaty of Amiens, they had come to Danziger together and had been enrolled in the naval arm of the Upholders of Tarbell Freedom.

They were solid spacers, men Daniel would have been glad to have in any crew under his command. Longridge, another former RCN spacer, had assigned the three of them to get the balky fall working.

The cable had several splices, which Schatt had said was the problem. Beauchamp had backed his partner against Daniel's opinion that the problem was in the block. When replacing the cable hadn't solved the problem, Daniel had neither complained nor said that he'd told them so. He'd volunteered to cut through the strop of the original block to remove it—a bitch of a job in free-fall.

Schatt opened the forward ventral airlock and led the way in, then initiated the lock-filling process when Beauchamp had closed the outer lock behind them. Daniel started unlatching his helmet as soon as he entered the lock and, with the others, took the helmet off when the chamber had reached half-pressure. No rigger ever waited for full pressure to build; seven or eight pounds was perfectly comfortable.

Beauchamp paused the mechanism, shutting the pump off. He looked at Daniel.

Daniel nodded with a faint smile. He didn't bother looking behind him because he knew he'd see Schatt watching at him with the same fixed grimness.

"Go ahead," Daniel said mildly.

"A lot of the spacers on *Upholder* are ex-RCN, Green," Beauchamp said.

"Right," said Daniel. About sixty percent of the present crew had come from the RCN. It was Krychek's way of hiding his—the Alliance's—involvement in the scheme. "I am too."

"The thing is . . ." Schatt said. His voice managed to sound grating even in the thin atmosphere. "Some of them say you look like Captain Daniel Leary. You've heard of him?"

"I have," Daniel said. "Go on."

"We been talking—you know, the crew; pretty much all of us," Beauchamp said. "We asked the spacers you came aboard with what they thought about it. And what they said was that it might be true."

"What do *you* say, Green?" Schatt said.

"I say that it might be true," Daniel said, still calm. He wished that Schatt were standing in front of him. He would like to have his smile as well as his voice keeping the situation positive, but he didn't think there would be a problem.

"Now," Daniel said. "You fellows have been asking me questions. Let me ask you one: how much do you love the rebel government, the Upholders?"

Beauchamp stepped past Daniel to put himself beside Schatt at the back of the lock. Daniel turned to face them.

"They pay good," Beauchamp said.

"Right," said Schatt. "And that wasn't always true with the RCN."

"Admiral Vocaine was afraid if spacers had their full pay at the end of a voyage," said Daniel, nodding in agreement, "that they'd manage to slip off-planet on a merchant ship instead of filling the next RCN slot Vocaine wanted them for."

"Did he worry my wife was going to ship out too?" Beauchamp snarled. "Though that's kinda what she did, left me for a chandler's clerk with regular pay."

"I wouldn't say the Upholders were much government, though," Schatt said. "Still, it's nice to get paid."

"What're you doing here?" said Beauchamp; the rough tone from describing his marriage was still in his voice. "Green, Leary, whatever your name is!"

"I looked at the situation and decided there might be money in it," Daniel said. He smiled more broadly.

"But you're rich," Schatt said, frowning. "Captain Leary's rich, anyway, from all that prize money. Are you saying you're not Leary after all?"

"What I'm saying..." said Daniel. "Is that there's a lot *more* money out there. More for me and more for anybody who serves with me. There's risk, too. You're old spacers, you know about risk."

"There's a lot of us RCN," Beauchamp said, choosing his words carefully. "But there's a lot who were Fleet too. And a lot who weren't either one. You know that, right?"

"Sure," said Daniel. "I said *anybody* who serves with me, I don't care who their last enlistment was with. I want spacers with guts, that's all. Do you two qualify?"

The riggers looked at one another. They were senior people, respected by their fellows. This had probably been arranged from the beginning, and Longridge wasn't the only other member of the crew who was in the business.

Instead of answering directly, Schatt said, "What would we have to do? If we wanted to, I mean?"

Daniel shrugged. "Your jobs, that's all for now," he said. "And maybe talk to your friends without giving them details. Just hint that this could be a really good thing for everybody."

"We don't *know* any details," Beauchamp said.

"That's true, you don't," Daniel agreed. "Which is best, don't you think? But you might just start wondering—"

His smile was as real as it was wide, because he was seeing his way clear to success.

"—about how much a heavy cruiser would bring in prize money, hey?"

He turned toward the inner hatch and restarted the pump.

The only possible problem was Captain Joycelyn, who struck Daniel as both smart and honorable. That was a job for Adele.

Or possibly for Tovera, which would be a pity; Daniel liked what he'd seen of Joycelyn. *But people die in wars*.

ABOVE ITHACA

Adele forwarded the coded message to Commander Braun just as her watch ended. Tovera stood beside the signals console, her face expressionless.

"Commander," Adele said on a two-way link. "I'm going off-duty. Over."

Braun's station was the astrogation console two places toward the bow from Adele in the portside rank. He grunted in response. Because of the link Adele heard him, but she wouldn't have prodded her superior for a proper acknowledgement regardless. She wasn't very interested in propriety herself, after all.

Tovera seated herself at the console as soon as Adele rose. "I'll be in my compartment," Adele said. She began to maneuver herself to the bridge hatch using the overhead railing.

On the *Sissie* she knew where the handholds were and more or less how much force to use in free-fall as she pushed herself from one to the next. The *Upholder* was still unfamiliar territory after a week aboard the ship, and she wasn't embarrassed to use the lubber line to navigate. She *was* a landlubber, for all that she had spent more time in space than some of the able spacers.

I have other skills.

The compartment Adele shared with Tovera and six spacers,

none of them former Sissies, was midway down the Level 1 corridor. The other personnel were spacers striking for a warrant rating. The bunks, two racks of four each, covered the outer bulkhead. The small stations on the corridor side were uncomfortable with more than four people trying to use them.

Adele had just entered the compartment when the speaker in the ceiling croaked, "Communicator Bethel! Report to Commander Braun at once in Compartment 124! Repeat, Communicator Bethel report at once!"

One of the sleeping spacers turned on his bunk and glanced at her; the other two did not. Adele showed no expression, but her mind was smiling in triumph. She went out to the corridor and began pulling herself forward again.

124 was Braun's own compartment, the size of the one Adele shared with seven other spacers. She tapped on the hatch, forgetting to hold on with her other hand. She was drifting backward as Braun jerked the hatch open.

He swore and tried to grab her by the wrist, but her feet touched the far wall of the corridor. She launched herself toward the hatch of 124. Fortunately for both of them, Braun got himself out of the hatchway in time to avoid a collision.

"You bloody fool, Bethel!" Braun said as he dogged the hatch behind them. "How can you have spent so many years in space and be so bloody clumsy?"

Because I'm skilled at my real job, Adele thought. Aloud she said, "Sorry, sir."

"Well, that doesn't matter for now," Braun said. "I want to know about this message from Coralville that you forwarded to me."

124 was double the size of a signals officer's compartment on a heavy cruiser. It held a fully functional console instead of a flat-plate display fed by a bridge console. The addition must have been made before Krychek turned the *Upholder* over to the rebels.

"I don't know what you mean, sir," Adele said, hoping that her lie sounded believable. "It appears to be a message sent by courier torpedo and downloaded to Harbor Control, then relayed to the *Upholder* when we linked with control when we returned to Ithaca orbit. It's in a nonstandard code, but I assumed it was one you had access to."

Of course Braun had access to it: it was the code he used to communicate with General Krychek, his immediate superior. The material which Grozhinski had provided couldn't predict which sequence the First Diocese would be using, but it offered alternatives which Adele had been able to refine when she got into Braun's console. She had done that as soon as Braun gave her access to the signals console.

"Yes, but when did it get here?" Braun said. "Get to Coralville, I mean. Can you tell that?"

"May I use this console?" Adele said, gesturing with her free hand to the unit she was holding on to so that she didn't drift off.

"Yes, yes!" Braun said, but Adele was already onto the couch. She strapped herself in and brought up all the messages which she had forwarded to Braun. She used the console controls directly instead of coupling through her data unit. That might concern Krychek's agent, though he knew that was how she handled the bridge console. He probably thought that his own console was protected against external entry.

"This string of numbers here..." Adele said, highlighting the line in pale blue for Braun. "Indicates that the message was received at Coral Harbor seven days ago, that would have been just after the *Upholder* transited out of the Ithaca system on the training cruise just ended."

What Adele said was true. In fact, however, she had downloaded the message with all its false routing data to Coral Harbor when the cruiser returned to Ithaca orbit.

"The origination data is this line," she continued, moving her highlight. "I would want to check, but I believe this is the locator for Ravenna."

The headquarters of the First Diocese was on Ravenna. Adele had added the qualifier because she might not have recognized the locator had she not added it to the counterfeit herself.

"Gods, gods..." Braun muttered. "A week!"

He was clinging to the back of the console so that he could look over Adele's shoulder. She found the situation uncomfortable, but she supposed it was really ideal for her purpose. Being uncomfortable was too familiar an experience for her to remark it.

"Is there a problem, sir?" Adele said blandly. She wondered if she should turn to face Braun, but that would have been unusual behavior for her. She instead brought up a miniature of his face on the holographic display.

"Why did the timing have to break this way?" Braun said in the tones of a man accusing the gods. "They'll think I've been doing nothing for a week and of course I haven't, I *couldn't* do anything. But are they going to believe that?"

"Who is going to believe that, sir?" Adele said. "You can't act on information you didn't receive, can you?"

The message was a directive under Krychek's personal signature to take immediate action against six agents of General Storn among the crew of the *Upholder*. They were all Alliance citizens and had served in the Fleet before being recruited by the Tarbell rebels. Captain Joycelyn was the most prominent, but the list included two lieutenants, the gunner, and two junior warrant officers on the Rig side.

They were personnel whom Daniel had decided were both loyal and capable—unlikely either to be turned or to be cowed by threats if the Sissies led a mutiny. They could be killed if necessary, but Adele had decided that it was simpler and even more effective to have the cruiser's political officer remove them at what he thought was Krychek's order.

"Look, you've probably guessed that I'm more than a signals officer," Braun said. He flung himself into a chair bolted to the deck and twisted his foot around it to stay seated. "I'm actually an investigator. They should have given me a proper staff, but I'm supposed to be undercover!"

Yes, you certainly are supposed to be undercover, Adele thought. Instead of blurting this to a stranger whose very competence should have raised red flags. She had intended the message to shock Braun, but she hadn't expected him to melt down like this.

Aloud Adele said, "Well, I think Selkirk and I have signals pretty well covered, so you don't have to worry about that part of your duties."

"I'm not worried about it!" Braun snarled. "I'm worried

because—because my headquarters ordered me to arrest six criminals a week ago and I just got the message now! And how am I supposed to arrest six people anyway?"

"Well, surely you can call on the ship's officers to help you, can't you?" Adele said. Another person would have enjoyed the situation, but she found that Braun's panicked incompetence made her queasy.

He should never have been put in the field. Adele wondered if the choice had been made because it got Braun out of somebody's office. *Krychek isn't being well served by his subordinates....*

"What if the ship's officers are the problem?" Braun said. "What then, hey?"

Adele met the angry man's eyes, wondering if he was about to explode into violence. Braun kept a pistol in a drawer of his console on the bridge, but he might well have one in his quarters as well.

"Well, we'll be on the ground in a few hours, won't we?" Adele said. "You can have the Shore Police waiting on the dock. You have some sort of authentication code to deal with the situation, don't you?"

Would you like me to bring it up on the screen for you? Adele thought. But even to think that meant that she was becoming really ill-tempered. She needed to be careful.

"Yes!" Braun said in sudden excitement. "So long as I've seen to the arrests before the, the criminals have gotten off the ship, it doesn't matter that the message was late being delivered to me!"

He stood and gripped the console. "You may go back to your compartment now, Bethel. Remember, there's a promotion in this for you."

"Thank you, sir," Adele said as she opened the hatch. Back in her quarters she would keep an eye on Braun's communications.

She had already decided that she would have a company of the Capital Defense Regiment on hand to back up the Shore Police. It was possible that some of those being arrested would consider resisting. Having overwhelming force on hand to deter such heroics was a good idea.

Adele was sure that Braun would claim the idea as his own after the fact.

CHAPTER 20

CORAL HARBOR ON ITHACA

The *Upholder*'s twenty-four thrusters roared at seventy-five percent output, beating the slip into steam and violence. The deck had a tilt serious enough that even Adele noticed it, indicating that the port/starboard thruster alignment wasn't as good as it should have been.

I've been spoiled, Adele thought wryly as she ran through her checklist of things she had to do before the *Upholder* lifted to orbit. She had gotten used to having Cory and Cazelet to handle part of such duties. She had also gotten used to an engineering crew run by Boris Pasternak, and overseen by Captain Daniel Leary.

"*All personnel prepare for liftoff!*" Captain Morseth announced. He had been commanding the destroyer *Justice* three days earlier. His sudden promotion and transfer to the heavy cruiser was in response to Captain Joycelyn's arrest. This was Morseth's first liftoff in his new command, so it was as much a shakedown cruise for him as for the *Upholder*.

"*Initiating liftoff!*" Morseth said. "*Increasing thruster output to full!*"

Adele carried out the last action on her list by locking out the antistarship missile batteries which defended Coral Harbor. This was sure to be discovered within an hour or two, even under a rebel command which wasn't as professional as would have been the case with an RCN installation. She had therefore waited to do it until the last instant.

Since Adele controlled the *Upholder*'s communications, it shouldn't be possible for anybody aboard the ship to request intervention when the Sissies moved to take over the vessel. Even if a signal did get out, the commanders on the ground wouldn't put a missile into the cruiser until they had spent a great deal of time trying to assess the situation.

Regardless, it was an easy precaution to take. Adele took it.

Cazelet was at present signals officer of the *Princess Cecile*, in orbit above Myrmidon, a nearby world now under rebel administration but too sparsely populated for that to matter. Cory was captain of the *Fisher 14*, which should be in what was supposed to be an uninhabited region of the surface of Myrmidon.

I don't need their help for anything here.

"*Lifting!*" Morseth said.

The roar of the thrusters sharpened as the captain sphinctered down the petals of the thrusters, focusing the exhaust into narrow jets. The *Upholder*, already rocking from side to side on a cushion of steam, began to rise.

Adele continued to work, running through her checklist for the next stage of the operation. A starship's acceleration was never abrupt, and the bigger the ship was, the more deliberate the process had to be.

The noise slackened. Though the console projected a sound-cancelling field, a ship vibrated violently even when its thrusters were perfectly balanced, causing the antennas and rigging to rattle against the hull. As soon as they had risen high enough that they were no longer buffeted by surface-reflected thrust, things smoothed out.

Adele reviewed the ship's spaces as they rose toward orbit. Normally that would not have been part of her duties.

All was well. Both rigging watches would go out on the hull to set the sails for the first time after liftoff. Port watch was in its bunks; starboard was at stations in the corridors where pull-out handgrips allowed them to anchor themselves against changes in thrust. This morning Woetjans—van Arp—had shifted all the Sissies to the starboard watch.

The High Drive motors started raggedly, for a moment adding their greater impetus to that of the plasma thrusters. The thrusters cut out to save reaction mass. The High Drives pushed the vessel along far more efficiently than thrusters, but in an atmosphere, antimatter which was exhausted without recombining would erode the motors themselves.

The normal altitude for switching propulsion on a habitable planet was about a hundred thousand feet, but there were many variables. The relative abundance of reaction mass and the relative wear state of the drive and thruster nozzles were generally factors, but the captain's whim might matter even more.

Thrusters vibrated in a deep note like heavy pumps. High Drive motors had a buzzing discharge like that of power hacksaws in steel; many people found the latter even more unpleasant. Adele worked through either. So long as she had a task in hand, nothing made a great difference.

"*Preparing to enter Ithaca orbit,*" Morseth announced.

Adele set a green telltale on the corner of Tovera's flat-plate display to alert her, then locked Commander Braun's console adjacent to her own. On a two-way link she said, "Commander, this is not a joke. The ship has been captured by agents of the Tarbell government."

"*What?*" said Braun. He touched the latch plate of the drawer holding his pistol and seemed surprised that it didn't open. Only then did he turn to look at Adele, holding the control wands of her data unit.

"Commander, don't move," Adele said. This was one of the times that she wished she could project emotion better; people hear emotion rather than words, even if the words are the difference between life and death. "If you move, you'll die."

"*I don't need a gun to take care of you!*" Braun said as he rose from his couch with his arms extending toward Adele. Tovera shot him through the temple. Wisps of hair flew. As Braun fell, Tovera shot him twice more through the back of the neck.

The High Drive shut off. Braun's corpse hit the deck, then bounced upward as the *Upholder* entered free-fall. Tovera was using a small pistol rather than the submachine gun which she preferred: a pistol for self-protection wouldn't raise eyebrows in a slightly built woman shipping in a starship's crew, but a submachine gun would have been hard to explain. The snap of the shots seemed to have gone unnoticed amid the High Drive's snarl.

Adele locked the port watch in their compartments, then idled all the bridge consoles except for her own. On the general push she said, "All hands. This ship has become an element of the Tarbell Stars navy. So long as everyone stays calm—"

The gunner's mate had replaced the arrested gunner. He stood up. He was an Ithaca native and young for his new rating.

Hale fired at him, trying for a head shot and missing. Her pellet disintegrated on the ceiling near one of the loudspeakers. Tovera shot the fellow twice through the top of his breastbone. He drifted upward. Two small blood splotches spurted toward the port bulkhead, driven by arterial pressure.

"Do not resist or you will die!" Adele said, hoping she sounded threatening or at least more threatening than she had managed so far. "No one needs to be harmed!"

Daniel sailed in through the bridge hatch while it was still cycling open at Adele's command. He touched the back of the missileer's console to correct his direction and gripped the command console, braking himself to a halt.

Hogg entered the bridge more like a boulder rolling downhill than as an acrobat like his master. *He's not any more agile in free-fall than I am*, Adele thought. On the other hand, Hogg would have been intimidating even without the knuckle-duster knife in his right hand.

"Captain Morseth," Daniel said; Adele piped the words on the general channel so that everyone aboard the cruiser would hear it. "I have to ask you to vacate the console. My name is Daniel Leary and I'm taking command of the *Upholder*."

Captain Morseth stood up. His face quivered like a frightened blancmange.

MYRMIDON: THE SOUTHERN HIGHLANDS

Cory had landed the *Fisher 14* on a high plain in Myrmidon's far south. Daniel and Vesey brought the *Upholder*—they'd obviously have to rename her now—and the *Princess Cecile* down on either side of the merchant vessel.

Daniel had mustered the crew into groups of twenty in the lee of the cruiser, each with coolers of beer and water. That was small enough that he could talk to them without amplification, but large enough that he could expect to get through over four hundred spacers in an acceptable length of time.

The wind blew bits of coarse soil into Daniel's face as he and Hogg walked toward the next section. It must have rained recently because the clumps of vegetation were in enthusiastic flower instead of huddling in woody tangles which tried to survive. There was probably an aquifer fed from the snowy mountains in the western distance, but it was too deep for the roots of these shrubs to penetrate.

Daniel had set no guards on the spacers. The Sissies and the former Upholders who had already signed on with the government were pulling normal maintenance on the two warships. The *Fisher 14* was back under her own Pleasaunce captain, Faenz. He and his crew were taking a relaxed attitude to the circumstances.

"Hello, Hijiro," Daniel said to a rigger he recognized by name among this twenty. "Sorry for the inconvenience, but I decided it was better to keep the port watch locked down for a couple days till I could get here and explain things."

"You don't have to explain!" a heavily built technician said.

His arms were tattooed from wrists to short sleeves, many of them including banners with the names of Fleet warships. "You're a bloody pirate and that's all there is to say!"

"I see where you're coming from . . ." A fragment of memory clicked into place at the right time; Daniel hadn't had time to learn the names of the whole crew, though he had made an effort. "Sobol, isn't it? I believe the matter is covered under the laws of war, though we won't argue. The ship there—"

He pointed with his whole arm.

"—the *Fisher 14* is ready to carry you and any of your fellows who want to leave to Danziger. You'll have to make your own way back to Ithaca because Captain Faenz refuses to land on a rebel world. He's a civilian simply hired for the job, but he's not sure he'd be treated that way by the folks we captured the cruiser from."

"Well, *I* want to go!" Sobol said, standing arms akimbo with his clenched fists on his hip bones. His arms were thickly muscled.

"Then so you shall," said Daniel. "But you'll listen for a moment first."

He hawked phlegm and spat behind him. "Hijiro?" he said. "I'd be grateful for a mug of that lager."

The little rigger grinned and refilled the mug he'd been drinking from. Daniel took a good swig from it. His throat really was dry—this was the seventh group he'd addressed; but it had also seemed like a good way to change the mood.

"The Tarbell government will pay you the same wages you've been earning from the rebels," Daniel said. "Most of you will keep your ratings and watches. There'll probably be a few transfers under your new officers, but I served alongside you long enough to know that this cruiser had a bloody good crew."

"I've met worse riggers, too," Hijiro said cheerfully. He was an able spacer, but Daniel had already decided that he was about to become a bosun's mate—though not necessarily on the *Upholder*.

"Now, the rebels probably told you it was going to be a walkover when they moved against Peltry—" Daniel said.

"Well, they would, wouldn't they?" called a man missing part of his left hand. They were getting into the spirit.

"Yes, they would," Daniel said, "but a month ago it really did look like the rebels were the smart-money bet. I can tell you it wouldn't have been a walkover, but when one side has a heavy cruiser and the other side had nothing bigger than a destroyer—well, that's long odds, isn't it?"

He grinned broadly. "It's still long odds," he said. "But it's the other way now."

There was general laughter. Even Sobol was grinning.

"Are you in command, then?" asked a tech, one of the few women in the *Upholder*'s crew. Daniel had seen her but didn't know her name.

"I'm the head of the navy of the Tarbell Stars," Daniel said, nodding with approval of a good question. "I report to the Minister of War, Christopher Robin, whom I can tell you is good. We had our differences at first, but we knocked some of the edges off each other—"

Adele had done that, but this was a recruiting speech rather than a debriefing.

"—and I can guarantee the ministry's full support."

Daniel paused and smiled broadly. "In theory Robin reports

to President Menandros," he said. "I don't guess anybody needs to hear my opinion of politicians, right? Regardless, I'm pretty sure the president won't try to get in the way."

There was more laughter. While Daniel waited for it to die down, he saw a glint of movement in the vegetation beyond the area which the cruiser's thrusters had burned off. It was a ripple of light which, when he focused, resolved into a flattened snakelike flyer with diaphanous wings and tail. It disappeared again into the brush.

Adele has probably downloaded natural history data on Myrmidon, but I've been too busy to think about it.

For a moment Daniel imagined a life in which he had leisure to really study the wonderful, unique life-forms of the planets he visited. Then he smiled again at the waiting spacers and said, "There's one more thing. Some of you have probably heard that my crews have been lucky with prize money. If you *haven't* heard that, talk to anybody who's served with me."

"How do you figure there'd be prize money now?" Sobol said. "Cruisers don't make prizes!"

"Pretty much true," Daniel said, nodding agreement. "But this cruiser *is* a prize, and every spacer in her crew gets a share of what the government buys her in for. I've got the minister's word on that, and you've got my word as a Leary!"

The gabble that followed was positive but too startled to be really loud. The crew was trying to take in what they'd just heard.

"*Every* spacer?" the woman said.

"Every spacer who takes service with the navy of the Tarbell Stars," said Daniel emphatically. "The share-out will be according to standard RCN rates—which is the same as the Fleet's if you came here by that door. I told you, the government's friends have deep pockets."

"And they've got you?" said Hijiro.

"Yes, they've got me," Daniel said, nodding. "*You*'ve got me if you enroll with the government."

He looked about the group again and said, "Now, any more questions?"

"How do we sign up?" asked a spacer who hadn't spoken before.

Daniel pointed to the cruiser's main hatch. "Right up there in the boarding hold," he said. "Hale and Woetjans are set up at a table to enroll you. Ah, you may remember them as Garrett and van Arp. For now you'll keep your original watch and berth, though there may be some sorting out after we arrive on Peltry."

There was still beer in the mug Hijiro had handed him. Daniel sloshed some of it around his dry mouth, then swallowed.

"One more thing, fellow spacers," he said. "You really are free to walk out of this whole business. Go over to the *Fisher 14* and tell Captain Faenz that he's to carry you back to Danziger. There's no paperwork, no questions: just leave."

Daniel finished the beer, gave the mug back to Hijiro. Spacers cheered as he and Hogg walked to the next group. The ones he'd been talking to headed in a straggling column toward the cruiser's boarding hold. Hijiro was leading, but Sobol was in the line with the others.

"How much of a passenger list do you guess Faenz is going to have?" Hogg said as they walked together. "Not long, I'd say."

Daniel was keeping an eye out for the flying creature he'd glimpsed, but it didn't show itself again. He wouldn't be able to make a real search before they lifted for Peltry, but at least he could see what the database had.

"There's two officers who were born on rebel worlds whom I'm not willing to trust," he said. "There'll probably be a couple others as well. Even so, we've not only added a heavy cruiser to the fleet, it comes with a crew of prime spacers."

All in all, this had been a very successful operation. But Daniel did wish that he could get a better view of that flying creature.

CHAPTER 21

NEWTOWN HARBOR ON PELTRY

Adele walked beside the Minister of War and General Bloemfontein as Daniel, leading with Admiral Quentin, made a broad gesture with his left hand. "Lady Mundy and gentlemen," he said. "The cruiser *Triomphante*, the most recent addition to the Navy of the Tarbell Stars. She'll win the war for us if we use her right."

Bloemfontein was the head of the army; Quentin had been head of the navy before Daniel's promotion. Adele had expected this briefing to be conducted in one of the ministry's conference rooms, but Daniel had decided that the quay alongside the just-captured cruiser would be better for their purpose.

"What kind of name is *Triomphante*?" Quentin said. "Not a Tarbell name, certainly. I think we ought to change it immediately!"

Quentin was a peppery little man with a brush moustache and hair dyed a brighter red than it had probably been in his youth. He was a Peltry native and had spent thirty years in merchant service before Robin had put him in charge of the navy. Quentin hadn't loudly objected to becoming subordinate to Captain Leary, but he wouldn't have been human if he hadn't felt *some* resentment.

"*I* chose the name, Quentin," said the minister. "Leary pointed out to me that she was *Triomphante* when she was a Fleet warship. Through skullduggery she was sold out of service as the *Gallissonniere*. By going back to her real name we're waving a flag at the crooks in the Alliance who sold out to the rebels."

Adele had made a thorough search of the ministry's databases. She was sure that Robin didn't know that General Krychek himself was working against the Tarbell Stars; Robin didn't even know the *name* of the First Diocese commandant. Neither was Robin sure of the forces supporting the Tarbell government.

The Upholders and the Tarbells were both pawns in a struggle of bureaucrats. Adele wondered what would happen if Christopher Robin realized that he was being manipulated by the Third Diocese of the Fifth Bureau rather than being supported by wealthy industrialists in both the Alliance and on Cinnabar.

Three antennas on the *Triomphante*'s spine and one on the starboard side toward the quay had been partially extended. Spacers and a number of dockyard personnel wearing orange tunics were crawled over them. Adele couldn't be sure, but it appeared that they were working on the joints as well as the rigging.

Daniel had chosen this location to emphasize the

Triomphante's size and power. The cruiser was impressive from where they stood, even to Adele, who had been close to larger ships during her RCN service. The two Tarbell aides gaped as they took in the massive hull, the triple missile launchers—three of the four sets were visible—and the turrets with paired fifteen-centimeter plasma cannon.

The turrets on the spine were raised and visible. The ventral pair were below the waterline and would have been retracted into the hull if the cruiser followed the practice Adele was familiar with on the *Princess Cecile*.

Christopher Robin was making a point of not displaying obvious amazement, but Adele thought he spoke in a reverent tone when he said, "Well, Leary...What *do* you consider the right way to use this warship?"

Daniel turned to face the minister, placing his arms akimbo. "By taking the fight to the enemy before they can respond to the change in circumstances," he said. "The rebels and the parties backing them have put all their hopes in their cruiser, *this* cruiser; *our* cruiser as she is now. Take a look at her and think of how you would feel if she were leading the rebel fleet."

"Well and good, Leary," Robin said, frowning. "But what do *we* do with her?"

"We set up a temporary base on a moon of the fourth planet of the Ithaca system," Daniel said. If they'd been in a proper conference room Adele would have provided a visual of the Ithaca system, but she didn't suppose that would have changed anything. "The *Triomphante* will keep station while the destroyers and corvette attack all ships trying to land or take off. We'll capture them if they surrender immediately but destroy them with gunfire if they try to get away."

"Are you mad?" said Quentin.

"Nothing in the Ithaca System is habitable except Ithaca itself," said Bloemfontein. "You can't put a base on a moon, there's either no atmosphere or methane."

"We'll use the *Montcalm* and *Montclare* as our temporary bases, living spaces for off-duty crew," Daniel said to the army chief, ignoring Quentin's blurted comment. "There's liquid water on two of the methane moons, not drinkable but fine for reaction mass. The transports will carry extra potable water as well as food for a three-month blockade. The rebels will cave before then. Remember, we'll have completely cut them off from the rest of the universe."

"That's crazy," Quentin said. From his tone that was his analysis rather than abuse; crudely put but a defensible position nonetheless. "The crews can't take being packed into a transport hold for that long! They'll all mutiny."

Though she didn't recall moving, Adele was seated on a bollard with her data unit in her lap. Proper use of the control wands required both hands, but they were enormously faster for an expert than any other input method.

Two moons of the giant fourth planet might qualify for a base, but one was so close to the primary that the surface was always dangerously unstable. The other was generally suitable, but the availability of liquid water limited the possible landing places.

She continued to search. This was Daniel's field and he'd certainly considered the relevant factors. Still, information was her business, even when it was redundant or apparently pointless.

"The crews of the lighter vessels won't mutiny while the

Triomphante remains solid," said Daniel with a brusque gesture. "I'll vouch for the cruiser's crew. For that matter, I'll vouch for the *Katchaturian*. Admiral, I think your personnel are of better quality than you do."

Christopher Robin had said nothing. Now he turned to Adele, who was focused on the data scrolling across her holographic display. He said, "Lady Mundy, what in your opinion should we do at this point? What should the Tarbell government's action be?"

Adele didn't look away from her display, but a twitch of her wands inset the minister's real-time image into a panorama of the surface of a moon in the Ithaca system. She wasn't so much gathering her thoughts as deciding on the phrasing.

Adele smiled minusculely.

Daniel hadn't been sure that Adele would look up from her display, but she did. Fixing her eyes on the Minister of War, she said, "I think the Tarbell government should take the course of action their expert recommends. Your expert in this matter is Captain Leary."

"Of course she'd say that!" Quentin snapped. "Look, I know Leary's a genius and walks on water, but use your common sense, Minister!"

"Minister, this is your decision of course," said Bloemfontein, frowning in agitation. "But it seems risky to me, very risky."

"Your opinions are noted," said Robin—without looking at his aides, and in a tone that wouldn't have encouraged Daniel to pursue the conversation. "Now, Lady Mundy: I phrased my question badly. Your record demonstrates your ability to analyze complex situations. On behalf of the government of the Tarbell Stars, please analyze the factors bearing on a government attack into the Ithaca system as Captain Leary outlined."

Adele looked at Daniel. He met her eyes, grinned, and said, "Please do so, Lady Mundy. I have more experience of your skill than the minister does—and therefore even more respect for your opinion."

Adele nodded twice, her eyes returning to her display. From Daniel's viewpoint it was a colored blur hanging in the air before her. Her wands flickered.

"Admiral Quentin is resentful of being superseded and would probably object to any proposal that comes from Captain Leary," Adele said. "Nevertheless—"

"Now just because I'm talking sense—" Quentin said.

"Quentin, shut up until I ask for your opinion!" Robin said without taking his eyes off Adele. Though he had sounded calm, even amused, when he talked to Adele, he was obviously keyed up by the situation. "Go on, Lady Mundy."

"Yes," said Adele. "Admiral Quentin is nevertheless more experienced in dealing with the quality of spacers to be found in the Tarbell Stars, while Captain Leary's experience is largely with RCN personnel. And if I might say so, with picked RCN personnel."

"Most of the *Triomphante*'s crew is ex-RCN, as I understand?" said Robin.

"The *Triomphante*'s crew is good material," Adele said, "but even that ship isn't properly worked up. In six months under Captain Leary the *Triomphante* would be as effective as any ship of its class in the human universe, but we're talking about today."

Daniel nodded. He was pretty sure that he could bring the cruiser up to full RCN standards in less than six months, but it was a valid point.

"Continue," said Robin. Quentin and Bloemfontein were watching blank-faced, surprised to realize that Lady Mundy was providing a real analysis. The Minister of War had examined her record, but his aides clearly had not.

"That isn't the real concern," Adele said as her wands moved and her display shimmered into a different pattern. "If the strengths of the parties remain as they are at present, Captain Leary will almost certainly bring the rebels to their knees as he expects. The rebels' off-planet backers cannot allow that to happen, however. Even if it means making their involvement manifest, they will have to change the odds."

"That's if they learn of the situation," Daniel said, frowning slightly. "While nothing is certain, I'm as sure as a human can be that we can prevent any ship from the surface of Ithaca from reaching the Matrix."

"That may be so," said Adele, her voice as emotionless as it had been when she described Quentin's jealousy. "The off-planet backers have sent vessels to Ithaca every seven to ten days since the beginning of the rebellion, however. Even if all incoming couriers are destroyed as soon as they become aware of the blockade, the sudden break in traffic will warn the principals almost as quickly as a message would."

She looked up, first at Daniel and then to Robin. "I must add," she said, "that there is a significant possibility that

Guarantor Porra is aware of what is going on and that he supports it."

"The Alliance is behind the rebellion?" Robin snapped.

"Lady Mundy spoke very precisely," Daniel said, jumping in before Adele could answer herself. She had been on good behavior thus far, but a serious misstatement of her own words might bring a sharper response than the minister was used to getting. "She identified the worst case and said that it was possible. I personally don't believe that Guarantor Porra is aware of the extent that members of his government might be involved."

"Yes," said Adele. "My data suggests that at worst the Guarantor might be willing to back a successful overthrow of the Tarbell government but that he would instantly disown a failure. We need to be sure that the rebellion fails, and that means not putting all our assets in a position to be destroyed by a quick stroke by the rebels with help from within the Alliance."

"If the Alliance is behind this, we don't have a chance," said Bloemfontein, sounding like he was practicing a dirge. "We may as well run now."

"If we surrender to the Alliance directly," Quentin said thoughtfully, "we may get better terms than the Upholders would give us. Particularly you, Minister."

"We haven't bloody lost!" Daniel said. "Lady Mundy just made the point that we mustn't give the rebels the easy opening that my plan provided. An excellent point, but it just means that we go at it a different way!"

Robin looked at him. Daniel met the minister's eyes calmly. *He can dismiss me, but I don't think he will. If he swings at me—*

Daniel grinned. He'd thought, *If he swings at me, I'll pull his arm off and beat him to death with it.*

Which suggested that he was getting a little edgy himself. The reminder settled him down.

Robin's face softened slightly as well. He turned to Adele and said, "Lady Mundy, you've outlined the problems with one course of action. What course of action would avoid the risks of the first course?"

"I told you before that I'm not competent to plan a naval campaign," Adele said sharply. For an instant she seemed about to take both control wands into her right hand, freeing her left. She saw Daniel's slight frown, nodded to him and smiled minusculely.

"Captain Leary?" she said. "What course of action do you recommend, based on the information now in your possession?"

"I suggest we move on Chevalier with the Tarbell navy and at least half, the better-trained half, of our ground forces," Daniel said. This had been his first thought after he reached Peltry with the ex-*Upholder*. "It's the closest rebel planet which has a real garrison. It'll provide live-fire training for the ground troops, and it'll give our fleet—"

The reality was barely a squadron, but this was a sales pitch.

"—experience in working as a unit under combat conditions."

"A victory on Chevalier would cut the rebels off from their bulk protein," Quentin said. "That's why they took it to begin with—the fisheries."

"And it would be, well, a *victory*," said Bloemfontein. "There haven't been many since the rebellion broke out. For them either, there hasn't been real fighting."

"What size is the rebel garrison?" asked Robin.

"About three thousand," Adele said, back at her display, "according to the figures in the Department of War in Coralville. Half of them are locally-raised and it isn't clear from the records that they're all armed."

"How did you get...?" Quentin began. He understood Daniel's broad grin and stopped there.

"We'll have nearly that many troops ourselves," Daniel said. "Ours will be concentrated, and we'll have the ships for fire support."

"How do you mean?" said Robin, frowning but not angry.

"You'll see," said Daniel. "I'll have my own officers demonstrate it first because we practice low-altitude maneuvers, but Chevalier will allow us to train all your crews. Short hops at low altitude aren't much of a trick."

That was a bit of an exaggeration, but he was still selling the idea.

"Excellent," said Robin, nodding. He looked at his aides and said in a harder voice, "I have planning to do, and I presume you gentlemen do also. Shall we get back to the ministry?"

"I'm going to check the *Princess Cecile*," Daniel said. "Lady Mundy, will you join me?"

Adele rose, slipping her data unit and its wands away as she did so. When they were a safe twenty feet from the Tarbell officials, she said, "I'm sorry, Daniel, if I misread your intent."

"You didn't," he said cheerfully. "I directed you to tell the truth, and you did so with the skill of long practice. Frankly, I hadn't been considering direct Alliance action as being as much of a danger as you've convinced me it is. Krychek may really feel that he's in a corner."

"Yes," said Adele. "He has a reputation for taking risks...
which is why we're here in the first place."

The *Princess Cecile* was moored directly beyond the cruiser
on this long quay. Daniel grinned reflexively as he saw her.
His ship.

"And to tell the truth," he said aloud, "most RCN officers
would have been as horrified as Quentin was. I'm glad you
said what you did."

"Most RCN officers..." Adele said, "don't have the
reputation Captain Daniel Leary does."

CHAPTER 22

CHEVALIER

The *Princess Cecile* thrashed and rattled as Daniel brought her through the atmosphere of Chevalier. The thrusters roared at very close to maximum braking effort. The corvette wasn't short of reaction mass, and there would be plenty of time to replenish what she used on her descent.

Daniel had set down many times on land rather than water, but he never forgot that it was a less forgiving surface. He was dropping at a more leisurely rate than he would if he had intended to land in the harbor.

Chevalier's settlement pattern was unique in Daniel's experience. The northern ice cap spread far toward the equator, while a belt of deep green covered the world's middle. Between ice and forest was a broad ring ocean bounded by a continent edged with lagoons.

Combrichon was one of the score of fishing communities located on those lagoons. Over a hundred trawlers were based there to harvest the schools of fish which browsed the nutrient-rich Northern Ocean. A branch of the low-speed maglev system connected Combrichon to the trunk line and thence to the capital and starport, Brownsville on Lake Eric, a freshwater sea to the south.

"Adele?" Daniel said, cueing the link. Their descent had stabilized: there was still buffeting, but the ship's course wouldn't need adjustment for at least several minutes. "Why isn't Brownsville on the ocean where most of the population is? The weather? Over."

"*No*," said Adele, as though she had been waiting for the question instead of correlating data gathered by the *Sissie*'s sensors from when they arrived in Chevalier orbit. "*The soil between the ring ocean and the highlands is a bog. Significant structures can't be safely built there without extensive pilings or being floated. It was simpler to locate the port on Lake Eric and build only shacks and light connector lines in the basin.*"

The *Princess Cecile* was low enough that terrain features were as clear as they could be through the scintillating plasma exhaust. The Northern Ocean lay to port. Near the shore its surface was green and bright blue with algae blooms.

Directly ahead the hull of either the *Montclare* or the *Montcalm* glinted above the treetops. Daniel adjusted the thruster angle three degrees forward to brake the *Sissie*'s forward motion to a shuddering crawl.

"*Six*," said Sun on the command link. "*There's tanks moving in the camp. May I lower the ventral turret, over?*"

"Negative, Guns," Daniel said as he opened the throttles slightly and returned the thruster angle to nearly vertical. The corvette moved slowly toward Combrichon, holding at three hundred feet above the rounded treetops. "We're coming in so low that you'll be able to use the dorsal guns if there's really any need, out."

Lowering the ventral turret would increase buffeting slightly, not a serious concern; slightly increase leakage of hot ions into the lower levels of the stern, also not serious; and risk damage to the High Drive motors on the outriggers. With some gunners that would be a serious danger, but Sun was skillful enough that it wasn't a concern here.

On the other hand, there was no need for the ventral pair of plasma cannon either. Gunners and missileers were proud of their weapons. They got very few opportunities to use them, so they wanted to make the most of those opportunities.

The two transports were in the lagoon, still wreathed in steam from their landing. The ex-Pantellarian destroyer *Mindello* lay between them and the town, and Schnitker had landed the *Katchaturian* across the maglev line just south of town. Schnitker had wanted to prove that he knew as much about coming down on dry land as any Cinnabar officer did.

That was probably true, though the boggy soil of northern Chevalier would be as forgiving as a normal slip. In any case the *Katchaturian* had come down neatly. With her bow turret aimed at Combrichon and the stern guns pointing down the maglev track along which any possible relief would have to come, the destroyer might have been enough by itself to convince the garrison to surrender.

It *might* have been enough. Daniel wasn't going to leave the matter to chance.

"Ship," Daniel warned over the general channel, "prepare

for landing. Do *not* open hatches, spacers. If a few slugs bang off the hull we're none the worse for it, but an open hatch will give the wogs an aiming point. Six out."

The *Princess Cecile* drifted above the western houses of Combrichon. All of them were wood-framed and many were roofed with wooden shakes, but Daniel didn't think that the corvette's plasma exhaust three hundred feet up was going to ignite them. If he was wrong, he would regret it—but he wouldn't lose sleep over the fires.

It was also possible that a brave man below with a stocked impeller could smash one or more of the thrusters while they glowed at high output. That was the reason Daniel hadn't even considered letting someone else bring the *Princess Cecile* in on this run. He was confident he could hold the ship against the sudden jolt of a thruster failing.

But it would take a *very* brave man to hold steady as he aimed into the blaze of white-hot ions.

The *Triomphante* with the destroyers *Albuquerque* and *Alfonso*, sister-ships of the *Mindello*, were in orbit to deal with any off-planet threat. The ships could also drop onto other communities quickly, but Daniel didn't see any reason to do that.

The only community more significant than Combrichon was the capital, Brownsville; it had a battery of antiship missiles. The Upholder garrisons in the ring of fishing communities kept them loyal, but the villages weren't really defended.

Kept the communities disloyal, Daniel supposed, since he commanded the navy of the Tarbell Stars.

He realigned the thrusters to vertical as he sphinctered the thruster nozzles open by ten percent without reducing the flow of reaction mass. The corvette dropped slowly without ever pausing in a hover.

Daniel had expected somebody to take a shot at them—out of cussedness if not for any military purpose—but the thick steel hull didn't ring at the impact of a slug. Spraying fiery tree limbs and clods of dirt baked to pebbles, the *Princess Cecile* landed in the park facing the town hall,. The vegetation had all been ornamental, too slender for a twelve-hundred-ton starship to notice as it came down.

If somebody had been picnicking in the park, Daniel sincerely hoped that they'd had sense enough to run as the *Sissie* came toward them. If they hadn't, they were probably well out of the gene pool—but he truly would regret it happening.

"Citizens of Combrichon!" Daniel said. "I am Captain Leary of the Tarbell Stars. You will not be harmed if you quietly return your allegiance to the Tarbell government,"

The speakers on the *Sissie*'s external hull were bellowing out his words, and he knew that Adele was transmitting them through the communications system of not only this town but also the entire planet. Combrichon was a lesson for Chevalier; more important, it was a lesson for the Upholder forces on Chevalier.

"Upholder troops who surrender will be treated according to the laws of war," Daniel said. "I'm a Leary of Bantry, and I say this on my honor."

The cooling thrusters and the *Sissie*'s reentry-heated hull drew a fierce wind off the lagoon, whipping the steam and smoke toward the two-story town hall. At first Daniel didn't see any human beings in the panorama which filled his display, but then movement and faces appeared at the windows of buildings.

"Some of you troops aren't rebels at all," Daniel said. "You're locals who got drafted when the rebels arrived and handed you guns. Throw your guns in the street and put on your civilian clothes again. If you do that, you're civilians in my book—but get rid of the guns *now*."

"*Six!*" Sun said. The dorsal turret rotated slightly, making the hull shiver. "*Tanks!*"

Daniel inset the gunnery screen on his own display. A pair of four-wheeled armored cars were driving up the road from the camp to the east, one ahead of the other. They had just come into sight of the *Sissie*'s dorsal turret.

"Upholder vehicles!" Daniel said. He hoped the cars had their own communications system, in which case he was bellowing directly to the crews. "Stop immediately and abandon your vehicles. Get out immediately!"

The second armored car stopped on the road. They didn't have turrets, just open-topped fighting compartments with an automatic impeller mounted on a pintle. They were police, not military vehicles and they were armored at most against small arms.

"Abandon your vehicles!" Daniel repeated.

Two people in uniform got out of the rear car and started running back the way they had driven. The leading car tried to turn around.

"Guns, hit 'em!" Daniel ordered.

The left four-inch cannon CLANGed. The leading armored car detonated. The bolt of ions had ignited everything in the vehicle which could burn, including the steel armor at the point of impact. The initial white flash swelled to an orange fireball twenty feet in diameter.

The plasma cannon's heavy iridium tube recoiled in its carriage, which in turn shook the whole ship like a giant sledge hitting a twelve-hundred-ton anvil. The shells loaded into the breech contained a bead of tritium in the center of a circular array of lasers whose only gap aligned with the center of the gun bore. When the lasers tripped simultaneously, they compressed the tritium into a tiny thermonuclear explosion vented out the barrel.

In hard vacuum, the jet of charged particles was very nearly as linear as a beam of light. In air, as here, the plasma scattered and quenched in a matter of hundreds or thousands of yards depending on the size of the bolt and the density of the atmosphere. The armored car was near the edge of the *Sissie*'s effective range—but still within.

The right-hand gun fired an instant after the left, a second aimed shot rather than a burst as Sun would fire if he were trying to nudge an oncoming missile out of its course toward the *Princess Cecile*. That was the strictly defensive task for which the plasma cannon were intended, but Daniel had realized early in his career that the ion bolts were devastating to ground targets.

Use in an atmosphere eroded gun bores very quickly, which Daniel regarded as simply the cost of doing business. Lethal business.

The halted vehicle exploded. Both running men fell down. One rose and staggered on, but the other continued to lie in the road. His uniform burned with smudgy black flames.

"Cease fire!" Daniel ordered. "Cease fire!"

Sun had already locked his tubes on Safe. Jets of liquid nitrogen were injected into the bores to cool the iridium and clear the tubes of debris.

Several houses were afire near the road where the cars had exploded. They could have been ignited by either side-scatter along the plasma track or by flaming fragments of the targets.

"Citizens and garrison of Combrichon!" Daniel said. "Surrender immediately or face complete annihilation!"

There was movement at the town hall. Somebody was waving a white cloth, probably a jacket. It had no pole, but it was good enough for the purpose so far as Daniel was concerned.

"All Tarbell forces, cease firing!" Daniel ordered. So far as he could tell, the *Princess Cecile* had done all the shooting there had been, but his words were as much to reassure the locals as they were for his own forces. "Break. Citizens of Combrichon, we'll open the ship in a few minutes. Prepare to send a delegation to make your surrender. Tarbell Navy out!"

BROWNSVILLE ON CHEVALIER

Adele sat at the head of the table in the Legislative Chamber. Master Jenshotz, Secretary to the Legislature, sat at her immediate left; Masters Plantin and Trenody, the president of Chevalier and the Upholder-appointed governor, sat in the bottom two of the four chairs to her right; and the figures on the huge, clumsy mural of Chevalier's settlement stared down at Adele from the end wall.

"The wife of the third-previous president, that was Henrik Hondius, painted it," Jenshotz said. He was a cheerful little man, a civil servant rather than a politician. "She was paid three thousand gulders, if you can believe that."

"I'm no judge of art," Adele said, looking hard at the painting. At least she understood now why it was there.

"Neither was she!" Jenshotz said with a cackle. "But by reputation she was a shrewd judge of a gulder!"

Another starship was landing in Chevalier Harbor. The *Triomphante* half an hour earlier had been deafening, but this lighter ship was merely background noise.

"Look, did you drag me out of my bed to discuss art?" Plantin demanded. His short beard and what hair remained behind his receding forehead would have looked better gray than the glossy black he had dyed them.

"No, Master Plantin," Adele said. She shrank her display so that she could look directly at the former official. It was a bit of theater prompted by her irritation at Plantin's attitude; she had a job to do, but if the former president had been courteous and perhaps contrite, she wouldn't have chosen to remind him of what and where he was. "First, because I'm informed that you were dragged out not from your bed but from your mistress's closet—"

"So true!" called one of the spacers from the legislators' seats on a dais above the central table for the officers. "And she was a right pig, too."

There was general laughter. Adele hadn't closed this interview. Most of the spacers whom Cazelet had directed to the officials' hiding places had stayed to listen to what happened next. There were others in the audience as well, including half a dozen civilians.

"Besides that obvious point," Adele said, "you're here to discuss gulders. Both of you appear to maintain several accounts which, though they draw from the Treasury, are for your private use."

"I knew it!" said Jenshotz. "But however were you able to find it so quickly, your Ladyship?"

"I'm told that it wasn't difficult," said Adele, "and that I could have found the accounts myself. In fact it was the work of Lieutenant Cazelet, who has accounting experience from his civilian career."

She nodded to Cazelet. He sat in the upper tier of seats with the spectators.

Plantin was swallowing repeatedly. Trenody, a younger man, leaned forward with a guarded expression. "Your Ladyship," he said. "Without discussing the possibility of accounting errors..."

He paused and raised an eyebrow.

Adele nodded. "Go ahead," she said.

"Wouldn't questions of past finances be matters for the local government?"

"Yes," said Adele. "Now that Chevalier has returned to the jurisdiction of the Tarbell Stars, I represent that local government until—"

"Ma'am?" called Sun from the chamber's outer door. "Robin's here from the *Triomphante*, the minister, you know? You want we should let him in?"

"Yes, thank you, Sun," Adele said.

Sun lowered his submachine gun. A moment later Minister

Robin bustled in with medals glittering on both breasts of his white uniform. He was obviously working to compose his lips into a smile.

"Your guards take their job seriously, Lady Mundy," Robin said as he walked past the spectators. He was trying to speak in a light tone, but his face was flushed.

"Yes," said Adele. "They aren't skilled in ceremony, but the four at the door are all good shots. And if they're afraid of anything, I haven't seen the evidence."

"That's as it should be, of course," Robin said. This time the smile was more or less real. "For a fighting man like Captain Leary, that is."

He looked at the civilians and said, "Speaking of Captain Leary, I expected to find him here."

"Captain Leary is reviewing the military side of the previous administration," Adele said. "These gentlemen"—she nodded to Trenody and Plantin—"are about to transfer all their private assets to the government of the Tarbell Stars. What further punishment they'll receive depends on your decision, Minister, and that of the president."

"All assets?" Plantin cried, jumping to his feet. "Now, there may be some question about—"

Onofrio, a rigger who'd been in the arrest squad, leaned over the railing and jabbed his stocked impeller like a spear. The muzzle prodded Plantin onto the table.

"Watch your tongue when you're talking to the mistress, wog!" Onofrio said.

Spectators laughed and cheered. The most enthusiastic were three old civilians who sat together.

Plantin edged around to the left side of the table without speaking. He seemed terrified.

Robin sat down across from Jenshotz. He looked at Adele and said quietly, "I suppose he would do the same to me?"

Adele glanced at Onofrio, who was chuckling with the other Sissies. "I don't know," she said. "Certainly my mother wouldn't have approved of Onofrio's manners or bearing."

After considering the matter, she added, "On the other hand, I don't think you would try to badger me the way Master Plantin did."

Robin grinned across the table at Plantin. "No, Lady Mundy," he said. "I would not."

An alert flashed red on Adele's display. She brought the screen back to full size. Cazelet's purple-bordered text crawled across the bottom: MAJOR GROZHINSKI IS LEAVING THE HARBOR. REQUESTS URGENT PRIVATE MEETING WITH YOU.

Adele shut down her data unit and rose from the chair. "Cazelet, inform him that we'll meet at the Founder's Statue in front of the building, then take my place here. And tell Captain Leary to join me!"

She started up the steps toward the door out of the chamber. Tovera silently fell in behind.

"Is there a problem?" Robin called from behind them.

"I don't know," Adele said without looking around. "If there is, we will deal with it."

CHAPTER 23

BROWNSVILLE ON CHEVALIER

"Ma'am, anything up?" Tech 3 Mullins called as Adele strode past.

"I need to meet a man," Adele said. "I don't expect that it will break the monotony. Sorry."

Mullins was in charge of the squad of armed spacers on the porch of the Legislative Building. They were a mixed group of Sissies and Tarbells, including two whom Adele recognized from the *Triomphante*'s crew.

Daniel had placed the guards there "in case." Chevalier had never been a rebel planet in the sense that any of the locals cared who was running the cluster government, but Adele agreed that some of the functionaries sent here by the Upholders might become violent if they saw the opportunity.

The reality Adele had found was that the Upholders had sent these particular functionaries to Chevalier to get rid of them. As far as she could tell from a quick pass over the records, Trenody was the only one who had enough ambition to steal on a large scale. There wasn't going to be a counter-coup against the Tarbell government.

The rectangular plaza in front of the Legislative Building had several flower borders—Adele assumed they would be flowers when they were blooming—and trees at the four corners. There was a gazebo at one end; at the other was a statue of Carlos Dumont, Knight of Benoit—the settlement leader.

Adele had picked the statue as a meeting place because she hadn't remembered the gazebo. When Grozhinski and Daniel arrived, they could move there or wherever her colleagues wished.

The trees at the four corners of the park had straight trunks and limbs that reared upward at a sharp angle. Wispy foliage covered the upper surfaces like fine reddish fur.

Adele suddenly wondered if the trees in the park at Combrichon had been of the same species. The *Sissie* had totally destroyed them in landing, but the video log should have a record.

She called up the log on her data unit. It was suddenly very important to her that there still be some record of what was gone, what was dead, what had been blasted to blazing splinters.

"Adele?" called Daniel from close at hand.

She looked up. They were alone save for servants, so he hadn't bothered with the polite formality of calling her Officer Mundy. There was guarded concern in his expression.

"Daniel," she said, "are these trees—"

She nodded toward the nearest corner.

"—the same as the ones where we landed in Combrichon?"

"No," Daniel said, looking over his shoulder. He didn't ask why she wanted to know. "These are native to Grenadine.

That park in Combrichon was all local vegetation. I guess they'll have to replant now, and they might want to haul in dirt. We tore up what was there pretty bad with the thrusters."

He faced Adele again and said, "I've seen trees like these on other planets, mostly Alliance worlds. They don't grow higher than forty feet or so, they don't spread, they're really very adaptable to weather—you probably think the limbs would break in heavy snow, but they just bend down and clear themselves. And I suppose some people like the color better than I do."

"Thank you, Daniel," Adele said. "Those trees at Combrichon still exist so long as you do."

He frowned. He said, "Well, there was nothing very important about them to begin with, you know. Or these either—"

He gestured with his thumb.

"—to tell the truth."

"That's quite true," Adele said, thinking of Colonel Colmard's body flying backward in a spasm. "No one needs to be concerned about it, not really."

Hogg and Tovera stood side by side at the base of the statue, but facing in opposite directions so that they looked both ways as they chatted. It was a fortunate thing for everyone, not least the Republic of Cinnabar, that the two very different servants got along so well together. So long as their masters worked as a team, so did Tovera and Hogg.

"Good morning, Major," said Daniel, calling Adele's attention to the man in spacers' slops walking briskly toward them. She tended not to notice people unless they were images on a display. "I gather there's a problem?"

"You might say that," Grozhinski said. When he stepped close enough to be able to talk quietly, Adele noticed the bite of ozone clinging to him. "Krychek has provided the Upholders with a battleship."

"Umm," said Daniel. "Which battleship is that?"

"The *Almirante* from Karst service," said Grozhinski. "In fact she's still *in* Karst service officially, but she'll be cooperating with the Upholder forces. She has a Karst crew— Krychek wouldn't otherwise be able to crew her and work her up in less than six months."

Adele projected holographic data on the *Almirante* for them. She chose to use RCN files for the purpose. When the battleship came into service fifteen years ago, Cinnabar and Karst had been close allies for decades. It was possible that the Alliance had better data on the ship's current state, but Adele was supplying the first ten years of its history.

Grozhinski looked at her in surprise. "Ah, yes," he said. "I was given files to deliver to Captain Leary, but they aren't— well, they certainly aren't *more* complete."

"What do you know about her crew and condition?" Daniel asked.

"Undercrewed, probably by about twenty percent," Grozhinski said. "The captain, Staples, is one of Karst's most senior officers and has combat experience as a lieutenant."

He smiled faintly and added, "Against Fleet destroyers in the Battle off Sugarball."

"Twenty percent short is as nearly a full crew as any RCN battleship could manage during the recent war," Daniel shrugged. "They may not be as maneuverable over a long run than they might be, but it won't affect their combat effectiveness in the sidereal universe."

"And their magazines are only half full," Grozhinski said. "Of course, that was true of the *Upholder* as well."

"And still is true of the *Triomphante*," Daniel said, "but..."

He grinned at Adele. She smiled back, though she knew that Grozhinski might not be able to read her expression.

"Major," Daniel said, "you can tell your principal that I have an idea, but it will take some planning to execute. And I'll need to meet with the Minister of War before I put it to my officers, because there's a degree of risk to this. Are you willing to join me in the discussion with Robin? Because I'd like him to be sure that his backers are fully behind me when I talk to him. If you are?"

"Captain Leary," Grozhinski said. "General Storn directed me to support you in any way I could. I'll do anything you request."

He smiled broadly. "Besides," he added, "I trust you as completely as the general does. Let's find the minister."

"Hello, Sun," said Daniel as he walked out of the elevator ahead of Adele, Grozhinski, and the servants. "Is Minister Robin still in the chamber?"

"He sure is," said the gunner. "He's talking to the secretary; the other two went off to the brig under guard."

He scowled with sudden concern. "Say, that's all right, isn't it, ma'am? I mean the secretary, I don't guess any of us care about wogs going to the brig."

"That's fine, Sun," Adele said. "I'm sure Master Jenshotz has entertained the minister usefully."

Daniel stepped into the doorway. The discussion had caused Robin to turn from the table where he and the Secretary were looking at something on the integral display.

"Minister?" Daniel called. "We'd like to discuss something with you in the reviewing balcony facing the park."

"We?" said Robin without rising. Grozhinski moved into the doorway so that Robin could see him.

"Ah, yes. I didn't know you were here," said Robin. He got to his feet and followed Daniel across the lobby to the glazed double doors opening onto the third-floor loggia. The minister entered with Daniel, Adele and Grozhinski, while Hogg and Tovera closed the doors behind them waited in the lobby.

Daniel glanced over the railing and into the park thirty feet below. He turned to his companions and said, "I suppose someone could train a parabolic microphone on us, but I don't think that's going to be a problem. I see only two men in the gazebo, and they're passing a bottle back and forth."

"Have you been here all along, Grozhinski?" Robin asked. There were chairs in the loggia, but only Adele sat down.

"No," said Daniel. "He just brought us warning that the Upholders have acquired a Karst battleship, though we're not sure on what terms yet."

When they met in the park, he'd caught a whiff of ozone clinging to Grozhinski's clothing: the major must have crossed the boarding bridge only a moment after the crew had extended it. That had either been insanely dangerous— the ions were literally blinding at that stage—so Grozhinski had either been blinkered by goggles or he was as confidently sure-footed as a rigger.

I wonder what Fifth Bureau training amounts to? Daniel thought, though Grozhinski might be a special case.

"A battleship?" Robin said. "A *battleship*? Good gods, what can we do about that?"

"Well, I think we can handle this, Minister," Daniel said. He kept his tone professionally upbeat; that really was the way he felt about the situation, though when he *thought* about it rather than feeling, he knew that there were quite a lot of problems. "We'll need to move promptly, but that's always a good idea in wartime."

Daniel stood with his back to the railing, looking past Robin's shoulder through the glass doors into the lobby. An officer in Tarbell uniform whom Daniel didn't recognize got out of the elevator, talked to another officer in the lobby, and strode purposefully toward the minister. On the other side of the door, Hogg shifted into the path of the Tarbell officer.

"Move how?" Robin said. His face was getting red. "Run, do you mean? That's easy enough for a Cinnabar citizen, but it might prove more difficult for me!"

The discussion in the lobby seemed on the verge of becoming heated. Several armed Sissies came out of the legislative chamber and headed for the Tarbell officer.

Adele's lips moved in her version of a smile, though she didn't look up from her display. Daniel remembered that Cazelet was in the legislative chamber.

"I wasn't hired to run from a fight, Minister," Daniel said, hoping that his tone hadn't been too sharp. "Especially a fight I think we can win."

"The *Almirante*, the Karst battleship," said Grozhinski

briskly, "is poorly equipped. Her missile magazines are only half full, and Karst missiles are single-motor units. There are still nearly three hundred Alliance missiles on Danziger. The rebels' first operation will be to load with those missiles."

"You said they wouldn't dare do that because it would expose their backers," Robin said, looking from Grozhinski to Daniel and back again. His voice was under control but the fear—or anger—underlying it was obvious.

"They will be willing to go public now," said Grozhinski. "At the point they arranged for the battleship, they gave up all chance of keeping their operations secret in the long run. Now their only chance of survival is to gain a total victory and offer the Tarbell Stars as a possession to Guarantor Porra."

"That'll mean war with Cinnabar!" Robin said, sounding desperate. "Porra will never do that!"

"You're more certain about Guarantor Porra's intentions than I am, Minister," Grozhinski said. "And I have spoken with him on several occasions."

Is that true? Daniel thought. It well might be. In any case, it was a perfectly believable statement which gave weight to Grozhinski's words.

"Are you going to push for your original plan of attacking the Ithaca System, Leary?" Robin said. "It was suicide then and it's even crazier now, even if the battleship is on Danziger for the moment! I *won't* allow it. Better to run!"

"I wonder..." said Major Grozhinski, looking at his well-manicured fingernails, "where you expect to run to, Minister? Because you won't have any friends in Alliance space, I assure you, and deserting Captain Leary and his backers pretty thoroughly cuts you off from Cinnabar and its possessions also."

"The question doesn't arise, Major," Daniel said, smiling at Grozhinski and hoping that Minister Robin would find his expression reassuring. "Placing our fleet in the Ithaca System and waiting for the *Almirante* to attack us would indeed be crazy. What I propose to do if we can agree here—"

He dipped his head to Robin in deference.

"—is to attack the *Almirante* at Danziger, where they won't be expecting us."

"Captain Leary and I have discussed his plan," Grozhinski said, nodding solemnly. "I think it has an excellent chance of success—"

That was an overstatement, unless Grozhinski had more confidence than Daniel himself did.

"—and in any case will convince my principals—who are your backers in the Alliance, Minister—"

Another nod.

"—that we've done all that was possible and that we can't be held responsible for the failure."

We're giving you back your bolthole.

"But can you defeat a battleship with a cruiser, even if you do take it by surprise?" Robin said. He still sounded doubtful, but there seemed to be a hint of hope in his voice.

"We'll be attacking the *Almirante* with three heavy cruisers," Daniel said with more certainty than he felt. "At any rate, the Upholders will think we are. Lady Mundy assures me—"

Adele looked up from her display and nodded to Robin, then went back to the display.

"—that she can give the electronic signatures of RCN heavy

cruisers to the transports *Montclare* and *Montcalm*. We'll make other modifications also to aid in the deception. My hope and expectation is that the *Almirante*'s Karst captain and crew will be unwilling to face what they believe to be an RCN squadron."

Robin's eyes narrowed. He was over the initial fright of learning that the Upholders had a battleship. He had returned to being the canny politician who had made himself the effective leader of a cluster in which he was an outsider.

"Lady Mundy?" he said, shifting his gaze. "What is *your* analysis of this plan?"

Adele looked up, then back at whatever she was examining on her display. "I think it has a reasonable chance of success," she said. "Captain Staples doesn't have a history of taking great risks, and he's sophisticated enough to know that attacking a pair of RCN cruisers will mean at least a Cinnabar punitive expedition directed at Karst. The interests of Karst aren't those of the Upholders or of the outside backers of the Upholders."

"But would you recommend that I *take* this action?" Robin said, sounding a little testy. He had wanted a yes-or-no answer and had gotten a nuanced one instead.

"Yes," Adele said. Her tone sounded thin also. "It appears to be the only way of accomplishing your objective of putting down the Upholder Rebellion. At any rate, *I* don't see another way."

Of course Adele doesn't give any weight to the risk to her personal safety.

"I see..." said Robin, who was probably beginning to. "Leary, will we return to Peltry before proceeding to Danziger?"

"No, sir," said Daniel. "That would add a week to our

transit time, and we're cutting it close as is. I really want to be in position when the Upholders arrive."

"But for reinforcements?" Robin said, frowning. "We weren't prepared to attack a battleship when we set off for Chevalier."

"No, sir," Daniel said. He was feeling buoyant as he considered the coming maneuvers. "But I've checked the stores here and aboard the *Triomphante*. We have sufficient for our purposes—and as for reinforcements on Peltry, there are none. None of the ships are serviceable, and I've taken all the spacers I'd want in a fight to crew our squadron here."

He was always this way at the beginning of a project, facing a complicated game with infinite possibilities. It might have terrified him, but instead it made him feel alive.

"Ah, Minister . . . ?" he added, suddenly considering another factor. "There are commercial ships in harbor here. We can commandeer one and put in a naval crew to get you back to Peltry so that you can resume your duties. Sir."

"I'm not a coward, Leary!" the minister said. "This is new to me, the whole way of thinking is new to me, but I'm not afraid!"

No one spoke for a moment.

"Very well, then," Robin said calmly. "Since you're all convinced this is the correct course, it's settled. I'll be aboard the *Triomphante* and in titular command of the squadron, but I know better than to interfere with any orders Captain Leary gives. Is that satisfactory?"

"Yes, sir," said Daniel. "Now it's just a matter for me and the rest of your navy to put down a rebellion for you."

"Then let's get to work," Robin said. He opened the glass doors and led the way back into the lobby.

The Tarbell officer who had tried to break in on the meeting was now sitting across the lobby; he popped up from his chair. Yahn, a tech from the *Sissie*, put a big hand on the fellow's shoulder and pushed him back. Beatty, on the other side of the Tarbell's chair, glowered down at the fellow.

"That's all right, Yahn," Daniel called. "He's the minister's problem now."

Robin gave him a crooked smile and went off to meet the officer. Daniel followed him with his eyes.

Hogg stepped between Daniel and the man walking toward him from the wall between the elevators, "Hello, Joycelyn!" he called. "I didn't expect to see you again."

Daniel looked past Hogg's shoulder; the servant had his right hand in his pocket. Captain Joycelyn, whom Daniel had last seen being frog-marched off the *Triomphante* on Ithaca, was wearing a Fleet utility uniform.

Joycelyn stopped, smiling, with his hands in plain sight. He said, "Hello, Master Hogg. I'm here because I hope to get a job with Captain Leary. It seems only fair, since he worked for me at one time."

"It's all right, Hogg," Daniel said. "I don't think Captain Joycelyn is the sort to pull a pistol on me."

He chuckled, hoping that he was right. Joycelyn had probably thought the same about him when he greeted the draft of Sissies aboard the *Upholder*.

"There are chairs on the loggia," said Adele. She made a curt gesture, drawing Daniel's attention to the group of people clustering around them, many of them locals. "I suggest we adjourn there to continue this discussion."

"Excellent idea," said Daniel, stepping back into the covered balcony.

"I'll leave you now," said Grozhinski. He strode toward the stairs, though the doors of one of the elevators were open on this floor.

Joycelyn nodded Adele ahead of him, then followed. Hogg would have come out with them, but Daniel shook his head and closed the glass doors.

"Hogg did bring up a good point, Captain," Daniel said, looking at his former commander. "How is it that you come to be here on Combrichon?"

Joycelyn struck a formal at-ease posture, his hands crossed behind his back. "Leary," he said, "I had a destroyer flotilla in the past war. I got a job as operations manager of a trading line when I wound up on the beach after the Treaty of Amiens, but boredom was driving me mad. When a friend in the Fleet Directorate told me that the Tarbell rebels were looking for an experienced captain, I made inquiries and was hired immediately."

"I can understand that, Captain," Daniel said. "But that doesn't explain why you're *here*."

"I joined the Upholders to fight," Joycelyn said. "I know you can understand that. And at the first rumor they decided I was disloyal and jailed me—until you stole the cruiser and they figured out what had happened. With *my* record, they thought I was a traitor!"

"They're traitors themselves, Captain Joycelyn," Adele said from her chair. She continued to adjust her display. "They see themselves in a mirror."

Joycelyn grimaced, then shrugged. "I suppose you're right," he said. "Anyway, when they released me, I decided I didn't want to work for them any more and headed for Danziger. When I heard that Captain Daniel Leary of the RCN had attacked Combrichon with the *Triomphante*, I signed on as second mate on a freighter to Brownsville. If you've got a use for a fighting officer, Leary, it'll save me having to learn how to pack frozen fish for transit back to Danziger."

"I *can* use an officer of your caliber, Captain…" Daniel said. "But before you make a decision, you should know that the rebels have bought or been given a Karst battleship. I intend to fight her."

Joycelyn raised an eyebrow. "We were told that there were people behind us," he said. "When I was with the Upholders, I mean. I didn't expect it to be Karst, though."

He shrugged. "I don't have any higher opinion of the Karst navy than you seem to, Leary," Joycelyn said. "I'm with you if you'll have me."

Daniel reached out and shook Joycelyn's hand. "Welcome aboard, Captain," he said. "I don't know yet where I'll place you, but I do know that you'll be better than whoever would have the job otherwise!"

CHAPTER 24

CHEVALIER, SOUTHERN HEMISPHERE

Reasonably, Daniel should have held this officers' meeting in the *Triomphante*'s large stateroom, though at least the Sissies present would have approved if he'd chosen the bridge of the *Princess Cecile* for sentimental reasons.

Hogg was probably the only person present who understood why they were standing in a glade overlooking the lake on which the ships of the Tarbell squadron floated. The foliage of the native trees was dark blue-green, nothing like the chartreuse of Bantry's vegetation, and the individual leaves formed long curling strips rather than flat quadrilaterals with sharp corners. Nonetheless it was a chance to be outside on a beautiful day, in a wilderness which had been completely untouched until the squadron arrived.

Now the forest on the north end of the lake had been cut to provide platforms, temporary shelters, and the rafts by which spacers were transferring spars and sail fabric from the *Triomphante* to the *Montclare* and *Montcalm*.

"Are we going to have enough sails?" said Cory, frowning at the bustling activity in the near distance. He was using the display of his personal data unit as a magnifier.

"Yes, I think so," said Daniel with an enthusiasm which was only partly assumed. "We'll want to keep the transports bow-on to the *Almirante*, but we'd be doing that anyway. I don't think we need be concerned about the sensor packs of the rebel destroyers."

"The *Ithaca* isn't new," said Captain Joycelyn, "but Lieutenant von der Main is a very good officer and she's got a crew of Fleet veterans. I don't think you should write her off as a fighting force. You can say what you please about the *Truth* and *Justice*, though, and I won't argue with you."

"The battleship's communications," Adele said, "are almost certainly set to Karst codes and protocols. The *Ithaca* is operating on rebel codes, which are a variant on a commercial code which is standard in this region. If it were the other way around there wouldn't be a problem, but I very much doubt a Karst crew will immediately adapt to unfamiliar codes and procedures."

"You're saying that the destroyers can't talk to the *Almirante*?" Vesey said. Her tone was neutral, but a slight frown suggested her doubts.

"They can talk in clear," said Cory. "And if the *Ithaca* is as good as the captain says, they may have Karst codes downloaded."

"She's a destroyer," Cazelet said sharply. "Yes, I know, the *Sissie* is a corvette, but you can't judge small-ship communications by Lady Mundy."

How much pain is he in? Daniel thought.

Though some of what he read as Cazelet's recent bitterness might have a psychological rather than a physical cause. Major surgery when the *Princess Cecile* had returned to Xenos could lengthen his femur, but according to Tovera, Cazelet would never again have full feeling and movement in his right leg.

"A battle involves risks," Daniel said. "Under normal circumstances we'd simply assume that the enemy ships could communicate with one another, so I don't see that we've anything to complain about if that's the case here."

He looked around the group of officers. The biggest question he was facing now was whom to place as captains on the vessels of his squadron, and—he grinned—as with most important questions, there wasn't a good answer to that.

Overhead three creatures circled. They were so high that with his naked eyes he saw only the light rippling from their diaphanous wings. The database said they had exoskeletons, but internal struts provided stiffening and muscle attachment points.

Not for the first time, Daniel thought of a life in which Daniel Leary was a field biologist, accompanied on his travels by information specialist Lady Mundy. Hogg would be happy living like that. It was hard to tell how Tovera would feel or if she had feelings at all, but she seemed to be adaptable.

"Lamson?" Daniel said, looking at the *Montclare*'s captain. "How soon will the spars and sails from the *Triomphante* be loaded aboard your ship?"

The Tarbell spacer, about fifty and clearly a man who had learned his trade by example, spat toward an insectoid which had just landed on a shaggy yellow mass of florets. He hit the creature squarely.

"Three hours more, maybe two," Lamson said. He grinned at Daniel's raised eyebrow and said, "Yeah, I know you think the sun shines up the ass of your own people, but me 'n' my boys've been striking down cargo for a lotta years. Maybe we can't get from here to West Bumfuck as quick as you can, sonny, but we know our own jobs."

Daniel grinned at the implied challenge. "Vesey?" he said without looking away from the civilian. "Do you agree with Captain Lamson's assessment?"

"Yes," said Vesey, whom Daniel had put in charge of the transfers. "The *Montclare* will be ready in that time frame. Ah—I'd like to add that some of the fabric which was loaded in Hold One has been transferred to Hold Six so that the large rolls from the cruiser will be easier to access in space when we mount them."

Lamson's smile was broad enough to show that he was missing upper incisors on the left side.

"All right, spacer," Daniel said with an easy grin. "You know your job. Now, do you have the guts to do the job *I'm* giving you? Draw fire from a battleship?"

"At the bonus you're promising, yeah, I do," Lamson said. "It's enough that I'll be able to buy a ship of my own. Okay, nothing as big and new as the *Montclare*, but I'll get there."

"You'll be paid the bonus," Daniel said. He caught the eye of Minister Robin, who nodded curtly.

He looked down into the lake, its deep blue brightened by reflected sky and clouds. When rafts moved across the surface or simply bobbed as they were loaded or unloaded, they sent out ripples. Movement gave the water life.

"Captain Burk?" Daniel said, turning to the other civilian captain. He was younger, thinner, and more sour than Lamson.

"We'll be loaded by nightfall," the *Montcalm*'s captain said. "We had a mare's nest in the holds from the sails you stripped from the merchant ships at Brownsville, but we'll have it struck down in six hours tops."

He turned from Daniel to Vesey, then looked back again. "I gotta say, Captain, it would've been a bloody sight easier to make the transfer in Brownsville where we had the harbor cranes and proper lighters. A little foresight would've gone a long way."

"I'm sure that would have been easier, Captain Burk," Daniel said, gesturing with his left hand to forestall Cory. "We're trying to conceal our intent from people in Brownsville, however. Whatever their politics, there are certainly some who would sell us out to the rebels for a good price."

Just as well I'm only meeting with the commissioned officers; Woetjans would've knocked him down before I could stop her.

"But we cleaned all the spars and fabric out of Brownsville, even stripping ships in harbor," Burk said, brow furrowing. "How's that a secret to anybody?"

"Burk," said Cory, facing the civilian squarely. "Everybody in Brownsville knows we're going off to fight, so it's no surprise that we're loading as much spare rigging as we can find. If they saw that we were shifting the spares from the cruiser to a couple transports that shouldn't even be in a battle—that's going to make them wonder."

"And if the rebels figure out what Six is planning," said

Cazelet, glaring from the other side, "then it's kitty bar the door. We have to take them completely by surprise. Particularly the *Almirante*!"

"Look, I said the *Montcalm* would be loaded in six hours," Burk muttered. "And if you don't mind, I'll get back aboard and see if I can speed the business up. All right?"

Daniel thought for a moment, then said, "Yes, unless anyone has further business. Anyone? Then, dismissed."

His officers began trouping down the slope to the docks and temporary housing at the edge of the lake. Adele and the servants remained behind, as did Christopher Robin.

The scars where trees had been cut for timber were ugly, but they would grow back before long. The spacers didn't have the sort of heavy equipment that crushes the soil to the consistency of brick. They had moved the felled trees on rollers cut from lesser trunks, pushed by the muscles of a hundred or more spacers used to working together.

The installations would rot away within years or at most a few decades. In fifty years, no one viewing the site would have realized that a squadron of warships had prepared here for battle.

The minister kept brushing at the tiny insectoids which flew about his face. They were drawn to the warmth of human flesh, but they didn't bite or sting because their chemistries were too different for people to be food. In long-inhabited portions of Chevalier, the parasites which settlers had brought along were just as annoying as they would have been on Cinnabar—or Earth, for that matter.

Daniel closed his eyes and rubbed his temples. "Sometimes

I need to remind myself . . ." he said. Adele and the Minister of War were listening—so were the servants, for that matter—but he was really speaking to himself. "That the other fellow's troubles look just as bad to him as ours do to me."

"Do you mean that this is a bad plan after all?" said Robin. "I thought . . ."

Daniel opened his eyes and smiled cheerfully at the minister. *I shouldn't speak my mind in front of laymen. Maybe I shouldn't speak my mind, period, except to Adele.*

"Not at all, sir," he said aloud. "I'm imagining that I'm commander of a Karst battleship. Far from home, supporting rebels whose command structure is more absent than rickety, dependent on foreigners who hold me in contempt. And well aware that if things go wrong, my home world will abandon me as a mutinous pirate. Why, if that were me, I'd be considering suicide!"

His analysis of the Karst admiral's position was accurate. The statement of his own probable reaction was not. Pleased as Daniel was at his squadron, he would *much* rather be leading the *Almirante* with her Karst crew against any cruiser in the galaxy.

"Well, I see what you mean," Robin said. "Speaking as a layman, which I realize I am . . . well, I'll be glad when it's over."

"That's quite understandable, sir," Daniel said with a bright smile. "Lady Mundy, is your part of the business ready?"

"The software is prepared," Adele said. "We won't be able to test it until the transports have been modified, since the fabric swathing will affect propagation."

She shrugged, then added, "We've completed as much as we can at this point."

"Then I think I'll give a last surface check to the ships," Daniel said. "I want to be sure that we're ready to lift off as soon as the loading is complete."

He smiled in bright assurance. *Screw it. Battles are fought by people, not equipment.*

SIDEREAL SPACE, BETWEEN CHEVALIER AND DANZIGER

"I'm opening her up," Tech 3 Shingawa, the pilot, warned over the PA system.

Barnes gripped Adele's right wrist while Dasi, on the other side, rechecked the catches of her air suit's helmet. Their caution was both excessive and irritating, but—Adele grinned wryly—her demonstrated clumsiness at any kind of normal shipboard maneuver was so far beyond the spacers' comprehension that she sympathized with their concern.

The *Triomphante*'s cutter supposedly held thirty personnel in its single compartment, but they would be squeezed in like canned fish if they were wearing any kind of protective gear. It wasn't a problem at present because Adele and her two handlers—both wearing rigging suits—were the only passengers, and the trip was a thirteen-minute excursion from the *Montcalm* to the docking ring above one of the flagship's forward dorsal airlocks.

The hatch popped open, venting the compartment's atmosphere. The cutter didn't have an airlock. They had boarded through a pressurized personnel tube already fitted to the *Montcalm*, but Adele was in enough haste that she didn't want to wait for one to be attached to the warship.

Dasi floated through the hatch, then pulled Adele after him by her safety line; he had already clipped the free end to the docking ring. The hatch was sized for big men wearing rigging suits and thus more than adequate for a slender woman in an air suit, but Barnes nevertheless hoisted her directly into his partner's arms.

Adele grimaced. The flat, undiffused light of vacuum caused her problems, so the riggers' care was more necessary than she would have chosen to admit.

Dasi handed himself down the ring to the hatch, which he opened. Only then did he gesture Adele to follow him—while he held firmly onto a second safety line. She entered the airlock with a gentle push from behind by Barnes as he pulled the hatch closed and dogged it.

The riggers started releasing their helmet catches immediately, but when Adele reached up to hers Dasi caught her hand. *How can it be dangerous for me if it's safe for them?* She didn't speak aloud, though.

When the telltale winked green, Dasi opened the inner hatch and Barnes lifted off Adele's helmet. They were treating her as though she were an infant!

"Barnes?" Adele said. "Would you give this kind of service to Minister of Defense Forbes?"

"I bloody well guess *not*," Barnes said.

"Ma'am, you're the *Mistress*," Dasi said with a look of puzzlement. "If we didn't treat you right, Woetjans'd break us down to Landsman. And she'd be right to!"

"The Minister of Defense never did a bloody thing for any of us," Barnes said. "You've saved our lives every time we got in a tight spot, and with Six leading us that's pretty bloody often!"

True enough, I suppose, Adele thought. It was a different—and positive—view of behavior which she had found irritating.

The whole squadron was in freefall. That simplified the job of shrouding the transports in sailcloth to bulk their outlines up to that of heavy cruisers, but it would have been a chore for Adele to traverse the rotunda without her escort. The volume was much larger than that of similar chamber on the *Princess Cecile* because it served two airlocks and four up/down pairs of companionways.

The two riggers were bosun's mates now and could have held bosuns' slots if they had been willing to leave the *Sissie*. Each grabbed one of Adele's arms and sailed across the rotunda to the bridge hatch.

A spacer from the *Triomphante* came out of a companionway at the wrong time; Dasi grabbed him by the shoulder and swung him out and behind. The maneuver looked casual, but Adele noticed that Dasi had used the fellow's mass as a fulcrum so that the contact didn't affect the line in which she and her escort were moving.

Daniel attracts good people…or maybe he makes people better. Myself included.

Hogg stood beside the open bridge hatch, ready to catch them if necessary. It wasn't: Barnes and Dasi swung their boots forward and clacked to a smooth halt, absorbing the shock with their bent knees.

Hogg took Adele's hand. Locking himself to the hatch

coming, he tossed her to Daniel, who had risen from his console. He and Vesey were using the stations at which Adele and Braun had been sitting when she captured the *Upholder*.

I wonder if all of Braun's blood and brains have been cleaned up? Well, it doesn't matter.

About a dozen of the stations were occupied; some of the cruiser's officers stood to get a better look at what was going on. Adele took the flat-plate station across the aisle and reached for her personal data unit. It was inaccessible beneath her air suit.

"We're on it," said Barnes, who with his partner must have followed her onto the bridge. He lifted Adele without ceremony while Dasi unlatched the suit's waist catches and pulled the lower portion off her. The stiff fabric slipped away more easily than Adele had ever managed when she was doing it herself.

"Want the top off, ma'am?" Barnes asked solicitously.

"This is fine," Adele muttered as she brought up her data unit. The remaining portion of the suit was slightly awkward to work in, but she decided she was sufficiently embarrassed already. Personnel who didn't know her from the *Princess Cecile* were gawping with amazement.

"Would you like me to clear the bridge?" Daniel said, bending forward to speak without bellowing. Though the ship was in freefall, the echoes of many hundreds of systems working in a large steel box were burdensome if not deafening.

"No," said Adele as her wands flickered. "But I'll set up a cancellation field for the three of—there. The three of us."

She had coupled the three stations into a single cell of active sound cancellation so that they could speak normally and not be overheard. The latter wasn't a concern at this point, because the squadron was sealed off from enemy attention until after they went into action.

"Should I leave?" said Vesey. "We were going over squadron tactics but I don't need..."

"Stay, I'm glad you're here," Adele said as Vesey started to rise. "The *Montcalm*'s short- and medium-wave transmitter is nonfunctional, has been nonfunctional for six months, that idiot Burk tells me. But he didn't think to mention it before I started to install my equipment and found there was nothing to hook up to."

"But they've been communicating?" Daniel said. "I've spoken to Burk, the *Montcalm* has sent normal reports."

"Using microwave and laser," Adele said curtly. "And their receiver works, so they were getting signals in normal fashion."

I mustn't take my anger out on innocent people, whom everyone but Burk himself is. Though if the signals officer had been doing his job, it would have been taken care of regardless of whether the captain saw the need.

"Mistress?" said Vesey. "If the *Montcalm* can still send, why is it a problem not to have short and medium wave?"

Adele looked at her. *Maybe I've been too hard on Burk, since I know that Vesey is competent and smart....*

Aloud Adele said, "In order to appear to be a particular ship, a heavy cruiser in this case, we need to send out all the electronic signals the cruiser itself does. Every electric motor, every switch—anything whatever which uses electricity is also a transmitter. Much of the noise is longer than microwave.

The missiles in their cradles are transmitters!"

She cleared her throat in embarrassment. "I'm sorry," she said. "I'm frustrated, but that's no reason for discourtesy. That was one of my mother's strongest beliefs."

Adele smiled faintly. She added, "It remains a belief which I personally hold."

In contrast to Mother's belief in the innate goodness of the common people.

Tovera hadn't accompanied Adele to the *Montcalm* for the installation. She appeared at the bridge hatch and hauled herself by the overhead rail to Adele's side. She hooked her toe beneath a seat frame as an anchor.

"Can we repair or replace it?" Daniel said. "I'm willing to pull the transmitter out of one of the destroyers if that's what it takes. Frankly, the best use I can think of for the *Alfonso* is to divide the rebel fire."

"On a merchant ship..." Adele said carefully. "This is all handled by the main console, the only console."

She hadn't realized how specialized her knowledge base was. Well, knowledge regarding starship communications systems. She had known from childhood that information gathering and data management were a blank wall to most people, though for the life of her she couldn't see what was difficult about it.

"Ah," said Daniel, nodding. "Which is responsible for astrogation and sail attitude among other things. Even if we could replace the console, we couldn't calibrate it in less than a week, even if we had a proper dockyard."

"Mistress?" said Vesey. "We'll have a destroyer keeping station as close to each transport as they can. To launch missiles, you see, because we can't rig the transports to do that in the time we've got."

"At anything less than ten light-minutes," Adele said, "the difference would be obvious to even a civilian console. The larger vessel would act as both a reflector and a barrier, depending on the angle to the receiving antenna. The console might not identify the transmitter correctly, but it couldn't be fooled into believing it was really a heavy cruiser."

She pursed her lips as a thought occurred to her. "If we could import the signals to the *Montcalm* through a cable," she said, "we could broadcast them *from* the larger ship. That would work, or I hope it would."

"We can hook a cable in normal space," Daniel said. "I was hoping to arrive with the deception in place, but if we can't, we can't."

"Six?" said Vesey. "I—I don't mean that I'm as good as you are, that anybody's as good as you are, but..."

She paused, looking stricken. She licked her lips to moisten them.

Adele felt her anger flare again. She deliberately looked away and brought up the list of biographies of officers on the *Almirante*—not because there was any significance in it but just to prevent herself from slapping the younger woman out of her funk.

That probably wouldn't be helpful.

Adele smiled and turned to her companions again. Her rational analysis of what anger was suggesting had quenched the anger.

"Go ahead, Vesey," Daniel said calmly.

"Six, I can hold the transport steady during an insertion," Vesey said in a whisper. "And you—*you* can hold station with me, I know you can. We can do this!"

"You know…" said Daniel slowly. "That might possibly be true."

He smiled like the sun breaking through clouds. "At any rate," he went on, "I think we're going to try it. Adele, figure out what you'll need for the hookup, and Vesey and I will come up with a protocol. That creates one new problem, though?"

"Six?" said Vesey.

"Since I've just moved Vesey from the *Triomphante* to the *Montcalm*, I need someone to captain our only major combat asset," Daniel said, his smile slipping.

Adele called up another biography, checked it, and said, "Captain Joycelyn is familiar with the *Triomphante*, as she is now. And his war record is very good."

Daniel and Vesey looked at her. Vesey said, "If we can trust him."

"I think," said Daniel, "that we can trust Joycelyn … but I'll put a safety in place just to make sure. Adele, please summon Captain Joycelyn from the *Ithaca*, and also call Midshipman Hale from the BDC."

He smiled. Adele thought he looked satisfied.

Hale entered the bridge fast. That was proper for an acting lieutenant responding to the captain's summons, but her expression betrayed an understratum of concern overlaid with a neutral gloss.

Daniel felt a twitch of embarrassment at having accidentally frightened an able officer. He gestured to the bulkhead station beside Adele's and said, "Sit down, Hale. I need a Sissie here on the bridge of the *Triomphante*, so I'm transferring you to the Signals slot. I'm moving von Golz"—a Tarbell lieutenant who had originally come from the Fleet; the current signals officer—"to the *Montclare*."

"Ah, yes, sir, of course," Hale said, confused now rather than worried. "But my understanding was that you would be commanding the *Triomphante* yourself?"

"My intention," Daniel said, "was to control squadron operations from the cruiser's BDC while Lieutenant Vesey—"

He nodded to her in the adjacent station.

"—commanded the *Triomphante* herself. That's changed because of an equipment failure on the *Montcalm*. Vesey will be commanding the transport, and I'll be taking over the *Princess Cecile*."

He smiled. The *Montcalm*'s commo failure was an irritation which made a risky plan even more dangerous, but he was glad that he'd be back aboard the *Princess Cecile* during the coming battle. The heavy cruiser had a fine crew which by now was reasonably well worked up, but the *Sissie* was home.

That will be a problem if I ever reach flag rank. Which in turn won't *be a problem unless we're luckier at Danziger than I'd give odds on.*

"Oh," said Hale, her face going blank. "Well, I—"

Hale looked at Adele, then back to Daniel. "Sir?" she said. "Six. I'm honored by your choice and I believe I can handle the commo work as well as the next space officer. But I'm not in a class with Lieutenant Cazelet. His leg won't keep him from doing the signals job, and he's got more determination than, well, than just about anybody. He *can* do the job, sir!"

Daniel listened, hoping that his surprise didn't show. Hale and Cazelet were simply two shipboard colleagues: her recommendation was completely disinterested.

He nodded and said, "Cazelet is very good, as you say, and I agree that he's physically capable of handling the commo duties. What he couldn't do, psychologically, is to shoot Captain Joycelyn if he began to act in a fashion not in the best interests of the Tarbell Stars."

Hale swallowed. She didn't speak.

"I think Cazelet could command the *Triomphante* in battle adequately in Joycelyn's place," Daniel added, giving Hale longer to process the information, "but Cazelet would never be able to do what was necessary to take control."

"I suspect you'd be a better combat commander also," said Adele. "I would put you in charge rather that Rene, even if I were on the bridge to murder Joycelyn."

She smiled. There was no humor in her expression.

"I have a great deal of experience in murder," Adele added.

"But, Six . . ." Hale said. "Yes, I'll carry out any duties you give me, and I didn't need the Academy to tell me that part of what an RCN officer might do was to kill the enemies of the Republic. But what if I'm wrong?"

"Lieutenant Hale," Vesey said. "We're about to fight a battle. It's nearly certain that some people will die, and possibly everyone in the Tarbell forces will die. Like the rest of us, you'll use your best judgment with whatever situation arises."

Her expression softened a little. "Based on what I've seen of your conduct..." Vesey said. "Your judgment is sound."

"Thank you, sir," Hale said to Vesey. She turned to Daniel and said, "Sir, do I wait for a formal announcement or do you want me to just move onto the bridge immediately?"

"Let me intrude," said Tovera. "People like me and Hogg generally keep quiet when our betters—"

She grinned. Daniel had no idea how Tovera saw herself in relation to human society, and he wasn't sure he'd find her joke funny if he did understand it.

"—are talking, but I have something to say."

Daniel looked at Adele. She shrugged and said, "Go ahead, Tovera."

"Mistress," Tovera said, nodding in acknowledgement. She looked down at Hale at the station on Adele's other side. "Hale, you're a crap pistol shot, right?"

Daniel thought of saying something but immediately smothered the reaction. He'd left the question of permitting Tovera to speak to Tovera's mistress. He wasn't going to second guess Adele in a matter which she understood much better than he did.

Hale didn't react for an instant. Then she said, "You saw the hash I made of it when we took over the *Upholder*, so there's no point in my arguing, is there? I know to get close this time, if it comes to that."

"Good answer," said Tovera, grinning like a happy serpent. She reached into her attaché case and handed her little submachine gun butt-first to Hale. "This is another answer. It's got lighter recoil than the service pistol you were using, but from here to the command console—"

She gestured with her left hand.

"—it'll slice him open as nice as Hogg could do with that knife of his. Aim at the waist and it'll recoil straight up."

None of Daniel's group said anything for a moment. Those on the bridge who'd gotten up to stare at Adele's arrival had gone back to their business. *They'd better have, or they'll learn that goggling at their captain isn't a good career move.*

Hale took the weapon and after a moment slipped it into the right side-pocket of her utility jacket to get it out of sight. "Thank you," she said carefully.

"You're welcome to the holster," Tovera said. "I think you'd be better off carrying it in your waistband, the way you did on the *Upholder*."

"Thank you, Mistress," Hale repeated. "Ah, isn't this—"

She touched her sagging pocket.

"—something you may need yourself?"

"Officer Mundy and her servant will be aboard the *Princess Cecile* with me," Daniel said. "I'm not expecting that sort of problem, but I'm confident that we can outfit Tovera with small arms should something arise."

"Yes, sir," said Hale. "I'll carry out my duties to the best of my ability, sir."

Daniel smiled at her. "As expected, Hale," he said.

Hale had been a classmate of Cory in the Academy. She had taken a common spacer's slot under Daniel on a private charter because she wanted to learn how Cory had changed from a dull cadet to a lieutenant with a name and a future.

Well, she's learning.

"Captain Joycelyn is in the airlock," Adele said, watching her display.

"Very good," said Daniel. "Why don't you and I—and you, Vesey, since you're still in command of the *Triomphante*, take him to the captain's duty cabin off the bridge and inform him of the new arrangements."

He got to his feet and smiled again. "Not your part of the arrangements, Hale," he added. "I don't expect he'll ever learn about that."

"If I'm sufficiently accurate," Hale said, "he won't learn even if things go tits up."

Vesey winced, but Daniel and the servants were all laughing as they shepherded Adele back to the rotunda to meet Captain Joycelyn.

CHAPTER 25

DANZIGER SYSTEM

Adele felt as though the right half of her body was missing and the left half was ice cold—all except her head, where the sensations were reversed. Extracting from the Matrix into normal space was always unpleasant but it was also always different—both as a personal experience and for individuals undergoing the extraction in the same ship.

I could collect and correlate reactions to extraction, Adele thought. *I could set up a program throughout the RCN, I have enough influence to do that, and I could probably expand it even wider*.

Her mind cleared, bringing her back onto the signals console of the *Princess Cecile*. There were worse reactions to returning to sidereal space than that you find yourself constructing silly plans, but neither was this a situation in which to dawdle idly.

The bulk of the *Montcalm* filled a large sector of the panoramic display at the top of Adele's screen. The transport was only a hundred yards away, too close for the ships to extend all their antennas without contact.

The distance at which hostile vessels could view the two as separate ships depended on the observing optics, the sharpening software, and the skill of the user. Adele believed that there was a high chance of success that their extraction into the orbit of the system's fourth planet would at least initially appear to be a single vessel.

Moreover, the optical fiber linking Adele's console to the transmitting antennas on the *Montcalm* had survived the Transit. That was truly an amazing piece of shiphandling for Vesey and even more for Daniel, who was controlling the *Princess Cecile* from a pulpit on the ship's hull, connected to the command console by a hydromechanical linkage.

The reason that trying to correlate reactions to extraction was a silly idea was not because the information would be useless. All knowledge was equal in Adele's mind, though she might not have an immediate practical need for most of it at any one time.

Rather, it was silly because the data would have to be subjective. Adele didn't trust subjective data. Though she could organize it, she would never in her heart feel that it was real. She supposed that was a failing in herself, but she doubted whether a practical, "normal" scholar would press her to carry out that particular research.

This had been the first real-world test of Daniel's outside control rig. He had added it after operations in the Sunbright System had proved how effective it could be in the hands of a skilled enemy.

Most astrogators didn't read the Matrix the way Uncle Stacy

Bergen had taught Daniel to do; Daniel in turn had taught his junior officers. Reading the Matrix had made Commander Bergen the most famous explorer in Cinnabar's history.

A different skill was to be able to follow another ship in the Matrix. That was a pirate's skill. Daniel had fought pirates. From sheer determination to master every aspect of his profession, he had taught himself to do whatever a pirate could do.

Shiphandling wasn't Adele's concern. They had extracted fifteen light-minutes from Danziger, as planned; they were within the orbit of the next planet in the system, though the planet itself was a quarter of its way around the sun.

The three rebel destroyers—*Ithaca*, *Truth*, and *Justice*—were orbiting Danziger. Initially Adele couldn't tell whether they had just lifted off or whether they were arriving and were preparing to land. There was no sign of the *Almirante*.

The *Katchaturian* was already on station, two thousand miles from the *Sissie*. The *Triomphante* extracted three seconds after the *Sissie* and *Montcalm*—which for this purpose were claiming to be the RCS *Powerful*—and about a thousand miles away, good station-keeping for proceeding in the Matrix.

The *Mindello* flickered into sidereal space at the same time, then vanished back into the Matrix when Cory realized that his charge, the *Montclare*—AKA RCS *Terrible*—hadn't arrived. Quick in-and-out maneuvers were brutally hard on the crew, as Adele knew very well, but there was no help for it.

When the *Montclare* arrived a minute later and two thousand miles out, the *Mindello* reappeared, then vanished into the Matrix for final adjustments out of sight of the enemy. When Cory extracted the third time, he was tucked almost as close to the *Montclare* as the *Princess Cecile* was to the *Montcalm*.

Even the best spacers would be vomiting and weak after that series of insertions. Cory had expected it—and had brought a pistol from the *Sissie*'s weapons locker before he returned to take command of the *Mindello* after a last conference with Daniel. If spacers who were not used to the standards of the *Princess Cecile* decided to mutiny, Cory would deal with it.

"Warships in the vicinity of Danziger," Adele said. "This is Admiral Beukes of the RCN. Identify yourselves and stand by for boarding, over."

She was sending on the twenty-meter band, the standard hailing frequency, using the *Montcalm*'s antennas. It would be fifteen minutes before the destroyers received the signal and another fifteen before their reply reached Adele, even if they responded instantly.

Daniel, wearing his rigging suit except for the helmet, clanked onto the bridge. He nodded to Adele as he passed on the way to the command console.

Farber, a lieutenant from the *Katchaturian* whom Cory had spoken well of, commanded the *Sissie* from the BDC while Daniel was on the hull. Daniel settled onto the couch and said, "*Command, this is Six. Farber, continue to conn the ship until I relieve you—which I may not do until after our next insertion. Over.*"

"*Roger, Six,*" Farber replied. "*I tweaked Thrusters Three and Four to match the transport's notion of one gee, nothing else. Control over.*"

"*Six out, break,*" Daniel said. "*Signals, what's the situation, over?*"

Rigging suits didn't have any form of electronic communication. In normal space that was only a minor disadvantage: riggers used hand signals and mechanical semaphores to communicate.

In the Matrix, not only would radios not have worked, the effect of RF signals on the sails would have been to drive the ship on a wild career through the cosmos. It was better not to fit suits with radios than to accept the results of the mistakes inevitable if the equipment was there to be used at the wrong time.

"The rebel destroyers are orbiting Danziger," Adele said. "There—the *Ithaca* has begun braking to land so they must have just arrived. There's no sign of the—"

As she spoke, sidereal space rippled, the precursor to a mass extracting from the Matrix. The center of the disturbance was equidistant from Danziger and the Tarbell squadron: roughly in the orbit of the fifth planet but leading it by as much as the Tarbells were trailing.

"Correction," Adele said. "The *Almirante* is now extracting. That is, extracted fifteen minutes ago. One moment."

She switched from intercom to shortwave again. The beams were directional, so she adjusted a second antenna to focus on the Karst battleship. The hardware would have been standard on a heavy cruiser, but they'd had to jury rig a fitment to the *Montcalm*.

"Warships in the Danziger system," she broadcast. "This is Admiral Beukes of the Republic of Cinnabar Navy. Identify yourselves and stand by for boarding, over."

Daniel was figuring courses on the astrogation display. Each sweep of his finger through the display was translated into alphanumeric notations on a sidebar; when he banged the Execute button on his keyboard, the calculations went to a compiler which translated them into adjustments to the antennas and sail plan.

"Warships in the Danziger system," Adele repeated. "This is Admiral Beukes of the Republic of Cinnabar Navy. Identify yourselves and stand by for boarding, over."

The rebel ships would not have received even the first transmission yet, but the repeated demand might disturb the rebels' composure. She went back to reviewing the chatter among the rebel ships for the fifteen minutes before the *Princess Cecile* had arrived in the Danziger system. It was an ordinary discussion of landing procedures, enlivened only by a question from the captain of the *Truth* as to whether the other ships knew the whereabouts of the *Almirante*.

They didn't, of course. Even a civilian sensor suite would have been able to spot a battleship within the confines of the Danziger system, so if the *Truth* couldn't find the *Almirante*, the *Almirante* couldn't have arrived yet.

It should have pleased Adele as a member of the RCN to learn that their enemies were stupid. She had quickly learned that it didn't: she had a romantic ideal of what human intelligence should be; though unlike her mother she didn't carry it to the point of denying reality.

Esme Rolfe Mundy had had as little as possible to do with the Lower Orders, whom she claimed contained an innate nobility which needed only to be directed by the leaders of the Popular Party in order to bring a new Golden Age. Adele had lived at the squalid bottom of society where what her mother meant by "the Lower Orders" were a ceiling above her; she hadn't noticed a great deal of nobility among them.

"*Signals*," said Daniel as he slammed Execute again, "*copy my course calculations to the* Montcalm. *Break. Cinnabar Peacekeeping Detachment*"—the squadron's public name—"*proceed to close with unidentified battleship. Peace Six out.*"

Daniel checked the Plot-Position Indicator. "*Ship*," he said, drawing on his gauntlets as he spoke, "*I'm returning to the control station on the hull. Farber, you remain in command until I reach my position. Six out.*"

He stomped off the bridge, lifting his helmet in both hands to clamp it in place as soon as he was in the airlock.

Adele looked at her intercepts, converted to texts on her display. The rebels still weren't aware of the Tarbell arrival.

"Unidentified warships in the Danziger system," Adele said. "Identify yourselves and stand by for boarding by the RCN peacekeeping force, Admiral Beukes commanding!"

Daniel stepped into the chest-high framework he'd had built just forward of the Dorsal A antenna. The enclosure had room for one person in a rigging suit and a pillar like that of the semaphore stations by which the interior of the ship communicated to the spacers on the hull.

Instead of a semaphore's six arms, this station had a joystick with a mode button, currently set for sidereal space. Daniel put his right gauntlet on the handgrip and clicked the mode switch to Matrix operation and then back to indicate to the bridge that he was in position.

The rigging watch waited, as motionless as the antennas and sails. Above them hung the *Montcalm*, her natural lines swollen grotesquely by a suit of sail fabric which gave her the apparent bulk of a heavy cruiser. She was barely maneuverable in the Matrix because her only controls were the transport's topgallants, all that protruded from the camouflage.

The coming insertion would be a short one and very simple: she and the *Sissie*, together the heavy cruiser *Powerful*, would in company with the *Triomphante* and the *Montclare/Terrible* extract within one light-minute of the Karst battleship. The battleship's captain would have—just—had time to digest the demand which Adele had broadcast at the Tarbell squadron's first appearance.

At one light-minute a battleship's optics would easily be capable of determining that the two transports weren't really RCN heavy cruisers. RF sensors, however, were the default system on most consoles, and they would continue to indicate the RCS *Terrible* and *Powerful*.

What happened then depended on Captain Staples' orders, and even more on his personal courage. Even a very brave man—and from his record, Staples wasn't a coward—knew that if he provoked Cinnabar to declare war on Karst, the best he could expect from his home government was a quick execution.

The universe blurred into a greenish haze as the *Princess Cecile* began to insert into the Matrix in accordance with the course Daniel himself had programmed into the command console. The *Montcalm* faded from a cold, reflective behemoth filling the heavens above him into a disruption. Daniel gripped the joystick, but he didn't take control yet.

Daniel always felt a thrill when he first stepped out into the light of the Matrix. The first time had been when he was seven, too small to fit into even the smallest air suit.

Uncle Stacy had wangled a child's escape capsule from a yacht and modified it with a clear panel at eye level. In it he and a trusted workman had carried Daniel when they brought him onto the hull during an insertion on a test lift. Daniel wasn't a religious man, but his feelings on looking out at the Cosmos arrayed as a shimmering light show—every bright point a bubble universe—couldn't really be described except in religious terms.

Hogg had been with the boy during that first view of the Matrix, but he hadn't helped carry the capsule. It was Hogg's first experience in the Matrix also, and he didn't trust himself not to make a fatal mistake.

When they were back within the hull and Daniel had been released from the capsule, Hogg had pinched the boy's lips closed to still his excited burbling. Then, with the same grim sincerity he had used when instructing Daniel in firearms safety, he had explained why Daniel never *ever* must let his mother know what had just happened. If gentle, loving Maude Bergen Leary learned, she would never again let Daniel visit her brother.

Later Daniel realized that Hogg would also have been expelled from the Bantry estate which was the only home his family had known for at least three hundred years, but that was at most Hogg's secondary concern. Lady Maude had made Hogg responsible for Daniel's well-being, and in Hogg's opinion the boy's obvious love for spacefaring should be indulged—even though Hogg's own opinion of the business was very close to that of Daniel's mother.

The *Sissie* was fully within the Matrix, a bubble universe among the myriad thousands of bubble universes which made up the cosmos. Daniel looked about him in delight.

Humans could not see the Matrix with their eyes, but their brains translated the perceptions into visual images. The *Montcalm* did not exist in the universe which had formed about the *Princess Cecile*, but the Matrix itself was blemished if you understood its infinitely changing structure. Daniel Leary had as much of that understanding as the next person.

He grinned tightly as he eased the joystick forward. *Unless the next person was a Qaboosh pirate. And maybe even then....*

The discontinuity had been fading; now it began to grow again, disturbing a wider apparent arc of the Matrix. Though the internal clocks of the *Montcalm* and *Sissie* were identical to the level of molecular movement, the constants of universes which the starships had formed about themselves as they inserted differed. Daniel was bringing them into closer synchrony by his vastly geared-down effort on the joystick.

The yards of the antenna immediately behind him were rotating, adjusting the angle at which Casimir radiation impinged on the sails. Daniel didn't have to turn to know what was happening: the vibration though the soles of his boots told him.

He had set the course: not the sail plan, that was determined by the console, but the point at which the *Princess Cecile* was to extract into sidereal space. Because of Daniel's long experience on the hull, he knew roughly how long it would take for the ship to transit that distance. The sail adjustment was the final route point.

Instead of shrinking, the ghost of the *Montcalm* began to fade. Daniel drew his joystick back to its stop at the six o'clock position.

The *Princess Cecile* jerked and shuddered into normal space. At each instant another—horrible—feeling wracked Daniel's mind. Normally he would undergo extraction while he was seated at the command console or at worst would be gripping an antenna or some fixed portion of the ship's rigging. This time he was plodding toward the airlock, not so much ignoring the pain as pressing on regardless.

He had to be back on the *Sissie*'s bridge as soon as possible.

He had to be back on the *Sissie*'s bridge in order to conn her into battle with a hostile battleship.

As the *Princess Cecile* extracted from the Matrix, Adele felt spiders walking on the surface of her brain. It was very unpleasant. *Very* unpleasant.

Why do I think they're spiders?

The surface of the brain has no sensory input nerves. Why do I think I'm feeling something on the surface of my brain? That's as foolish as it would be to think that a rock hates me!

Adele's silent reflection had the useful effect of bringing her fully alert. Usually extractions bothered her less than seemed to be the case for others, though since the whole business was subjective she might simply be patting herself on the back for being exceptionally tough. That thought was worse than the spiders, even though she hadn't spoken out loud.

Tovera was slumped over her side of the console. Perhaps the fact that the *Sissie* and the transport were linked had made the effect worse than it usually was. That would be very unfortunate, because the crew of the *Almirante* weren't sharing the discomfort.

"Karst battleship, this is the Cinnabar Peacekeeping Force, Admiral Beukes commanding," Adele said. At this range it was to be expected that an RCN warship would have identified the origin as well as type of a major warship. "Lay to and prepare to be boarded by RCN officers. RCS *Powerful* over."

She had no idea of what the rebel vessels—she included the *Almirante* among them—might have been transmitting during the period that the *Princess Cecile* had been in the Matrix. If there had been time she would have entered the logs of the hostile ships and extracted the records, but there most certainly was *not* time now.

Tovera had sat up again. Adele hoped that the rest of the bridge crew were recovering also, but there was nothing she could do if they weren't.

The PPI on the bottom of Adele's display—commo had the top half—showed that the *Ithaca* was clawing back up from the gravity well it had started to enter. Its captain must have heard "Admiral Beukes"' challenge and decided to face the issue directly.

The other two rebel destroyers were accelerating hard; the *Truth* was even using its plasma thrusters to boost the output of its far more efficient High Drive. As Adele's eye fell on the display, the icon for the *Truth* blurred as the ship inserted. A moment later the *Justice* followed its companion into the Matrix.

They might be on their way to join the *Almirante*, but Adele very strongly doubted it. They would wait at what their captains considered a safe distance—a light-hour or more—while the heavy ships decided the issue. If the *Almirante* drove off or destroyed the three cruisers, the destroyers would reappear to support the victor. If the cruisers took control of the Danziger system, the destroyers would run for Peltry. The deception—her deception—had at least worked that well.

The *Montclare,* with the *Mindello* clinging tightly to its skirt, appeared three thousand miles away only a few seconds after the *Sissie* and *Montcalm* extracted. The *Triomphante* was thirty seconds later but within a thousand miles of the *Sissie*, extremely good astrogation.

Normally Adele would have guessed that any deviation from the plotted rendezvous point was the fault of the other vessel, not the *Princess Cecile*. Under the present circumstances the transport, maneuvering with only her topgallants, was the limiting factor on accuracy. The *Sissie* went where the *Montcalm* led; if the *Triomphante* extracted in close proximity, Captain Joycelyn had every right to be proud of himself.

Daniel shambled past in his rigging suit. He had looked ill after they transited into the Danziger system; now the normally ruddy skin of his face was drawn so tightly over his skull that he looked as though he were a pallid caricature of himself.

"*Cinnabar vessels, this is CKS* Almirante," a male voice replied on the twenty-meter band which Adele had used in hailing. "*Karst is an independent principality at peace with your republic. You have no authority to halt or search our vessel. We will not comply with your demand, over.*"

The speaker's tone wobbled between haughty and frightened, with haughty seeming to gain strength as the transmission went on. Adele had found Karst to have the typical arrogance of a minor power whose leaders don't understand how trivial they are in the greater scheme of things.

Because of the near parity between Cinnabar and the Alliance, the superpowers had for decades been more than polite to the Headman of Karst and his henchmen. That had fueled Karst's feeling of self-importance.

Besides, the *Almirante* was a battleship. Three aggressively-handled heavy cruisers could put up a fight, but the weight of metal was still comfortably on the battleship's side.

Daniel pulsed a red icon on Adele's display, meaning he wanted to take over. Adele immediately ceded the transmitter to him.

"*Karst vessel,*" Daniel said, "*this is Admiral Beukes of the RCN.*"

The real Beukes commanded a cruiser squadron of the Home Fleet, based at Harbor Three on Xenos. He had a good war record and was a likely candidate to head such a peacekeeping squadron if the Republic lost its collective mind and became openly involved in the Tarbell Stars.

"*In the name of the Republic of Cinnabar, I am ordering you to either lie to and be boarded by my officers,*" Daniel continued, "*or to immediately remove yourself from the Danziger System. If you do not obey my orders, I will use all force necessary to bring you into a condition of obedience. Beukes over.*"

Adele's software translated a wiggle in the electronic noise emanating from the *Almirante*. She said, "Daniel, the battleship has opened the shutters of its missile tubes." Someone who knew her as well as Daniel did would be able to read the urgency which didn't actually reach her voice.

The *Almirante* began to launch missiles.

"Cinnabar Force, engage the enemy!" Daniel ordered. He noticed that his order was not only being microwaved to the ships of the Tarbell squadron but was also being broadcast in clear on shortwave so that Captain Staples of the *Almirante* would receive it.

Daniel had forgotten to tell Adele to do that. Fortunately the choice was as obvious to her as it was to him.

"*Missiles, launch two*," ordered Lieutenant Farber, the captain of the *Princess Cecile* properly executing the orders of the squadron commander. The ship rang as Chazanoff pressed his launch button.

About a cup of water in the breach cavity was flash-heated to steam. That shoved the multi-ton missile out of its tube into hard vacuum where its twin High Drive motors lighted. The missile accelerated on a preprogrammed course toward the Karst battleship. By the time it had exhausted its reaction mass and split into three parts, the missile would have reached a significant fraction of light speed.

Each separate projectile weighed more than a ton. They didn't have warheads. Explosives—even nuclear weapons—

were vulnerable to countermeasures and at missile velocities would add little to the kinetic energy of the impact.

A second *clang!* Chazanoff had launched the *Sissie*'s other loaded missile. A corvette carried the same missiles as a battleship, but not nearly as many of them and with only two tubes for a salvo. The *Almirante* could launch ninety-six at a time, enough to overwhelm the defenses of even another battleship—if they were well aimed.

The *Princess Cecile* shuddered as reload missiles moved from the magazine to the launch tubes. From the harmonics, Chazanoff had more than two missiles moving on each rollerway. That made reloading faster, but it would take serious effort to move five-ton missiles back up the rollers into the magazines again if they were not launched.

That was a problem for after the fighting had stopped. Launching at maximum rate increased the chances that the fighting would stop at a point favorable to the *Sissie* and her crew.

The *Mindello*, huddled against the *Montclare* to mimic the RCS *Terrible*, launched two missiles—one from each pair of tubes—and two more in five seconds. That was enough of a delay that the leader's High Drives wouldn't damage the following missile.

The *Triomphante* herself—the only major warship involved in Daniel's deception—also launched two missiles. That was a good choice, again one that Daniel hadn't thought to order. The *Princess Cecile* and *Mindello* were limited to two or four missiles in a salvo. The heavy cruiser could have salvoed twelve, but by limiting his own launch Joycelyn was suggesting that the small salvoes were a matter of "Admiral Beukes"' choice rather than necessity.

The *Almirante* in her initial probe had launched six missiles toward the *Triomphante*. Now she rippled out twenty-two, probably intended to be twenty-four; again she was aiming only at the *Triomphante*. Presumably Captain Staples still hoped not to involve his nation in a war with Cinnabar, even though he believed that two RCN cruisers were launching at him.

The *Katchaturian* under her Nabis captain was keeping decent station three thousand miles outboard of the "*Terrible*." She had launched two missiles at the *Almirante* and now launched three more.

"Squadron, launch at maximum," Daniel ordered. The *Princess Cecile* carried only twenty-two missiles with her magazine full—as it had been at the start of this action. There was no reason to conserve them at this point. The *Mindello* had sixty, though most were single-converter models.

The *Alfonso* had advanced toward the *Almirante* as Daniel ordered, but either her captain's astrogation was *very* bad or he had chosen to extract two light-minutes from the Karst battleship rather than the plotted one minute. The destroyer was not launching, though in fairness she was so far away from the *Sissie* that her officers might not have had time to understand and obey.

The *Albuquerque*, the third Tarbell destroyer, had entered the Matrix when the heavy ships did but hadn't extracted—or at any rate, hadn't extracted close enough to the region of battle to show up on Daniel's Plot-Position Indicator. That didn't actually prove that Captain Tremaine was more interested in saving his skin than in fighting, but Daniel would discuss the situation with him when matters quieted down.

If any of us survive—but you can die stepping out of the shower.

Instead of engaging the incoming missiles with her plasma cannon as Daniel expected, the *Triomphante* inserted into the Matrix before the first of the Karst rounds reached her. Daniel frowned.

Joycelyn had plenty of time to evade the salvo in this fashion: the Karst missiles were single-converter units which accelerated at half the rate of the double-converter missiles used by both Cinnabar and the Alliance. The *Almirante*'s salvo hadn't been well-aimed.

If Daniel had been the *Triomphante*'s captain, he would have batted away the few missiles whose trajectories might have posed a danger. Plasma cannon left a miasma of charged particles clinging to the vessel firing which had to dissipate before the ship could enter the Matrix.

If the *Triomphante* had stayed in normal space and launched a full salvo of twelve rounds, there was at least a chance that the additional threat would have been enough to frighten the battleship off the field. Had Hale been too hesitant to take over when Joycelyn had lost his bottle? Or had Minister Robin intervened?

"*Karst warship!*" Adele broadcast. She didn't raise her voice, but she had the tone of command which her family had honed during twenty centuries in the forefront of Cinnabar politics. "*Cease firing at the Cinnabar Peacekeeping Squadron. You are committing piracy and will assuredly be hanged by your own government if you survive this action!*"

The Tarbell vessels had been able to rough out their attacks before they transited: their target was a fixed point and their computers knew the location at which they intended to extract. The results were quite good. Nothing else appearing, one of the missiles from the *Princess Cecile* and one from the *Mindello* might strike the *Almirante,* and even one from the *Triomphante* had a chance.

Not even a battleship could shrug off a missile at terminal velocity, but there was no realistic chance of a hit from the projectiles launched thus far. The *Almirante* had time to maneuver out of the path of most, and her eight twenty-centimeter plasma cannon directed enough energy that a single bolt could easily defeat a ton and a half of steel. The blast of ions didn't make the projectile vanish, but it vaporized enough of the mass to shove the remainder away at a sharp angle.

"*Cinnabar forces, cease your attack!*" the battleship broadcast. "*We are the CKS* Almirante, *a vessel of a friendly power! Cease your attack.*"

A destroyer—the *Ithaca*—extracted some thirty thousand miles from the *Almirante.* The *Sissie* launched two more missiles—one and one. Their sharp blows punctuated the hull's rhythmic flexing as additional missiles came down the rollerways.

In a normal battle the *Princess Cecile* would be maneuvering and probably making quick insertions into the Matrix. Daniel couldn't do that while they were linked to the *Montcalm.*

He wasn't sure that their deception was still working, but it certainly seemed to be. Deception was their only real hope against a battleship, and he wasn't going to give it up.

The *Triomphante* extracted thirty light-seconds from the *Almirante* but at ninety degrees to the plane of the previous action. Joycelyn hadn't inserted to dodge missiles, he was maneuvering for a closer shot and a different angle on the battleship. The cruiser was barely in sidereal space again when it began to launch missiles.

Daniel had an enlargement of the *Almirante* on a corner of his display.

It was a further minute before the battleship began to react to the *Triomphante*'s attack. Her massive plasma cannon were carried in pairs in four turrets. They all rotated to meet the incoming missiles.

The battleship launched a missile salvo—thirty-seven, according to the readout on Daniel's display. They weren't especially well aimed: the *Almirante*'s missileer was reacting to a target at an unexpected angle. Indeed, it seemed obvious that the battleship's captain and crew hadn't been prepared for a battle, period.

The weight of metal accelerating toward the *Triomphante* was nonetheless enormous. The cruiser opened fire with her fifteen-centimeter guns. She had maneuvered in the Matrix with topgallant sails alone, and Joycelyn had placed her at an angle which permitted all four turrets to bear without being blocked by the rigging.

The *Almirante* didn't fire in her own defense. Instead, the battleship faded into the Matrix, barely before the first of the cruiser's missiles could have reached her.

We've won!

"Ship, this is Six," Daniel announced. "The Karst battleship has withdrawn, leaving us in control of the Danziger System and therefore of the Tarbell Stars. We have achieved our objective. Six out."

There was cheering on the bridge and the command channel. A heartbeat later Daniel realized the mistake he had made—and worse, that Captain Joycelyn had made the same mistake.

"Squadron, engage the *Ithaca*," Daniel said. "Break, Chazonoff, I'm taking over Missiles, Six out."

He'd given Joycelyn as much warning as he could, but the cruiser was thirty seconds away. Cory had understood immediately, however, and the *Mindello*'s four-inch plasma cannon were already lashing at the rebel destroyer.

Joycelyn had focused wholly on the battleship. He had aligned the *Triomphante* to respond to the missiles which the *Almirante* was sure to launch. The rebel destroyer had extracted while the cruiser was still in the Matrix, however, and her presence had gone unnoticed in the majesty of the battleship's seventy-five thousand tons.

The *Ithaca* had launched four missiles at the *Triomphante*. One had malfunctioned, ripping itself apart as its High Drive lighted. The other three were well-aimed. Though there was more than enough time to engage them or even to maneuver the cruiser out of their predicted tracks, Joycelyn and his gunners thought only of the *Almirante*'s salvo until it was too late.

For most naval captains plasma cannon were purely defensive, used the way the *Triomphante* was using hers now. Daniel had from his first command seen how effective plasma bolts could be offensively. His officers had absorbed his philosophy, and Cory was putting it in practice now.

The *Ithaca* was too distant for the *Mindello*'s bolts to seriously damage her. Even riggers in hard suits on the hull would probably be safe, because over nearly a light-minute the slug of ions had expanded into a diffuse spray.

Daniel finished his calculations and pressed Execute; the first and then the second missile clanged out of their tubes. He had decided it was quicker to program the launch himself instead of explaining the change of target to Chazanoff... and besides, Daniel wanted to do something to make up for having failed to warn Joycelyn about the new danger.

It was too late, though. The rebel destroyer had already begun to fade from his display.

The icon for the *Ithaca* suddenly sharpened to full brilliance again. The *Mindello*'s well-aimed plasma bolts had disrupted the rebel destroyer's electrical balance enough to interfere with Captain von der Main's attempt to escape into the Matrix.

Daniel launched another pair; the *Sissie* had only six missiles remaining on board, and four of those were on the rollerways now. It was a long carry, but if the *Mindello* could keep the target pinned there was at least a chance!

Four of the *Triomphante*'s cannon had slewed quickly enough to fire on their new targets. Daniel didn't set his own display to calculate the incoming missiles, but the fifteen-centimeter rounds had eight times the energy of the four-inch guns of the *Sissie* and of most destroyers. There was a good chance—

The bow of the cruiser bloomed into a distorted white bubble. The missile's impact had heated the steel of her hull into lambent flame.

Almost in the same instant, the icon for the *Ithaca* swelled and faded from Daniel's display. *Did she insert after all?*

But a real-time image showed an expanding bubble of gas. A fragment that might have been a mast was the only solid object visible even at the console's greatest magnification. A missile had hit the destroyer squarely.

"*The target is destroyed*," a voice declared in a broken transmission. "*I repeat, the target is destroyed. Schnitker out.*"

A missile from the *Katchaturian* had made a direct hit on the *Ithaca*.

If the priests were right, perhaps that pleased the late bridge crew of the *Triomphante*.

CHAPTER 26

ELAZIG ON DANZIGER

Adele had gathered a great deal of data from the *Almirante* during the battle, but there hadn't been time to process it. Here in Elazig Harbor, she began to go through it as a break from the information which Cazelet had forwarded from the residency.

Cazelet had gone back there as soon as the Tarbell Squadron had landed. None of the office personnel had commented on either his presence or his previous absence.

That might have been the case in even a normal Fifth Bureau residency. The staff here in Elazig remembered the way Cazelet's predecessors had been removed, however. Indeed, there were probably spatters on the walls if you knew where to look.

Traffic through Port Control ran as a column of text along the right margin Adele's display. Over twenty ships had lifted or landed during the three days since the battle. That was at the normal rate for the past year and a half, higher than that for traffic before the outbreak of the Upholder Rebellion. War had been good for neutral Danziger.

The movements were being recorded also. Adele didn't imagine—she *couldn't* imagine—that she would ever have use for Elazig's traffic logs, but it was unlikely that she would ever have another chance to collect them.

ELAZIG CONTROL, THIS IS AFS KING WILLIAM. ON BEHALF OF ADMIRAL PAUL OF BRUNSWICK, WE REQUEST DOCKING FACILITIES FOR THE ALLIANCE FRIENDSHIP SQUADRON IN ELAZIG HARBOR. OVER.

Adele immediately pinged Daniel, who was busy on the *Triomphante*. He had boarded the crippled cruiser and brought it down in Elazig Harbor after transferring most of the crew to the transports. He had downplayed the risk, but Cory had told Adele that one or more trucks of thrusters might have separated during descent because of unnoticed fractures when the hull flexed.

Adele hadn't tried to convince Daniel not to take the risk. It was his business. She would not long survive him, though: that was *her* business.

"*Elazig Control acknowledges transmission from* King William," the ground controller replied. Adele had switched to audio. She routed the transmission to Vesey's console in the BDC; Daniel had not responded. "*What number of berths are you requesting, over?*"

Adele tried to enter the *King William*'s systems through Elazig Control, but without success. The warship's communications console was properly isolated from the rest of its systems, and Control's hardware couldn't handle Adele's more subtle tools.

Danziger had a rudimentary satellite communications

system but no orbital information-gathering systems for Adele to use. The *Sissie* was in harbor and there were no Tarbell warships in orbit—which was probably a good thing, given the chance that a flustered and inexperienced Tarbell officer would try to interfere with the Alliance squadron. It wouldn't be worth using the sensors of the two tramp freighters in orbit.

"*Control, we have two battleships, two light cruisers, and a flotilla of eleven destroyers,*" the *King William* responded. "*We can stage them in if necessary. We want to take on reaction mass and replenish our supplies of fresh fruits and vegetables, and we hope to purchase some stores. Over.*"

Adele had data on the *King William* open in a sidebar. She and her sister ship, the *Crown Prince*, were modern vessels; they had been assigned to the Pleasance Squadron after the Treaty of Amiens, where they remained in service instead of being put in ordinary.

"*Acknowledged*, King William," said Control. "*We can accommodate all your ships in the outer harbor, or the destroyers and cruisers in the inner harbor and the battleships in the outer harbor, over.*"

Harbor Control was desperately trying to rouse someone in the civil government but thus far without success. From the excited chatter among the controllers—Adele was listening in through the control room's security system—they had decided on their own to bring the ships down, mainly because they had no way to stop so massive a force.

Adele approved silently. The controllers were using good judgment in a crisis. That didn't affect her or anyone for whom she felt responsible, but it always pleased her to see people behaving well.

Daniel would answer when he could; Adele refused to become concerned about it . . . which was a lie, basically, but she hadn't said it to anyone else and she didn't believe it herself.

She called Cazelet's direct line. "Stanfleet Organization," he responded promptly.

"Clear everything connected with Cinnabar or our sponsors and get out immediately," Adele said. "There's an Alliance squadron landing and I expect there'll be a Fifth Bureau presence with it. Ah—will you need additional manpower? They haven't started landing yet."

"I've kept things pretty sterile," Cazelet said. "I even removed the storage element on the security video that showed the leadership change, though the staff might be able to identify you."

"I'll take that risk," Adele said. "Report to the *Sissie* when you're done."

Tovera would be happy to execute all the potential witnesses. Tovera had attached herself to Lady Mundy, however. She knew that Adele would make choices that were more survivable in the long run than her own—sociopathic—choices would be.

Daniel called just as Cazelet rang off. There was a query from Vesey on Adele's display also, but she let it continue to pulse. She had nothing to tell Vesey beyond what the forwarded Alliance landing request already contained.

"Daniel," Adele said, "an Alliance squadron of two battleships and supporting vessels is in the process of landing.

They're calling themselves the Alliance Friendship Squadron under Paul of Brunswick."

She hadn't bothered with preamble. This was a crisis, and she hadn't been good at small talk even when she was quite small herself.

"*Do we know which faction they're supporting?*" Daniel said. He sounded calm; but then, so did Adele. She knew that *she* wasn't.

"I can't get any information from them in orbit except for the names of the ships," Adele said. She had forwarded that data in a packet, though she wasn't sure whether Daniel would be able to view it yet. If he was using a handheld communicator rather than a commo helmet, perhaps not.

"But Daniel," she continued, "this is a detachment of the Fleet. Its cruise must have been authorized at a level higher than a Fifth Bureau diocese. Guarantor Porra is at least complicit in what is happening."

"*Ah,*" said Daniel. "*I believe...that I'll stay here on the* Triomphante, *just as I would do if I were making a port call and a warship of a friendly power arrived. I'll tell Vesey not to let any more of the crew go off on liberty but not to try to recall those who are off the ship already.*"

The hesitation was so slight that Adele might have believed Daniel had been planning his response for days.

"*I'm sorry not to have gotten back to you sooner,*" Daniel added. "*Pasternak and I were down in the bilges, deciding whether any of the converters had shifted during whipping when the ship was hit.*"

"All right," said Adele. A sound of approaching thunder

meant that the Alliance ships were descending to land. The first must be one of the cruisers; as loud as it was, it wasn't the earthshaking commotion of a battleship.

"Daniel?" she said. "When Cazelet arrives, I'm going to put him on communications. I'll come and join you."

"*I'm always glad of your company, Adele,*" he replied.

Neither of them said that it might be the last opportunity they had to see one another. It all depended on what orders Admiral Paul and the squadron's Fifth Bureau contingent had received.

Adele went back to trying to get through the squadron's shielding. When the Alliance ships were nearby in harbor she would have more options, but that wasn't a reason for her not to try before then.

"Pasternak!" Daniel called as he followed his chief engineer down from the forward strut of the *Triomphante*'s starboard outrigger. "Use the bloody ladder! I'd rather scrap this bloody cruiser right now than have you drown on me!"

Pasternak was over sixty, an old man by spacefaring standards. Though a jury-rigged ladder had been welded to the other side of the strut, he wore gauntlets and used the teeth of the extension gear to clamber down hand over hand.

If he falls into the slip, I'll have to see how well I swim in boots and gauntlets, Daniel thought.

The *Triomphante* should probably be scrapped anyway, but Daniel didn't feel it was his job to make that decision. He smiled wryly. He supposed it was in the hands of whoever was in charge in the Ministry of War, though the news that there was an opening at minister level might not have reached Peltry yet.

Or we could leave it for Admiral Paul to decide. The cruiser properly belongs to the Fleet, despite having been mislabeled as scrap when she was transferred to the Upholders.

Daniel laughed aloud.

Pasternak dropped to the dock and looked back. "What's so bloody funny?" he called, misunderstanding Daniel's laughter. "When I can't do a spacer's job I'll stop shipping as one, but you've got no call to put me out to pasture yet!"

"Chief," said Daniel stepping down beside him, "there's an Alliance squadron landing out there."

He gestured generally in the direction of the battleship which had landed some ten minutes earlier. "I was wondering if they were going to charge me with damaging their cruiser here, since I think it properly belongs to them."

"Damage, hell," said Pasternak. "She's right and truly wrecked, Six. But if you give me the dockyard hours, I can put her back in shape in three months."

Not in the docks here on Danziger, Daniel thought. *Back home at Bergen and Associates, just maybe...but it still wouldn't be economically viable.*

"The strut torqued so bad when the missile hit..." mused Pasternak, looking at the great outrigger. "That we had to blast the extension loose in its channel to extend it. And I wouldn't trust a weld to hold for landing, so we drilled and pinned the sections."

"You did a great job, Chief," Daniel said. "I knew that

when you said it would take the strain that I didn't need to worry about it."

"None of the ship's own crew believed we could use high explosive to clear the strut," Pasternak said, turning to Daniel again. "But you'd put me in charge of getting her in shape so they did it anyway. Worked out pretty good."

Then he said, "It'd be a pity to scrap her, wouldn't it, sir? She took a hell of a whack and she was still ready to fight if there'd been anybody left to fight, right?"

"Right as rain, Chief," Daniel said. "But it's not our decision."

An ex-Fleet lieutenant in the Battle Direction Center had become the ranking officer aboard the *Triomphante* when the bridge had vanished in a fireball. Daniel wondered how she would have performed if the *Almirante* had returned. Probably as well as anybody could have, though that wasn't saying much.

"I have to say I'm glad the fighting was over, though," he added, and *that* was the truth if he'd ever spoken it.

A van drove down the quay toward them. Something in the mechanism squealed until the vehicle stopped at a line of bollards. Tovera and a moment later Adele got out.

"It's a belt, not a bearing," Hogg said. He sounded apologetic. "I tightened it before I handed the bitch over to Tovera, but I need to get on it again."

"I'll talk with Officer Mundy now, Pasternak," Daniel said. "I think I'm clear on the *Triomphante*'s status."

"Whatever you want, Six," the chief engineer called cheerfully to his back. "We can handle it!"

"Pasternak seems more optimistic than I would expect

from seeing the ship," Adele said, looking at the cruiser. Hogg had joined Tovera beside the van.

The first twenty frames of the bow were gone, down to A and B levels: the impact had been quartering from slightly above. Icicles of congealed plating hung from the edges of the cavity, pointing down and back in the direction of the *Triomphante*'s thrust when she was hit. Several cracks starred the hull aft.

"Pasternak regards the *Triomphante* as a technical problem, which he's confident he can solve," Daniel said. "He's shading the job on the hopeful side as people do, of course, but I'd be willing to back him—as a technical matter. Economically—"

He shrugged. Like Pasternak, the spacer in him would like to try.

"—fixing her is nonsense. You can't see it from this angle but both forward turrets are off their races. Forward dorsal's barbette has been crushed as well."

Daniel cleared his throat and asked the question whose answer he was afraid to hear: "Adele, are the Sissies going to be all right? In your judgment? Because I can tell them to scatter now and get off Danziger the best way they can. They're all trained spacers that any captain would be glad of in his crew. That means civilian officers'll hide them from the rebels—or whoever, the Alliance—for their own sakes."

"General Storn was Paul of Brunswick's political officer for ten years and two promotions for both men," Adele said. "Our crew knew nothing about the background of why we're in the Tarbell Stars, so I don't imagine that Paul will attempt to kill them."

She pursed her lips and added, "I could be wrong, of course."

"But if Paul and Storn are allies..." Daniel said as he absorbed what he had just heard. "Then we've won, haven't we? That's what you're saying, isn't it?"

There was a glint of light above the western horizon: another ship approaching to land. The exhaust roar hadn't reached Elazig yet, but the ultraviolet glitter promised that it was coming.

"No," said Adele with a cold edge in her voice. "It *probably* means that General Storn has the advantage over his rival General Krychek and may even have destroyed him. General Storn's goals are not identical to our goals, however—yours and mine. If it became public knowledge that Storn had conspired with enemies of the Alliance—"

Her smile was as quick and humorless as a snake's strike.

"—which I think describes us accurately, his own position in regard to Guarantor Porra would become very difficult. Potential problems could be avoided by eliminating all those who know of his connection with us."

"He can't..." Daniel said, then treated the question as a problem for solution instead of simply reacting to it. "He could *try* to have Minister Forbes assassinated, but there'd be a considerable chance of it going wrong. Even if he succeeded, there's at least a toss-up chance that it'd mean resumed war between us and the Alliance. Storn doesn't want that!"

Or does he? How much of Daniel's belief was simply wishful thinking?

"Forbes isn't a risk to Storn," Adele said. "A Cinnabar minister's statement is scarcely compelling evidence that a Fifth Bureau official is a traitor. You and I, however, are another matter."

The incoming vessel was close enough to be a background rumble. It must be a big one, perhaps even the remaining battleship.

"I see," said Daniel. He thought of pulling his goggles down, then simply turned his back on the searing actinic radiation. "I had the impression that you and General Storn were, well, on good terms."

"You started to say 'friends' but corrected yourself," Adele said with another flash of that grim smile. "The correction was proper. I have helped General Storn in the past, and he certainly will consider the possibility that I might help him further in the future...but we aren't friends, and in the last analysis it wouldn't matter to him if we were. Do you worry about the spouses and offspring of the crews of ships you attack?"

"That's in war," Daniel said, surprised by his own anger.

"Life *is* war to people at General Storn's level of the intelligence services," Adele said. "Everyone is expendable."

The ship on landing approach was a cruiser, still loud but not so loud that it seemed to turn the world inside out for those near the harbor.

"You're not like that, Adele," Daniel said. He raised his voice only slightly; he wasn't sure that he had wanted his words to be understood.

"No," she agreed. He was reading the words on her lips. "That's why I wasn't better prepared for the situation. I apologize, Daniel. I didn't consider the wider implications until we had arrived in the middle of them."

The cruiser's thrusters shut off. The waterfall-hissing of metal cooling in the slip continued in a diminishing background.

Daniel suddenly felt the humor of the situation. "Adele," he said, "I took on this project and asked for your assistance. I didn't think it would be without risk. The factor that *I* hadn't allowed for is the arrival of an Alliance squadron. That's what's upset things."

A thick-wheeled vehicle pulled up beside the van that had brought Adele. This was a dockside runabout with a small cab in front and a short lowboy behind it. The driver, a very big man, got out.

I've seen him somewhere.

Hogg and Tovera faced the vehicle. Neither held a weapon—Tovera deliberately set her attaché case on the ground beside her—but they were tremblingly rigid.

General Storn got out of the passenger seat. He was wearing a civilian business suit, and the driver was his bodyguard.

"Master Hogg?" Storn said in a carrying voice as though Hogg were standing twenty feet away with Daniel and Adele rather than directly in front of the speaker. "Might I have a word with your master, please?"

"If he's come alone," Daniel said in a whisper that only Adele could hear, "then we've won."

He walked toward the line of bollards so that he could be heard when he said in a normal voice, "Do you want to speak with me or with my friend, sir?"

"Good morning, Captain Leary," said Storn. His hands and those of his bodyguard were at their sides. "I was hoping that you and I could have a quiet discussion somewhere. Lady Mundy would be quite welcome, but—"

He turned and looked over his shoulder. An aircar with a four-place cabin and a separate cab for the driver landed behind the two ground vehicles. Dust and debris puffed away for an instant before the fans shut down.

"—I believe she has other obligations," Storn concluded. He smiled.

Commander Huxford, also in civilian clothes, got out of the cabin. He started forward, then actually looked at the three servants facing him from the line of bollards. He stopped, swallowed, and called, "Lady Mundy? A lady has asked that you join her for lunch. I'll carry you to her, ah, when you're ready."

Adele had followed Daniel forward. She looked at him and said, "Daniel, would you like me to accompany you and General Storn?"

"Ah ...?" he said. He nodded in the direction of Huxford.

"We were discussing priorities a few minutes ago," Adele said, looking at General Storn. "I suspect that Mistress Sand already knows that I place the duties of friendship ahead of other obligations. If she doesn't know that, it's high time that she learns."

Daniel grinned. "Go have your lunch," he said. "General, there's a construction office there—"

He pointed to the frame building at the open end of the quay.

"—which I can empty if it isn't empty already. I suspect it's secure simply because no one would have seen a reason to bug it, but I'm sure you can search it before you say anything if you're concerned."

"I'm not concerned," said Storn. "Now, if I can join you ...?"

He cocked an eye at Hogg.

"Let him through, Hogg," Daniel said. "You and the general's driver can probably find something to talk about while you prevent anybody from walking in on us."

Hogg stepped aside. He nodded the general through, then followed with the big driver.

Storn turned and called, "Have a pleasant lunch, Lady Mundy. It's always a pleasure to see you again."

CHAPTER 27

ELAZIG HARBOR ON DANZIGER

Adele got into the aircar after Huxford. Though the vehicle was featureless on the outside, the interior of the cabin was covered—cushions and panels both—with pebbled leather.

I wonder if Daniel could identify the animal? Adele thought. She clipped an image with her data unit to show him later.

It had been built on Cinnabar by Bevis and Sons, according to the car's computer. *Better, I could run the car's specifications through the manufacturer's database when I return to Xenos.*

"Are you going to invite me in, Commander?" Tovera said to Huxford. She grinned. "Or shall I get in without an invitation?"

"I was directed to let Lady Mundy bring any companions she chooses," Huxford said, sitting on the rear-facing seat across from Adele's. "It's entirely up to her."

"Get in, Tovera," Adele said. At this point she was willing to let bygones be bygones with Huxford. Her servant was not, however, and Adele didn't feel compelled to protect the fellow from discomfort his arrogance had brought on him.

The door shut with a heavy thump and the car lifted smoothly. The cabin was windowless, but where windows would have been, real-time images were instead. The considerable noise of the fans was muted to a background whisper.

"Is this car armored?" Adele said.

"Yes," said Huxford, "though it can't be very thick and still fly, of course. The vehicle is part of the regular outfit of the communications vessel which brought us."

Adele checked her data unit. She hadn't been aware that a Cinnabar ship was accompanying the Alliance squadron, but there it was, the RCS *Themis*; in harbor not far from the *Princess Cecile*. According to the harbormaster's records, it had landed immediately after the battleship *Crown Prince*, on which Storn had arrived.

"I see," said Adele. She wasn't surprised that Mistress Sand could demand the use of one of the few RCN communications vessels, shortened cruiser hulls which retained the warship's full set of antennas and sails. It was very surprising that the *Themis* was travelling in company with an Alliance squadron, however.

"Does it bother you to have been demoted to errand boy, Commander?" Tovera said. "You must have thought you were on the way up when you decided to put the mistress in her place. You certainly learned what her place was, didn't you?"

"That's enough, Tovera," Adele said. The interior of the car was shielded, so she was linking her data unit to the vehicle's own communications system.

"I have been chastised for that error in judgment by the highest authorities in the Republic, Lady Mundy," Huxford said bitterly. His cheekbones were flushed. "The yapping of a nasty little animal don't concern me."

Tovera giggled. "That's right," she said as she opened her attaché case. "I'm not even human."

Adele looked at the submachine gun Tovera had taken out of the case. "What is that?" she said. Her voice was neutral but probably harder than usual.

"A friend of Dasi's, a fitter in the power room, took four inches off the barrel of an issue gun," Tovera said, ejecting and then reseating the magazine tube. "At the receiver end so that he didn't have to splice the coils. Now it fits in the case till I can replace the one I gave Hale."

"I see," said Adele. Tovera had made friends within the crew of the *Princess Cecile*. Spacers didn't think in philosophical terms about what constituted a human being. They stood up for their own, though, and the Sissies knew that Tovera was one of them.

As was Tovera's mistress.

The car began to descend. Adele hadn't been paying attention to the view outside. When she looked, she saw they were banking around a rectangular building set in a moat. Inside was a paved courtyard.

"We leased a villa beyond the city proper," Huxford said. Perhaps they were all glad to change the subject. "It was possible on such short notice because of help from Alliance officials. From General Storn, as you know."

They curved into the courtyard; it had a cobblestone surface. Rather than cut his throttles abruptly, the driver eased them off so that the low skids didn't bang down.

Huxford got out on the right side; Adele and Tovera got out also, on the left. "You're to go in through there," Huxford said, pointing to double doors in the south wall. "She will be waiting in the Great Hall, where you'll enter."

Beside the doors was a small building, half-timbered to match the look of the courtyard interior. A doghouse, Adele assumed, though empty now. The dog must have been the size of a small horse.

Tovera gave Huxford a hard look, then moved in front of Adele and pulled open the right-hand door-valve. She stepped through, then backed up with a look of surprise.

Isn't it Mistress Sand after all?

"Come in, Mundy," called Elisabeth Forbes. "We have things to discuss. And feel free to bring Tovera if you like, though I don't think I'm really *that* fierce."

Adele's meeting was with the Minister of Defense of the Republic of Cinnabar.

No one was in the office when Daniel opened the door. There were three desks of different sorts; several lengths of high-pressure tubing lay on top of one. Windows on two sides were open; papers had blown to the floor long enough ago that the edges were curling. There was also a used condom and a bag with the remains of someone's lunch.

Storn turned one of the chairs to face Daniel and sat in it. There were connections in the walls but no electronics in the building. Daniel similarly turned the chair at the adjacent desk and said, "I'm surprised to see you, sir, and I'm *very* glad you're not from General Krychek."

"Master Krychek is pursuing other opportunities, Captain," Storn said. His smile reminded Daniel more of Tovera's than of any other expression he had seen. "As for agents, no one alive today would admit to being an agent of his."

Storn raised an eyebrow in question and said, "Would you care for a drink? I certainly would. Does one ever get used to the feeling of extraction from the Matrix?"

"No one I've ever heard of did," Daniel said with a grim smile of his own, "and that includes my Uncle Stacy who had about as much experience as any man born. As for a drink, I doubt there's anything here—"

He glanced around the shed; there was nothing at all, as he expected.

"—but I suspect my man Hogg can promote something pretty quickly."

Storn reached under his tunic and brought out a flat silvery flask. "I'll offer you some of mine," he said as he unstoppered it, "if you're not too proud—"

He took a swig from the mouth of the flask, then held it out to Daniel.

"—to drink from the bottle."

Daniel laughed, thinking of some of the things he had drunk from in the past. Including a dancing girl's pump, though for the life of him he couldn't remember why. He probably hadn't known at the time either, because he'd been very drunk already.

He sipped the liquor. It was whiskey, but it left a tingle in his mouth like that of hot pepper. He sipped more, then returned the flask.

Storn capped it. Instead of putting the flask inside his tunic, he set it upright on the desk beside him and said, "General Krychek, as he was until very recently, had been under investigation for some months, but his decision to involve the Commonwealth of Karst shortened the process. Guarantor Porra came to suspect that Krychek planned to replace him."

"Did he?" said Daniel, frowning.

Storn shrugged. "It was a possible interpretation of Krychek's actions," he said. "Whether or not it deserved the weight it received in the report which went to the Guarantor is a moot point now."

Daniel remembered Adele's description of life at General Storn's level. *Well, it was to my advantage this time*, he thought; but he was still uncomfortable at the cool brutality of Storn's attitude.

Daniel said in what he realized was a hard voice, "Then the war with the rebels was all waste effort? The deaths?"

Storn's tone was as hard as Daniel's own. "Waste? Of course not! If Krychek had brought the Tarbell Stars into the Alliance, I'm quite sure that his position would have been reevaluated. He had many friends and a great deal of influence—until he failed in a humiliating fashion. Thanks to you, Captain."

He twisted and looked back through the grimy windows toward the *Triomphante*. It occurred to Daniel that though Storn was now an intelligence chief, he had spent ten years as political officer of combat units. He had first-hand experience of war at the sharp end.

"When we learned that the *Almirante* was under way for the Tarbell Stars," Storn said musingly, "my son—you've met him, I believe? Major Grozhinski?"

"Yes, I've met him," Daniel said. "Though I believe most of his contacts were with my colleague, Lady Mundy."

The relationship explained Storn's choice of a go-between. Even now, however, Daniel couldn't see a family resemblance between the spare, ascetic Storn and the beefy blond Grozhinski.

"Mikhail believed that our only chance of success," Storn said, "was to provide the Tarbell government with a battleship to counter the *Almirante*. I said that the best result of that would be for us to be executed beside Master Krychek. Besides—"

He turned to face Daniel again.

"—I was more optimistic than my son that the Tarbell government could survive without such obvious support from the Third Diocese. Though I couldn't imagine *how* you would do it."

"We had good luck," Daniel said. He remembered how his gut had twisted when he saw the *Triomphante* unexpectedly insert—to flee, he had assumed. "And very good personnel, not all of whom survived. Captain Joycelyn was a loss to the Fleet when he took service in the Tarbell Stars."

He smiled wryly. "Also we were fortunate in our opponents. If Lieutenant von der Main and her crew had been in the *Almirante* instead of a destroyer, I probably wouldn't be here talking to you."

"You fought a battle and there were casualties," Storn said. "Captain Joycelyn did indeed have a fine combat record, which he lived up to above Danziger. His comparable level of success with the wives of senior officers made his decision to leave Fleet service a wise one, however. I dare say he wouldn't have greatly regretted the way his career has ended."

"Your agent, Christopher Robin, was on the *Triomphante*'s bridge also," Daniel said. "I doubt *he* would have been as happy with the way things worked out."

Storn smiled again. "Perhaps not," he said, "but I don't think I need to pretend loyalty to a man simply because he was a recipient of my aid. As it turns out, the chance of Minister Robin's death has simplified the next stage of events."

"Go on, please," said Daniel, trying to smooth the frown from his forehead.

"Minister Robin was an able and strong-willed man," Storn said. "President Menandros is neither of those things. Admiral Paul will shortly take the squadron to Peltry. I'm confident that the president will realize immediately that the Tarbell Stars will be better off as an Alliance protectorate than they were in their previous fractious independence."

Daniel said nothing for a moment. Storn's level gaze met his with neither concern nor challenge.

"My understanding..." Daniel said slowly, "was that under the terms of the Treaty of Amiens, neither Cinnabar nor the Alliance of Free Stars would expand its possessions. Their empires, that is."

Storn is telling me this. He came to me to tell me this. That means the situation can't be what I think it is.

But what in hell is it?

"The matter has been the subject of discussion at high levels," Storn said evenly. "I'm sure that you will be informed of your government's position by the proper authorities, but since you were in the Tarbell Stars at my request I thought I should personally alert you to the situation."

In other words, this is above your pay grade…which is true.

Daniel took a deep breath. He said aloud, "I appreciate your candor, General. I will await further information through my chain of command."

He grinned at Storn. It had taken a great deal of personal courage for the general to face him this way. Courage was a common virtue in the RCN; you could be as thick as two short planks and be promoted to admiral, but cowards were very rare. Daniel still valued a brave man more than he did a clever one.

"If you don't mind my saying this…" said the general. "My government has taken unofficial notice of the fact that Cinnabar citizens were a major factor in bringing about this desirable state of affairs. This has been to the benefit of your government in the discussions."

I wonder how Midshipman Hale would have felt about that? But that was a foolish question: you did all the important thinking before you took the RCN oath. After that you went where you were sent and took your chances.

Daniel gave a short laugh. Storn raised an eyebrow again, his hands still.

"Midshipman Hale wasn't on active RCN duty when she was killed," Daniel explained. "She volunteered to follow me to the Tarbell Stars. I am quite certain that she was aware of the risks of her decision."

"She was aboard the *Triomphante*, was she not?" said Storn, proving how little he had left to chance in planning this meeting. He took the flask again and removed the cap.

"Then I suggest we drink to her memory before I go off on my business."

"Yes," said Daniel. "I'll certainly drink to that."

"Mistress Forbes!" said Adele. She grimaced and corrected herself: "My apology, Minister Forbes."

"Come in and sit down, Mundy," Forbes said from a wooden couch. She patted the seat beside her. "And shut the door. Your Tovera is welcome also. She isn't going to repeat what she hears, and I'm not worried about her shooting me unless you tell her to."

Adele walked in. The hall was paneled in dark wood to mid-height and was whitewashed above that. The ceiling was steeply arched with exposed beams. There was a display of projectile weapons—old ones—on the wall at the far end, and rigging suits in niches at the corners. The suits looked fake to Adele, though she would have to get closer to be sure.

Behind her, Tovera said, "She doesn't need me to shoot you, Minister. I think I'll go talk with the commander."

Adele looked over her shoulder. Tovera grinned and hefted her submachine gun by the pistol grip. "I make him nervous, which is fun to watch."

Tovera closed the door behind her. Her mistress had more important things to think about now than what happened to minor officials who had once insulted Mundy of Chatsworth.

Adele sat at the other end of the couch from the minister. It creaked and was no more comfortable than it had looked; in particular, the top back railing projected inward and caught

Adele across the shoulder blades. She shifted slightly so that she was leaning on her arm rather than her back.

"I took the place for privacy rather than comfort," Forbes said with a smile. "Some of the other rooms may have better furnishings, if you'd like to move?"

"Don't worry about it," Adele said. "What do you want with me?"

Forbes smiled, then said, "First, to tell you that the Senate sent me here with full authority to negotiate an amendment to the Treaty of Amiens. The arrangements I have agreed have already been approved in closed session by the Senate, and therefore by the Republic."

"Go on," Adele said. "I've never been concerned with political maneuverings except as they touch me personally."

As when my immediate family was proscribed, executed, and their heads displayed on Speaker's Rock. Everyone but me, because I had just left to finish my education on a world of the Alliance.

"Second," Forbes said, "Mistress Sand is aware of my remit and is in favor of the proposed settlement—if I was able to negotiate it."

Forbes smiled slightly. From what Adele had seen, the minister's relations with Mistress Sand were professional rather than collegial; which was good enough, of course.

"Mistress Sand told me that she doubted whether I *would* be able to reach the hoped-for agreement," Forbes continued. "Thanks to you and Captain Leary, I have been able to do so."

"Go on," Adele repeated. She didn't like to hear someone crowing about getting the better of Mistress Sand, but

Forbes was giving information. She would give more if Adele continued to act as a good listener.

"The Tarbell Stars will shortly align themselves with the Alliance of Free Stars," Forbes said. Her quick smile was forced, and Adele could see the tightness in the older woman's cheeks. "The Republic has no pressing interests in the Tarbell Stars, so we're giving up nothing of significance."

Except the principle of parity on which the Treaty of Amiens is founded, Adele thought.

"I see," Adele said aloud. "Go on."

"Yes," said Forbes. "I don't believe you were in the audience hall on Karst when I brought the Republic's greetings to the new Headman, were you, Mundy?"

"No," said Adele, "but I watched and recorded the events as they occurred."

Headman Hieronymous had been a boy when he succeeded his uncle, Headman Terl, a close ally of Cinnabar for thirty years. His advisors had suggested that Hieronymous assert his own personality in dealing with the Cinnabar delegation, headed by Senator Elisabeth Forbes.

"I'm sure you haven't forgotten the way we were treated," Forbes said. "But though you watched, the insults were sharper to those of us in the hall receiving them. I think Captain Leary would agree with me. Insults to the Republic, but to us personally as well."

"Yes," Adele said. "I presume you're correct."

"Because of the war between us and the Alliance at the time," Forbes said, "the Republic couldn't teach Karst the lesson the Headman's behavior deserved. And because of the terms of the Treaty of Amiens, we couldn't deal with Karst afterwards either."

"I see," said Adele. Pieces were falling together in her mind. They formed a structure from what had moments before been a pile of disparate, generally unpleasant, incidents.

"The Tarbell Stars were General Storn's *quid pro quo* for giving Cinnabar a free hand to deal with Karst," Forbes said, smiling. "The considerable help which Cinnabar personnel provided in quashing General Krychek's attempted coup permitted Storn to convince his superiors. More accurately, his superior."

"I'm pleased to hear that news," Adele said. *I'm pleased that you're not a buffoon, that Mistress Sand hasn't lost her mind, and that Midshipman Hale really did die in the service of the Republic of Cinnabar...unlike what I believed a few minutes ago.*

"Speaking as the Minister of Defense," Forbes said, "I am informing you that Captain Leary is being recalled to Cinnabar and to active duty. There will be formal orders to that effect before close of business, but I would appreciate it if you would inform Leary of the situation when you next see him."

"Thank you," said Adele, rising to her feet. "Am I dismissed, Minister?"

"You are," said Forbes, who also got up. "Commander Huxford will return you to where he picked you up. Whereas *I* will take a hot bath, because the water lines to the suites of the *Themis* cracked on the third day out!"

EPILOGUE

Huxford rode back to the *Triomphante*'s dock with Adele and Tovera, but none of them spoke. Either Tovera had wearied of her game, or she had caught the air of cheerful excitement as Adele came out of the building. It would probably have been all right to speak in front of the commander, but there wasn't any reason to do so.

The aircar lifted from the dock as soon as Adele and Tovera had gotten out. At the sound of the fans, Daniel, Pasternak and Hogg came out of the construction office; Daniel waved and started toward them with Hogg a pace behind.

Adele paused and looked up at the damaged cruiser. "When I was younger," she said quietly to Tovera, "I would have believed that if the *Montcalm*'s transmitter had worked, I would be dead and Hale would be alive."

"And me dead as well," Tovera said with a shrug. "You and Six would have been on the bridge of this one—"

She nodded toward the *Triomphante*.

"—and Hale would still have been in the BDC, as safe as if she was back on Xenos."

"Perhaps," Adele said. "Perhaps. As I've gained experience of the world, I've come to realize that book solutions aren't the only things that can happen. Daniel might have been more alert to the *Ithaca*'s missiles than Captain Joycelyn was. Sun would probably have transferred with Daniel to the cruiser and might have been more alert than the *Triomphante*'s gunner. And our defensive fire might have diverted the missile into our stern instead of our bow."

Tovera shrugged. "I suppose," she said. "It doesn't really matter to me, except that I have to replace a submachine gun."

Tovera looked at the cruiser again and grinned. "It was a tool," she said. "There are thousands just like it. Tools break and you replace them; or you break and somebody replaces you. We all break eventually."

"Yes," Adele said. "That's quite true. I need to stick to facts and not speculate. I'm not very good at speculation."

"How did your meeting go, Officer Mundy?" Daniel said. He was smiling, but Adele could see that he wasn't relaxed.

"Quite well, Daniel," Adele said. "The Minister of Defense informed me that we—all of us, I gather, though she didn't mention the *Princess Cecile* specifically—are recalled to Cinnabar and active duty. Formal orders are coming shortly."

"Indeed," Daniel said, still expectant. "Did she say what sort of duty we can expect on our return?"

"My understanding is that we may have dealings with Karst," Adele said. "I don't have any details as yet, but I hope to learn more shortly. I expect that matters will proceed in a more satisfactory fashion than they did when we called at Karst a few years ago."

"You know," Daniel said, "I don't think I could've heard anything that would have made me happier," he said. He was beaming.

"The minister also mentioned that the internal water pipes of the *Themis* broke on the way here," Adele said. "I suppose they'll be repaired by now."

Daniel shrugged. "Not necessarily," he said. "The trouble with communications ships is that they mostly sit in harbor, but when they're used, they're strained way beyond the norm. Remember the air-handlers in the *Aggie*'s bow section?"

"I was a civilian when you came to Kostroma aboard the *Aglaia*, Daniel," Adele said quietly. "I was a civilian librarian at the time."

"I forgot," Daniel said. "That was really a long time ago, wasn't it?"

Adele nodded. "A lifetime," she said.

"Well, what I was saying," he went on, "is that you get whole systems going out. They'll fix the leak, sure, but there's a good chance the lines will break somewhere else as soon as they make a few insertions and extractions."

Adele felt herself smiling, something she did very rarely. This seemed a suitable time to smile, though. She said, "Do you think we could get back to Cinnabar more quickly than the *Themis* could, Daniel?"

"Umm?" he said. "Under Captain Murgatroyd, isn't she? Murgatroyd's quite good—she wouldn't be captain of a communications ship if she weren't—but I know this region of the Matrix better than she does. At worst we could give the *Themis* a run . . . and I *think* we might be able to do better than that. Though I say it who shouldn't."

"Then I suggest we offer Minister Forbes the option of making the voyage on a ship whose water pipes have always behaved properly," Adele said. "Does that seem reasonable?"

Daniel laughed. "It does indeed!" he said. "If you'll make the offer on behalf of the owner of the yacht *Princess Cecile*, I'll see about getting our crew back aboard. Fortunately, I've got most of them right here, working on the *Triomphante*!"

ACKNOWLEDGMENTS

Dan Breen continues as my first reader. I make mistakes. He catches as many as he can.

Dan, Dorothy Day, and Karen Zimmerman, my webmaster, store my texts against a disaster which engulfs central North Carolina. (Well, if it gets all of central North Carolina, Dan is gone also. Which I would regret if I were around.)

Karen and Evan Ladouceur provided continuity help when I asked for it. It's probable that I should have asked more often than I did, but my focus is always on the story and I tend to ignore other stuff. I know that there are people to whom the continuity is very important and I apologize to them, but that just isn't what I care about.

John and Val Lambshead not only guided me to settings which I later used for scenes but also provided logistics support for the research. This became an acute problem when my business credit card was blocked (my fault) and could not be cleared while I was out of the US (very much the fault of the Bank of America).

I had various computer adventures. (Actually, I'm having another one as I type this, but thus far it's only affecting one of my notebooks.) My son Jonathan saved me each time, among other things by converting all the machines to Win10 and recreating the local area network (which didn't survive the upgrade).

(Come to think, one problem I fixed myself. After a week I realized that the cleaning lady had moved the wireless router to a place she thought was more attractive but which blocked the signal. During that week I used flash drives to transfer my data. I'm not very computer literate, but I'm very good at finding work-arounds.)

My wife Jo keeps house (which I'm sure is frustrating, because she knows not to move stuff, and I'm messy when I'm working...which is most of what I do), and feeds me fresh food cooked in tasty fashion. I'm in good shape for a man of my age, which is as much due to the meals I'm fed as to my daily exercise.

To them and to those whose help I've forgotten to mention, my sincere thanks.

— Dave Drake

ABOUT THE AUTHOR

David Drake was attending Duke University Law School when he was drafted. He served the next two years in the Army, spending 1970 as an enlisted interrogator with the 11th Armored Cavalry in Vietnam and Cambodia. Upon return he completed his law degree at Duke and was for eight years Assistant Town Attorney for Chapel Hill, North Carolina. He has been a full-time freelance writer since 1981. His books include the genre-defining and bestselling *Hammer's Slammers* series, and the nationally bestselling RCN series including *In the Stormy Red Sky*, *The Road of Danger*, and *The Sea without a Shore*.

THE LOST FLEET

JACK CAMPBELL

DAUNTLESS
FEARLESS
COURAGEOUS
VALIANT
RELENTLESS
VICTORIOUS

BEYOND THE FRONTIER:
DREADNAUGHT
INVINCIBLE
GUARDIAN
STEADFAST
LEVIATHAN

THE LOST STARS:
TARNISHED KNIGHT
PERILOUS SHIELD
IMPERFECT SWORD
SHATTERED SPEAR

After a hundred years of brutal war against the Syndics, the Alliance fleet is marooned deep in enemy territory, weakened and demoralised and desperate to make it home.

Their fate rests in the hands of Captain "Black Jack" Geary, a man who had been presumed dead but then emerged from a century of survival hibernation to find his name had become legend. Geary must find a way to inspire the battle-hardened and exhausted men and women of the fleet or face certain annihilation by their enemies.

For more fantastic fiction, author events, competitions,
limited editions and more

VISIT OUR WEBSITE
titanbooks.com

LIKE US ON FACEBOOK
facebook.com/titanbooks

FOLLOW US ON TWITTER
@TitanBooks

EMAIL US
readerfeedback@titanemail.com